"JUST WHEN
NOTHING N
THE SERIA

—Ed Gorman, *Mystery Scene*

ALONG COME
OBERT W. WALKER'S *INSTINCTS* . . .

KILLER INSTINCT

Th   debut of Dr. Jessica Coran, an FBI pathologist track-
ing   rinking "Vampire Killer" . . .

"Chilling and unflinching."   —*Fort Lauderdale Sun-Sentinel*

FATAL INSTINCT

*Jessica Coran faces a cunning, modern-day Jack the Ripper nick-
named "The Claw"* . . .

"A taut, dense thriller. An immensely entertaining novel
filled with surprises, clever twists, and wonderfully drawn
characters."   —*Daytona Beach News-Journal*

PRIMAL INSTINCT

*The Hawaiian beaches are awash in blood. The relentless "Trade
Winds Killer" is loose* . . .

"A bone-chilling page-turner."   —*Publishers Weekly*

PURE INSTINCT

New Orleans plays host to the notorious "Queen of Hearts" killer . . .

"Perfect for Patricia Cornwell fans."   —*Mystery Scene*

DARKEST INSTINCT

*From Florida to London, a copycat killer strikes, and Jessica Coran
faces double jeopardy* . . .

"Walker takes you into a world of suspense, thrills, and
psychological gamesmanship." —*Daytona Beach News-Journal*

continued . . .

EXTREME INSTINCT

A psychopath on a Satanic mission is terrorizing the American West . . .

"Robert W. Walker combines the best of Cornwell with Koontz."
—*Midwest Book Review*

BLIND INSTINCT

A bizarre series of crucifixion murders haunts the darkest corners of London . . .

"If you're a fan of Patricia Cornwell, you'll enjoy *Blind Instinct*."
—*The San Francisco Examiner*

BITTER INSTINCT

The Poet is loose. His words are toxic. His parchment is human skin . . .

"A very frightening police thriller . . . captivating."
—*Midwest Book Review*

UNNATURAL INSTINCT

A judge has been kidnapped and sentenced to death in a madman's private hell . . .

"Fascinating medical details, a unique murder method . . . [a] gruesome story. For fans of Patricia Cornwell." —*Booklist*

GRAVE INSTINCT

A killer who removes his victims' brains plans to give millions of Americans a front-row seat to his next atrocity.

"Walker can always be counted on to create an exciting crime thriller with a villain that readers love to hate."
—*Midwest Book Review*

Titles by Robert W. Walker

ABSOLUTE INSTINCT
GRAVE INSTINCT
UNNATURAL INSTINCT
BITTER INSTINCT
BLIND INSTINCT
EXTREME INSTINCT
DARKEST INSTINCT
PURE INSTINCT
PRIMAL INSTINCT
FATAL INSTINCT
KILLER INSTINCT

FINAL EDGE
COLD EDGE
DOUBLE EDGE
CUTTING EDGE

ABSOLUTE INSTINCT

ROBERT W. WALKER

BERKLEY BOOKS, NEW YORK

THE BERKLEY PUBLISHING GROUP
Published by the Penguin Group
Penguin Group (USA) Inc.
375 Hudson Street, New York, New York 10014, USA
Penguin Group (Canada), 90 Eglinton Avenue East, Suite 700, Toronto, Ontario M4P 2Y3, Canada
(a division of Pearson Penguin Canada Inc.)
Penguin Books Ltd., 80 Strand, London WC2R 0RL, England
Penguin Group Ireland, 25 St. Stephen's Green, Dublin 2, Ireland (a division of Penguin Books Ltd.)
Penguin Group (Australia), 250 Camberwell Road, Camberwell, Victoria 3124, Australia
(a division of Pearson Australia Group Pty. Ltd.)
Penguin Books India Pvt. Ltd., 11 Community Centre, Panchsheel Park, New Delhi—110 017, India
Penguin Group (NZ), Cnr. Airborne and Rosedale Roads, Albany, Auckland 1310, New Zealand
(a division of Pearson New Zealand Ltd.)
Penguin Books (South Africa) (Pty.) Ltd., 24 Sturdee Avenue, Rosebank, Johannesburg 2196,
South Africa

Penguin Books Ltd., Registered Offices: 80 Strand, London WC2R 0RL, England

This is a work of fiction. Names, characters, places, and incidents either are the product of the author's imagination or are used fictitiously, and any resemblance to actual persons, living or dead, business establishments, events, or locales is entirely coincidental. The publisher does not have any control over and does not assume any responsibility for author or third-party websites or their content.

ABSOLUTE INSTINCT

A Berkley Book / published by arrangement with the author

PRINTING HISTORY
Berkley hardcover edition / August 2004
Berkley mass-market edition / December 2005

Copyright © 2004 by Robert W. Walker.
Cover design by Steven Ferlauto.

ISBN: 0-425-20715-3

BERKLEY®
Berkley Books are published by The Berkley Publishing Group,
a division of Penguin Group (USA) Inc.,
375 Hudson Street, New York, New York 10014.
BERKLEY is a registered trademark of Penguin Group (USA) Inc.
The "B" design is a trademark belonging to Penguin Group (USA) Inc.

PRINTED IN THE UNITED STATES OF AMERICA

10 9 8 7 6 5 4 3 2 1

PROLOGUE

We know that the complex human brain cradles every conceivable sort of evil and madness, as seen on 9/11. But more specifically for the murder investigators are designs born of a mind imprinted with the seed of Cain: the seed science now knows as the DNA strand forming a predisposition to become Cain.

—Dr. Jessica Coran, M.E., FBI
from *The Neuronet Map to Murder*

Millbrook, Minnesota
November 17, 1987

THE boy sat cross-legged, scrawny at a mere forty-eight pounds in seven years, big-headed, awkward, sickly at birth and all his life, and now set on a path to cure himself, to fill out the flesh, to strengthen muscle and tissue, to raise the sunken eyes as in his drawings of himself, but now he had gone too far. Thin and sticklike, his body battled the diseases of his father, evil curses he'd never be rid of. His mother believed it with a certainty after seeing what he'd done to harmless, inoffensive little Squeakums.

Giles had been in and out of hospitals all his life, but tests always proved inconclusive, and no one could tell Larina Gahran why her son remained only half formed. Giles's body was his enemy—the overactive metabolic rate kept him pinched and angular. He looked like an Eastern European WWII refugee, a survivor of Auschwitz, or one of those dead-eyed children on TV ads about Africa or South America. She fed him and fed him, but Giles's frail body somehow remained malnourished and starved-looking. And now he was seven years old and defying her, not eating *anything* she put in front of him anymore. He was now living on Coca-Cola and junk food filled with sodium and calories but nothing substantive.

Giles had the demons inside him, fighting for his soul, the demons that had stolen his father's soul before him—the sins of the father shall be visited upon the child—for how many generations? Three, four?

"Perhaps I should have taken Giles off that respirator when he was born," she confided to her priest in the confessional. "Perhaps the girl I was . . . I should not have rushed Giles to the hospital that time when he fell from the apartment window, two stories, breaking his leg, collar bone and his back. All that pain in his back for months afterward had to play havoc with his mind. Perhaps I ought've crushed his skull in, claimed it as part of the fall."

"But you didn't, did you? That speaks good of you. Your motherly instincts were absolute, unbreakable, resolute. You are to be—"

"No, Father, don't misunderstand. This is a small town with small-town cops, but given today's forensic science detectives, like the ones you see on TV, they'd figure out in an instant that it was murder."

Now this.

The boy had killed her cat and had hidden the body in the basement of the old apartment house, stuffed little Squeakums behind the hot-water heater where it now stank of decay and desiccated flesh; dried blood and bile were matted in the dead calico hair. This sent a particularly horrendous odor throughout the building vents. Giles had killed Squeakums, his mother's only pleasure, the jealous little miscreant had murdered poor, innocent Squeakums, his latest outrage.

A little pleasure ball that never did harm to a single living soul, and now to find Squeakums like this, after thinking her only in the ranks of the lost. The truth hurt; it felt so painfully wretched.

Larina's eyes filled with tears. She found a box to put the poor creature's remains in, saying, "I'll see you get a proper burial, my sweet little Squeakums. I'll take care of you now."

She'd been having nightmares of lost Squeakums out in the dark, lost, cold, alone, and frightened in the grid of the city of Millbrook, Minnesota—a small town some twenty miles from the Twin Cities where she had met Giles's father at Millbrook Memorial, where she had once worked as an admitting nurse.

Giles's father had charmed her out of her own life. Swept her off her feet. But he turned out to be the Devil incarnate, as attested to by his having been arrested on charges of murder. He'd left her with promises and pregnancy, and then got himself locked up in an insane asylum—a federal facility for the criminally insane.

She reached in with gloved hands and pulled Squeakums from the corner behind the hot-water heater where she'd been wedged in between the heater and the stone wall. The body was actually warm, she assumed from the warmth of the metal heated by the hot water.

Then she realized as her eyes and hand simultaneously saw and felt the huge rent in Squeakums's back, a gouged out elongated hole from the base of her little brain to the end of her backside, and the curious lightness of the cat's corpse combined to make Larina look closer at the enormous wound. She put the cat's body in the box she meant to bury it in and placed it on an old desktop below a light she had already switched on. Steeling herself, she again examined the puckered wound that was filled with dried, matted hair thick with blood. She also noted that the cat's skull had been caved in by some sort of blunt object.

"My God," she muttered as she peeled back the hardened edges of the long gash down the cat's spine. "My God, he's cut out her backbone, but why? For what possible reason?"

There could be only one purpose, one obsessive, mad goal as satanic as the intent of the Antichrist himself. "Just like his father," she said aloud, "just as insane. He's got the same lunatic psychotic gene, the mark of Cain."

Then she heard a noise, a strange knocking together of metal balls, a creaking crackle of a noise, followed by a slurping sound, and it was all coming from behind a closed, several-times-painted-over door to a little used storage room.

So this is where he's been hiding? She took tentative steps toward the door and reached out to take hold of the doorknob. Her hand suddenly froze over it, shaking, unsure, as unsteady as her mind. She stood there for some time, listening to the sounds from behind the faded multicolored door. Giles was in there doing something unspeakable, something evil and horrid. Conjuring up demons? Playing a game, a little harmless game of divination? Or worse? Far worse?

Her hand continued to hover over the knob as breathing became harder and harder. She knew most certainly she'd be needing her inhaler to get through this but it was upstairs. Should she fling open the door and see something so entirely gross and disgusting as to bring on an asthma attack and be unable to get to her inhaler, should she keel over in one of her fits and become helpless to move or breath, would little sickly Giles rush upstairs for her inhaler doing all in his power to save her? Or would he brain her with a hammer and cut out her spine and take it into the dark storage room and do with it what he might now be doing with Squeakums's?

She knew she had to find a lawyer, make out a will, and see to it that her own body was cremated to keep it from ever falling into her son's hands.

Slurp, slurp . . . more noises from the other side of the door. Little boy sounds of gratification, possibly masturbation. Certainly quenching his thirst as if he had a pitcher of Kool-Aid in there.

Larina Gahran steeled her resolve and found the strength to grab hold of the doorknob in complete inch-by-inch stealth. She turned it slowly to be imperceptible. So far, she felt absolutely certain that little Giles hadn't the least notion she stood here with her cat in a box, angry as hell.

She now had the doorknob turned as far as it would go. She need only to snatch it open and dare to look at precisely what her son was. She hesitated again, wishing her inhaler was at hand, feeling the first shivering rumble of an attack in her cells, subtle but wanting to escape and invade her lungs.

To open or not to open, her mind struggled. She'd come this far, and for Squeakums's sake, and for her own fiery curiosity, she tore the door wide open and stared into the semi-darkness, a weak light from an outside lamppost struggling through the grimy windowpane.

Silhouetted and unaware of his mother, seven-year-old Giles Gahran held the cat's backbone overhead and sucked on its end. A clear yellowy, oily fluid spilled over his lips. With a penknife, he then dug deep into the bone and pulled out chunks of a dried bloodlike substance, the bone marrow, and he consumed this.

Larina stood watching the thing in the shadows that moved with the clumsiness of a child and the precision of a monster all at once. It grunted, moaned in pleasure, licked its chops, touched itself all over, rattled the bones, shaking them for more fluid, more marrow in a kind of eternal squatting animal dance where Giles, cross-legged with arms raised and hands holding on to the cat's spine appeared in the throes of a bliss that she herself had never known, one at once fascinating and terrifying.

A squealing board underfoot gave her away and Giles's catlike, penetrating eyes burned through his mother.

"Get out of here, Mother! Away with you! Now!"

His voice raged out of control, a gravelly, draconian, motorized metallic thrumming thing fueled by venom. Indeed, a child possessed in need of serious help, a child, possessed of a demon.

She dropped Squeakums and the makeshift coffin to race upstairs. She was panting, feeling faint, certain she would die here and now, and terrified that Giles would do to her what he'd done to Squeakums—feed on his own mother's spinal fluid and bone marrow.

Once upstairs and in her kitchen, she fought to maintain control and conscious behavior, tearing into a cupboard for a fresh inhaler and grabbing a knife from the butcher block only to see a larger slit in the block wink back at her.

Gasping, panting, feeling light-headed, and fearful, she leaned heavily against the island block in the kitchen when she heard his footsteps coming up.

"Mom? Mom!" he called out. "I know what it must look like," he calmly spoke as his form materialized from the darkness, "but it's not a bad thing. Just *practicing* for the day I become a surgeon. You said Father was in medicine. I'm just a curious kid is all."

"You fucking killed my cat!"

"No, no! Poor thing, she got hold of something bad, a neighbor's poison, maybe . . . Least I think so . . ." He'd stopped short at the top of the stairs and remained in the doorway to the kitchen, staring at her.

"St-st-stay the fuck away from me, Giles."

"Ahhh, Ma, don't make a big deal of it."

"Of what?"

"Of what you think you saw."

"And what . . . did . . . I see?" She gasped between each word now.

"A little kid experimenting, curious about life's all. I think maybe I'll grow up to become a doctor maybe. Or an illustrator for medical books. I just like to know what makes things . . . and people run, you know?"

"Is that what I saw? I saw Squeakums's head caved in is what I saw, Giles. You killed my cat!"

"No way. I just put it out of its misery. It was suffering bad. In pain and suffering, and I did the right thing is all."

"And you saw fit to cut out her backbone and—"

"It's called a dissection, Mom."

"—and . . . and feed on it?"

"I was curious when I smelled the stuff inside, so I sort of tasted it. You just happened to barge in at the worst time, that's all."

"I don't want to ever hear of your doing anything even remotely like this again, do you understand, you little monster? You little bastard . . . so like your sick father."

"Sure, Mom, sure. I'm really not any kind of monster."

"Then go to the bathroom where I keep more inhalers and get me another one, now!"

He made a step toward her and she flinched. "Sure, I'll go get the inhaler."

Alone again, Giles's mother feared she might catch his madness, his and his father's. She wondered if she dared try to institutionalize him. She wondered if she could. The worry brought on a new wave of fast gasps for air and a coughing jag at once.

She thought of the years yet ahead of her with him as her child. She wondered what might become of Giles, wondered again if he would ever contemplate robbing her of life for her spinal column the way he had Squeakums's.

In the will, she would insist on him never being left alone with her body. She would insist on immediate cremation.

She got a mental image of him feeding on her bone marrow, his lips and tongue slick with her spinal fluid.

He had enjoyed it too much with the cat.

ONE

Millbrook, Minnesota
November 14, 2002

Louisa Anne Childe closed a dying fist around the blood-soaked charcoal drawing she'd so loved—the impeccable image of her sitting in the park across the street, doing what she loved, feeding the late winter birds. With a trapped breath in her throat, believing it her last, she knew—feared—gasped. Her only hold left on this life—her sketch. Perhaps in the next life, things would be as peaceful as in the black-and-white drawing. Still, birdlike breaths of air fluttered, perched, and then struggled past her lips and into her lungs; and when she felt the dagger rip into her spine, she wished desperately that it had been her last breath.

Cheated, she felt a wave of anger against God for allowing this murder—her murder. She'd always imagined herself dying peacefully in her sleep. Instead, she would die a *fool*, a victim of murder, by a cunning killer who had led her down a grim-rose lane with a mere bit of artistry, the sleight of hand of flattery playing no small part. He had been so good for her ego . . . until now. What would Papa say . . . ? He'd say she was a fool woman, that's what, and that she'd be left with the now-worthless sketch and her own disgrace.

Disgrace at being found dead at the hand of a man she had invited past her threshold. How stupid was that? How disgraceful her body would present itself. She feared her spirit would hover, witness to the disgrace. The thought of it, the horror of a scene involving paramedics, policemen and women, detectives, coroners . . . it was simply horrid. She feared being manhandled by those strangers, certain none would look like Basil Rathbone, Clark Gable or George Clooney. She feared strangers seeing her nude form, her clothes ripped from her, her naked body bloated and ugly with the passage of time, as she had no one.

No one would come looking until the rent was long overdue. Even more painful, the truth: She had literally put herself into an early grave by a murdering con artist. Louisa felt this humiliation above all, even above the pain of the cold giant chasm now being opened down the length of her spine.

The last earthly words she heard, he whispered in her ear, "You will still sit for me, *won't* you, Louisa." It wasn't a question, more a statement. Little wonder he had failed to sign her charcoal drawing.

Louisa Anne Childe had endured the flesh-separating blade, feeling it course from the nape of her neck and race to the bottom of her spine. When the second cut snaked from the bottom up and up, and finally returned to the nape, Louisa still clutched the drawing. Her killer had seduced her with the enticement of charcoal drawings of her in the park, sitting, feeding birds.

She now fell into unconsciousness, her fist frozen about her favorite of four sketches.

By the time the rectangle of flesh was removed from her

back, Louisa had died from hemorrhagic shock. She didn't feel a thing when her murderer's gloved hands latched on to her spine with one hand and worked a rib cutter with the other. He cut the twelve thoracic vertebra of the rib cage from their hold on the spinal cord. This finished, twisted wirelike nerves snapped as he tugged and ripped the backbone, but it jammed and held.

"Godfuckingsonofamotherfuckingbitching bastard!" he erupted and immediately covered his mouth with his gloved hand to silence himself. "Like fighting with a metal snake," he added as he continued to tug. Finally, the spinal octopus let go and came free, almost sending Giles tumbling over.

The sketch-artist killer liked the heft and weight and feel of the bone snake in his hands, freed of all its moorings.

Strangely supple and beautiful in its shape, the human spine had always fascinated Giles, even as a child. And now he had one in his possession, to have as his own, to do with as he wished, and he had a plan. In the waiting room of a chiropractor's office, in a collection of newspaper clippings favoring the laying-on-of-hands science over pills and surgeries, he had read that every person on the planet had slight individual differences in their spinal development— some quite subtle, others as remarkable and as lurid as those of the Elephant Man. Certainly no two *racks* were ever exactly alike. So he now held a unique backbone in his hands, Louisa's, dripping with bodily fluids and blood.

The blood splatters, pools and puddles amounting to a great deal of red, reflected in Giles's delighted eyes as he turned the spinal column in his hands, closely examining it. "A true work of art," he muttered. "But I can't ever do this again . . . never."

He saw the woman's cat, "Archer" she'd called the little creature. Archer stood on his paws as if they'd turned to arrowheads, prepared to dart or pounce or race off, but his marble-green eyes froze wide at the fear he swallowed in a growl. Staring from behind a doily-covered sofa, Archer's nose went busily atwitter with the odor of blood and what wafts up from an opened body.

Giles reached a tentative hand out, calling, "Here, kitty, here kitty-kitty!"

But when he tried to pet Archer, the cat slipped below the sofa and disappeared in one fluid motion. "Don't want nothing to do with me. Smart animal," Giles muttered. Then he near shouted, "I've yanked out a few cat spines in my day!"

Giles then turned his attention to the human spine in his left hand, Louisa's gruel-dripping backbone. He laid the spinal column across the dead woman's buttocks. As he busily collected her blood in small, empty honey jars he'd cleaned and brought with him—sample-size jars he'd pocketed from the hotel where he'd been staying the entire time he had staked out Louisa's place, having stalked her from her beloved park bench to her most private corner of the planet. He briefly flashed on *Grendel*, which he'd read as a child, and how touched he had been by the monster's cave. How cold and unhappy a place it was, and the creature's absolute aloneness—an Adam without an Eve. And so poorly misunderstood, the sad oversized hairy beast, and how very pathetic it all became, his story. How he had no choice but to attack and destroy those men who sat about the warm hearths chomping on their muttonchops and raising their ale glasses and whoring with their women. How he'd see the lights of men in the company of men, and how he must absolutely hate them for their happiness.

Giles shook off the remembrance with a strange psychic shiver he little understood. Time to finish up with the blood collection and pack up the spine for transport, but then his stomach churned with a clawing hunger, a reminder of the deserted corned beef on rye that Louisa had made for him, left unattended in the kitchenette.

From a kneeling position over the body, Giles pushed off the bloody carpet to stand over Louisa's remains. Her spine was as beautiful and intricate as he'd imagined all those days and weeks of stalking her. It reflected her beautiful soul, Giles thought before stepping over the mutilated body, going for the sandwich. Once in the kitchen area, he stood contemplating whether or not he had left behind any trace of himself when he saw the red footprints on the Italian marble tiles he'd just walked across.

A small oval mirror—a homey Midwestern message stamped onto the glass—stared across at him where he leaned against the counter, chomping down large bites of the corned beef. He thought it odd how his reflected eyes formed little blue bull's-eyes in the final two O's in the *of* and *of* in the familiar, apropos message: *Today Is The Last Day Of The Rest Of Your Life.*

Giles hadn't removed his hat or his tight-fitting gloves on entering her place, even when she offered to turn on the gas-driven fireplace. He'd argued it was unnecessary and that he'd only be a few minutes. So he had kept hat and gloves on, as they were now in the mirror. But he had also admitted that his fingers and toes remained numb from being outside, and that's when the mother in Louisa leapt out. She insisted he stay for a sandwich and a tumbler of whiskey "to warm his giblets," as she'd put it.

With the gloves on, he needn't worry about fingerprint evidence. The hairnet he wore below his winter knit cap would keep hairs from falling, but there was always fiber evidence, and now his footprints in blood. He had to consider everything. As he did so, his cobalt-blue eyes surveyed the kitchenette, which in its heyday surely must have been top of the line, fabulous even. As he looked about the small space, he heard the crunch of glass.

"Damn me!" he cursed, lifting his shoe off the glass tumbler she'd earlier knocked from his hand in her panic at realizing that Giles had come for far more than money for the charcoal drawings he'd done of Louisa in the park. The broken glass underfoot lay shattered in countless pieces now, whereas it had been neatly shorn into three large, easy-to-dispose parts before he had clumsily stomped on it. Earlier her cheap whiskey had gone flying when she lashed out at him with a broomstick. Any minute amount of saliva on the shards of the glass would carry his DNA. He scooped all the larger pieces into his gloved hands and tossed them into the trash container. He then located broom and dustpan and swept up the residue of granular-sized glass, the sandy stuff mixing with hair, fiber, dust, all discarded into the plastic container lining the trash can.

He next stared at the counter, littered with the paraphernalia of apartment living: obligatory spice rack, bottles, jars, can opener, skillets, dirty dishes—*she'd not been expecting him so soon*—nickel-plated silverware, used-up E. coli–infested sponges and dish towels. Amid this, he had located his half-bitten corned beef on rye piled high with tomato, lettuce, mayo and mustard that Louisa had lovingly prepared for him, remarking on how cooking for a man was tantamount to a gesture of true love, blushing as she said it, the old dear.

A gnat-sized banana fly flit into and out of his peripheral vision as if *lift off* had come from the center of his sandwich. Louisa's lithe little soul in the guise of an insect—a black Tinkerbell perhaps? Highly doubtful, but the possibility the thing had been crawling on his sandwich the entire time he'd been taking bites from it disturbed him enough to make him toss it into the trash bin with the broken glass.

Giles left the bag open to receive his bloody clothing and shoes. Naked now, he next lifted the broom from the floor. Firmly holding on to the broom, Giles painted his bloody shoe prints into swirls and eddies created by the nylon bristles. He stood back and studied the beauty of patterns he found unexpected. The patterns made the red circles look like giant fingerprints, but they'd be useless to authorities, these giant, mocking prints. The thought of it created a strange but welcome shiver along the length of his epidermis from scalp to toe.

This finished, he stepped back into the cramped living area. He stepped over Louisa's body and placed the bag alongside his other two bags near the door, readying to leave once dressed. But first, seeing additional red shoe marks stamped and drying against the carpet, he quickly swiped at these with the broom. His finished product here created a river-stream effect of red against the thick pile to blot out his footprints as he worked his way backward toward the door and the bags he'd placed there.

He looked down at his victim, the woman he thought an absolutely useless human being. Mousy brown hair just turning to gray, the first signs of old age beginning to crease her face, a woman tired of life, Giles imagined. Had never been with a man, he further imagined, never dared anything, never lived. The dash between the dates on her tombstone will stand for nothing, he told himself. Still, she had been sweet to him, kindly, motherly even. He hadn't expected the depth of her concern, and he'd felt ill at ease with it, though certainly he'd cultivated her trust. A double-edged sword; part of the game. While Louisa had, in effect, made things far easier for him as a result of her trusting kindness toward him, the end result was accompanied by a strange feeling in Giles, a twinge of remorse. Such regret surprised him.

In a way, Louisa had shared with Giles a handful of similar, if not identical, characteristics, just as *he* shared with the monster Grendel. She was trusting, wanting to believe the best in human nature, even good-hearted. In another time, another place, another upbringing, with other parentage, Giles believed he'd have been as kindly, as good of heart as Louisa any day of the week. His mind tumbled over the notion that it could not wrap around, trying to form thoughts, the thoughts trying to form words, to get a fix, a hold on the facts and keep them in order. She got what was coming to her in the long run, her damnable, milksop, cookie-baking, Millbrook kindness notwithstanding, something he'd encouraged sure, but he'd wanted it to be false, not true, a kind of Midwestern traditional mask, all bullshit, her mewing at him like a kindly mother, her treating him as she did her precious damned Archer as if she meant it, as if it meant anything, when all it managed to do was cloud his determination, blur his purpose, and make things more difficult. The bitch'd made things easy only up to a point; even after death, she somehow managed to make things hard. Certainly harder than doing dogs and cats. In fact, thanks to her damnable sandwich and whiskey and doting, she'd made it the hardest thing Giles had ever had to do. Still, he congratulated himself on having stood his *ground* and having done the deed.

Earlier he had visually scouted the walls and shelves, any surface for photographs but found no family pictures. After taking Louisa's spine, he'd searched drawers and boxes and beneath her mattress for any personal letters or envelopes lying about. Aside from bills, nothing. Apparently she had no ties, just as his intuition had led him to believe. No one to miss her passing.

Giles had watched her go in and out of the building. Louisa only came out to cash checks, visit the corner grocery for birdseed, food and liquor. Her only recreation or joy at all appeared to be in feeding the birds across the street at that run-down children's park he stared at now through her apartment window. His artist's eye—studying the patterns of snow-laden November leaves—saw the mosaic of color, texture and line created about the dry earth, rendering ocher and orange amid patches still green with life alongside the blight of dirty snowdrifts piled high, each a counterpoint to the other like the tug of war between seasons.

Giles had begun to frequent the park, and had begun to follow her to the her grocery, carrying his art supplies on his back. At the grocery, he'd watched her pay with food stamps and guessed that she lived on disability checks. A miserable life, yet one she prized more highly than he'd imagined. For two weeks now, he'd watched and waited, approaching with great care and a foolproof plan to play on her vanity—what little she still possessed.

Giles recalled how surreptitiously—how like old Archer still hidden somewhere nearby—he had encroached on Louisa's tree-lined territory there in the park to gain her attention. His sketchbook in hand, he set up at her favorite bench, where he busily replicated her birds. Giles suspected that her birds must be the only thing in life more prized than her drink. Certainly, she interacted far more with her birds than with anyone in the neighborhood.

"You're drawing the birds," she had said to him only this morning.

"I find them *fascinating*."

"Really? Someone of your generation?"

"My generation? I've read Conrad Deueval's books on bird behavior, how very much they are like—"

"—like us," she finished for him. "Deueval is marvelous. God what insight he has into people as well as birds."

Giles had read in the man's introduction that he had never known how to interact with his parents, was alienated all his school life, failed miserably at every endeavor, and could not stand working or living in the same environment with people. Giles easily empathized. But his interest here was in catching and dissecting Louisa Anne Childe for her spinal column with its sweet meats and juices. Still he got caught up in Deueval's musings. When the man came into money, he built a four-story house off Bird Cove Key on an island bird sanctuary in an apparent deal too good for the state of Florida to turn down. He had the house built with no doors and no glass in the hundreds of window frames, allowing free access to the bird population—video cameras everywhere, running twenty-four hours, seven days a week. The biggest birdhouse on the planet.

Giles learned all he could, to intersperse his knowledge into the conversations he hoped to have with Louisa in order to wrangle an invitation to cross her threshold. Once inside, he knew he could proceed with his own fanaticism which did not include birds.

"Conrad Deueval earned his doctorate in the natural sciences and with his Ph.D. and his books chronicling bird activity and behavior, he proved there is little difference in the working brain of a bird and that of people, especially promiscuous men!" she said and laughed, blushing red. Giles recognized the little girl in the aging face, amid the pudgy cheeks and crease of her smile from nose to chin.

"Have you . . . did you read his last book?" Giles asked.

"*The Frightening Truth About Ourselves?* I have it on order at the local bookstore."

"I could get it far more quickly for you."

"How?"

"I know the author," lied Giles.

"No! You don't! How?"

"My uncle's roommate in college knew him."

"But Conrad Deueval's never finished college. He bought his degree sometime later. He could not be confined and chained down by academic bureaucracy and ballyhoo. A great man, a brilliant mind."

"Do you want the book tomorrow?"

"You have that kind of access to the man?"

"Well, two days. Give me two days."

"All right, you're on, but I insist on paying for your troubles."

"Only one kind of payment I would accept from you," Giles replied, knowing he had her in his grasp.

"What . . . what exactly did you . . . that is . . . do you have . . . in mind, young man?"

"Oh, oh, please, nothing like that, ma'am, no! No way."

She flushed, embarrassed. She pointed and spoke to cover her blushing cheeks in the frosty air. "Look at them."

He followed her finger to the begging birds.

She added, "Watch how they play and fight among themselves."

"Just like people. Just as Deueval says." He went back to his sketching of the birds as if he'd forgotten something he had to either touch up quickly or lose to memory. This invited her to come near, to stare over his shoulder at the sketch book, curious.

In his ear, she made a sound with her teeth. "Is it for a book? A magazine?"

"What? This, the picture? No, I'm really not that good. It's just practice. I'm taking classes, you see."

She examined the charcoal sketch he'd crafted.

"How much?" she then asked.

"Oh, I don't sell them. I'm not that good. Besides it's *unfinished*."

She pursued him. "Name your price. I want at least four."

"Four? One for each wall?" he'd asked, joking.

"Yes as a matter of fact."

"Okay . . . Okay . . . I'll give you the bird sketches if you'll *sit* for me."

"Sit for you? You mean as . . . some sort of—"

"As centerpiece to my homework, as an integral part of my getting a decent grade without having to hire some fake actor. I draw you, now, right here amid the—your birds."

"Oh, they're not *my* birds. They're *free*. No one owns these footloose feathers."

At that moment, she seemed to him more lonely than reclusive. "I've seen you out here before, feeding them." He allowed her a closer look at the work. "It calls for you to be in it," he added and smiled. "The final drawing . . . perhaps a painting to follow . . . you should be in it alongside the birds, really."

"But if I sit for you, and you give me your work free of charge . . . what's in it for you?"

"I learn my craft. It's a . . . you know . . . a challenge."

They exchanged first names.

Wasting no time, Giles had then speed-sketched her into the work in progress, having earlier left a space for her likeness. She fit perfectly, looking like St. Francis amid the birds. Louisa loved it, taking it to her breast and asking for three more pictures just of the park and the birds.

"When and where can I bring the other sketches to you?"

She pointed to her building. "One-oh-six is the number."

He had watched her walk off, the November wind tugging at her coattails.

"She's the perfect choice, isn't she?" he asked the birds.

HE had choked on the stuffy air in her hallway. When he'd knocked, she was careful to call through the door, asking who it might be—as if she had frequent visitors—a pretense born of pride and embarrassment, Giles imagined.

"It's Giles . . . I have your finished drawings."

She cracked the door, and seeing him, she threw it open. "You can't possibly be finished already!"

"But I am. They were easy." He held out the charcoal sketches. "They weren't hard, really."

She looked at each one, praising each in turn. "Let me pay you something for these. They're beautiful." She saw that he stared at her. "Oh, where are my manners? Come in . . . come in! It's become too cold out, hasn't it? I'll get you something that will warm your giblet. You must be hungry, too. It's so wonderful to be able to create like you do. It must be so fulfilling and rewarding. Such a gift. Such talent. Were you born with it? Of course, you were, but you must have had to cultivate it as well. Like the seed into the flower, to see it flourish, you must see it nourished, as they say. I once tried my hand at watercolors . . . once . . . once was enough." She twittered instead of laughing. "Everyone in the class was so good, and my stuff . . . it was . . . well, pitiful."

Giles gave the appearance of caring to listen to her nonstop chatter. It'd been as if a floodgate were opened. Once inside, with the door closed, Giles heard a man's voice through the thin wall say, "Plumber, ma'am! You called for a plumber?"

It registered with Giles that he mustn't give Louisa a chance to scream out.

Giles had grown somewhat fond of the bird lady. While not decrepit or elderly, Louisa seemed far older than Giles's twenty-two years—perhaps by some fifteen or twenty years—he thought. She was neither pretty nor ugly, only plain—like her choice of clothes, her face a featureless sky, no life in her eyes until and unless she were speaking of or *to* her birds.

She had turned her back to him and gone straight into the kitchen. Once there, she poured him a drink—Jack Daniel's, softening it with water from an Ice Mountain bottle. She immediately began building him the sandwich, and offered him breadsticks while he waited. In between she said, "Take your hat and gloves off. Stay awhile."

He patiently waited, biding his time, alert to the right moment when it came. The creation of the sandwich finished, and it handed to him, Giles took a couple of bites and swallowed down some whiskey.

She went back to the sketches she'd laid on the kitchen table, glancing at them with admiration. "The sketches . . . I'm going to frame each and place each one up on the walls. Now you must take *something* for your troubles, Giles. I insist."

She gazed to her purse on the table, placed the sketches down and lifted the purse. Rifling through for cash, she turned toward him.

"I don't want your money, Louisa." His tone made her look up from the purse and into his eyes. From a darkened corner, her cat growled and hissed at him, and she said, "Now, Archer, bad cat! You stop that now. This is our guest—Giles. You remember, I told you all about Giles, and that he might be coming by to visit with us."

"If you really want to help me, you'll sit for me," he said. "But please, I won't take your money."

"I can do that, sit. In fact, it's one of the best things I do, indeed." Lightly laughing at her own little joke, Louisa again lifted the sketches, studying them. Then she said, "Giles, you didn't sign the sketches."

"Forget about the sketches for the moment and concentrate on me," he said, staring into her eyes. She saw something she could not read flash across those cobalt-blue eyes. He still hadn't taken off his gloves or his hat, only the overcoat.

"Giles, why don't you take off your hat and those gloves?"

"I'm still cold," he repeated.

"Jack Daniel's'll help with that." She poured him a second tumbler full and went to the fridge for the water.

"I want you to sit for me *now*, Louisa," he told her as she placed the glass in his hands.

"Why didn't you sign the sketches, Giles? They're beautiful. You must see that. You, young man, are an artist of extraordinary talent."

"Careful of that word. Talent usually means the end result of years of preparation." He put aside his barely tasted sandwich. "In the living room, on the floor, Louisa. I want to sketch you lying on the floor."

"Lying on the floor? Really? Now?"

"In the supine position."

"You mean lounging on pillows?"

"Yes, with your clothes off."

"Nude! I hardly know you, Giles."

"I only want to draw you, Louisa. I have no intention of taking advantage of you or to lose the mutual respect and admiration we have. Besides, our age difference alone is . . . is . . ."

"Is what?" she sounded scolding.

"Ahhh . . . incompatible."

She shook her head, almost laughed but frowned instead. "Incompatible, indeed."

"I mean it could only lead to no good, and I wouldn't dare jeopardize our newfound friendship."

In the back of his head, a voice told him to get on with it, to drop all pretense and take what he wanted and swiftly.

She smiled. "You're right, of course, but you have a lot to learn about how to flatter a girl . . . ahhh . . . woman." She blushed at the underlying suggestiveness, and that they were dancing around such a subject at all. "I suggest you read *Men Are from—*".

"*Mars . . . Women . . . from Venus.* I have, but it hasn't helped." He laughed on cue.

Having made him laugh struck her as amazing, and he saw that, for a millisecond, she appeared to fight back a heart-wrenching tear. A quiet coyness filtered into her voice. "I'm not sure if I should be pleased about this age difference thing, or if I should take offense."

"Calmly now, Louisa, go into the other room, get comfortable with the idea and the pillows and the floor and the nudity. You will be beautiful when I am done with you, I promise. I promise."

Louisa only stared in response. "I-I-I couldn't . . . not without weeks of workouts . . . you know, the cellulite, flab!"

"What?"

"I just couldn't . . . really, Giles. Not in a million years." She shivered from within. "We hardly . . . I hardly know you. It's out of the question, and I think . . ."

"How much more do we need to know about one another? This is just false modesty, Louisa."

"No . . . no . . . nothing false about it. I have plenty to be modest about."

"But you're beautiful."

She dropped her gaze and shook her head. "I know better. All life has taught me different."

"Just do it . . . like the ads say, just do it, Louisa." His impatience filtered through.

"I really can't see myself doing that, Giles."

"But that's precisely how you do it. You psych up for it, mentally, picturing yourself there"—he pointed to her living room floor—"lying nude there for me to paint. Look, I've gone to the trouble to bring all my tools and supplies for the job. You really must, and I insist."

"With a lady, you don't insist on anything, not in my house, Giles, and if I'm uncomfortable with the idea, why then—"

"What's a little moment's awkwardness and discomfort if it serves a larger purpose and—"

"I-I-I would like you to leave now, Giles."

He didn't move. "Leave?"

"Now. Now, Giles. I want you to leave, yes . . . please."

Still he did not budge.

A slow quaking fear slithered along her spine like a warning, an instinctual bell tolling inside her frame. "Out! Out this minute, Giles. I want you out!" She went to the table and lifted the charcoal drawings and said, "Our arrangement is over! You can have these back!"

She held out the drawings, and he reluctantly took them. His eyes downcast, he looked like a petulant boy.

But instead of leaving, he laid aside three of the sketches and held one out to her. "You must keep this one, Louisa."

She had instinctively clutched on to the broom to use as a weapon, should she need it.

"Take the sketch and don't be foolish. I'm *leaving*, Louisa, and I'm so sorry. The last thing I wanted was that you should feel a moment's distress around me, really," Giles assured her. Indicating the broom, he added, "You can put that down. It's totally unnecessary, Louisa. We don't need shit like this between us. We're still friends, right?"

She eased her grip on the broom but stood her ground. She stared at the single drawing, her favorite of the four, extended to her.

"Of course, you're right."

"I mean, who couldn't use another friend. No such thing as too many friends, right?"

She nodded, saying nothing, as if embarrassed, and she further loosed her grip on the broom. The moment she took hold of the charcoal drawing of herself surrounded by birds, Giles grabbed for the broom, frightening her. With the sketch clutched against the handle, she brought the broom up and knocked the glass from his hand. It rained across the floor in miniature thunder. The broken pieces winked up at the odd pair—recluse and would-be killer.

"Please, Louisa, you're beautiful . . . a beautiful person resides deep within you. In your soul, and I want to get at it. That's all, that's all."

She softened in both body language and tone. "That's all?"

"Yes, that's all I want is to sketch you. After that, I want to do you in oils, that is to *paint* you. You see, I sketch first, paint last."

She hesitated. She tightened her grip on the sketch in her hands.

Giles quietly said, "All I really want for Christmas is your spine, Louisa. You can keep the rest."

"What?" she said, confused. "What did you say?"

But even as she asked this, he pulled a small, hefty hammer from the loose overalls he wore, and the ugly tool came crashing down, bloodying her scalp. She stumbled to the floor and crawled into the living room, dazed, disorientated, still clutching the sketch, wondering where she was and what had happened to her. Even dazed, she felt him standing over her. Something instinctive told her to face him, but she could not stand. Doing the next best thing, she turned onto her back to face up. "Come close, closer . . ." she croaked out a whisper.

He leaned in over her. "You have some final words?" he asked.

She whispered so low that he could not hear. When he came within reach, she tore at his face with her nails, shouting, "Bastard!"

Her fighting back had surprised Giles; he wondered why she wanted to live. To hang pictures of birds on her walls? To feed her cat? To clean her sink of dishes? Some other mundane chore in her dull existence?

She'd passed out, and needing to get at her entire backside, he ripped her clothes from her. The entry through the back must be completely unfettered. He next located the sketches and began to stuff them into the bag. But he was stopped when he saw the blood stained sketch she clung to. He decided to place the last three he'd done on the walls as she had planned. He hunted down her tape-and-scissors drawer and got it done.

Backing up, studying and admiring his hung *Collection of Birds in the Park*, he imagined what she had had in mind. With the right frames and in this context, it might have been lovely. Too bad he could not take credit, a bow for the work. *It was good.*

He next returned to his tools and pulled out his scalpel and rib cutter.

The actual killing had taken less than a minute; the working up to it all these months, was a different story altogether.

Still, getting in and out of Louisa's apartment had taken far too much time. Giles now felt an urgency to vacate without being seen. He lifted the hand she had scratched his face with; she had left him with a scar from chin to Adam's apple. Using the rib cutter, he snapped off each fingertip at the joint, dropping each into the trash bag alongside the broken glass and his partial sandwich. One of the round-nailed fingertips missed the bag, seemingly leaping to freedom, rolling away toward the sofa chair, when in the same instant Archer the cat darted and snatched it up and was gone again.

"Damn you, cat!" he bellowed. He coaxed but failed to lure the cat from its hiding place; kneeling low, looking up under the sofa chair, he learned the damn thing had simply vanished, along with Louisa's fingertip. "Fucking cat!"

Giving up on the cat, Giles turned back to Louisa's body and stopped momentarily to stare at how beautiful the geometry of her form lay there, splayed open, limbs forming a kind of human swastika, each aligned in a spontaneous akimbo, but what struck him most remained that damnable charcoal drawing clutched in her dying hand. The sight caused him to give up cutting off any more fingertips. He reasoned it out: She had to've torn at him with her only free hand, and since he resided somewhere under the police radar here in Millbrook, Minnesota, he had acted accordingly to remain that way, removing any possible DNA he may've left in the apartment or on the body—all save the DNA the cat would hopefully consume.

"Isn't likely they'll cut open a cat for evidence they don't know is there," he muttered to the empty room and corpse.

For some minutes, he stood clear of the blood while regarding her in death, moving round the body with care in his bare feet, considering every angle. He made mental notes for later. He'd want to depict her exactly as she lay here, only in the abstract—caught like a butterfly on a pin within the context of his art.

No, he needn't bother with her right hand. She'd only scratched him with her left, and only the once before falling back.

"Got to get out of here," he told Archer from whom he caught snatches of contented birdlike murmurs coming from the gut and throat, somewhere below the sofa, happy with his prize. Out Louisa's window, he saw a man walking a poodle past a service truck of some sort. He ruminated how people foolishly attributed warm, cozy feelings to their animals so as to feel better about themselves, as if they had some kind of reciprocal even symbiotic relationship with

their pets, as if the pet cared. And people did this so routinely and without the slightest sense or dared thought. The
same people who made light of a man like John Edwards,
the TV psychic, attributed an entire array of emotions and
feelings of love that their cat or dog *provided* them, when in
fact the animal liked your smell, and why'd it like your
odor? Because when your smell was nearby, they knew
they'd be fed. And this Childe woman with her birds and
this crazy belief system she had built up around them, as if
they spent time thinking about her, placing her in their little animal dreams and thoughts, as if they gave a shit about
her when all they really cared about came out of a bag of
feed in her hand. The woman had come to think of herself as
a kind of Uncle Remus—like in a Disney film—birds flit-
ting about her cheek, stealing kisses, or a St. Francis of As-
sisi in a skirt, animals whispering in her ear the secrets of
the universe and peace on fucking Earth. And all that crap
about the complexity of the bird's brain written by that so-
called naturalist who bought his degree was exactly that—
crap. "Birds're as smart as my left nipple," Giles allowed.
"Bird Man of Alcatraz only proved one thing—birds contract as many diseases as we do, but it took the brain of a
man to combat those diseases."

Poor stupid self-deluded reclusive Louisa Childe. Her
last thoughts were likely of her birds and Archer.

Giles went back to the door he would exit from, and
there he removed what might be taken as a big blue easel
bag, struggling to bring it from deep within his backpack.
Successful, he dug from the bag a large towel. Using the
towel, he lifted the woman's spine from where he had left it
on her buttocks, wrapping the serpentine rack of bones in
the towel and carefully working it, section by section, into
the oblong bag without its coming apart.

The vertebral column filled the blue bag, creating a
somewhat irregular line, but Giles had read somewhere
that the eye saw only what the eye wanted to see. He wor-

ried little that anyone would stop him to ask what might be inside the bag. After all, it wasn't as if he were transporting a body. It would appear to anyone he might pass that he carried an easel inside. Nothing sinister about an easel.

He then located his change of clothes. He quickly pulled on a set of clean underclothes, pants and a pullover sweatshirt to accompany his hat and gloves. Finally, he replaced his shoes and socks with what he'd brought. He then threw on his coat, filled his hands with bags, and with a final look around, surveying the charcoal drawings on the wall, and the one clutched in Louisa's hand, he bid adieu to the place and the woman who had supplied him with what he needed. He inched out the door, careful to make no noise.

As he walked down the hallway, the bagged spine over his shoulder, he located the incinerator shaft and dropped the trash bag with glass, leftover sandwich, fingertips with his DNA embedded (all save the one the cat had squirreled away), and the bloody clothing he'd been wearing. It would all burn with the Tuesday morning trash as it did every Tuesday morning on the corner of Cologen and Geldman streets, a crossroads intersection with a stern green light in the middle of icy Millbrook, Minnesota.

The cold air fired brisk chilling needles into the pours of his face.

"Thank you, Miss Childe for a lovely evening and a fine trade," he said to himself as he stepped out onto the street. Surprised, he found that the plumber's van had remained parked out front of the building the entire night. "Looks like someone else got lucky at Number Forty-eight Geldman," he muttered, hefting the bone sack and sauntering casually toward the bus stop.

Giles loved riding buses. Loved people watching.

TWO

My days are in the yellow leaf,
The flowers and fruits of life are gone,
The worm, the canker, and the grief
Are mine alone.

—LORD BYRON

Milwaukee, Wisconsin
November 12, 2004

"MOTHERS . . . you gotta back pain in dem joints? Den back outta dem joints."

"I'd say the cure was worse than the patient."

"Yeah, surefire way to get rid of that pesky ol' sciatica . . ." muttered Special Agent in Charge, Xavier Darwin Reynolds to the others from the crime-scene unit, who were gathered about the victim, each in turn taking a verbal joust at the impossibly insane crime scene.

Not only had the victim's back been splayed wide open by an as-yet-undetermined blade, but her insides looked out at the detectives—shyly hiding, peeking out through a bloody rectangle in her back the size of a French-louvered window.

All surrounding tissue and remaining bones had collapsed inward on organs untouched by the killer and the

bone cutter used to extract the spinal column from its calci-
fied moorings. And so the *back window* stood open like some
bizarre pirate's chest, literally plundered as if an archeologi-
cal dig, and the plunderer had made off with a strange treasure indeed, leaving all the rest. He had not cored out her
eyes. Had not taken any teeth. Had taken nothing of her
features, asked nothing of her breasts, nothing of her geni-
talia. Only the serpent of bone.

An enormously disturbing sight for which the only defense seemed stark, grim humor which now, thanks to the
lead investigator's having joined in, opened the floodgate
wide.

"Least she had—with an emphasis on *had*—backbone."

"Somebody really had a *boner* on for her."

"Gonna need one helluva big pot to flavor the ol' bisque
with that ham-bone!"

"Ham-bone, ham-bone!" sang a tall female agent.

"Gone are the days of *spine* and roses," said a photographer.

"Gives new meaning to the old spinal tap, don't it?"
came another.

"Render unto us a few bars, Jerry, 'Take me BAAAAACK
to ol' Virginy . . . ' "

"Guy needs serious *back up*."

"All right, enough with the vertebral backgammon,"
said FBI Medical Examiner Dr. Jessica Coran, who stood
staring from the small foyer leading into the apartment. Jessica had just arrived from the airfield, her auburn hair bur-
nished and gleaming in the light filtering through the
apartment windows. Jessica's keen eye immediately crossed
swords with the awful wound done the victim, when a large
policewoman stepped between her and the body—cutting
off her line of vision. Jessica silently thanked the woman,
wondering if it were intentional or otherwise.

The small army of men and women of the Milwaukee,
Wisconsin, FBI field office crime-scene unit fell silent. The
others watched this guru of forensics who'd flown in from

Quantico, copiloting the FBI Lear Jet from Virginia to oversee their case.

Jessica quickly donned a hair net over her ample hair, which had been pulled tight in a ponytail for the work. She slipped a pair of gloves over her smooth, suntanned fingers and worked them over each hand. She wondered if any of the others could read what was going on behind her shining eyes. Eyes now sending messages to a brain that truly didn't want to cooperate with the image she'd seen only photos of until now. She stalled for time, swallowing back the bile that threatened to erupt on her first sight of the god-awful hacking the victim had taken.

"Ever see anything like this in the D.C. area?" asked one of the field ops, a strikingly large young woman with a blue jacket over her vomit-stained business suit. It appeared from her nonchalance that she'd been in and out of the crime-scene area, and that she'd popped something akin to Prozac. Her dangling name tag read Amanda Petersaul.

She extended a gloved hand and Jessica pumped it. "I'm Agent Petersaul. Everyone just calls me Pete."

"You mean the boy's've decided you're OK, so they graced you with a nickname."

"Exactly."

"What do you make of it so far?" Jessica indicated the deceased.

"You can't be in this crime scene without steppin' in it, so you'd best—"

"Put on the booties, I can see that," replied Jessica. A curving river of blood painted the carpet all round them there in the foyer. They stood on the dried stuff and it felt crunchy beneath Jessica's shoes. She placed on the booties and tied them about her ankles.

Jessica looked toward the body a second time. Agent Pete's considerable size continued to act as a kind of blind from which Jessica could safely view it without anyone seeing her pained wince. She'd been trained not to show emotion under any circumstance at a crime scene. Her number of years and experience had taught her the only way to gain the trust and authority required to take control in mutilation murder cases was via an aloofness and professional acumen that could not be questioned.

"This is like looking at a war wound," commented Agent Petersaul.

"You come to us through the military?" asked Jessica.

"How'd you guess?"

"Psychic powers and that pendant around your neck, GI issue."

"Had it made at great expense." She fingered the golden numbers: *101st Airborne.* "First in, last out."

"You see duty in Iraq?"

"Pakistan and Iraq. Fucked up place in a fucked up world, yeah."

"Fucked up? Which one?"

"Both."

"Oh, yes, of course. How're we doing there in the Mideast now? Think we'll win the post-war economic crisis?"

"The natives have gone ape-shit for American goods, means and ways. They love all things Western and are embracing apple pie, Elvis, McDonald's and Fox News Network."

"Sounds like Japan."

"Been there? Tokyo?"

"Yeah, that and Beijing, China—worlds apart. Beijing is 1930 America, while Tokyo is futuristic America—*Minority Report* time." Jessica looked into the hefty agent's wide face, and the full-figured Pete smiled back. "Best I get to work, Agent," Jessica added now.

Petersaul nodded and stepped aside. "Yeah, best, but"—she broke into an Elvis oldie—"didja-eva, eva get, eva get one, eva get one-a-those girls boys . . ."

Smacks of a virgin to such horror and trying to compensate, Jessica thought, likely her first year out of the academy with a lot of questions and horror ahead of her, unless she dropped out of this line of work. Jessica calmly replied, "I believe I've seen every kind of iced and diced corpse, male and female, in the book, thanks to my boss at Quantico, Agent Petersaul."

"So I've been told by Darwin. Sexual mutilation murders, hearts ripped out, vaginas and breasts butchered, cranium's opened and brains scooped out."

Others listened in with interest.

"However, I can safely say that I've never come across a victim with so horrid a gash of flesh removed from her body as this unfortunate woman."

Unfortunate, she rolled the word over in her mind. The understatement of the century, for this crime rivaled even the Skull-digger's work. Where he robbed his victims of their gray matter, cannibalizing it, whoever had done this latest, most-warped atrocity had robbed his victim of her entire vertebral column.

"Whataya suppose he does with the spine?" asked the young lady agent.

Darwin craned to hear Jessica's reply.

"I couldn't begin to speculate at this moment. Some kind of voodoo soup calling for backbone . . . who knows?" Jessica moved closer to the corpse, taking in the scene around the body, her gaze following the hardened, dark brown and bristled flow of blood radiating outward from the deceased toward the door—a river true to current, origin the body. "I can tell you this much, the knife he used was no bowie or other hunting knife, but a precision instrument. Whoever he is, he's done this sort of work before. Perhaps not as extensively as this, but he's trained on precision cutting tools, possibly started as a kid on small animals, insects even, rodents, working his way up to cats, dogs, rabbits, anything he could save his lunch money up for."

The tall, black and mustached Xavier Darwin Reynolds, the local special agent in charge, was the man who had per-

sonally lobbied to put the crime scene on hold until Dr.
Jessica Coran could get there from FBI headquarters in
Quantico, Virginia. "Sick but slick *sonofamotherlessslut*
whore . . . He used that mop." He pointed to a bristling-
with-blood mop resting in a corner. "Used it to cover his
shoe prints, as he backed from the crime scene and out the
hallway, but we got a partial bloody scuff on the outside
hallway carpeting."

"Yeah, I saw the cutaway patch," she replied.

"It isn't much, but we're doing our damnedest to make
something of it, maybe get it blown up, find some sort of
shoe sole markers."

"But no one saw this guy coming or going?" she asked,
knowing the answer. "He had to have been covered in
blood."

"We suspect he brought a change of clothes," countered
Agent Reynolds.

His badge read X. Darwin Reynolds. Jessica thought
the man in the wrong time, age, and profession. He ought
to be a sixth-century king of Nubia as he towered over
everyone in the place, his skin beautiful and onyx. Jessica
had to crane her neck to make eye contact with the man.
She imagined him at home on the streets where he grew up
here in Milwaukee, at the neighborhood bar, likely a gold
necklace bulging below his dark dress shirt and tie, and yet
he somehow fit in here at the gruesome crime scene, too.
Perhaps the blood of kings, that genetic seed, did reside in
Darwin, the genes of African royalty transplanted to the
small kingdom of an FBI field office in a midsize, Midwestern Mecca.

Reynolds had the bearing of a man aloof and in absolute control of his own emotions and circumstances,
even giving off the illusion of controlling the environment
immediately around him. She imagined him to be one of
those men who somehow remained dry even in a thunder-
storm. Yet the wisp of a shadow of a tear formed in his eye

for Joyce Olsen, which he quickly wiped away with a harsh utterance designed to cover the emotion. Jessica liked that. She knew now that the man who had called Quantico and had specifically requested her help cared deeply about this victim. Why? Had he known her? Or had the sheer horror of the crime perpetrated against the woman moved him? Either way, he'd scored points with this FBI medical examiner and profiler. Jessica felt an instant rapport and bond with X. Darwin, her very own Samuel L. Jackson look-alike if you shaved off twelve, maybe thirteen years.

At the same time, she hated Milwaukee, hated having taken on this horrid mutilation murder, hated Darwin for dragging her away from the ranch she and Richard Sharpe now cohabited just outside Quantico among the dogwood in the Virginia hills. The case had literally pulled her from their bed, from Richard's embrace in fact. Not to mention all the safety of all that comforted her both physically and emotionally. The call had pulled her from several ongoing, urgent cases as well—cases she'd had to dump on John Thorpe's shoulders.

Staring again at the godforsaken, god-awful evil and butchery done the victim, Jessica wondered why she continued in this line of work, why she didn't take early retirement, return to private practice and save her sanity.

"Playing safe cases for insurance fraud scoundrels?" Richard had asked in his most biting sarcasm, tinged all the more since he had a British accent. "Right you are, Jess."

"I could. And I'd be damn good at it. Like a Sue Grafton character," she quipped.

"Or rather become another in the new breed of ex-coroners selling their expertise to the highest bidder."

"You mean like the fellow—what was his name? Bayless, Baydum, Baylor—who testified for the O. J. defense?"

"Balden?"

"Always going to sue people for blackening his name when he's done such a good job of it himself . . ."

"Like the M.E. who did the same in the Blake trial, and then the Peterson trial?"

"I couldn't live with myself." She knew herself too well to ever settle into such a life. "But I could take up where I left off before I was invited into the FBI by Otto Boutine—God, so long ago."

"Back to the pain and turmoil of running the D.C. Coroner's Office? How wonderful that they're offering you your old job, but their facilities have not changed in twenty odd years!"

"The State of Virginia Medical Examiner's Office is state-of-the-art, and they want me there."

"Take early retirement and take up a hobby. Read all those Joe Konrath suspense novels you've been hoarding and start one of your own, as you keep threatening to do."

"If you think an autopsy is hard, try writing a novel. . . . I'm just not talented at juggling a thousand decisions at once."

"The hell your aren't! You absolutely write circles around that Madeleine Cromwell person, and you could easily knock her silly ass off the bestseller list," he said, adding, "and I so loved that short story you did, *The Unread*."

"I'll never write a bestselling novel. I can't write that much cheese into it."

He laughed at this. Nowadays, with Richard at her side, she was seriously contemplating the possibility of a writing career. She'd already written two successful nonfiction titles mixing forensics and philosophy, harrowing true-crime tales and hard-won pearls of wisdom. Still, to do a full-blown crime novel with the intricacies of characterization, setting, dialogue, to keep twenty plates in the air at once while riding the unicycle of plot across a high-wire of tension? Book reviewers had a lot of balls to complain about *anyone* capable of putting a novel together, perhaps the most complex piece of artwork on the planet, not unlike sculpting images from stone. She so admired authors like Matheson, Bloch, Konrath, Castle, Weinberg, Jens, Bonansinga, Geoffrey Caine and Evan Kingsbury. She only dared dream she could replicate their success if given the freedom and time to write, drawing on the cases she had worked over the years as backdrop to her fiction. "No one would believe my cases if I dressed them up as fiction," she'd told Richard. "They're hard enough to believe as truth."

"No one could make the graceful lie sing so articulately as you, Jess," Richard, ever encouraging, encouraged. "Go, do it!"

"Perhaps after this thing in Milwaukee is put to bed," had been her final reply.

"And after Milwaukee? What? Another and another. The calls won't stop until you decide they will stop, Jess."

"You are sounding more the husband every day."

"Is that such a bad thing? I'm only concerned for you, dear, not the bureau and certainly not the state of evil on the planet. You are not a Marvel comic character in one of those Edgar deGeorge fantasies."

Virginia's forensics lab wanted her badly at their state-of-the-art facility in Richmond. The drive would be horrendously long, but Richard—a helicopter nut—had the perfect solution there, too, if she wished to make that career choice. "Why we'd purchase a helicopter, of course."

"Oh, yes, of course," she'd chided back.

"But it's that simple."

"And do you have any idea how foolish that'd make me look?"

"Foolish?"

"Take my word for it. It'd go over real big with the people I'd be supervising. Me dropping in from the sky each morning onto the roof like . . . like some cross between Tinkerbell and . . . and—"

"Superwoman, of course, and why not, like an avenging

angel each day, still fighting crime yet capable of maintaining a stable—*well, almost stable*—home life. It would befit you, descending on the state crime lab," he had quipped.

"As an angel of vengeance?"

"We'll arrange for wings to go with your lab coat."

They had begun to talk more frequently of marriage, but as yet they had not set a date. Things were simply too good between them to spoil or to risk spoiling, and so they remained lovers and friends rather than man and wife. Although they had passed the ongoing test of having lived together now, happily, for six months, each felt a reserve of emotion that feared the litmus test of actual marriage vows. Vows changed things. Upped the ante. And for now, they were happy and having fun, something Jessica hadn't known for a long time, and she feared losing that even to a marriage certificate.

Richard's own consulting work had made a diplomat of him, taking him to the far corners of the earth on various missions for the State Department—missions cloaked in secrecy. He primarily trained other intelligence forces across the globe in the tactics of Scotland Yard and the FBI. And while he was busy at the far-flung corners of the planet, Jessica's work sent her to such holes-in-the-wall and armpits as Paris, Texas; Rome, Georgia; Corinth, Mississippi; and even Hong Kong, New Jersey—with its claim to a six-story, Disneyesque McDonald's with a decidedly Asian theme replete with the two-headed dragon Ferris wheel.

And now, Portland, Oregon, or Millbrook, Minnesota, might well be her next stopovers if Darwin had his way. If the killing here in Milwaukee appeared the work of a maniac some years back who had dispatched someone else in the very same manner. In the Portland, Oregon, case, the victim's husband now awaited lethal injection for her murder. As with the Milwaukee case, the salient feature of the crime, of course, was the missing spinal cord that'd been literally ripped from the Portland woman's back, the rack of bones stolen and never recovered. Something similar had occurred in a small town in Minnesota as well, and Darwin appeared bent on building a reputation for himself by tying the cases together and hunting down the real killer, a serial killer in his mind, someone other than the man on death row in Oregon.

On meeting the enthusiastic Darwin at the airport, the huge black agent had begun to spout on about how he had read the FBI bulletins and the *Journal of Forensic Sciences* relating every detail of every case Jessica had ever worked, and he had been loud about it, his voice booming across the tarmac as he shouted her name in a mantra of praise, "Jessica Coran! I can't believe it. Jessica Coran, here, in Milwaukee. Jessica Coran. I cut my eyeteeth on your crime-scene techniques book! God, Jessica Coran. I'm working with Jessica Coran!"

His enthusiasm was infectious. She blushed and accepted his praise.

Later, in the car on the way to the crime scene, he leaned into her and near whispered, "I tell you, I am so absolutely and instinctively certain of my ground—that these cases are related."

"Let me be the judge of that, Darwin. It's what I'm here to determine, remember?"

Now they were here in the death room, and the noise and chatter around Jessica rose and fell with the predominantly male crime-scene unit people giving voice to feelings similar to Jessica's own. No one had ever seen such inhuman injustice done to a victim. The corpse did not always have everyone's sympathy, such as the Diamondback, Louisiana, father who had brutalized and raped his own children and had been murdered by his children and son-in-law when they schemed to get him into a New Jersey junkyard with mad dogs they had infected with rabies. The murder had worked but the cover-up had not, and while no one in Diamondback mourned the monster's passing, the responsible parties were brought to trial.

No, the corpse seldom had every man and woman in the place wanting vengeance for her. But this one did, as if her ghost had plunged a cold dagger into each detective's heart to make even the jaded feel again—*even if it was a sharp iciness*. Even the hesitancy with which the official FBI photographer's camera clicked, unlike the usual frenetic *snap-snap-snap* of each frame, spoke volumes about the awful horror and sheer awe that this killing engendered. Jessica tried to imagine worse, but she simply could not. Perhaps at an inquest in 1888 London during which the mutilated body of a Ripper victim was displayed before the gallery, literally *hooked* to a wall for all to see the brutality. At least today, authorities treated the body with the professional courtesy and reverence it deserved, taking all precaution to preserve the dignity and to keep it in as intact a form as humanly possible under the rigors of an autopsy. In fact, laws had been enacted since the days of Jack the Ripper to safeguard and maintain that very integrity.

Reynolds came to stand near her, and he said, "Are you all right, Dr. Coran?"

Her nod was a lie. "In the old days . . . not so old, really, a hundred and fifty odd years ago, when something of this nature occurred, people in the immediate vicinity . . . anyone who'd had anything whatsoever to do with the deceased—friends, relatives, neighbors, landlords—came to the inquest. Only thing missing was the popcorn."

"Yeah, it was like a public forum, a hearing?"

"Like, no . . . It was a public forum, an inquiry into cause of death. Conducted much like a trial today."

"We sure don't need an inquest here." He indicated the body. "Fairly obvious here, wouldn't you say?" Reynolds's Midwestern twang made him a native, and his tall frame placed him a head taller than Jessica. He had black-on-blue eyes, piercing, questioning. Any woman could get lost in them. A powerful build, he stood at just over six-foot-four, and his close-cropped hair accented a wide, intelligent forehead.

"Here, you oughta put this on." She handed him a hair net from her bag.

As Jessica searched her valise for a pair of gloves for him, she added, "I've read about the bizarre proceedings at the death inquiries in the cases of Jack the Ripper."

Accepting the hair net and a surgical mask and a set of gloves, Reynolds replied, "Ol' Jacko's got nothing on our Milwaukee, Wisconsin, boy . . . least not in the butchery department."

"Agreed, but why the spine?"

"That's why you're here, Dr. Coran, to tell us exactly that. You're the profiling expert."

"Thanks, but this . . . this defies any profile on record."

"Not quite. There're two other cases that we know of in which women have literally lost a backbone."

"Yes, Oregon . . . the guy on death row. And the other? Some Minnesota woman?"

"Yes, and this very same pattern emerges in each case. Also, Millbrook, Minnesota, is only three hundred miles from Milwaukee."

"But Portland . . . That's over half a continent away, and you think this guy in Oregon innocent, wrongly convicted—"

"Towne, Robert Towne."

"You believe him innocent. That it's all a mistake. His arrest, trial, conviction?"

"Larger mistakes have happened in the judicial system of Portland, Oregon, especially where black men are concerned."

"Then Towne is black?"

"Yes, he is as black as . . . as me."

"But suppose Towne did it to copycat the Minnesota killing? And by extension, suppose someone here did it to copycat Towne for some sick, perverted reason?"

"Three separate guys tearing out backbones? I don't buy it."

"Stick to your guns, Agent. I like that in a man," Jessica said.

"There's more than happenstance and coincidence at work here. I feel it in my bones. No pun intended."

"Trust me, none taken."

Two photographers were snapping pictures now, one centered on the body and everything in relation to it, every stationary point of reference. The other cameraman fired off shots of the bloody mop propped against the wall beside the door where presumably the killer exited, leaving his wake of blood. Photographic shots from all angles exploded one after another, the photographers having latched on to competition as a way to get past the horror of their subject.

From somewhere down the hall, the sad melody of a Hank Williams tune droned on, the words a surreal fit: "the mooooon just went be-hind a cloud to hiiiiide its face and cry . . . I'm so lonesome I-ah could die . . ."

More shots of the body from all angles. The second photographer now took shots of the swirls of blood on the carpet. She looked from the busy photographers and back to Reynolds, but he had stepped away. Special Agent X. Darwin Reynolds now stood alongside Dr. Ira Sands, the Milwaukee M.E., and together they studied several cellophane-wrapped charcoal sketches.

At first, Jessica assumed the sketches were created by a police artist, but Darwin informed her, "We believe her killer drew them and left them behind."

Now everything about the case felt *surreal*, even her thumbing through these lovely charcoal sketches. Sketches left by the Spine Thief himself. "Why'd he do it? Take the time to do all these?"

"And when did he do them?" asked Reynolds.

"Are they telling us something? Are they his con? How

he wormed his way past the threshold?" Jessica mused aloud.

"Dr. Coran . . . like to introduce you to Dr. Ira Sands." Reynolds stood between them, the obvious message being that she and Sands should work together.

Sands instantly shot out his hand and took hers, pumping it in a vise grip, his smile wide and welcoming. "We are so lucky to have you, Dr. Coran, so very fortunate indeed. I've read all your abstracts and bulletins."

"Thank you, Dr. Sands. I've heard only good things about your crime lab." Jessica knew that paying him this compliment was the highest praise he sought, as it was with any M.E.

"My lab is at your disposal, of course."

"That's wonderful to hear. Thank you, Dr. Sands." Like every FBI field lab boss, Sands thought the government-issue lab was his and his alone. She prayed he was being genuine and not simply politically correct.

The short, stocky Dr. Sands said, "Beginning with these"—Sands pointed at the sketches of a dog and the dead woman in Jessica's hand—"we are covering every base."

Nodding, Jessica again examined the finely drawn, beautifully wrought charcoal drawings of the victim, three in all, one of a frolicking golden retriever chasing birds and two depicting the same dog with the victim in different poses, kissing and hugging one another.

"Where's the dog?" she asked.

"Animal control took him out," said the heavyset Wyatt Abrams, the Milwaukee police chief, who'd introduced himself downstairs where he'd been taking a smoke break. "Poor dog had matted blood all over him from sleeping up against her for a week. 'Fraid he . . . ahhh . . . gnawed on some of the flesh cutaway from the woman, too, but you can't blame the animal."

"Animal instinct," she muttered.

"No, the SOB of a landlord let the dog howl for days before he decided to check on things, and even then only after the stench caught his attention."

Darwin Reynolds took the sketches from Jessica and handed her another set, but these additional six were faxes. "From the other two cases, and I'd bet my pension it's the same artist leaving his calling card."

"Two other cases *not* here in Milwaukee?" commented Sands, rolling his aged eyes.

Chief Abrams exploded with, "I think Reynolds is reaching."

"Never discount gut instincts," Jessica countered, coming to Reynolds's defense. "My own have served me well over the years."

Smiles all around except for the stodgy chief, his forehead a road map of confusion. "Unfortunately, the law doesn't work that way, and neither does it put a man away for no good reason. We gotta trust the authorities in Oregon are every bit as competent as we are."

"And just how competent is that?" joked Sands, laughing lightly to himself.

Reynolds's eyes showed rage, but he spoke with cool reserve. "Competent? Like the Smollen case, and the Byrd case before that? Competent? Try incompetent nincompoops. I tell you, Wyatt, they've got the wrong man on death row for this, and now it's a certainty. Given this murderer's robbing his victim of her spine."

Reynolds had peaked Jessica's curiosity, but Dr. Sands said, "Look, Darwin, for the moment, we have our hands full with this fucking mess"—he indicated the horrid mangled body a few feet from them—"and we're losing light, and I haven't eaten anything since my morning coffee roll, so if you don't mind. Dr. Coran, let's get down to business, shall we?" Sands swept his arm out in a gesture that said, *You first*.

Jessica went to the body and knelt beside it. Dr. Ira

Sands did likewise across from her. She saw that the hefty local coroner wanted to get nearer. "Darwin," he near whispered to Jessica, "is on a tear to prove this is the third such death in a series, but I've seen nothing to convince me of it. Regardless, we have enough in hand for the moment, wouldn't you agree?"

"I do indeed." Jessica steeled her own spine as she viewed the enormous gash in the dead woman's back. She'd seen disemboweled victims, dismembered victims, victims with eyes removed, god-awful drowning and burn victims, but this went beyond the pale, beyond any hope of speculation. With disembowelments came necrophilia and even cannibalism, which served as motivation, albeit a sick one, something in the human experience and collective psyche hanging on from cave-dwelling days. And even with mutilations brought about by lust murder, there resided some modicum of explanation a profiler might work with to assuage her own guilt at being human. With dismemberments, there usually followed facts uncovering a perpetrator's pure hatred of the victim, or an attempt to reduce the very real problem of body disposal—a hatchet job borne of fear of discovery. Even a butcher who butchered for the sake of butchering at least had a "reason"—even if it was as despicable as "I just love the feel of a cleaver going through bone." With an eye-gouger—in the end, at interrogation—he'd say the fear of the victim's eyes staring at him, even in death, drove him to his brutal act. But often, after a little judicious questioning, he will confess to having been at it for some time, beginning with the eyes of dolls. Working his way up to wanting Jessica's eyes even as they spoke of it across a table in the federal facility for the criminally insane. "What can I say? I like eyes," he'd confess after months and sometimes years of incarceration. One madman named Gerald Ray Sims, who did much more than take the eyes, told Jessica, before taking his own life, that the dead girl's eyes could see him even in death, and that after he cut them out, he realized that they were not dead but the all-knowing, all-seeing eyes of God Himself. "And the only way to stop them staring at me," Sims had added, "was to put them into my pockets."

Even Sims had a reason for his mutilations, albeit a lunatic's expedient answer to the ever-present need of his interrogator to know why.

"Her eyes kept coming back open, even though she was dead," Zachary Durning—the Daylight Stalker of Starkville, Mississippi—had chanted in mantra fashion throughout his arrest procedure when taken into custody. Jessica later recovered the eyes found in a pickle jar on a shelf in the Bar None Grill that Durning ran for the tourists trade, catering to their insatiable curiosity of the antique remnants of the kind of Wild West Mississippi saloon Durning kept. The tourists came off the Mississippi River excursion and casino boats, and Zach Durning's place had long been a fulcrum for strange disappearances over a period of years—as his father had begun the first killings as robberies gone bad. Zachary's last victim had been a tourist, and the daughter of a U.S. senator, who never returned to the boat. As serial killers went, the man proved a sad bore, rather more the recluse spider who struck only if you got too close to the center of his web. He never stalked a single victim. He didn't have to.

Alongside Jessica now, Sands spoke into a tape recorder. "The female victim, one Joyce Olsen, is in her late forties hideously stripped of her spine. Noting the deep, wide canyon created along the length of her back, this was done with a certain precision and knowledge of depth and length measurements required. In my opinion . . . a practiced cut. Exact measurements of the wound will be taken to determine this further, of course, along with the precise extent of damage. Blood loss is considerable. Apparent cause of death: hemorrhagic shock due to this wound. Blow to the head caused a serious fracture, but it appears an unlikely death blow. Alongside the corpse, we see the window of flesh that the killer opened in order to get at the spine."

Jessica now reached out to lift the single large, long piece of flesh that'd been cut from the dead woman's back—a large trout-sized piece of flesh, discarded by her killer. Jessica meant to secure it in a sterile polyethylene bag for later microscopic analysis for fiber and hair evidence, perhaps traces of fluids not belonging to the victim, a DNA sample perhaps. But latching on to this big fish with her two gloved hands, Jessica found herself in a tug of war. The tussle was between her and the dried blood pool the back section had lain in for so long. The fleshy bottom wall of the thing had dried hard and fast to the stained light gray carpet below, bonded as it were.

Angry at this killer and his awful leavings, Jessica whipped out her scalpel, the gold-plated one given to her by her father upon her graduation from medical school. Agent "Pete" Petersaul, holding the bag open to receive the enormous tissue sample that Jessica meant to pry from the carpet, stared fixedly at the shining scalpel for something to concentrate on. Jessica used the edge of the blade to free the flesh from the carpet piling. Carpet fiber clung like a sticky web to the flesh. This made it necessary for Jessica to work slowly and with care all along the length of the fleshy prize.

"It's little wonder I sometimes feel like the ogre in all this," Jessica muttered to Petersaul and Sands, who also stared and gulped at the work she'd begun.

Finally, she freed the bile-inducing, sumptuous and serpentine block of flesh and fat and dropped it into the bag held wide by Agent Petersaul, who stilled her own quaking hands to get the job done.

"Some three-foot-long party sandwich this'd make for a cannibal killer, you know, like that guy you put away in New York, the Claw," said Agent Reynolds.

"That was over a decade ago, and he ripped open abdomens and fed on the intestines and organs like a frenzied mad dog, but he didn't take any bones off with him to bury someplace."

Sands stated the obvious, "This case is not about cannibalizing flesh, otherwise he'd never have left this." He hefted the snake of flesh in the bag.

Sands gave Petersaul instructions, "See that our several pounds of flesh go with the body to the lab for autopsy."

"If he's not a cannibal, what the fuck is this freak? A blood drinker?" demanded Petersaul.

"From the amount of blood spilled here, again, I'd say no," said Jessica. "Matisak was a blood drinker, and he controlled the bloodletting to maximize his treasure with each killing. No, this Spine Thief is something new, something I've not encountered, nor do I know of anything like it in all the literature of police science and police history."

"Whataya think he does with the spines?" pressed Petersaul, her curiosity palpable.

Jessica looked at Darwin Reynolds, seeing his own need to know there in the black depths of his eyes. "Bone marrow perhaps. Perhaps he feeds on the marrow he can can extract from the vertebral column."

Petersaul uttered a string of expletives and added, "Uggh . . . euuuu, no . . . ykkk!"

"Maybe he has some fucked-up notion that spinal fluid has life-giving properties . . . wants to feed his immune system to keep trim and forever young," Jessica continued. "Or he thinks it replenishes his own spinal fluids to do so, to vampire off someone else's manna. Or some such ridiculous notion, since ingesting the stuff can only send it out his ass."

"Kinda like a spine vampire maniac, isn't he?" said Darwin.

"You might argue that . . . That he likes his blood thick and congealed. Consommé as opposed to bisque, cold as opposed to liking it fresh and hot."

"But why? Where . . . I mean how does any man ever get such a notion?" Darwin asked.

"Rather, how does any man *act* on such a notion?"

Sands's voice, as he continued to tape, interrupted their conversation, "Serious blow to the head appears to have been caused by a blunt instrument, possibly a tool such as a hammer, given the diameter of the wound."

SOME time had passed as they processed the crime scene when Ira Sands shattered the silence. "With what we now have, Dr. Coran, I believe we can begin thinking of closing this crime scene down."

"I'm in agreement."

"And back at the morgue, if you will follow my lead, I feel we can get most, if not all, necessary tests under way. Unless you care to lead this dance."

"Generous of you to offer, Dr. Sands, but no, I am happy to follow your lead, sir."

"Are you all right?" he asked. "You look a bit peaked. Airline food, perhaps?"

"No, I came by FBI jet. I will be fine, really."

"That was some operation you performed, separating flesh from carpet. Enough to excuse anyone a bit of queasiness, my dear."

Jessica had again been staring at the enormous gash to Joyce Olsen's backside, the missing serpentine section of flesh that left a gaping hole large enough for a small animal to climb into. She thought of the dog trapped with the dead woman for over a week. Out of one eye, she saw the bag with the flesh in it being forced down into a large Tupperware container, the lid snapped and patted down by Agent Petersaul.

"Tupperware party?" joked another agent with Petersaul.

"I'm hosting a big one," she snapped back.

Light laughter followed.

"Is it all right?" Ira Sands was saying to Jessica. She only half heard him. "Do you understand?" he continued in her ear.

Jessica could not recall the last time the sight of a wound had so disturbed her to the core. Jaded, having seen so much, it crept up on little cat feet, this dizzying combination of clamminess, perspiration, and nausea. Surprised she could still get this affected, her thoughts returned to her first FBI case: the body of a young woman called Candy found hanging by her ankles, the fly infested leavings of Mad Matthew Matisak after he'd jammed his now-infamous handheld Spigot into her jugular, in order to control the flow of her blood as he robbed her of every ounce.

It had been Jessica, the novice FBI M.E. who had discovered the small, telltale hole made by the spigot within the massive throat slashing, which had been done to mask the mark of the spigot. But while she eventually put him away, it had been at a dear price, losing her first real love to Matisak's madness.

He had maimed her physically, too. She'd had to use a cane for almost two years following his attack on her. To this day, the psychological scars he'd inflicted remained.

She felt some strange and eerie connection here but could not make it out. Just a feeling, a foolish one, as foolish as Darwin's notion that the killer was like the Claw. This maniac was no Matisak, either. Still, she felt the same iciness and fear of this demon as she had with Matisak. She felt it in her throat, her chest, her heart and her stomach.

"Come now, Dr. Coran," said Sands in a bid to help color return to her face. "I've read your book. You've seen bodies without hearts, others missing their brains even."

"All . . . all the . . . same, not . . . notwithstanding, I fear, Dr. Sands, I'm feeling just a might . . . light-headed." She finished with a little gasp.

"Go out and come back in. No one else need know. Go," he encouraged her.

She stared into his kind eyes, studying them, as another voice inside her head advised she stand her ground—her father's voice. Her tough, uncompromising military father's old advice. He, too, had seen some awful deaths—horrid battlefield wounds—and in his days as a medical examiner for the military, he had learned discipline and mental toughness, but she could safely say that not even her father had ever seen anything like this. Nor had her mentor, Dr. Asa Holcraft who'd done thousands of autopsies. How was one to combat such a sight as this?

Sands placed a hand on hers and said, "Would you like us to step out together?"

She heeded his advice, getting to her feet. To hell with what the men at the crime scene thought, she told herself. She announced clearly, "Yes, Dr. Sands, I'm sorry, but I need to take a moment."

He pointed toward the balcony off the bedroom. She stepped out into the November breeze, and she watched as the others, including Sands, filed out and into the light. They had merely needed someone to say "uncle" and to lead the way.

THREE

Is God himself a detective in the dark void,
trailing a killer the deity himself created, trying
to uncover the unknowable unknown created from
the whole cloth of his own inner tensions?

—EVAN KINGSBURY, *FLESH WARS*

MILWAUKEE awoke with the sound of blaring horns and rush-hour traffic jamming the nearby interstate. X. Darwin Reynolds hovered nearby, taking a protective stance over Jessica, acting as a shield. Along West Allis Boulevard Jessica could see the signs of commerce dotting the horizon, Exxon, Econo Lodge, H&R Block, Burger King, Popeyes, KFC, McDonald's, BP, Cooney's Funeral Home, Bridgestone Tires, Schwinn Bike Outlet, Costco, Jewel-Osco and Joe's Crab Shack.

Jessica said to Darwin, "Imagine a Milwaukee resident of a hundred or even fifty years ago, standing here, staring at the once tree-lined avenue and asking, 'What have they done to my home, Momma, what have they done to my home?'"

Before entering the death scene a second time, Jessica filled her nostrils with Caine's All-Purpose Odor Firewall. The scent was an improvement on the old Vicks VapoRub.

The brutal sight was no less brutal, but the odors of a week-old corpse were somewhat tamed by Caine's Firewall, first developed for firemen and crematorium workers and anyone else working with burn victims, such as police officials, paramedics, pathologists and medical examiners.

The scene must be tolerated in order for her to perform her duties. She'd come way too far to be here just to crap out now. No walking away from this, not even in her mind. But she must somehow remain aloof, above the horror in order to deal with it in a controlled, professional manner, and to stand her ground with Darwin Reynolds and the other men and women present, especially the young ex-marine, Petersaul.

She composed herself with great gulps of the last vestiges of the early morning Milwaukee air. She said to Darwin, "Air here· is supposed to be filled with the fumes of . . . what . . . ninety-nine local breweries? My best friend and right hand in the lab, John Thorpe, told me that if things get too hairy in Milwaukee, the natives just suck up the brew from the fumes. Does it work?"

"Takes the sport out of drinking. Most of us like to sidle up to a bar and down a tall one."

"One big swilling *swear-never-to-get-drunk-again* fest, eh? I understand, every Friday and Saturday night."

"We gotta be imaginative to compete with neighboring Chicago somehow."

Traffic below seemed like the world was rushing by the open balcony with the death room inside; the jaded world, ignoring the collection of squad cars and coroner's vehicles that had converged on the apartment house in this residential neighborhood. People in Milwaukee appeared as world-weary of strobe lights and sirens as military men were to exploding bombs lobbing overhead. Still, the requisite crowd had gathered, curious, asking questions, pushing at the barriers. Newspapermen and camera crews in particular clamored to be on the inside, gathering news. She heard a

familiar phrase from the beat cop holding everyone in
check, a kind of mantra at such scenes:"Can't let out no
names or take any pictures till the next of kin's been notified. You know that."

Jessica thought again of the worst monster she had ever
chased down and killed, Mad Matthew Matisak. No creature of the night she'd ever hunted compared in utter brutality, until now. This ripping out of a woman's spinal cord,
this ranked a Tort 10 on the torture scale if the victim were
alive when he splayed open her back, and from the coloration around the naked wound, it would surprise Jessica
to learn otherwise.

Matisak's blood-drinking measures had exacted a slow
kind of torture, the draining of his victim's very lifeblood,
and so it had rated a Tort 9 on the torture scale. The scale of
torture represented in the spine-thief case she looked at today did not compare with regard to the time it took to die.
The Olsen woman did not suffer long. Still, in Jessica's
book, this monster rated a ten for sheer animal brutality,
and it made her wonder if it were not some sickening animal need that drove him, some genetically predisposed urge
toward gnawing on bone, a throwback to the caveman mind
dwelling in us all.

It felt in her own bones—scuttling like a spider along her
own spine—as if the putrid disease of evil carried about by
the criminally insane Matisak had unaccountably returned,
maybe had never really left. Perhaps in a new guise, a new
shape, a new form, but the same evil nonetheless. "Cut of
the same satanic cloth, this one," she muttered to herself.

"What's that?" asked Reynolds, his forehead creased in
consternation.

"Confound bastard is like a fiery coal from hell's own
hearth." She took in another deep breath. "Should've
brought some whiskey along."

Jessica reentered the death room and stepped to the body

again. "This one," she said to the others in the room, "this one may lead me into early retirement. You say she lived alone, that she hardly socialized or went out?"

"That's right, a reclusive type," replied Agent Reynolds. "Vic's name's Joyce Dixon-Olsen, aged forty-eight, a loner, lived with her dog, Shep. Dog's at his vet's . . . nice, good-natured as all hell."

"I suppose it'd be asking too much to hope that some-one in a forensics capacity got to the dog before he was shampooed?"

Sands frowned and shook his head. "Gone long before I got here, I'm afraid."

"He was one hell of a mess, a long-haired cocker spaniel," Reynolds replied apologetically. "First on scene took better care of him than he did securing the body, I'm afraid. Dog lover."

Jessica kneeled beside the blood-soaked corpse, and looked into the woman's face, turned as it was sideways against the carpet. Jessica mentally traced the features, thinking she had character written right into them, that she appeared to be someone who had seen and overcome much adversity until now. *That which does not kill us, makes us stronger*. She might be anyone's mother or aunt. "No fam-ily?"

"Ex-husband passed away two years ago. Some distant relatives in Nebraska. They've been notified," said Reynolds in his resonant voice.

Jessica placed the ruler end of her scalpel against the wound to Olsen's cranium. "Diameter of the wound is less than an inch; the work of a small blunt object, likely a ham-mer of some sort as Sands said. From the concave appearance an educated guess says the hammer blow came from a ball peen styled one."

Darwin Reynolds now knelt alongside the cadaver, too. Reynolds's black skin was as ebony as one of his African ancestors—Nigeria or Ghana, Jessica guessed from his bone structure and height. He had a broad, strong face, and a nose any Roman would kill for, all beneath those black, probing eyes. *Every girl's dream,* she thought, *but not mine. I've got Richard.*

Milwaukee Police Chief Wyatt Abrams, who had remained sullen and silent throughout, a great anger seething below his calm, had also partaken of the balcony air. A big man not to be missed by anyone, his footsteps alone announced his return from outside. Everyone else had returned ahead of Abrams. Staring down at the scene, at Reynolds, Sands and Jessica all on knees perched about the body like so many ghoulish scavengers, Abrams erupted, "I don't fucking suppose you people in Washington have anything like this in your data banks! We gotta catch this *motherfuckingfreak* before he strikes again."

"I couldn't agree with you more," she replied.

"Not in my city . . . not here. I can't look at this kind of thing again, not ever, Dr. Coran."

"Sir . . . I completely understand."

"What about those international guys you guys check with all the time, Interpol? They ever get anything remotely like this overseas someplace? Say just off a military base? Maybe our guy is some sort of military butcher or even a military medic type."

Jessica stood and went to Chief Abrams. She walked with him away from the others. "Checked with Interpol and every law-enforcement agency that cooperates with the FBI worldwide, Chief. Sorry, no one anywhere has ever seen anything like this save Portland, Oregon, and—"

"I know, Millbrook, Minnesota."

"But this is the first one to fall under the lens of the FBI's Behavioral Science Unit. It's a . . . a uniquely sick MO . . . nothing like it in anyone's computers."

Reynolds had followed them, listening. He added, "Wyatt, it's got to be related to the Towne case in Portland, Oregon, over a year back. Ex-husband, a regular mountain man type, a black Jeremiah Johnson for the modern age, and he's on death row for the crime. He supposedly hated her enough to do something like this." He pointed back to the mutilated corpse. "Can you really imagine that two men on the planet could conceive of and execute this exact atrocity?"

"Yeah, I can if they turn out to be bunk mates in a prison cell, or two nuts meeting on a train or at a window placing a bet, and your boy Towne in Oregon spent a lot of time in prison cells from what I gather."

"He's locked up. Can't have done this here in Milwaukee, and there's no proof he had ever been in Minnesota, Chief."

Abrams spoke to Jessica. "Remember that case breaking on CNN?"

She nodded.

"Reynolds thinks it's somehow relevant to this murder."

"Didn't he say he killed the woman for her spine because she always called him spineless?" Agent Pete shouted from the kitchen where she was using Luminol spray and a blue light to scour for useful blood evidence. Obviously by now everyone in the apartment was involved in the speculation and debate.

"And in his confession," added Sands, getting into the foray. "What was it he said at the trial? Let me see if this old brain still has it tucked away. Oh, yeah . . . yeah. He said, 'I guess in a way I did kinda get her hackles up. Got those spiney bones breaking skin on her backside once't -or twice't . . . kinda made her what she was—all spine and blister.' " All but Darwin Reynolds laughed at this.

Abrams shouted, "The man had an insanity defense at trial, and at the time, the guy *was* a lunatic, but jail time sobered his ass up, and now he claims his entire confession was a bold-faced fabrication!"

"To end an eighteen-hour, marathon interrogation," countered Darwin.

"Were there sketches at the Portland murder scene?" Jessica asked.

"Matter of fact, yes."

"Charcoal drawings?"

"Yes."

"And what did they depict?"

"The dead woman and her horses."

"Horses?"

"She loved horses . . . a real horse lover."

Sands broke in. "Didn't the husband say she slept with her horses?"

"Actually, he said she'd rather have fucked a horse than ever get down with him again," replied the resident expert on Towne, Darwin Reynolds, and this brought on laughing jags all around and a halt to the discussion, and everyone took a moment.

Dr. Sands turned his attention back to the body and began probing the ugly wound, taking a few more measurements. Abrams said he needed a smoke, but remained.

Reynolds didn't let it drop, however. "Look, the victim was white, and Towne's only prior was an aggravated battery charge, a domestic, and that only once, but him being a black man—"

"Oh fucking hell, here we go again with the poor black man's wrongfully accused defense because he's black shit," countered Abrams. "Pah-lease, Darwin."

"A black man beating on a white wife," continued Darwin. "It conjured up every redneck's primal prejudice— images of O.J. and Nicole—and it was all that came up on every Portland cop's radar screen."

"The woman was found with her spine ripped out," stated Abrams. "And *his* prints were all over the place."

"The man lived there for years. And as for her spine, it was never recovered. Neither was the one in Minnesota or here to date."

"Aggravated battery, hell, I'd be looking close at him for

his wife's murder even without that, but with it on his record, Darwin, it's not about race," argued Abrams, his face reddening.

"I'm not so sure. Way people behave in this life, seems everything is about race. And you know the fact is the other two victims were white women approximately the same age."

"Yeah, so what, Darwin?"

"Dr. Coran, will you please tell these backward Milwaukee yahoos how damned *rarely* a serial killer kills outside his own race? Tell 'em, Dr. Coran."

"True. There's even less chance, statistically speaking, for a black man to kill outside race," she added.

"Towne was convicted on highly suspect, circumstantial evidence alone. And now, with this at our feet, hell, it becomes even more suspect!" Darwin paced, adding, "The first victim two years ago in Millbrook, Minnesota, also lived alone, no relatives. She was found clutching a charcoal sketch, too."

"All information the cops up north let out to the press, so anyone could copycat it," added Sands, *tsk-tsk*ing his disapproval.

"No one was ever apprehended for the murder."

Jessica recalled what little she knew of the Millbrook case—a small burb outside the Twin Cities. She told Reynolds, "FBI field office wasn't called in. It was handled as a local murder by the Millbrook authorities. Kept relatively quiet given the sensational way in which she was dispatched."

"Case went nowhere," replied Darwin. "There were no repeats, so for the most part, authorities were pleased it just went away, that it didn't become a recurring nightmare."

"Then it happened over a year ago in Portland," said Abrams.

"A year in between the first and second killing," said Sands. "Not your typical bad boy, this one, and now this, a year later."

"Agreed," said Jessica. "Highly unusual if all the killings were done by the same man. Spacing his killings so far apart."

"The Oregon black mountain man case," began Chief Abrams, "got play on Court TV. High-profile case. Guy was put on psychoactive drugs and claimed later, after getting his head straight, that he didn't do it."

Reynolds finished for Abrams, adding, "Towne then refused any appeals made on his behalf. He's on death row, end of story for everybody who wants to look the other way—just about the whole world, because he's decided to regain control himself with institutional suicide."

"I remember reading something about it at the time," said Jessica.

Reynolds added, "Towne has till the end of the week, a handful of days."

"Then he's toast," Abrams put in.

"He's been on death row for over a year now," added Darwin. "Third Strike law . . . Nature of the crime . . . Speed Law of the West."

"Everybody's anxious to see him die. Isn't that right?" asked Sands as he worked to place a stray particle of lint beneath a slide. "Even *he* wants an end to it."

Jessica, returned to the body to continue her pre-autopsy examination.

"Are *you* that anxious to see him die?" asked Reynolds of Abrams.

Sands looked up to see Abrams's reply.

Abrams said, "Frankly, until this discovery here . . . Frankly, Darwin, I hadn't given much thought to the case."

"Until now." Reynolds held his gaze. "Until this." He indicated the Olsen body.

"Right . . . until now. Now that we have a spine-theft murder in our own backyard—what to me appears a copycat of Towne's work."

"There's not a shred of evidence to say so."

Abrams waded back in, his eyes traveling the room to see who was paying attention. "Look, Reynolds, the man tried the insanity defense and lost, and then he wanted a *sanity* defense? And now he wants a quick execution?" Abrams punctuated this with laughter. "Come on!"

"That's some new Johnnie Cochran–style twist his lawyers must've come up with," added Pete as she wandered in from the kitchen.

"Yeah, who's he got? O.J.'s dream team?" commented another tech team member.

A third leapt in with, "Come up with the insanity to sanity defense. Straight out of the Johnnie 'Confuse 'em' Cochran School or that guy Roy Black."

Jessica stayed out of it and kept working.

Reynolds kept on Abrams, ignoring the side remarks. "Look, Abrams, his lawyers are saying he deserves another hearing in light of the way his confession was gotten, in light of this crime, and the fact he couldn't be tied to the one in Minnesota."

"If Robert W. Towne is innocent I'll—"

"You'll what? If Towne is innocent, and we find out too late, how will that play, Chief?"

Jessica had motioned for the photographer to take close-ups of the head wound she'd cleaned, and the man moved in with purpose. Jessica said to Darwin, "Are you personally involved in the Oregon case, Darwin? You seem to be."

"I see a wrong I'd like to right. That's the extent of my personal involvement."

Jessica considered this as she finished the depth measurements to the killing wound down the length of Joyce Olsen's back. "My guess, Dr. Sands, some sort of surgical scalpel, a large one . . . A very controlled cut."

"Didn't use a machete or a scimitar, that's for sure."

"The M.E.'s in Portland and Minnesota concluded the same," said Reynolds firmly, his gaze probing hers. "In all three cases, there are commonalities, Dr. Coran."

"Those being?"

Darwin spread the fingers of his enormous left hand and ticked off each item. "The obvious—a missing spine—for one. Each victim lived alone. Each had next to no family. Led a sedate life. Heavily committed to their pets—their pet preoccupations, as it were. And each of the victims had sketches drawn of themselves while involved in a favorite pastime with their pets, and there's the way the guy smeared the blood with a mop or a broom to cover his footprints. In Minnesota and Portland he used a broom in each case, here a mop. He uses a scalpel or scalpel-like knife for the incisions, and a bone cutter, not a noisy Stryker saw to detach the spine fully from the body."

"Obviously, you've given this a lot of thought."

"You're going to find that he used a bone cutter to remove the Olsen woman's ribs, too."

"How long have you been working on this, Reynolds?" Jessica asked.

"Since things in the Oregon case didn't add up to me. I don't believe Towne's guilty of any of this. In fact, he claims there is—floating around somewhere—a photo of him at a lake at the Canadian border where he was fishing with a friend when his wife was being murdered."

"Gone fishing? That's an awful alibi. I could cite you hundreds of foolish men who used it, including Scott Peterson."

"But in Towne's case, it's true. He's an avid fisherman and hunter."

"Who owns a deboning knife, a rib cutter, and a ball peen hammer, I'm sure," said Sands with a shake of the head.

"And a bow and arrow, and a collection of hunting rifles rivaling Sears Roebuck." Reynolds dropped his head, nodding. "All of which was carted into the courtroom to prove him some sort of animal."

"Then why the hell did he confess?" asked Petersaul.

"He was out of his mind at the time."

"What's the source of your information?" asked Jessica.

"All right, there is a personal connection. An old friend of mine is on the defense team, and I can assure you Towne couldn't afford a Roy Black. They started an appeal but Towne, shown of sound mind at the time, refused any appeals made on his behalf."

"So you're saying that the Minnesota case, and now this awful butchery, that this constitutes new information for Towne's defense?"

"I've always maintained he could not have done the Minnesota killing. I've already faxed the broad outlines to Oregon, but they've wired back that the governor's not buying it. The DA's somehow gotten the time of death changed by a day to counter claims that Towne was in Canada at the time."

"I see."

"So much for that. The governor can't be convinced of a stay of execution, citing the fact that Towne himself refuses any further appeal!"

"Meanwhile, you uncovered all this coincidence surrounding the murders." Jessica put a fiber slide together as she spoke. "Like the sketches left at the murder scenes in both Millbrook and Portland, and now here in Milwaukee."

"According to my experts, done by the same hand," added Darwin. "And Towne has no history of artistic ability whatsoever."

"How do you know that?"

"Let's just say that I've seen what he can't do with the back of a napkin."

"So you're maintaining that he can't have created the charcoal sketches," said Abrams, still playing devil's advocate, "and I gotta agree, not here with the Olsen woman and her dog since he's sitting on death row. But this could just be a copycat killing. Your boy Towne could've done the bird lady in Minnesota, and his wife."

This drew some laughter.

Darwin dropped his head as if defeated. Jessica saw his

frustration as he realized he could not change any of their minds. She jumped in, asking, "Agent Reynolds, when Towne was in his insanity phase, did the defense use schizophrenia as a mitigating circumstance?"

"Afraid so, yes, but—"

"And so, did he ever in any other personality show any artistic—"

"None, I tell you."

"And you have the autopsy reports on the two other crimes?" she asked.

"As a matter of fact . . ."

"I'll be happy to look them over, but I must tell you, I am skeptical, at least as skeptical as Dr. Sands and Chief Abrams."

"Understood."

"But I am also equally skeptical anything can be done to save Towne from execution at this late date."

"Skeptical is fine, perfect actually. I want your skepticism, Dr. Coran. It's what makes a good M.E., correct? And when you are convinced, it will mean something to Oregon."

Skepticism is the hallmark of the medical examiner, she thought. "But for now I have, as Dr. Sands says, my hands full."

Reynolds held up his hands in the universal gesture of retreat, and he did just that.

"I'LL give you transport to the crime lab," Darwin Reynolds offered Jessica when it became apparent that she and Dr. Sands could do no more at the scene. "I'm sure you can trust Ira and his people to maintain the chain of evidence, Dr. Coran."

She'd automatically begun to search the room to see what final steps needed to be taken before leaving the crime scene. "Once we let it go," she said, her gaze sweeping over everyone and everything remaining, "it's gone. No longer ours. Any mistakes we make now. All that."

Even as she and Reynolds started toward the door, Jessica couldn't help but again regard the smoothed out dried blood running from the body to the door where it had been purposefully disturbed—mopped. She noticed the techs placing plastic bags over the mop ends and rubber-banding them. Another pair of men zipped up a body bag, having lifted Joyce Olsen's remains up and into it. Jessica's last glance met the woman's features, a mildly chiding reproach in the dead eyes. Now, in the hands of God, the eyes of the victim shone on Jessica like some sort of scolding preternatural light that insisted "find my killer."

Such had fallen to her countless times before, and the responsibility and burden only grew as more was learned of the victim. Joyce had been a librarian who walked to and from her job, kept a steady schedule of walking her dog, Shep, in the nearby park, and according to a diary entry, read by Darwin, as Jessica and Sands had worked over her corpse, she adored the roasted sweet corn at the West Allis Fairgrounds during the state fair, a place the librarians and their relatives went each year to celebrate and party. She had had to go alone for the past two years, and Joyce lamented about this in her private book.

At the elevator doors in the hallway, Dr. Sands was already swamped, surrounded and captured by newspeople who'd finally gotten past the uniforms below. Sands appeared to revel in the attention. Reynolds snuck Jessica out via a back stairwell. Behind them, Jessica heard Sands saying, "Boys, whoever the devil is, he's pretty well destroyed any chance at blood spatter evidence of any sort."

"What kind of weapon'd he use on her, Doc?" came a question.

"From the neatness of the incisions, I'd say our killer used a scalpel or a very good deboning knife."

"A deboning knife?" went up the cry.

"Damned handy with it, too."

"Is it true that her entire spinal column from top to bottom was extracted, Dr. Sands?" asked a female reporter, her voice shivering with the words.

Sands regarded her. "Scary as hell, isn't it? The very idea. The man used rib cutters or a bone saw to extricate the thoracic vertebrae. My guess is rib cutters."

"Why rib cutters?" another reporter came back.

"No one in the building heard anything like a bone saw. Bone saw sends up a noise like a wailing woman. Whereas bone cutters just toss off these snap, crackle, pop sounds."

"Why? Why'd he do this? Why'd he take, of all things, the spine?" asked the lady reporter. "It's horrifying . . . maddeningly so."

"No one knows. If we knew, Briana, it might help lead us to him," replied Sands.

Jessica realized that Sands did love the attention. At his age, he had learned to play the press to his advantage, and it appeared he made no excuses to his superiors.

Reynolds pulled Jessica away and guided her through the stairwell door. "I'm sure you don't want to be part of the circus."

"Absolutely right about that, and I'm not so sure I like Sands giving up so much of what we have. It's not wise."

"Hey, it's Ira, all right? What can I say. He runs his office the way he runs his office. He's ahhh . . . garrulous. Has lost a lot of jobs over the years over his outspoken style. Funny as hell."

As they made their way down the stairs, Jessica asked, "Funny good or funny bad?"

"He tells the funniest stories about having been fired from hither, thither and yon, and he has a bag full of hilarious stories about on-the-job stuff as well."

"Does strike me as a character."

"That he is . . . that he is."

The ease of step here on the stairwell made Jessica recall how the carpet in Olsen's apartment had crackled underfoot like Rice Krispies, hardened as it had become with Olsen's dried blood. She wondered if she'd ever get that sound out of her ear, or the image of a river of blood out of her head. There were no Caine's eardrops, earplugs, or sleeping pills to help.

She looked askance at Reynolds as they descended the two flights. She believed him ruggedly handsome in a Dick Tracy sort of way, and his stony onyx-black eyes showed a depth of intelligence that easily mesmerized others.

"Time for Towne is slipping away like the proverbial sand through the hourglass," he muttered.

"Why've you taken such a personal interest in Towne?"

"I hate the death penalty. We have to find another way. Too many on death row are innocent, there for the same reason as Towne—a confession beaten from them, if not literally so, then figuratively."

"But there's more to it than that. And you have to know from my record that I have sent a lot of men to their deaths on the row."

"Yes, I know your record and where you stand on the issue."

"The death penalty is too good for some of the scum we see. That aside, you've uncovered something else about these spine snatchings, haven't you?"

He stopped midstep, turned and stared deeply into her eyes. "I went back to the case in Millbrook, Minnesota. Went over it with a fine-toothed comb, but not until I talked with the detectives who worked it, did I realize how identical our killings this side of the Mississippi are to Towne's 2003 case."

"I see. And just what did these detectives have to say?"

"Come with me," said Reynolds, going toward the back exit of the apartment building. His car had been brought around by another agent. They got in and he peeled away, the diminishing blue strobe lights of the squad cars on the street reflected in Jessica's side-view mirror, growing smaller. It felt like escape.

She curled up in the leather seat. Fatigue claimed dominance, her eyes heavy with it, as if lavished on with a brush.

"Picture the Olsen kitchen again. You were there, you saw it, right?"

Jessica joined him there. "All neat and tidy."

"I had a look in the trash bin. Guess what I found inside?"

"I haven't a clue."

"Nothing."

"Nothing . . . hmmm . . . should I be impressed, Sherlock?"

"Freshly cleaned out. Same as in Millbrook. Now look into the dishwasher," he added as he "opened" an imaginary dishwasher between them in the cab of the car. "The killer is our neat freak. He even turned on the dishwasher and did the dishes." He paused to let this sink in. "A check with her landlord, and I'm told Joyce Olsen was *not* obsessively neat about the place."

"Still, how do you know she didn't do her dishes?"

"There are six dishes inside. No way is a woman going to wash four cups and two saucers. It's not economical, and from all accounts, Olsen *was* economical. Besides the noise of the washer would drown out the noise of *his* bone-saw activity."

Jessica found herself playing devil's advocate now. "She was expecting him, perhaps, so she put her dishes away when the doorbell rang . . . out of habit or nervousness."

"Look, the broom in Minnesota used to smear all the blood and any tracks and here . . . here it's a mop swept over the evidence."

"Done in Portland as well?"

"Not to mention the size and depth of the wounds, and the M.E.s all agreeing that he used a scalpel-styled knife, and a bone cutter, for the removal of the spinal cords."

Darwin allowed all he'd said to settle in.

Outside the car, the bustle of traffic in downtown Milwaukee moved like a herd of water buffalo going across a wide stream—slow going at best. Neon lights, electronic billboards and display windows vied for attention.

"All right, I see the similarities," Jessica conceded. "No great stretch."

"I tell you, Towne is innocent, and the real killer has surfaced again," pushed Reynolds.

"I can see that you believe this."

"You will, too, if you take the time to review the Portland and Minnesota cases. In Oregon, a moblike mentality prevailed in the community—a fucking witch-hunt engineered intentionally or not around the same kind of brainless thinking as . . . as went into the guilty verdict in *To Kill a Mockingbird,* or countless real-life cases I can give you chapter and verse on if—"

She held up her hands in mock surrender. "So, you are saying that they railroaded a conviction based on his being black? Come on."

"Worse than that. They rammed it to him for being black and supposedly killing a white woman. The machine ran a single-minded track and steamrolled over an innocent man."

Her silence telegraphed the fact that her skepticism hadn't significantly diminished.

"I'm telling you that's how it went down. They railroaded Robert onto death row. Oregon's still got that Wild West approach to law and order, an inherent vigilantism is at work there. Rob Towne *didn't* get a fair trial, and he'd never get a fair appeal, either, so he says why bother?"

"What does the governor think?"

"Hughes? Ahhh . . . He's persuaded—that is, moved by the political winds—and is persuaded that no way can he overturn a Court TV verdict. He's the consummate—"

"—politician, I'm sure, and easily led by his political advisors."

"Exactly, but he's begun to listen somewhat. There is hope, Dr. Coran, and you're it."

"Me? Meaning?"

"Meaning that I'm going to send Governor Hughes a copy of your report."

"You mean you're going to shove it down his throat, right?"

"Perhaps, yes."

"Does Hughes know you're a cross between James Earl Jones and Michael Dorn?"

"I've met with him. First time was the day after the trial verdict last year. Yeah, he knows I can hurt him, but I don't operate like that."

"Sorry . . . meant no offense. That was rude . . . thoughtless of me."

"I'll forgive your insensitive response, Doctor, if you'll seriously look over the evidence and report your findings to Hughes."

"So this has been a setup? Hughes is expecting a report?"

"Yes, he is." Darwin hesitated just a beat. "Hughes wants us, you in particular, to put the Millbrook and Milwaukee killings alongside what he has in Portland, kind of overlay each atop the other to see what comes of it, forensics-wise, I mean."

"Do you really expect me to believe that the governor of Oregon asked for all this to come his way? That he's anxiously awaiting my opinion?"

"Evidence is evidence."

"And state's evidence is state's evidence. Hughes isn't likely to want to pick a fight with his own people, to reverse the process that arrested, tried and convicted Towne. *Come on*, Darwin. Out with the truth. I can't work with you if you're going to play fucking games."

"This is the truth! I've dogged the governor's office since Towne was convicted, and I've wired him about you, about the new findings. He's gotta listen to us. I'll make him listen to us."

"Whataya going to do? Corner him with a sucker punch? You know governors of state, you know they hate granting reprieves, even short ones. And look at what you've done with me. You've blown it with me."

"How have I blown it with you?" he sounded genuinely surprised.

"Come on, Darwin. You've already prejudiced and compromised me, by—"

"—by informing you? That's all I've done."

"You've told me your opinion and that you fully expect your opinion to be upheld by my findings. In forensics, that's putting the cart before the horse—*conclusion made*, now go prove it. Besides, you're lying about Hughes's level of interest in reviewing Towne's case."

He pulled the car into an underground police crime lab facility that looked like a bank, nondescript with no indication it was FBI. Once in the lot, as he located a space and pulled into it, Darwin leaned heavily into his steering wheel and sighed. "All right. I'm sorry. You're right, of course, but I simply want you to review the facts and keep an open mind."

"Who is Towne to you? Really?"

Reynolds lifted his gaze to her, his jaw set. "He's a black *brother*, and I'm a member of For Blacks Only. Look, Towne is just another in a long, long line of black men who've been shafted by the American judicial system."

"Are you saying this is some sort of crusade, a cause?"

"It's as good a cause as any, Dr. Coran. An innocent life at stake."

"And you're not clouded by the passion of the crusade?"

"Not in the least. All right . . . perhaps some . . . All the same, I'm right and Oregon is dead wrong."

"And this guy Towne couldn't possibly be guilty? Couldn't possibly have done this to his wife, not even a

chance he'd read about what happened to the Childe woman
in Minnesota and—"

"I understand your skepticism, and I applaud it. Fact is, I
want you to pit it all against the case files, and I am certain
you'll see that Hughes and his state attorney's office are the
guilty party here."

"Towne could as well be proven *guilty* by my scrutiny,
by DNA testing, Darwin. Are you ready to accept that
possibility?"

"I am prepared for whatever verdict you decide, Dr.
Coran. Will you review the material I've amassed?"

She sighed heavily now. "Tonight, I'll go over everything
you want to share on the cases. But for the moment, I have
an autopsy to get to."

FOUR

*Fear is a disease that eats away at logic and
makes man inhuman.*

—Marian Anderson, American singer
(1897–1993)

THE modest, claustrophobic changing area for female doctors at the Milwaukee FBI crime lab run by Dr. Ira Sands left little shoulder room between the lockers. As a result, Jessica had donned her surgical garb as quickly as possible to join Ira Sands out in the larger arena of autopsy room #1. There Joyce Olsen's now cleaned and stark white body lay awaiting her attention, lying not on its back as in any normal autopsy, but on its front atop a gleaming metal slab, built-in suction tubes running down either side, to carry away any loose or falling matter.

Overhead vents filled the room with a steady flow of humming air, clean and antiseptic, and another pair of vents worked equally hard to shoot air out in a constantly moving current.

She pushed through the double doors with sterile hands in gloves, mask in place, her eyes meeting those of Dr. Sands. In a corner of the room stood the tall, imposing Agent Reynolds. "Observing," he announced.

She nodded.

"Nothing new, really," said Sands. "Darwin is often here . . . observing. He's a lifelong learner."

"Shall we get to work then, Dr. Sands?"

"I have begun already with the preliminaries, and have examined the fingernails."

"You mean with microscopic lens?"

"Exactly."

"Anything?"

"Afraid there's no evidence of tissue under her nails."

"None whatsoever?"

"No evidence of a struggle," Sands replied. "Some material we could not readily identify is being analyzed now by our toxicology guy, Grant."

"Grant?"

"Our go-to guy for toxins, yes."

"Barring we find any toxins in her system, and given the nonfatal blow to the head, then Joyce Olsen expired of gross loss of blood—hemorrhagic shock," Jessica stated for the recorder, to be transcribed later.

"A sure indicator she remained alive when he began his butchery," added Sands, heavily sighing. "Hence the coloration around the wound itself."

Under the bright lights of the lab, Jessica said, "A week to ten days she'd lain there in her own blood."

Sands agreed, nodding. "It'd take at least that long for the larvae to be planted and to hatch."

Jessica and Ira stared at the insect life phoenixing from the very womb of decay and death. "Kind of like new blades of grass wriggling amid the dead matted forest floor, wouldn't you say, Dr. Coran?"

"Almost a Hallmark card in there somewhere," she replied. "But frankly, I hate the grubs."

His eyes dimmed at once. She'd finally let him down. Then Sands groaned and winced with some internal pain.

"Are you all right, Dr. Sands?"

"Old sciatica kicking up. Damn strange how the longest nerve in your body can be such an evil to you."

"I am sorry to hear it. Do you have any medications, pain killers we can call for?"

"Any more and I will OD, no. Besides, they don't touch this thing. Nothing does." Sands struggled on. "I'd say, from the position and angle of the wound over her left ear, that the killer hit her from behind," he said.

"Yes, my guess is she turned her back on him, and she never saw it coming."

"I agree. She was comfortable enough around him to turn her back on him."

"And when she did, he brought the hammer down—one quick blow, so says the tattoo left behind," Jessica said, directing a video camera to that area. "Blunt-force trauma from a rounded edge."

"A ball peen hammer most likely."

"The Claw in New York used a hammer to subdue his victims before he ripped them apart."

"She was most likely unconscious when our killer ripped open her back, but the pain to the back, I suspect, would jolt anyone from an unconscious state. I fear our original diagnosis at the scene correct, Dr. Coran."

"That she suffered greatly."

"Most assuredly, she felt the great rent and tearing of flesh from her back, yes."

Jessica nodded, her body rigid, braced. "Until hemorrhagic shock set in."

"We can only pray for that small mercy," replied Agent Reynolds, pacing before making his way to the exit, where he stopped and turned and filled the echoing room with his voice. "Creep did all that and had the presence of mind to strip away his clothes and destroy them, to use the mop to wipe out any tell-tale shoe or footprints, and to leave no trace of his DNA behind."

"He's definitely an organized killer, one who thinks

through his every move, planning for months at a time before striking," replied Jessica, while her thoughts revisited the blood-painted, stiff and unyielding mop head. It, too, was being processed and analyzed for trace evidence.

"I gotta get outta here for now," said Darwin. "Get some air. When you're finished here, Dr. Coran, I'll . . . I'd like to talk further."

"When I get done here, I'm going to want to shower."

"I'll see you get to your hotel. I'll be just outside."

Jessica understood Darwin's need to get out. Back at the Olsen apartment, she herself had felt the walls closing in more than once. The only improvement in the situation here as opposed to what had been Joyce Olsen's safe little cozy corner of the world—home for her and her dog, Shep—was the reduction in number of people milling about and the sterile environment. In terms of space, the lab was close quarters, especially given the horrendous decay and mind-numbing wound.

A glance at her watch told Jessica the hour now neared 2 P.M. She marveled at how time seemed at first compressed, then stopped completely at a mutilation murder scene such as the one they had collectively endured today, and how amazingly time had vanished as a result of her focus and concentration on the job.

Sands now said to Jessica in a near whisper as he worked, "That boy Darwin's got a tear on for this monster. Can't say I blame him."

"Darwin believes it's all the work of one man, these three separate murders." Jessica hoped to get Ira's feelings on the matter.

"Covered his tracks well if Darwin is to be believed. Not an iota of DNA left at the other two crimes scenes. Kills at opposite ends of the country . . . unusual if it is a single killer. So who'd notice?"

"Who'd notice? Apparently Xavier Darwin Reynolds," Jessica said, a half grin creasing her features. "I can't count the number of times intuition alone led me to unmask a killer."

A valet stood outside Darwin's unmarked FBI car below a huge golf umbrella with the Wyndham Lakefront Hotel's logo clearly marked. He appeared to be held in check as he watched the arguing couple inside the car. A light drizzle had begun to speckle the lit windshield where Jessica and Darwin sat below the Wyndham's marquee.

"I am willing to accept your final verdict, Dr. Coran. I know you are the best the FBI has to offer."

"You're that sure?"

The light drizzle began slapping hard at the car, turning into a downpour, encouraging Darwin to swear and pull further up under the crowded carport-canopy.

The young valet and a bellhop with another logo-stamped umbrella pecked on the windows. Reynolds rolled his down and popped the trunk from inside, saying, "Bags are in the rear." He then turned to her and asked, "Well? Do we go over things tonight after you're refreshed or am I to leave?"

"All right. You can buy me dinner."

"Thank you. I'm sorry to be so damned pushy, but we don't have a lot of time, Doctor, not if we're to stop this execution."

"Give me half an hour and then call. We'll put our heads together on Robert Towne's behalf. No promises. That's the best I can do."

Darwin grinned and almost crushed her hands in his. "That's all I can ask . . . all I can ask. Thank you, Dr. Coran. Thank you."

As Jessica slipped from the car beneath the umbrella held for her, she stuck out a hand to the rain, enjoying its touch. "At last, something straight outta Mother Nature. Something real. I love it," she muttered, while within she wondered when she had last been as passionate about a case as young Darwin Reynolds felt about this one and its relation to the impending Towne execution over half a continent away.

Jessica rushed for the warmth and safety of the well-lit lobby. Her mind kept at her, begging the question, *When did you lose that enthusiasm and passion for hunting and running down evil, Jessica Coran?* She wondered how she'd become so jaded and casual about something so absolutely awful, so terrifyingly and horribly unique as a murder case like this one—bodies stripped of their spines. To some degree she'd been thinking it was just another case, just another in a long line of jobs to be gotten through. Perhaps the time had come for her career with the FBI to be through. She wondered how many cases she compromised, how many people she hurt, including herself, while in her present frame of mind. A frame of mind she did not fully understand but one which painted her as an accountant in Hades—enumerating body parts, the remnant leavings of mutilation murderers— as if each body part formed just another bead on a rosary of evil, as if she were counting bones, organs and tissue for Satan's ledger.

Darwin had followed her in. "I have a few things to do, but I'll call up to your room in thirty or forty, and we'll have dinner, and I'll leave you with the murder books from Minnesota and Portland."

Too tall to stand below the umbrella held by the bellhop, Darwin had gotten wet. He'd helped load the bags onto a four-wheeled cart, and he had tipped both bellhops for taking charge of the bags, and the valet for allowing the car to remain in place for a short span.

"If you get no answer when you call up, I will've fallen asleep," Jessica warned.

"Shower and you'll be refreshed," he reminded her. "If I get no answer, I'll pound on your door."

"Pushy man."

Jessica left him for the registration desk, acquired her key and made her way to the elevator. She felt a certain relief in watching the passionate and sure of himself young agent disappear through the revolving doors toward his waiting car. He was an exhausting man to be around for one thing, and for another, she had gotten by so far without the murder books. Perhaps he'd have second thoughts, perhaps he'd get involved elsewhere, and perhaps she could get a good night's sleep. Not a likely thing while within arm's distance of a man so filled with kinetic energy.

AFTER showering off the taxing day, Jessica sat on the bed in her white terry-cloth robe and pulled the phone into her lap. A red light signaled messages. She ran through them. One from Eriq Santiva, checking in, asking if she needed anything in Milwaukee, and wondering if this horrible case she was working on might signal a serial killer or not. After Santiva, it was John Thorpe, with a few pleasantries, saying he missed her at Quantico, and that everything was functioning quite well in her absence.

"Thanks, J.T. You always know how to make a girl feel needed," she said aloud.

The third message was Richard Sharpe, calling from their Virginia home. He had called to tell her how much he missed her.

Jessica smiled at the sound of Richard's baritone voice. He sounded like the actor Richard Burton.

She immediately went to her suit jacket and pulled out the PCS Vision phone with built in camera that Richard had purchased for her—or them rather. It'd been a special gift, a way to see one another despite the miles between them. This particular model had a feature that allowed real-time panning of a room or vista.

Using the gift, she now called her live-in lover and best friend. She had first gotten to know him as Inspector Sharpe of the New Scotland Yard, London, England. They had met when Richard had come calling at Quantico in search of help, and she had gone back to London to work with him on a curious case there involving millennium-phobic cultists and crucifixion murders. Richard, nowadays a working consultant and liaison between the FBI and the State Department, had only recently returned from an overseas assignment, and now she had to leave him at their home in Quantico, Virginia. Richard kept up a half-kidding needling of her to marry him, but she had remained reluctant, fearful of such a heady commitment.

He came on, standing in the yard at a white fence, horses playing over his shoulder as he smiled at her. His first words on hearing her voice were direct, as always. "When are we going to *tie the knot*, as you Yanks say? I'm feeding apples to Ben and Porsche. Bet you wish—"

"I was there, yes! As to *getting hitched*, things between us are too good to sacrifice to a marriage license," she firmly replied, waving into the camera for him to see.

"That room behind you could be our wedding suite," he persisted.

"Are you kidding, Richard? I'm going to want Maui or Tahiti, maybe New Zealand, but certainly not Milwaukee for our . . . But why am I even talking about this?"

"Because, you secretly want it as much as I?"

She quickly changed the subject. "I've gotten myself involved in quite a strange case here, Richard." He became instantly curious on hearing the details of the bizarre Milwaukee case and Agent Reynolds's theory that it could be connected to two other murders years apart from one another.

"Does his theory have any credence?" Richard jokingly asked Ben, one of the horses nuzzling, when a second horse shoved him completely off camera. Jessica heard Richard shout, "Porsche! That's not very ladylike at all!"

More apple slices calmed both horses.

"As a matter of fact, Darwin's theory has a great deal of

credence, just not enough hard evidence to get a man off death row. We have no DNA, no fingerprints to match, not even the killer's blood to make any comparisons with. And Towne's defense went from pleading insanity to denying this, and then he apparently stopped any move toward an appeal made on his behalf."

"Sounds like a confused man this Towne. Still, young Reynolds may have a case, but how can you be sure? About the first crime scene. Just how bungled was it?"

"Hard to tell from here. But like I said, the kid's made some compelling arguments."

"Fill me in."

She rattled off the similarities in the three cases and added, "The only thing that distinguishes them as not being the work of the same killer is—"

"—the disparity of time between each."

"Exactly, yes." She nodded, her image reaching him but breaking up. "From all we know of serial killers, they strike within days, weeks, months at best, not years apart."

The horse tugged off Richard's hat in a bid for attention. Richard laughed his full rich laugh. "And given our predilection for accurate bureau statistics, such an aberration frightens the hell out of us, doesn't it?"

"You're going to make those horses sick if you feed them any more apples. Put an end to it, for goodness' sake," she suggested.

After a moment's thought, Richard said, "Speaks highly of this fellow Reynolds, I'd say, his catching these killings spaced so far apart both in time and geography."

"He's awfully good and awfully young for an Area Special Agent in charge. I mean to be in charge in a field office as large as Milwaukee. I suspect he has a sterling record."

"Else he knows how to suck up!"

"Don't think he needs to. He's enormous. Even on his knees, he'd find kissing up impossible. More likely has something to do with placing more blacks in high-level decision-making positions, not that he isn't talented from what I have seen of him."

"Quotas, really? In the FBI?" Richard's mock grimace sold his sarcasm. "Does sound as if he's made an impression."

"He does make an impression, yes."

"Good bloke, heh?"

Jessica loved Richard's English accent and idioms. "Wish you were here," she said.

He replied, "In Milwaukee?" But his imagination was sparked now, his rapt attention had left her for the burgeoning details of her case. Over the videophone, she recognized that his mind burned with curiosity.

"So then, we only have days if we're to save this chap in Oregon from the barbarous electric chair."

"Three after today, and it's not quite so barbarous. They use lethal injection in a pristine sterile environment."

"Like putting down a dog, huh?"

"And what do you mean by we? 'We only have days'?"

"If the man is innocent then I want to help."

"How, Richard? How will you help?"

"I'll get on a plane for Millbrook, go over their tracks."

"I'm not even convinced that Reynolds is right."

"But you are convinced of his sincerity. I can tell that much."

"True. I believe he believes."

"And we don't have the luxury of debating it. This lapse in time between the murders could simply mean the killer himself has, at times, been incarcerated either in prison or an asylum."

"Else he has the patience of evil," she suggested.

"It may be what is meant by vengeance being best served up cold."

"Well this is damned cold. If he knew any of these victims, they didn't know him. There's nothing in their backgrounds to warrant any of them should have ended life as mutilated victims."

"I'm just suggesting he likes his bone soup served as a consommé."

"I tell you, Richard, you have a cookbook inside you wanting to get out."

"You must know the Buddy Holly title, 'Love Waits,' right?"

"Of course, but—"

"Hate waits longer."

"Still, can't help the doubts. A sociopathic monomaniac capable of this . . . I hardly think him capable of timing his killings to coincide with mid-November, spacing each by a year of interim quiet. A fantasy life for these guys is twenty-four-seven."

"There's always the exception. But speaking of fantasy life . . ."

"I miss you, too, darling."

"Another reason to join you on the case. So suppose that this Millbrook, Minnesota, place was in fact his first time, and it frightened hell out of him, learning what he was capable of?"

"So he lives with it for a long time, and then something else in his life intensifies, and with a sudden volley of stress placed on him, say the death of his mum, the loss of his income, a bout with depression all at once . . ."

"And so in Oregon later," mused Richard, "he has a new and overpowering urge to do it all over again, to again kill?"

"And the same thing happens in Milwaukee," she added. "But it's not like he's a loose-cannon, spur-of-the-moment type who leaves a trail of clues. Rather he goes at this thing in calculated fashion, hence the drawings. This is highly organized, premeditated stalking and butchering."

"Certainly doesn't appear anything random about it, save perhaps how he selects his victims, and even then there may be some hidden agenda. All of them being matronly in age and appearance."

"This creep apparently wants the bones still wet with the victim's bodily fluids and blood, because his damnable brain is telling him that something special resides therein, the victim's soul perhaps, her *anima* perhaps."

"Imbued with the essence of the known victim," suggested Richard. "Look here, I've finished up with that North Korea affair in China. To great ends, I might add."

"Congratulations again."

"I tell you the mucky-mucks running the country are so like the Russians of the fifties, that they could still screw it up. I could push them from the bloody balcony in a heart's beat. It's like stepping back in time going to Beijing, and not only did they destroy a lovely name for a city— Peking—but the pollution is horrendous as well. And what's frightening is that they are meat eaters in a country where not so much as a single swine, sheep, goat, bovine, antelope, deer, dog, cat or chicken may be found, only birds and rats."

"Can it be that bad? Really?"

"Really, yes! All livestock lost to extremely poor planning to say the least at the last emperor's feast I suppose, where he kept a continuous feast going for fifty years, every day of the year, every hour of the day and night for his thousands of honored guests like there was no tomorrow. It's no wonder—"

"Black market thrives," she finished for him.

"No wonder they love to go to the zoos and stare at the animals in the cages, and why they hunt down and eat wild animals like those cats, celts are they called, suspected of carrying SARS?"

"It's sad really."

"Now, except for what you can get on the black market, everyone is served some sort of mystery meat at every meal—a true mystery, my analytical sweetheart. One you could certainly sink your teeth into."

"What do they tell you when you ask about the food?"

"Chicken . . . everything is chicken or fish. Even the

meat with the four-inch bony tail, chicken. Sometimes they get cute and tell you it's the fish that walks on land."

They laughed over this and said tender good-byes, blowing one another kisses via the video link.

"I'll call you from Millbrook when I can!" he shouted and hung up.

Just like Richard to drop everything to help out, she thought. She knew no other man who'd be so willing to get involved in such a nebulous cause.

JESSICA put away her PCS Vision phone and dropped back on the bed, exhausted and hungry. Still no call from Darwin. She wondered what had become of him when there came a knock at her door. She remained in her terry-cloth robe, her hair still stringy from being wet.

She went to the door and peeked through the one-way telescopic peephole and found Darwin on the other side with a large room-service cart filled with food.

"I took the liberty of ordering!" he shouted through the door.

She pulled it wide, shaking her head at him. "What is this?"

"I feared you'd be too exhausted to come back out after all you've been through, and I know how I am after my evening shower. Last thing I wanna do is go back out. Just wanna curl up is all," he spoke as he wheeled the cart into the center of the room.

"You can be honest, Darwin. You saw a woman dead on her feet and you took pity."

"Ahhh . . . that, too, yeah, so I brought dinner to you, along with the murder books."

"You had the casebooks all along?"

"Trunk of my car."

"You do have it all worked out, don't you, Darwin." She closed the door and grabbed a huge strawberry and dipped it into a small vat of chocolate, chomping down, famished and unable to wait.

Agent Darwin Reynolds arranged everything on the balcony at the table there, even the two thick facsimiles of autopsy and police reports bound in the covers of what police officials called murder books—all the paper that made up the Sarah Towne murder investigation in Oregon and the Louisa Childe murder investigation in Minnesota.

"A working dinner then," she said, accepting the chair he held out for her.

Jessica lifted the cover off her meal, a steamy chicken marsala with a side dish of spaghetti in marinara. Between bites, once he sat down and joined her, taking up his meal and pouring wine, she told him about Richard Sharpe, who he was to her, and how he was on his way to Minnesota.

"To do what in Minnesota?"

"To find whatever blood or DNA evidence might help the cause."

"DNA evidence? But authorities in Millbrook told me they had no DNA evidence from the crime scene."

"Perhaps there's something hiding in the old evidence lockup. We don't any of us know for certain, now do we? If anyone can inventory the evidence and see beyond the obvious, it's Inspector . . . ahhh . . . Agent now, Richard Sharpe."

"Maybe this Sharpe fella can rattle their cages. I'll certainly keep my fingers crossed."

"Sharpe has indeed rattled a few cages in his time, and I'm betting Millbrook's finest will be no match for a former Scotland Yard investigator."

"Those guys in Minnesota who worked the case seemed genuinely concerned and professional."

"You want to explain your disappearing act?" she asked.

"Whataya mean?"

"Where you've been all this time, if you had the murder books in your trunk?"

"Phone calls. I still have a life."

"I'm glad one of us has, and one day I damn well will carve one out for myself." Jessica got quickly back to Richard. "Agent Sharpe cares, and he will do a thorough job in Millbrook, leaving none of the proverbial stones unturned."

"I doubt he'll find anything useful after three years. What blood they processed all turned out to be the victim's. Don't really see that going there is going to, you know, accomplish anything. Still, I do appreciate his help."

She forked up more food, famished from the long day of not eating, of being unable to stomach anything. Wiping her mouth with the large cloth napkin, she said, "Millbrook police are as prone to mistake as any agency, and autopsy folks make errors more often than I care to tell. We're not all as adept and agile as the perky young things on *CSI*, Darwin. And Richard is trained on the scent that *ineptness* leaves behind. Trust me. Or rather, trust Richard Sharpe. He has absolutely perfect instincts."

Darwin replied, "One of the detectives on the case passed away not long ago. The other guy keeps his cards close to his chest, and he hates it that this case has gone unsolved. Damned angry and defensive about it."

"What's your point?"

"Sharpe is going up against a wall there in Millbrook. I mean I appreciate his effort, but it will be a wasted one."

"We don't know that."

The sound of the street, like a strangely languorous melody rose up to the balcony where they dined. Jessica asked him what he knew of the medical examiner who had prepared the autopsy report on Louisa Childe.

"Nothing really. Seems competent enough for a small-town M.E."

"I know him well. Have met him on occasion at conventions of the American Medical Examiners Association. I've heard him speak. He does shoddy research from what I know. It's bound to spill over in his day-to-day. So, perhaps there is something lurking in Millbrook we have no clue about."

"And when you need a clue that's not there?"

"Send in Scotland Yard."

The rattle of stainless-steel utensils against dishware diminished and died. They sat looking across at one another, Darwin lifting his wineglass to accept her toast. "May we all be successful in our endeavors, you, me, Sharpe."

He drank to this.

"Then again, you are wise to be skeptical. After all, a two-year-old case gets a lot of cold on it."

"Still, it could save an innocent man if we can connect this murder to the other two."

"I hope we can find some hard evidence to bolster your cause, Agent. Now, let me read what is before me."

"I'll shut up and be patient then."

"Thank you." She sat back and lounged with the first murder book, that of Louisa Childe, propped atop that for Sarah Towne.

She sipped at her wine as she read. "You can walk me through the reports. I assume you've read both carefully."

"Nine and ten times over yes."

"And what strikes you as the most salient feature or point of comparison between the two?"

"The missing spine, of course."

"What else?"

"The control he obviously exerted over the situation in both cases and the killing here in Milwaukee. Cold and calculated, hence the use of the charcoal drawings."

"Let me read on through each book." Her unfocused eyes steadied and met his. "If there's any stone left unturned, we'll find it and exploit it."

FIVE

*Demons are among us, and we must learn to spot
them before they feed on us.*

—DR. JESSICA CORAN

The same night in Milwaukee

GILES Ramsey Gahran walked out into the evening air on
Loomis Street, going toward Lucinda Wellingham's art
gallery. Under a slight, tapering-off drizzle, his thoughts
wandered back to his mother. Lucinda reminded him
vaguely of his mother, something around the eyes, the curve
of the strong chin and the upturned nose, that perpetual half
grin. He fantasized at length about Lucinda falling in love
with his artwork and with him. Something he had never really ever had: honest, unwavering, unquestionable true love.
Even his mother had disliked him, always deriding him,
beating him, telling him he was just like his father, but
never telling him anything substantive about his father, only
nebulous references to his having been a horrible husband, a
loser, a callous, thoughtless *monster*, a major disappointment
to all who had known him, a failed artist, a teacher fired from
every position he'd ever held, a jobless bum, a *disappearing
act*. He was all of these things, and Mother was ever mindful
that Giles looked like him, and so must *be* like him.

Mother had no education. Mother knew nothing, only her prejudices and hatred of men, all men, including her own son. Moments before she died, she pointed a finger at Giles, and that bony worm shook before his eyes for the last time as she spoke in broken words. "You've a c-curse on ya, Giles Gah-ran, God and I know. I've pro—" A cough threatened to shut her up but she fought past it. "Pro-tec-a-ted ya from it, fr-from y-your very na-nature . . . all these years." More coughing gave Giles hope she'd shut up before saying another word, but it was no use. She meant to say it all with her dying breath. And some part of him wanted to hear it all again, to absorb it, take a morbid pleasure in her choking on it, her own *creation tale* of how he came into being one night when she got drunk with the Devil and spread her legs for Satan himself.

"But w-with me g-gone, you'll suc-cumb to your base n-nature to become *him* again—that monster that spaw-spawned you. Spawn as in the Devil's own seed."

She found voice now, taking sail on it, adding, "You have his eyes, his face, and his genes. He's in your core, boy, your every cell, your DNA." She'd then grabbed his hands in her cold, bloodless, knuckle-ugly grasp. "You ought do yourself and the world a favor, son, and come to eternity with me here, now. *Take your life.* Drop out of this existence *now*, before it's too . . . too late. Trade your ugly soul in for anything but what you are!"

Fucking bitch for a mother, he thought now. Louisa Childe had looked something like Mother. Joyce Dixon-Olsen and Sarah Towne to a lesser degree.

Mother had left him with a dust-laden box as well, telling him that everything about his father resided inside that box, and if he did not believe her ever before about the awful nature to which he was heir, that he need only open that ornate antique box.

He had all these years never opened the damn box, several

times taking it as far as the incinerator to burn it, but never going through with the destruction. Instead, he had placed the box back in its keeping place beneath his bed, unopened.

Lucinda had said to meet her at her art studio in downtown Milwaukee only blocks from the museum at seven-thirty, and that they would go to the Orion exhibit at the museum together. Lucinda was both young and wealthy, a patron of the arts who enjoyed nothing more than discovering new and unique talent. After all, she had discovered Keith Orion, now the toast of the elite of Milwaukee, Wisconsin, his work on display at the Living Art Gallery inside the Hamilton Museum just down the hall from the masters, da Vinci, van Gogh, Rembrandt, Matisse, Chagall, Picasso, Monet and Manet—all of them. Just off a room filled with exquisite sculptures from Donatello to Rodin to Moore.

Tonight Giles had been invited by Lucinda herself to see Orion's so-called magnificent oil paintings on display at Milwaukee's Hamilton Museum's Fine Arts Center, popularly known as the Living Arts Gallery. Giles thought Orion mediocre at best and did not understand all the to-do over his oils. Lucinda's taste in art swung left, right and center, and her shows had been known to fail miserably, but she had hinted at the idea that Giles's own discovery, his "breakout breakthrough" loomed close at hand.

Giles had dressed for the occasion, all in black, no tie or tails, only his leather coat and sleek shirt and pants along with fake Gucci shoes. He hopped onto a downtown bus to get to Lucinda's gallery near the arts center.

He recalled the day they had first met. He had a letter of recommendation from an art promoter in Minneapolis, Minnesota, that she simply could not be impressed by. Nonetheless, she looked over the portfolio he'd brought in. Still, she remained cool to his work. Even the photos of his two best sculptures—his finest work, requiring years to complete—hadn't impressed Lucinda, and he quickly began to feel she had no taste for what was truly unique and authentically from the heart. But perhaps he could win her over, if only she would come to his studio flat and see the two finished sculptures, and his work in progress. So he pleaded that day with Lucinda to come and have a look at his most recent works.

Back in Millbrook, he had shown one of his sculptures—his best work—to another art exhibitor, Cameron Lincoln. The man had claimed to love it, that it was world-class work, that it could easily fit into any gallery in the nation or the world stage, and that together they could make a fortune selling such works for Giles. But he told Giles that he needed more like it, a grouping, he called it, of at least six or seven "related" sculptures to be a part of a show he wished to promote. Giles showed Cameron his other works, created long before his master work, but Cameron's reaction was as tepid as cold soup to the work that "had no backbone." Cameron Lincoln absolutely loved the "unique and inspired use of the spinal vertebrae as artistic metaphor" in the sculpture.

"If you can get a grouping together before next April," Cameron had promised, "I can put your work on display alongside Minneapolis St. Paul's finest artists."

Giles could hardly believe his luck, but he could not possibly put together that many sculptures in so short a time. It had taken him a year to complete the sculpture that Cameron so admired, not to mention the time involved in getting together all the parts. As a result, Giles proposed a grouping of six or seven oil paintings with similar motifs in which spines figured heavily, one his *snake pit* of spines, all alive and hissing and writhing. Others were paintings representing sculptures he had dreamed up—plans for similar sculptures as the one Cameron so admired. Giles had already sketched these in charcoal, and he had rushed them to Cameron.

Cameron had stared at each sketch, finding them fascinating. "The attention to detail, even in black and white is remarkable, Giles. Christ, you know every bone and cusp in the backbone, don't you, boy?"

"Some people call the spine the Devil's tail."

"Really? I'd never heard that."

"Says it explains why men are evil."

"Women, too. They got backbones so they hafta be just as devilish, huh?"

Ignoring the question, Giles had replied with a question of his own. "If I do these sketches in oil, can you exhibit the paintings alongside the finished sculpture?"

Cameron had again stared at the sketches or rather into them. They pulled him in, and he felt mesmerized by them. Giles worked so beautifully with the human form, creating fired clay images of women in various poses, birds and animals at their sides. In the spinal sculpture that Cameron so admired and in the sketches, the human vertebra shone through the back as if to tell a story of courage and fortitude, as if the skeletal snake had a life of its own. Uniquely done, the faces were filled with pathos. Life-sized, everything stood in proportion, except that the spines lay outside the otherwise natural, peaceful body, floating overhead like the bony wings of angels. Cameron said, "It is the disarming, stark imbalance that creates a reaction in me that I must believe others, too, will—must—feel. At the center coils the knotty, snakelike cord painted a daring, hellish red. I love it, Giles . . . love it, love it, love it. So, we've gotta get more done and quickly."

"It takes time to build a bridge."

"Giles you've accomplished serenity alongside human misery, no small task for any artist."

"Sounds like you really like it. Do you? Really like it, I mean?"

"I love it, Giles. We can do the exhibit as oils. I will be terribly surprised if they do not evoke a great response," added Cameron.

However, before the exhibit ever got under way, the show fell through when Cameron was arrested for art theft and fraud. Sometime afterward when Lincoln was out on bail, Giles, in a fit of artistic rage and frustration killed Cameron.

Giles's bus now arrived in Milwaukee's downtown area, and he stepped from it and onto the pavement. He walked east on Milwaukee Boulevard the two blocks to Lucinda's gallery. She was locking up, readying to go without him. Sometime during the evening, he must ask her again if she could find the time to come to his loft to see his work in progress.

She turned from the door and gasped at his sudden appearance. "Oh, Giles! You frightened me. You made it after all."

"Sorry I didn't mean to scare you. Running late, I know. Glad I caught you."

"How've you been, Giles?"

"Fine and you?"

"Have you been working?"

"You know I'm always working, always."

"All work and no play," she chided.

"When are you . . . Are you going to come see it?"

"Oh, absolutely!"

He stopped and she stopped with him, and he stared deep into her eyes. "When absolutely?"

"Oh, I'm sorry, Giles. I don't want you to think I'm just blowing you off like that, no!"

"Then just say when."

"Sheeze, you can be pushy for a shy guy. All right, as soon as ever I can find time. Now you mustn't become a pest about—"

"What about tonight?"

"Tonight?"

"After the Orion exhibit. Come back with me. Promise me."

"I can't promise you it will be tonight, Giles. Perhaps sometime tomorrow."

"Promise? Really."

"I give you my word, but you know how busy my schedule is, so please don't be disappointed if . . . Oh, don't pout. Now you've learned my secret horror! My word is worthless!" She laughed nervously and patted his hand. "I will get there, soon. Not tonight but soon, I promise, Giles. OK? Tell me it's OK. I'll just die if you don't."

"Yes, I see . . ." *The bitch is never going to see the work*, he thought.

They walked the few blocks to the Fine Arts Center. She spoke of Keith Orion and Keith's melancholic nature, and Keith's showmanship, and Keith's genius, and Keith's wonderful chances for a showing in Chicago. Giles wanted to kill Keith before ever having met the man, and once they arrived, Lucinda immediately latched on to Orion's arm without a thought of introducing them. Giles was left to wander about the center on his own.

Orion was all that she'd said and more. He even dressed like a successful artist in the most expensive clothes Lucinda could find for him. He'd been well turned out, and his booming, masculine voice, good looks and charm filled the gallery. But an hour into the showing, Orion and Lucinda had a posh but loud falling out with one another on the gallery floor, and even in this short measure of time, Giles realized that the show had quickly sagged of its own weight. In Giles's estimation, and obviously in the estimation of the combined Milwaukee, Wisconsin, art critics' circle, Keith Orion had relied too heavily on his David Copperfield imitation, his charm thinning rapidly, and too many of Orion's oils and sculptures derived from Picasso and his disciples, showing nothing really original save the colored lighting and the special effects around and outside the frames, with little to recommend what was inside the frames. The sculptures, too, had taken on the feeling of Moore derivatives. Nothing unique. Nothing challenging to the eye, and certainly nothing leaping out at the audience, grabbing hold, and holding it hostage. Nothing like Giles's work.

"I sculpt circles around this clown. I make him look like a Boy Scout," he told himself, but others near him overheard and moved away as if he might pose a threat.

Still Giles felt happy, and if not happy, hopeful. Guardedly hopeful. He could clearly see that the public reaction to Orion's work proved disastrous. The comments of the evening spelled death for Orion in Milwaukee, and so Chicago was a pipe dream for him now.

Giles didn't see Lucinda again; she'd simply disappeared. Never going up to Orion, not bothering to pursue any contact, Giles inched toward the huge glass doors and left. Outside, he located a cab and went home to his sculptures.

Milwaukee was a loss. Besides, showing his work so near his scavenging could prove unwise and unhealthy. Lucinda had told him of a small cafe in Chicago where she knew the owners, and she felt his work would fit perfectly their little *galeria de' artes*. To this end, she had penned a letter of recommendation, should he ever care to use it.

Perhaps the letter represented an earlier brush-off, he now realized. Perhaps it was time to move on. Lucinda had led him by the nose long enough. Fuck her. Fuck this city. Fuck this state.

However, when he got home, Lucinda stood in his doorway. "I'm sorry about earlier. I apologize, and I've come to look at your work, Giles."

It shouldn't have surprised him. She needed to bankroll a new artist. Still he said, "That's surprising."

"What do you mean? I've always said I'd take a look, see if you're as good as you say." She gave him a coy smile.

"All right, if you're sure. . . . Come on up." He led her to his studio.

The surprise visit worried Giles, as his work in progress hadn't had the final touches applied, and one spinal cord remained in a solution and hadn't as yet been painted.

Inside the dimly lit room, he quickly placed a towel over the tub in which Joyce Olsen's spine lay in a saline solution. He then turned a spotlight on his two finished sculptures and his work in progress. She stared at the lifelike clay representations of serene looking women with pleasant smiles and an aura of peace, while backbones bulged outside of their backs, floating just above them, hovering in dragonlike grace in the air. And it stirred something inside Lucinda. "My god . . . Giles . . . who . . . who is your model for these? Don't tell me. Your mother? Beautiful . . . the perfect expressions . . . the perfect ages . . . so tranquil . . . and the touch of life in the skin tones, and the animals milling about their feet, and their bloodred backbones bulging through their backs—such a . . . so startling a contrast . . . such a juxtaposition of materials, motifs . . ."

Giles beamed. He saw she meant what she said, saw it in her gleaming eyes. He dared say nothing. He held his breath instead.

"It makes me at once agitated, excited by the work, and perhaps a bit fearful . . . uncomfortable—no, agitated—no, disturbed, yeah, that's it. Disturbed to my core. And the animals are a stroke of genius. What a touch. Birds, how sweet."

She then turned her full attention to the work in progress.

"This one's without animals?"

"A dog this time. Being finished in the other room, along with a horse."

"A horse? Really. How soon before all of them are finished?"

"Not long, really. I just have to attach the parts I'm working on."

"The animals and to this one the spine, right?" she asked.

"Right . . . that part takes time."

"The sculptures are so . . . so unusual, Giles. Photos don't do them justice, not even the oils you showed me do the work justice. Have you only the three pieces?" She went straight for the towel he'd covered the tub with and snatched it away, gasping at the sight before her. "My god, it's so lifelike. How did you get the lifelike tones? And why is it in water?"

"It's not water. It's a special solution that gives the clay a sheen so the paint adheres better."

"So you sculpted it of clay? Amazing. It doesn't look like clay."

"It's a discovery of my own making."

"It's so lifelike, not like the two red ones on the finished work. Why do you paint the bones red? It might look better if you used this natural bone color."

"I use a specially mixed paint on them that sends a message. Red stands for life, the lifeblood in us all. It represents our essence. I want to capture that in my work."

"Yeah, but you're missing the point."

"What point?"

"Don't you want to . . . I mean isn't your aim to disturb your audience?"

"Disturb on the one hand, enlighten on the other, to find eventual peace. I want them to find peace and comfort in my work."

"Really . . . That's beautiful." She turned toward Giles and said, "I wish you had maybe two or three more completed. We could launch a showing first at the gallery, charge a mint for these, and then, who knows, if it's successful . . ."

"That's my dream," he replied. "But these take time to create."

"How much time do you need?"

He feared answering her. Feared losing his chance. "What if we put these three up alongside the oils?"

"I've only seen the two paintings you brought to the gallery, sweetheart."

"Let me show you more. Come over here." He guided her

to a bedroom area where the walls were lined with oil paintings of women in various poses with animal friends about them, their spinal columns showing like an exaggeration of those starving Nigerian refugees seen on TV.

"The paintings do have a certain strange appeal," she said. After looking closely at each painting, Lucinda sat on his bed, took his hands in hers and guided him to stand facing her close in between her legs. Giles wondered if this was how Orion had gotten an exhibition of his work. He decided, danger or no danger in showing his work here in Milwaukee, he would go for it.

He pressed his lips to Lucinda's, and he began to fondle her, giving her what she wanted. As he began making love to her, he thought of the box his mother had given him to be opened after her death, and her repeatedly saying, "Your father's in that box. All you've ever wanted to know about the bastard, you have in that box—my final gift to you, Giles, your legacy. It isn't much but it will tell you why you are the way your are, trust me on that score."

The sagging bed on which he made love to Lucinda bounced over the lid of the large box bequeathed him where, so long as he had resided in Milwaukee, the box had rested, still unopened and unexplored after all these years—just waiting for Giles to find the nerve and the right time and place to delve into it, and to learn about Father.

Giles pushed it from his mind now as the joy of sexual release and the eroticism of sleeping with a rich, spoiled brat who held his career in her hands began to excite him to greater and greater passions.

Lucinda moaned and brayed under him, the rod of his manhood ramming into her, his perspiration falling into her eyes.

Part of him stood in the corner and marveled at the double-backed, four-legged crab created of their bodies there on the bed. But one of the eyes of his second self wandered to the beautifully carved wooden and leather-bound box tied with ribbons still smelling of Mother's perfume, wafting up from just below the lovers.

SIX

When did man become the higher form?

—DR. ASA HOLCRAFT

WITH Darwin using her restroom to throw water on his face and freshen up, Jessica sat on the terrace under light flooding from the room. It was nearing one in the morning. She'd been poring over her copy of Asa Holcraft's *If Christ Came to New York and the Ensuing Autopsy*, part coroner's memoir, part handy, compact compendium of information on all facets of the human body and body parts, from organs to eyes and back again to see what her old mentor had to say about the spinal column.

After dining, they'd ordered up drinks, and after a couple of beers and whiskey sours, Darwin had become somewhat drowsy and was now working toward getting his second wind. Jessica called to him from the terrace, asking if he were all right and getting no answer, she stepped back into the room.

Darwin had removed his shirt and his rippling muscles shone in the half light of the bathroom. He came nearer, toweling off his hair, replying, "Must be getting old. Past my bedtime." Darwin spoke through the towel.

She stared for a moment at his enormous pectorals and

felt a momentary attraction she quickly put in check. *I'm old enough to be his mother*, she thought, lifting his shirt off the back of a chair and throwing it at him. "Get dressed. We've got a lot of work yet to do."

"Sure . . . sure," he replied, working the buttoned shirt over his head and slipping into the sleeves. *What would I do with a twenty-six-year-old Sidney Poitier–Vin Diesel look-a-like?* Jessica wondered.

She rushed back out to the terrace, a safer place. There she sat at the table and opened Asa Holcraft's book again. She'd been going from it to the murder books and back again, looking for answers.

"Maybe the sick motherfuckingsonofabitch has begun his own stem cell research in an effort to find a cure for whatever ails him," she half joked.

"That may not be so far-fetched," he replied, stepping out onto the balcony.

Jessica sipped at her whiskey sour as she continued to read.

"Asa was a genius, a somewhat obsessive one, to have put together so much arcane and scatological and lost-to-time information between the covers of a single volume."

"Never heard of his book," admitted Darwin.

"Unfortunately, the thriving publisher that Asa earned a great deal of money for, Pendant, allowed its Pax Books division to go under as a write-off, and Holcraft's invaluable work, along with countless others, has joined the innocent yet somehow disdained horde of out-of-print titles left to die on the vine." This had happened the year before Asa's death. It had hurt the old man deeply to think that his years of backbreaking toil to bring this information to light, to put it into perspective, and to place it into every forensic student's hand had ended in such ignominy. The publisher, of course, had as much as told Asa it was somehow his fault as it must have been with all the authors in the Pax division who'd been used as tax write-offs.

"That's too bad. Guess every horror story you ever hear between writer and publisher is true, huh?"

"That's right. But I've got a contact who's very interested in reprinting Asa's work. She is as determined to see it back in print as I am."

She located the section that discussed the human spinal column, and next scanned down the page looking for what information she could find on the vertebral column in man. There were sections under *S* for spine and *V* for vertebrae and *B* for backbone. She hefted the book and stood, pacing to the terrace railing, reading aloud to Darwin. " 'Made up of thirty-three segments, the spinal column breaks down into five groups. One, *cervical*, the seven vertebrae making up the bones of the neck; called the first cervical vertebra and appropriately the *atlas*—' "

Rubbing the back of his neck as if in sympathy pain with the victims, Darwin interrupted, " 'Atlas'? Why 'atlas'?"

"Because it supports the universe, the known world—the head."

"Got it." Darwin stood and stretched, groaning with the effort.

Jessica read on. " 'Two, *thoracic*, or *dorsal*, twelve bones attached to the ribs, completing the rib cage and making up the trunk bones.' "

She moved one hand to her own rib cage.

"And three?"

" '*Lumbar*, five bones in the small of the back or loins; four, *sacral*, five bones in the rump, lying between the two haunch bones, and forming the back wall of the pelvis; in the adult these are fused together into a triangular bone called the *sacrum*.' "

"All right, so what's the fifth section of the spine?" he asked.

" '*Coccygeal*, four small bones forming the coccyx which is Greek for cuckoo—' "

"It's all Greek to me."

" '—so named from its supposed resemblance to the shape of a cuckoo's bill. The coccygeal vertebrae correspond to the root of the tail in animals.' "

"All of this scientific mumbo jumbo gobbledygook is only putting me to sleep," complained Darwin. "It isn't going to catch a killer, Dr. Coran."

"I happen to find it fascinating," she countered, waving the book at him. "Look, we all know that the vertebral column encloses the spinal cord, a basic part of the nervous system without which a person can't function, cannot even . . . ahhh . . . slither in snake fashion as our limbs would be paralyzed without it. Hell, if the spinal column and cord had not evolved as it has, we'd be big-headed slugs incarcerated in our reptilian beginnings, likely still in the sea using a dorsal fin to guide us and a series of clicks to communicate."

Darwin put up his hands in mock surrender. "All right, all right. I know it's all important. I just want to get something on this guy, and I don't think we're going to find it in any books other than the case files."

"You may be right, but listen to this." She again read from Holcraft's book. " 'The spinal cord and vertebrae hold endless fascination for early mankind and the shaman in particular who rattles the bones of fallen warriors overhead. It was both symbolic and concrete proof of deboning a man, rendering his flesh and his spirit helpless to ever harm his enemies ever again. The backbone was revered by ancient peoples—our cannibalistic ancestors cleaned the bones with their teeth and saliva.' "

"They used the bones of their fallen enemies to summon the gods or something, right?" Darwin asked.

"Or something. Holcraft talks about looking past the mere function of an organ or a set of bones or nerves and muscle to understand the value and symbolism a people placed on say the eyes, the heart, the brain, and in this case the backbone."

"All right, so you think our killer might place some kind of crazoid notion of importance on the spinal cord, so he has to have it—repeatedly. But it has to be plucked from a living human being. No five-and-dime knockoffs, no substitute for the real thing."

"Maybe . . . perhaps he has some notion of it carrying magical powers, that it can bring him powers. There is that possibility."

"I can just see some old crazy shaman shaking 'dem bones overhead at the sky, railing at the gods and rattling his rattles."

"A rattle of vertebral bones," she replied. "Indo-Europeans believed that the soul of man, like a fire or flame, fed on the cerebrospinal marrow."

"Is that what this monster is doing?" he shouted, his grimace and shake of the head telegraphing his disbelief turning to belief. They remained silent for some time, contemplating the horrid possibilities. She returned to sit at the table and poured from an open bottle of wine now. The wine, a rich burgundy, in this light, held a kind of purple hue. She poured him a glass as well, and she raised hers for a toast. "To feeding on the cerebrospinal bone marrow of his victims."

She downed a large gulp, but Darwin stared at the dark liquid. "Cannibalizing the marrow . . . maybe the spinal fluid . . . in some sick belief that maybe both can provide him with life-giving, power-granting strength and renewal?"

"Whatever he's doing with the spines, we are dealing with a sick, twisted mind that likely has cultivated an equally twisted fantasy and a liking for it."

Jessica read on as Darwin set aside his wine. " 'An injury to the spinal cord between the first and second vertebrae causes instantaneous death; between the third and fourth vertebrae produces an arrest of breathing; below the sixth vertebra, an injury gives rise to paralysis of the chest muscles; injury lower down causes paralysis of the lower limbs, bladder and intestines.' "

"And, as we know, removing the entire damn thing causes death!" he scoldingly added. "Come on, Dr. Coran. We don't have time for a science lesson."

Jessica ignored his tirade and sipped more wine between revelations found in Holcraft's account of the ancient religious symbolism of the backbone. "'The spine has been called a road, a ladder, a serpent, a rod, a tree. The spine is for many millions on the globe a *replica* in the human body of the primal cosmic tree, and the brain, as its *efflorescence*, corresponds to the expanse of heaven.'"

She had to stop to take all this in, and she tried to imagine some maniac who may or may not have read a similar description of the spinal cord in some arcane book on early rituals and beliefs of mankind.

"Can you imagine that," Darwin commented, leaning now over the edge of the terrace railing, staring down at various late night crawlers on the street below.

She found her place and continued to scan Holcraft's words, reading aloud, "'In ancient Thrace and Macedonia, people thought that the backbone of a dead person in time turned into a snake. The Egyptians believed that the sperm came from the spine, and the hieroglyph "ded" stood, among other things, for the spinal column or the sacrum of the god Osiris. In the mystery cult of Abydos, the sacral bone was set up on a pillar, and upon this the head of Osiris was placed, after which the god declared, "I have made myself whole and complete."'"

Darwin wheeled, his face a mask of anger. "Is 'at what this guy goes home and does? Lifts the bones over his head and chants, 'I am whole and fucking complete now'? Bastard. We gotta catch this guy, Doctor!"

"It's possible, and it's just as possible that he feeds on his victim's vertebral marrow. I get an image of a beast gnawing on a bone."

He gritted his teeth, the image coming full in his own mind.

She lifted his wineglass back to his hand. "Drink up. Become him, Detective, and you may just have a chance at catching him. Cerebral pursuit, I call it. For this kind of monster, I know of no other way."

Darwin grasped the glass and downed the remainder of the dark burgundy in one fell swoop as if to take her challenge.

She gave him a look of approval. "But beware the journey into the inferno. Put on all your armor and arm yourself with every weapon at your disposal."

"You're talking about emotional armor."

"Body armor and emotional armor."

"Teach me, Dr. Coran."

"You're sure?"

"I'm putting myself in your hands."

"You're talking about going into an abyss like none you've ever seen before, Darwin."

"I have my reasons."

"I'm sure you must."

GILES slept soundly and deeply now that he believed a showing of his work was inevitable, that Lucinda's money could and would make it happen. But Lucinda lay awake, making plans for exactly how they must proceed. She didn't want a repeat of the Orion disaster. She pulled herself from Giles's embracing arm and stood. Naked, she slipped out into the studio and returned to the sculptures, admiring them from every angle. Beside the tub with the incredible likeness of a human backbone lying in it, sat a jar of red paint. She reached down and stared at the jar. It had a strange label, simply marked *JO*. He'd said he made his own paint.

Perhaps the paint could be merchandized, she thought. Curiosity told her to test it out. She found one of his brushes sitting in a can of linseed oil. Wiping it clean, Lucinda returned to the bloodred paint and opened the jar. She was immediately struck by the odor, and it lay thick on the brush. She tried to place the odor. The slightly metallic smell brought back a memory of a childhood injury. Then it hit her full force. *Blood.* It was blood. Blood labeled *JO* with which he meant to color the spinal cord lying in the solution.

She set the jar aside with the brush in it just as a shiver rippled over her skin. All the same, she crept on hand and knee nearer the spinal column in the wash tub. Reaching out to touch it, she realized her hand was trembling as it went into the solution.

Her fingers lightly touched bone. She immediately realized that the backbone, like the blood, was real.

"Don't touch it!" he shouted from behind her.

She pulled back, the words *It's real . . . the damned thing is real* repeating in her head. Hadn't she overheard someone at the gallery say a woman had been murdered in Midtown? Hadn't something been said about missing bones? At the time, she hadn't paid attention.

Naked and vulnerable, her back to him, she replied, "Giles, you startled me."

"Couldn't sleep?"

"Just so excited about our collaborating. Your work is so . . . so beautiful, so unique." She then slowly rose and turned. Giles stood naked as well, leaning against the door-jamb twirling her panties. Lucinda glanced at the hallway door and quickly back at him, wondering if he had followed her gaze.

I'm closer to the door than him, but can I get past the lock before he grabs me? she wondered.

Giles Gahran had struck her as peculiar from the day she'd met him. Now her brain put him together with a mutilation killing, robbing someone of her spine—three spines, in fact—and creating some kind of sick, twisted evil thing he called art, and she had for a time *swallowed* it as art. His so-called art was actually murder, and he had the positive arrogance to want to display it in a public gallery.

His eyes widened with a congenial smile. "I'm excited, too, Lucinda, but it's three in the morning." *Shit, she's ruined everything. First Cameron in Millbrook, and now her. Fucking art dealers. How many of them do I have to kill to get my showing?* "Are you coming back to bed?" He must calmly entice her back into that sense of security she'd felt with him before now, but how?

"This thing in the tub, it just looks so real. . . . I can't get over it, baby. What an artist you are! It's so lifelike, so real," she repeated. "You really must consider leaving it unpainted. At least on one of your sculptures." *Sculpture hell. This is a damn nightmare.*

He stepped deeper into the room, his arms welcoming her back. She watched his gaze go past her for a brief second. She knew that he'd seen the blood jar, and that she'd tampered with it. Again, she glanced at the exit door.

He dropped one arm and extended the other out to her. "Come on, Lucinda, I see you opened a jar of paint. Now you know one of my secrets, that there's ox blood mixed in the paint. You know, blood, sweat, and tears."

"Giles, I'm sorry for snooping, but . . . but you gotta know this . . . well, it's all so—"

"In fact, you're finding out all my secrets tonight. The bones in the solution are real. I'm sure that's fueled your imagination."

"I'm sure there's a perfectly good . . . ahhh . . . explanation for . . . I mean a reason for . . ."

"Exactly, let me explain. People never understand artistic creation that is in the least foreign to their parochial thinking."

"I know . . . I know . . . like the guy that did the Pieta in elephant dung. Talk about thinking outside the box!"

He glanced back into the bedroom to make certain she'd

not also tampered with the box he kept secure below his bed. *Untouched.* "Ahhh . . . good, exactly," he said. "The true artist does not have to explain himself, not to anyone. I'm glad you understand that."

"I do . . . I wouldn't be in this business if I didn't understand the . . . the artistic mind. Hell, I'm the only one I know that got *Being John Malkovich*, you know? The movie . . . about the artistic mind?"

"Good, that tells me you do understand what I'm doing here. You know, scatological art, art with a grounding in the arcane, down to earth, gritty, real. You knew from the moment you looked at the sculptures that my work stands out . . . stands above . . . that it's important."

"Yes, Giles, I do understand, and . . . and I want to help you succeed on . . . on every level you wish, to overcome all obstacles and to reach your ultimate goals."

"I'm glad we're able to talk . . . about this, Lucinda. I've kept this secret for a long time. Never had anyone I could really open up to and just talk about my work. Not even Mother, I guess especially not Mother."

"It's a new vision, Giles. I see that. A new way of portraying the mother and child. I can see that clearly now."

"You have to know that acquiring the bones is difficult and time-consuming . . ."

"How . . . how *do* you acquire them?"

"Allow me to keep at least one secret for now. Look, Loose . . . Can I call you Loose for short?"

"Of course, yes. Cute the way it . . . rolls off your lips, sweetie."

He sensed she hated being called Loose or Lucy or anything short of Lucinda, but that she'd tolerate it for the moment. "What matters most in the world to me, Loose, is the gallery showing that will lead to a museum showing and maybe Chicago."

"Me, too. Me, too."

"Great, then we're on the same wavelength." He watched her every movement.

"Giles, honey, if we're to get a showing like we want—and I don't mean some raunchy little neighborhood cafe on Chicago's northside—we'll need *more* to exhibit."

"More?"

"I'll need far more to work with. More spinal sculptures. I just know they'll be so outrageously popular. The way you've got them floating there like dragons."

"You want to exhibit my work badly, don't you?"

"Yes, I want that Giles, so let me help you. The bones must be extremely expensive. I can help with that. It's some sort of black-market thing, isn't it?"

She sounds so sincere, he thought. For a moment he almost believed her. *It would be wonderful to share my art with her*. But he knew better.

"Yeah, you could call it a black-market thing, and you *can* help, of course." He stood rigid, pacing about her now, going from side to side. She realized his zigzag steps had shortened the space between them. The exit looked farther away than before. "After all, anything in the name of art," she added, forcing as normal a smile as ever she'd faked.

She backed farther from him. "You could have told me the truth from the start, Giles. I got a little sophistication, even though I am just a Milwaukee kinda girl, you know? Gave me a little shock sure . . . when I learned the truth, that's all, Giles."

"Sorry I frightened you, Loose." Her words sounded one bell, but her body language another. "Why do you keep moving away, sweetheart? I want to hold you, touch you, make love again."

"I . . . I need to find the bathroom, Giles. You go back to bed, and I'll join you in a few moments." She continued backpedaling until she slipped on the blood jar, spilling it over the hardwood floor, doing a dance in the blood and paint mixture, pirouetting to stay afoot as he watched and laughed. Her attempt to recover sent her falling and grasping the lip of the wash tub, spilling its contents, sending the spine slithering toward Giles.

Giles swore and attempted to catch the slithering spine but instead, he slipped on the water and fell across the bony vertebrae, the thing cutting open his back as if in revenge. He heard the soft crunch as one or more of the vertebrae snapped to the pain in his now-bleeding back.

Lucinda got up and raced for the door, while he got to his knees and held up the one end of the violated cord. He lunged at Lucinda with it, swinging it like a club, striking her in the back of the head.

Lucinda had managed to unlatch the door, but just as she'd opened it, she felt the body-numbing blow to her head. She slid down the door, her weight shutting it tight. As she fell into unconsciousness, she heard him say, "You wanted to be a part of my success story, Lucky Lucy. . . . Well now you can be. How's the old proverb fit here, Loose? Success is getting what you want . . . but happiness, ah, happiness is wanting what you get. I hope you like statuary immortality."

SEVEN

Millbrook Police Evidence Lockup

RICHARD Sharpe stood outside the cage in the basement of the one-story Millbrook police station, eye to eye with a bored officer in a two-tone brown uniform who had unhappily searched down evidence in the case of Louisa Childe, box number 1479/RJ6. The noisy, ticking overhead clock read 1:22 A.M. and the lockup guy couldn't hide his annoyance at not being alone, his body language signaling the fact in no uncertain terms. He'd been on the phone with someone as well, and Sharpe had heard the words "Federal Bureau" come up more than once.

Sharpe's tall frame made him uncomfortable in the cramped, damp quarters here. His time at the New Scotland Yard had enamored him to policemen like Sergeant Pyle of the Millbrook Police Department's evidence room. Richard tried to ignore it, but he wanted to tell Officer Pyle that if he so hated his work, then he should put in for any other duty or get out of the uniform altogether.

Instead, Richard quietly took the box to a nearby table, sat down with it and opened the lid, placing it to act as a catchall for anything he might quickly discard. The evidence box was the size of a file box, and it had been stuffed with a pair of bloody overalls and an equally bloodied shirt. Beneath this, he found some shards of broken glass, and nothing more. This confused him.

"What's become of the bag itself?" he muttered. "Officer Pyle, tell me, is it common practice to discard the trash bag the items were found in?"

"A bag's a bag, Agent Sharpe, whether you're from D.C. or Millbrook."

"Was it a plastic bag, as in a grocery store bag, or was it unique?" he pressed Pyle.

Pyle replied, "That label dates the case back two years. How the hell do I know about some bag?"

"Yes, I see."

He looked again on the manifest of evidence brought in as a result of Louisa Childe's murder.

It listed four fingertips and a half eaten corned beef on rye. Alongside each of these items a small square marked *M.E.'s Office* had been checked in faded red. He realized such perishable items could not possibly keep for two years in a box in a warm, humidity-drenched basement. If they were findable at all, it would have to be with the Millbrook M.E.

He spread the denim overalls and the shirt out across the table, and seeing this, Sergeant Pyle said, "Hey, we eat lunch on that table."

Before Sharpe could answer, someone barreled through the door and replied to Pyle, "Come on, Sergeant, when's the last time you guys washed that table?" He went to Sharpe and introduced himself as Lieutenant Daniel Brannan.

"Yes, Irish are you?" Richard guessed that Pyle had gotten Brannan out of bed.

"American Irish. All Paddy and proud of it. Understand you're with the FBI, former Scotland Yard man. I suppose I should be impressed, a man of your caliber snooping about a two-year-old case in this fucking hole. My case, by the way."

"I'm quite aware of that much. There've been two similar killings since Louisa Childe, and we're attempting to determine—"

"If they be related, sure. It's that Milwaukee business, isn't it? What's his name? That black guy, Darwin Reynolds? He put you up to this, didn't he?"

"In a round-robin way, yes. I got it through an FBI medical examiner, an associate."

"Does Reynolds really have anything? I mean, if I thought there was something to it . . . Well, does he?"

"Quite possibly, yes." Richard turned back to examine the blood spatters on the overalls. "These blood spatters have a story to tell," he said to Brannan.

"The M.E. didn't think it helpful since all the blood belonged to the victim."

"Look here." Sharpe carefully tucked the shirt into the overalls, recreating how they were worn. He then pointed with a pen to an area about the chest and the overall straps. "From what I know of blood spatter evidence, it appears that a spray of blood on the shirt matches up with blood along the straps, all about the chest area."

"Yeah, I see what you mean."

"The size of the shirt and pants give us some indication of the killer's size."

"That much is in both my report and the M.E.'s protocol." Brannan shrugged to emphasize this point.

"If these spatters had come as a result of the first blow to the victim's head, it means the victim had been facing her killer at the time, and that he stood over her, a taller person by at least a head. How tall was Louisa Childe?"

"I don't recall."

"Perhaps your partner, George Freeman, would know."

"George died in the line of fire a year ago come October. A drug bust."

"In sleepy little Millbrook? Sorry . . . I know how it is . . . losing a partner."

Sharpe rifled through the paperwork and found the answer to his question. "Five-seven, so that puts her killer at perhaps six or six-two if I'm right about the trajectory of the blood."

"Six, six-two . . . Wow, Agent Sharpe, that really narrows the search," Brannan said with a smile.

"Death-row inmate Robert Towne in Oregon is five-eleven."

"Reynolds did put you up to this."

Sharpe ignored this. "Look here," he said, pointing at the overalls again. "From the matted blood on the legs and stomach area, her killer appears to have straddled her backside when he cut into her and she bled out, the jeans absorbing it at the crotch."

"You're pretty sure of yourself, Sharpe, but that was all determined years ago, and it didn't help us then anymore than it helps us now. And it's not going to get Robert Let's-All-Cry-Tears-For-Towne gettin' off death row."

Sharpe understood Brannan. No cop wanted a cold case of his reopened, because it also reopened wounds in him. Every detective who could not solve a case went away from it limping inwardly and invisibly scarred. Brannan was more than merely touchy on the subject; he was defensive.

Sharpe asked point-blank, "I'd like to know if the glass fragments yielded any DNA evidence whatsoever."

"You think they'd be dumped in Pyle's dungeon in this box if they had anything to tell us? M.E. found no usable sample, not even a partial print, all wiped clean."

"What about the other evidence found in the trash bag? Where do I go to have a look at it, and who do I talk to?"

"Perishable evidence is at the crime lab, across town. I'll get you there."

Sharpe worked the glass fragments, overalls and shirt back into the box, and he returned the sad assortment of death-by-murder artifacts to Pyle. He then followed Brannan out into the institutional-gray corridor.

"Whatever became of the sketches the killer supposedly left behind?" he asked Brannan.

"I've got 'em."

"Really? On your wall or under key?"

"For a long time they kept me mindful of the fact this killer's still out there somewhere alive and living while Louisa Childe is in her grave. When I heard what Towne did in Oregon to his wife, I knew then and there I could stop taking those sketches out and staring at them."

"I'd like to see them sometime. In fact, I think the authorities in Milwaukee would like to have them examined side by side with sketches left at the crime scene there—a case, as you know, with some striking resemblances to yours, Lieutenant."

"I finally flush this case from my system and now this. You really think Reynolds is onto something?"

"I trust Jessica Coran's instincts."

"Dr. Jessica Coran?"

"FBI M.E., yes."

"The one who nabbed and killed Mad Matthew Matisak in a New Orleans Mardi Gras warehouse after Matisak left a trail of blood throughout the Midwest, the prairie states, all the way to Louisiana? That Coran?"

"That would be her, yes. Now . . . there's also a little matter of the authenticated sketches from Oregon and Milwaukee being identified as having been created by the same hand."

"Jessica Coran," Brannan repeated.

Sharpe kept speaking. "This alone must give you pause. Towne could not have committed this latest murder in Milwaukee as he was serving time on death row."

"Whose to say that Towne didn't pay someone to do a copycat killing? You know, just to get leverage to make his case."

"Be a pretty heartless bastard then, wouldn't he?"

"Which one, Towne or the guy that pimped it for him?"

"Even if that were so, a different man leaves different tracks as surely as a different animal. The striking similarities in all these cases are simply too many to ignore."

"You're sure of that?"

"I tell you, Brannan, in my experience, seeing modus operandi work as it does, whoever is responsible for each of these deaths, he meticulously designed his every move."

"All three were precisely, perfectly designed spine thefts."

"*Despite* their having been years apart in execution."

"The other two same exact way, the taking of the spine, same modus operandi, you're sure?"

Sharpe felt exasperation wantonly flirting with him now. He let out a long breath of air with his "Yes, veeery."

"Call me Dan."

"Richard."

"And just how well do you know Dr. Coran? You know, I've read her book on the nature of evil, one hell of a research job. Damn, I had no idea how far back it all went, and how bad it was before the advent of forensic sciences and mass communications."

"Indeed, the world has been plagued by murder since before man was man," agreed Sharpe. "Survival of the fittest animal in the jungle, all that. Murder began as feeding, and little wonder it remains in our genetic makeup."

"Then you believe in all that business of what she says about the aggression gene, and brain implanting, and conditioning . . . Brainwashed and predisposed to murder and that we'd better learn to accept it so we can deal with it, and all that stuff about us evolving from killer apes that damn near wiped out all other species comparable?"

"I do indeed."

"Let's get a cup of coffee. Kick this over, huh?"

"Perhaps after I've concluded my business in Millbrook. You can get me back to the airport. I saw a little coffee shop there."

Brannan nodded affirmatively. "Sure . . . sure thing. What was the name of her book again?"

Sharpe didn't miss a beat. "*Neuronet Map to Murder— Brain Maps and the Evil Inherent in a Beastial Lifeform.* Kind of a reverse *Origin of Species* or *Ascent of the Killer Ape.*"

"Oh, yeah . . . right. Weird title but it made sense, all of it. And where'd she come up with all that scientific evidence?"

"U.K. mostly, over several trips. We were first to develop DNA fingerprinting, you know, and now we're ahead of you Yanks on brain mapping. Jessica is pioneering it here and linking it to hereditary issues."

"An amazing woman."

"And agent. An agent for good, you might say. Listen, do you think we can open up the M.E.'s office here?"

"You mean like now?" He glanced at the clock which read 2 A.M.

"A man's life is at stake and the sand is emptying on his life each hour."

"Reynolds sure has a crusade going on."

"Yes, and it is now the FBI's crusade as well. Can you get the M.E.'s office open for me?"

"I'll call Krueshach. He's the only one who might authorize it at this hour."

SHARPE followed Dan Brannan into the building where they traveled through a maze of corridors to locate the M.E.'s office. As they did so, Sharpe complimented Millbrook on its resources. Brannan replied, "Still, it's never enough to wage the war we're in, is it, Sharpe? You wouldn't know it to look down our quiet, well-manicured streets lined with red maples and chestnuts that this town harbors a hotbed of lunatic drug dealers, pimps and prostitutes, but we do. We get the spillover population of crap from the Twin Cities."

Brannan had called and gotten the M.E. out of bed to meet them here.

"Right-o . . . I'm sure."

"You can bank on it." Brannan banged open the interior lab door and announced himself with his enormous bulk alone until he shouted at the local M.E., "Like I warned you, Herman, we've come to have a look at a two-year-old sandwich and Louisa Childe's frozen fingertips."

"The fingertips were returned to the body, buried with it, Dan. You know we scraped them for anything useful but found nothing. Since we didn't need the actual fingertips, I saw to it they got back to Miss Childe, to take to eternity with her."

"And you found nothing under her other nails?" asked Sharpe.

"We didn't bother with it. She was lying there stiff with her right hand clutched around one of the sketches. You remember, Dan, and the super said she was left-handed, so I assumed if she had had a chance to scratch her assailant, it would be with her empty left hand."

"I see," said Sharpe, trying to follow the man's logic and finding it questionable at best. Perhaps rationalizing away anything that might cast doubt on the Millbrook police.

Sharpe knew that Jessica would explode if she heard that last line about not bothering to scrape the nails of one hand belonging to the victim of a brutal mutilation murder. "Well, then, I guess I've come a long way to see a two-year-old sandwich."

Brannan smiled at this. Herman Krueshach said, " 'Fraid I have to disappoint you there, too. Remember, Dan, it was sent over for orthodontia forensics for that partial bite mark we had, and some idiot there forgot to put it away, and a night watchman discovered it . . . and I'm afraid the man ate it."

"This before any tests were run?"

"Well, we did get a plaster cast of the bite mark."

"But no DNA tests? So you really don't have any DNA on file for this guy?" Sharpe fought to contain himself, fought back what he wanted to shout. *Calm, Richard . . . stay calm, old man*, he silently warned himself.

" 'Fraid not, but we know his distinctive bite marks. We have the cast taken from the sandwich bite mark."

"Like fingerprints . . . without a suspect to match the bite to . . . fairly useless," Brannan said.

"The marks could be compared to Robert Towne's bite. Were they used when you sent them to authorities in Oregon?" Sharpe's tone grew in intensity with each word, and from the look on the M.E.'s face, Sharpe read a disturbing truth. "You never sent the impressions to Oregon, did you?"

"They never asked for dental impressions," replied Krueshach. "Tell him, Brannan. It wasn't our case or jurisdiction."

"But Reynolds must have asked you do so."

"Reynolds is not the Oregon State Prosecutor's Office or the defense team up there." Krueshach now merely shrugged as if he'd won a point in a handball match.

Brannan, ever the skeptic, added, "Not likely those little marks'd convince a jury of his innocence."

"But it might help the governor to decide. Still," continued Sharpe, pacing now, "we really hoped for a DNA sample to be absolutely conclusive, but you failed to take nail scrapings on the right hand."

" 'Fraid so." Krueshach obviously knew to say as little as possible on the subject.

"I want it done," said Sharpe, "and I want it done immediately."

"What? What can be done? What do you want us to do?" asked the befuddled M.E.

"Take scrapings from the right hand."

"It's been two years, Sharpe," Brannan uselessly reminded him.

"Look, it makes no sense for the killer to've cut off the fingertips of her left hand if there was no DNA evidence to be found there. You said the man was meticulous about leaving no clues, that he seemed up on what we do nowadays with electron microscopes and scientific investigation, and yet he slices off only the woman's left fingertips which carried no DNA from him, so why? Why?"

"I don't follow you, Sharpe," said Krueshach.

Brannan said, "Why did the killer cut off her damned fingers to begin with if . . . yeah, Herman, think about it. He wanted the nails off and incinerated along with everything else he threw down that garbage shoot. He had to've been scratched by her. He wanted the nails off."

Krueshach's only reaction to Brannan's sudden excited state was another shrug. *Is the man suffering Tourette's syndrome or a bad case of palsy?* Sharpe angrily wondered. Finally, the M.E. said, "But there was *nothing* under the nails."

"So . . . so he got confused as to *which hand* she used. That's what Agent Sharpe is driving at."

"He disfigured the wrong hand," said Sharpe. "Like the rest of you, he was thrown off by the sketch she clutched."

"Do you think *she* knew what she was doing?" asked Brannan.

"I don't know . . . I don't know how clever she was. But if she did scratch off some cells and blood, we've got the DNA then. But fuck, it's inside her coffin with her." Sharpe heaved a sigh and raised on his heels, rocking a bit. "Look, the two of you, I understand she had no relatives, so there's no one to stand in the way of an exhumation."

"That's rather extreme," Krueshach argued.

"It's the last hope of a man on death row, and it may be Louisa's last hope of resting in peace. If you don't arrange it, Brannan, Dr. Krueshach, then I'll arrange it through our field office here and take the case entirely out of your hands."

"You know what, Sharpe? You do that. You just fucking do that," Brannan shouted.

"Where are the sketches?"

"My desk. I've looked at them every damn day since the murder. That is, all but one."

"All but one?"

"The one she was clutching in her fist the day I walked into that room and found her with her back splayed open like a melon. Louisa took that sketch into death with her, and I believed she wanted to take it to the grave with her, and I saw no reason why not. I put it in her hand just before they lowered her."

"The road to hell is paved with good intentions. Will you arrange for an exhumation today?"

"The earliest would be tomorrow morning," said Dr. Krueshach. "But the order must come from the chief of police recommended by the principal detective on the case. Other than that, you'd have to go through your federal channels."

"Then that is what I'll do." Sharpe pulled out his cellular phone and dialed Eriq Santiva to wake up and get a court order. He was in mid-sentence, having awakened Eriq, when Dr. Krueshach waved Sharpe down, protesting.

"All right! All right, I'll sign off on an exhumation."

"Then do it," he said to Krueshach. Turning to Brannan, he stated, "Detective, are we agreed?"

"All right, all right if Herman's going to sign off on it. We don't need to involve a lot of people. I'll make the necessary phone calls."

Krueshach had gone to his file cabinet and pulled out a blank document. "Here's the exhumation order. You'll need to sign alongside my signature."

Sharpe took the form and signed it, handed it back and thanked him. "I'll see you at the exhumation."

Dr. Herman Krueshach nodded but said nothing. A man of few words, Sharpe thought, or a man with a guilty conscience. Jessica would call him incompetent to lose so much in the way of evidence.

Brannan said he'd awakened the mortuary and cemetery people who would meet them at the burial site on the outskirts of Millbrook. Together Brannan and Sharpe exited Dr. Krueshach's office.

As they climbed into Brannan's Oldsmobile, the Millbrook detective softly excused Dr. Herman Krueshach with something about incompatible software systems, horrible budget cuts, little assistance, and no incentives.

Sharpe didn't want to hear it.

EIGHT

Milwaukee, Wisconsin
Same night

A shadow moved across the page she sat reading. Looking up, Jessica found Reynolds staring down at her in a kind of silent examination. "I'm sorry to interrupt you, but I was hoping we'd have come to some conclusions about what next."

"What next?" He seemed awkward, his white shirt open, the linen contrasting sharply with his black chest. "Where do we go from here."

"Enough with the arcane science lesson, huh?" she replied. All the wine was gone, but she tipped the bottle anyway, studying it as if to have some focal point. "I think to bed is where we go."

"What?"

"I'm sorry. I meant to sleep, to sleep."

"Oh, yeah. What time is it anyway?"

"Three, three-ten in the A.M. Not even conventioneers . . . not even God is awake at this hour," she lamented.

"Let's just go over the Sarah Towne killing one more time."

"I can do it in my sleep, I promise you, Darwin."

"They're still taking orders at room service. I can get us another round of drinks. Whiskey sour, right? Jack Daniel's with a lime, lemon, cherry and an orange slice."

"You are a quick study, Detective. Know just how to tingle a girl's backbone all right, but no, no, and no."

"I'll just order that right up."

"Along with your gin and tonic."

"Hold my seat."

"Will do."

With his return, again dropping into the chair opposite her on this cool night, Jessica again noted how tall and imposing a man Darwin was. She watched him grab his shirt for an invisible pack of cigarettes. "Trying to give it up," he muttered.

Somewhere from another balcony, a piano player made beautiful music, reminding her of Billy Vaughn. Whoever this imposter was, he proved extremely good on the ivories, now playing "Danny Boy." No doubt a music student.

Whoever he or she was, the pianist slipped unnoticed into an equally beautiful rendition of "I Can't Help It (If I'm Still in Love with You)." The melody made Jessica think of how far apart she was from Richard.

"I wonder why the hell I'm here in the beer capital of the world chasing yet another monster," she confided in Darwin. "I'm not sure I have the stomach for it any longer, Darwin—the process necessary to locate, capture, and put an end to the career of a man bent on ripping out people's fucking spines. Maybe this is a job for younger—"

"What the fuck is this, why-me-whine-fest time?"

The fatigue and the booze conspired against her having any reply to this.

Darwin firmly added, "You are here, Dr. Coran, to teach me, remember? And because you're needed."

"You have any idea how tired I am of chasing down these

fucking freaks, these inhuman humans? And in the chasing, how often I've lost myself, my own soul, Darwin? And you keep at it this way, you'll join me in hell."

"How can you say that with your record of—"

"The price is high, Darwin. No winning. You lose even when you win. You lose repeatedly. Repeatedly you lose a larger and larger portion of yourself—"

Darwin stared, momentarily stunned at her admission.

"Along with family, along with lovers, along with any chance at happiness, two point five children, a white picket fence, a lapdog, a home and roots?"

"Sure, I understand, Dr. Coran."

"The hell you do."

"You got so close to evil, close enough to touch it, and the closer in you get, the closer you are to . . . to accepting it as . . . *as normal*."

"Then maybe you do know something, young Xavier Darwin Reynolds."

"I know what I've read in your books."

"As normal . . . the things you begin to accept as normal as Mom's apple pie—evil plunked down and hunkered like a gargoyle right in our faces, but it is all verboten for us to fathom why because it's all part of God's grand schematic plans. His unknowable design, and so the sickest most twisted things man can do are all in the human makeup, and so this is indeed *normal*. And then it gets scary."

"Scary? You want scary go to the neighborhood I grew up in. Come on, Doc, maybe you've had a little too much to drink."

"I see it in myself, you see it in yourself, in our species, Darwin, in our race, and in our self-of-selves, where we can't hide . . . And, yeah, we see it in our cells, our collective, unconscious DNA cells, and so I give you *particularly* scary."

Room service arrived with additional drinks. Darwin saw to it, tipping the bellhop. When he returned with her drink extended, he said, "Perhaps, Dr. Coran, we both ought to call it quits on the alcohol after all and get some sleep. We have the follow-up postmortem scheduled for eight-thirty sharp."

"Sharpe, how I miss Richard Sharpe." Jessica was beyond exhaustion now. She only grunted and sipped at her whiskey sour. Darwin's eyes lingered over his glass, then at her as he sipped at the ice tinkling at the bottom of his glass. He next exchanged it for his new drink.

"Don't worry about my getting up in the morning," she said, "especially since it would appear I am not going to sleep anyway. Don't worry. I'll be there on time," she assured him.

He gave her an approving nod, hefted his glass, waited for her to do the same and toasted, "If you're sure, then, to a speedy end to this, and to saving a man in Oregon from state-sanctioned murder."

"I don't know that we can save Robert Towne, Reynolds."

"We can and we will."

"Oh, yes . . . of course. All right, Darwin. I do like your enthusiasm."

"I had hoped to find more fire in you for the case."

"Fire . . . me . . . oh, sorry. Guess I'm fatigued from the flight, all that we saw today, and maybe, just perhaps a little . . . just a little jaded."

"That might explain the book in your hand, and you sitting working this case alone as if I'm not even here."

"Just looking for answers." She held up the book's back cover to show him Holcraft's photo. "One of the best men in forensics I ever had the pleasure of working with."

"Really? I wouldn't've guessed it on my own since I'm only an FBI detective. From his picture, your man Asa, looks like Santa Claus incognito—donning a suit and tie but failing miserably to fool anyone."

She glared at his irreverence toward her American idol.

He took the book from her and examined the write-up, the cover and then the marked page where she had left off.

He began to silently scan its pages, physically jolted by something he read. "Oh Christ."

"What is it?"

"Listen to this," he ordered and began reading. " 'In Hindu esoteric physiology the spinal column has an astral counterpart in what is known as the *brahmadanda*.' "

"And that is?"

"According to your friend Holcraft, 'the Rod of Brahma, an invisible shaft, which starts from a place between the anus and the tailbone, and proceeds upward along the spine to the base of the skull'."

"Yeah, I was reading that part when you interrupted me. So?"

"So, 'within this shaft is the *sushumna*,' " he continued reading.

"Meaning what?"

"Something to do with the pleasure centers in the brain . . . means 'pleasing,' something about the largest of the subtle arteries of the body. But what the hell is a subtle artery?"

"A 'subtle artery' is a mythical medical belief in an invisible system of connecting arteries between major organs, the eyes, the phallus and the brain."

"I think I see . . ."

"No, you don't. It's a fallacy. It does not exist except in the minds of some Hindu clerics who have never let go of the past, including medical *misinformation*."

"Medical mis-in-for-ma-tion," he slowly intoned.

"At one time, there was a generally held belief that the soul resided in the pancreas, too."

"This guy Holcraft . . . He didn't believe all this shit, did he?"

She shook her head vehemently. "No-no-no, but there are people who do, and that's the point . . . that some still do."

"You mean it was a kind of hobby of his to collect this kind of stuff even though much of it is a pack of lies?"

"Asa was fascinated with what people could make of something as simple as cartilage and bone, the human nose, the ears, the eyes, the skull cap, you name it."

"Is that right?"

"From A to Z, he researched all this arcane information about scatological practices and beliefs from every culture, race, religion and time period."

"Scat-o-logical? Does that mean it's logical to scat?" he joked, but she could hear the fatigue in his voice.

"Scatological refers to bodily functions, autonomous stuff, weird shit."

"Got that right. This is some weird shit. Says here, 'According to the Chinese system an exceedingly fine tube starts at the sacral'—whatever that is—'extremity and goes up the spine and enters the skull, and is connected with a reservoir of marrow called *t-t-t-t'ung te* situated at the back of the head.'"

"From tailbone to skullcap," she commented, nodding. "Pleasure points in body and mind."

He read on, "'The Tibetans took over this notion and added a refinement by introducing a system of *boo . . . ahhh . . . bu-gu-chan* veins.' Sounds like *moo goo gai pan*."

She frowned and took the book away from him. "'These veins,'" she read, "'branch out of the spinal column and then loop back again forming a network of tiny channels filled with a vaporlike essence. This system of veins is responsible for vitalizing the blood, semen and other "wet" elements of the body.'" She lifted her final dram of whiskey sour to toast these words. "And here's to wet elements." She downed the whiskey. "And I do believe it is time for me to retire."

"I appreciate all the time you've taken, Dr. Coran."

"On the case or on your crusade?"

"I assure you they are one and the same."

"Then we will make it so, one and the same."

She staggered, dog tired and tipsy, back into the room.

He followed. "Lock that window up for me, will you? And get outta here, will you, Xavier Darwin Reynolds? I'm off to see the wizard." She set her alarm as she spoke. She laid across the bed as he made his way toward the door.

"Good night or rather morning, Dr. Coran."

"You know, Darwin, you could be wrong every step of the way on this thing, and especially the part about an aging FBI M.E.'s having any sort of clout with authorities in Oregon to get a man off death row." In her foggy mind, she once again rifled through the photos as she spoke. "Still, there are some damn striking similarities here, even to time of year. Another pattern. Always in the fall, mid-fall, right? Only a year apart . . ."

"Two years ago come November fourteenth in Millbrook, Minnesota."

"Yeah, Millbrook . . . How big is this place, Millbrook?"

"Size of my left toe. One fire hydrant town. Farming community. More cows than people. I figure our guy may've just been raised there, and with too much time on his hands . . . who knows . . . maybe he read your friend Asa's book or he's read Evan Kingsbury's god-awful novels depicting Lovecraftian monsters feeding on human beings."

"The possibility that Asa's book set him off . . . that would upset Asa, I can tell you."

"Why the bastard needs a crocodile-sized bone *God alone* knows!"

She said, "Something to fuck, something to cuddle with in bed, something to take walks with, who knows what goes through the minds of these fucked freaks that can do this kind of thing to another human being."

"More likely it's like you said. He's extracting the bone marrow and cannibalizing it."

Propped on her elbow on the bedspread, she replied, "I said that? Oh, yeah . . . least that'd be my guess if I dared venture one. Possibly thinks it gives him some magical power or eternal life or some such nonsense." She flashed on the crime-scene photo showing the charcoal sketch Louisa Childe clutched in a closed right hand fist. Another photo showed that the fingertips of her left hand had all been removed. Removed by the killer himself. These had been recovered, unlike the backbone.

"Tell me again what was in the picture Louisa Childe had clutched in her hand."

He let go of the door and moved a few steps back into the darkened room. Darwin's skin glistened here in the room as if it came alive in the dark. "A charcoal drawing depicting the victim—"

"Right . . . feeding birds in a park."

"Not just any park, but the one directly across from her apartment, one she frequented. Three other drawings of the park and the birds had also been left clumsily tacked to the walls."

"That's some con to run . . . quite a segway into a woman's apartment."

"And Minnesota authorities believe the butcher did the artwork."

"Was it a good likeness?"

"Good likeness?"

"Did he do his subject justice. Did it look like her, you know, a decent job?"

"From what I gather, it was quite good, along with the other prints found tacked to the walls—all determined to've been done by the same artist."

"Strange . . . strange he would leave such a calling card. Especially in so rural an environment. People there could recognize the hand at work."

"Unfortunately, that hasn't happened."

"How much time does Robert Towne have before they drop the acid?"

"Forty-eight hours, and nothing I've been able to do has had the slightest effect on authorities and the governor there, including our field office in Oregon."

"Do you know the governor? What kind of a guy is he? Can you get cooperation?"

"He's a cowboy and an asshole. He's made up his mind, and why not? He has the entire fucking state, along with all of Portland, behind him."

"Tell me more about Towne and his wife."

"They were estranged, had enjoyed a long separation. He had no motive to kill her. No insurance, no kid problems, no alimony, no motive. The brainless cowboys out there just want a show, and he's the main attraction. Apparently, she was some sort of sainted beauty queen and cheerleader once, so the media had no problem creating a beast out of him."

"And now Joyce Olsen in your town."

"Under my nose."

"Is that your personal interest in this, why you're so passionate about it? That it happened on your watch?"

He hesitated a moment. "Damn straight it is."

She thought for a moment she should read something into his hesitancy and his reply, but she was too foggy and fatigued now to try. "Get out. Tomorrow is another day. G'night . . ."

Millbrook, Minnesota
5:16 A.M.

All of Millbrook, Minnesota, slept. Her quaint tree-lined streets silent save for the Sunbeam bread truck, the milkman's van making its predawn rounds, a farmer going door to door with fresh eggs. A place out of time, Richard thought as the car he and Brannan rode in rushed past disinterested raccoons that'd gotten into garbage back of the Millbrook Diner. The animals simultaneously rummaged, fed and fended off a barking dog barring its teeth at the family of four. Noticing Richard's interest in the raccoons, Dan Brannan said, "Little ones are cute as hell."

They followed two cars turning onto a back road out of town that took them trundling across a wooden covered bridge over a stream called Paintbrush Creek on a green sign. Ahead of them in the lead car, now wending its way toward their dubious destination, was the cemetery caretaker who doubled as the small city's undertaker for The French and Parker *Arrangement Center*—a euphemism for a euphemism—what Sharpe learned was the new term for funeral *parlor*. Mori French of French and Parker had slipped FBI Agent Richard Sharpe his advertisement which was called a *Funeral Decision Guide*, and in it Mori and partner Garrett Parker had summed up their service philosophy in a paragraph. The guide pointed out that French and Parker wanted only to help people make the single-most important decisions of their lives—decisions about death and "arrangements" for death in one's own absence. It made Sharpe think of Woody Allen's famous statement on the subject, which he shared with Dan beside him. " 'I'm not afraid to die, I just don't want to be there when it happens.' "

Dan laughed in response. "Got that right."

Sharpe returned to the brochure Mori French had whipped out from his inside coat pocket even at this hour, even though Sharpe would not be using his services. "These guys running the local funerary have this down to a science, selling their services."

"Lotta money in it. If maybe I'd been smart," muttered Brannan. "Hell, we see death all the time, too, but we don't make near the bucks off it Frenchy and Parker do."

"Listen to this," said Sharpe, reading now from the soft blue brochure with a cloud-filled sky, bright with beaming light, as backdrop to the bold lettering. " 'French and Parker's Arrangement Center provides you with an array of choices: Ground Burial, Cremation, Mausoleum, Funeral Services, Local and Long Distance Shipping to Anywhere in the Continental U.S., Winter Storage (during permafrost season only) and Veteran's Special Arrangements. Free Arrangement Decision Guide.' "

"They've got the territory covered all right."

Following Mori French, Dr. Herman Krueshach sleepily bounced along in a family station wagon. Sharpe imagined Krueshach blinking into his rearview mirror and cursing under his breath, disenchanted with the idea of digging up a two-year-old corpse on what he believed to be a wild goose chase.

They had driven through the chill damp fog that crept into the cab of the car and into Sharpe's bones. Despite the season, the predawn drive felt icy cold, its destination and outcome grim like any funeral motorcade, but worse yet since their purpose was at opposition to French and Parker's normal "arrangements." Nothing on their guide about exhumations. In fact, no one in Millbrook's entire history had *ever* been raised from the dead.

They'd rolled out past the city limits sign, past silent tractors sitting in fields and patient cows lined up at barn doors. Now in the distance, Sharpe heard the backhoe—a result of his court order, going *thrum-pump*, *thrum-pump*, *thrum-whosh* just as the motorcade of three vehicles turned in under a black wrought-iron gate. The cemetery gate reminded Sharpe of old black-and-white American cowboy films when Gregory Peck or Gary Cooper, sitting astride a horse, staring at the big cattle ranch announced an intent to take a stand. The overhead arch was oddly draped with a banner flapping in the cold November early morning light. The new, temporary banner proclaimed the fog-laden cemetery as The Henry Knox Memorial Cemetery.

"Just had a rechristening ceremony out here a week ago," explained Brannan as if apologizing for what appeared to have been a celebration. There were even a few dead balloons left hanging in a surreal fashion from the iron gates.

"I see," Sharpe replied as they entered the narrow unpaved paths inside the gates. Ahead of them, the yellow

monster backhoe that'd begun its journey here on a flatbed
an hour before, coming from *Alvin's A to Z Rental* in town,
materialized from the fog, its formless noise now taking on
clearer meaning. Form and function and mechanical effi-
ciency amid the weeping trees and fallen headstones of what
appeared to be an ancient plot of ground. Sharpe wondered
how old the cemetery might be, and he again wondered why
Louisa Childe had not been buried in any one of the three
cemeteries within the city limits, the Catholic cemetery, the
Baptist cemetery, or the Episcopalian one. Brannan followed
the succession of cars as each pulled up against the line created in the fog by Alvin's huge flatbed truck which had
come to this point in roundabout fashion so as to disturb as
few gravesites as possible. Their presence, the cars, and the
flatbed absorbed some but not all of the enormous noise
shattering the stillness of this place as the backhoe continued its work.

Sharpe saw a huge gash had been taken out of a lovely
oak that, by day, must provide ample shade throughout this
area for Louisa and her neighbors.

Everyone climbed from their cars and gathered about the
large hole being dug. They looked like men who would go
out of their way to watch a machine of this size do its job.
The sun remained just offstage, its predawn light muted by
the overcast morning, while ominous, dark, roiling clouds
threatened to complicate the morning's work with a downpour. But there seemed already so much moisture in the air
that it would be difficult for raindrops to pass through it.
Sharpe sauntered up alongside Krueshach, Mori French, and
Detective Brannan. Nothing was said. The sound of the
backhoe was king.

The serene invaded by the chaotic needs of men with
questions.

"It's Millbrook's second cemetery for its second-class citizenry, transients, homeless and uninsured," Dan Brannan
said in his ear.

"I see."

"Is that what they're going to put on your tombstone, Sharpe? 'I see'?"

"Quaint place," he replied, surveying the nearby tombstones, thin as parchment some of them, some with dates going back to the 1830s. None of the more recent markers had names, only numbers.

AT the same time that Richard Sharpe exhumed Louisa Childe's body, Jessica awoke sprawled across her luxurious Wyndham Hotel bed, amid paperwork on Sarah Towne of Portland, Oregon. She recalled having reviewed the Towne case the night before. She didn't remember tossing the files on the huge bed or falling asleep for that matter, or saying good night to Darwin Reynolds.

Rolling over, her eyes growing accustomed to the notion of opening, she saw it was still dark outside—overcast with roiling thunderstorms off in the distance and a pitter-patter against the windows that gently rocked her back into numbness and sleep. So she closed her eyes again and contemplated what lay ahead of her, and wondering if she'd been too exhausted last night to set her alarm properly. *Why hasn't it gone off by now . . . Must be seconds away from ringing . . . How can I sleep knowing that?*

She wanted to see Joyce Olsen's body one last time, perhaps to verify that it had ever happened. Most certainly for a final, closer look, wishing to find the secret message in the dead woman that she ought to be able to discover. Joyce Olsen's wrong-side-up or upside-down autopsy had been a strange postmortem indeed. Cleaned of blood, the wound had been like a gash torn from the body of a battlefield victim hit by heavy mortar fire. All the parts disfigured, out of place, surreal.

Jessica wondered now if she was losing her touch, her edge, her instinct for the chase. She had learned nothing

new in the autopsy. Perhaps it was to be so and to remain so
with this particular victim, but it nagged at Jessica. In the
past, she had often discovered something that had gone unnoticed by others, including other medical examiners. But
not this time. Not now. Perhaps it was the attitude with
which she approached the Olsen woman's body. Jaded, unfeeling, all the emotion knocked from her at the scene. Or
perhaps she simply expected too much, expected that the
very way in which the killer had carved Joyce Olsen up
might lead to something, might tell them something, might
grant them some small insight into the mind capable of
such a monster's appetite. But neither the body, nor the
enormous insult to it, nor the autopsy itself had revealed
any great insights. And another go-round—the continua-
tion of the autopsy with Sands this morning—she rather
doubted would net anything new or useful, either. Still,
Sands was going to "dig" deeper, and so, Jessica felt she'd
best be present.

In his own subtle way, Ira Sands seemed to want to best Jessica, given this opportunity to work alongside the FBI's finest
forensic detective. He'd turned it into a macabre competition
she wanted no part of. No doubt he had the body prepped,
ready and already waiting.

She pulled herself up against the headboard, and
squinted at the clock: 6 A.M. She'd set the alarm for 6:30.
She clicked it off so it would not ring in her ears. She next
worked gummy sleep residue from her eyes. Then she
looked across the room at the table where she and Reynolds
had spent some time early in the evening yesterday working
before they'd gone out to the terrace to work there.

Suddenly, the massive dark shadow at the table registered in her waking mind.

My god, it's Darwin. Here all night. He never left. She realized that Reynolds had fallen asleep there, too, sitting up-
right in a chair, the autopsy report of Louisa Childe lying in
disarray on both the table and at his feet. He looked like one

of those big Klingons in the *Star Trek* movies, his eyes closed, head back, slightly snoring.

Shit, how in the hell did this happen? she asked herself.

Pulling her robe on and tight around herself, Jessica rolled from bed and grabbed clothing from her unpacked bag. Reynolds blinked and yawned, coming around. "What time is it?" he asked matter-of-factly, as if no time had passed at all.

Jessica decided she had to cover any sign of embarrassment. "Six-oh-five. We both flaked out. Wake up, will you? Call down to room service for a pot of coffee while I freshen up and dress."

She disappeared into the bathroom, and Reynolds staggered to the phone.

After showering, she rejoined Darwin, and while doing her makeup and hair at the mirror, she summed up what they had discussed the night before, ending with a solemn, "OK, then, I am convinced beyond doubt that the deaths are indeed, in some fashion or other, related."

"I knew it! I knew you'd see it my way!"

"Curb your enthusiasm, Darwin. We've got a long way to go."

"But you believe me? You believe me!" He stepped out on the balcony and yelled a hurrah to the sky and the morning traffic.

Once he had calmed and returned from outside, an enormous smile on his face, Jessica calmly said, "After seeing all this?" She pointed to the circumstantial but compelling evidence he had lain out before her. "Yes, I'm onboard with you, Darwin."

Darwin's large black hands exploded, sending a thunderclap bounding off the walls. "Excellent. Think of it. Dr. Jessica Coran's backing. That'll cut the governor's cheese."

"Thanks for the vote of confidence, but what the governor of Oregon knows about Jessica Coran is not likely to be much."

"Are you kidding? With your rep? With all the FBI cases you've solved? All that behind you?"

"Damn but you make me feel old, Darwin Reynolds."

"I-I-I didn't mean it the way it came out, I swear."

"I'll bet you didn't. Look, Darwin, seriously . . . Trust me, I don't pull a lot of weight." She said this as she pulled a brush through her long, rich hair.

"Trust me, you do. You make a big difference."

"I think there's another insult in there somewhere."

"What?" He looked confused.

"Con yourself if you like, Darwin, if it helps, but I'm not so sure." She paced the room, thinking aloud. "Now, as I see it, we need to put out an all-points bulletin on this creep's MO."

"Sure, right."

"Should be forwarded electronically to every law-enforcement agency in the country to alert them to *anything* smacking of these uniquely gross murders, and *anything* in the way of peculiar sketches being left at a crime scene."

Darwin nodded, taking notes. "Yeah, we want to be notified immediately if a similar killing takes place anywhere in the country."

"Right. We've got to proceed under the assumption of zero help coming out of Minnesota or Oregon, since we've no way of knowing if Richard will be successful or not." Jessica returned to the mirror, sat and continued brushing out her wet hair as she spoke.

Reynolds watched the shining auburn hair pick up the morning light coming through the balcony windows. "The man who sketched the charcoal drawings did not sign his work, but his signature is all over the drawings."

"Yeah, if someone pops out of the woodwork and happens to see them, and happens to know the artist, we have it made. But you're right, of course. We need an art expert to tell us what he can about our boy."

"I've already got a guy."

"An expert who will back our contention that in each case, the artwork is the same hand at work."

Darwin insisted, "I've got it covered, and I'm satisfied with—"

"Who's your expert?" she challenged.

"My wife's brother."

She dropped her brush and her chin.

"Now wait a minute! Ronnie's an art major at Columbia. He knows this stuff."

"No, Darwin, no! We gotta get art professors and dealers *plural* to cover our asses on this," she argued. "Multiple opinions, understood? If it's to cut any ice with the governor in Oregon."

"Yeah . . . you're right, sure. Important thing is you're with me now, one hundred percent!"

There was no curbing the man's enthusiasm now.

NINE

The same time

As Giles Gahran worked with hammer and nail, putting his fully packed traveling crates together, he thought of how often he had done just this, picked up his entire circus and left town overnight, bleary-eyed from lack of sleep. He looked in over the lip of the collapsible crate he'd finished assembling, readying to hammer the lid shut. Inside lay Lucinda's naked body wrapped in absorbent packing materials. From Lucinda's purse he'd gotten Keith Orion's mailing address in Chicago where the other artist hailed from, and he had affixed a label addressed to Orion on the lid. He now placed the lid overtop of Lucinda, gave her one last look and blew her a kiss as he muttered, "Such a waste, so sorry . . . too bad. We could have made a beautiful partnership, Loose."

He'd taken her life and one other additional irresistible item—her backbone—and why not? It was there for the taking. Why waste it. Besides, she had so wanted to be a part of his art. Now she would play a major part for all eternity.

A short time after Giles had knocked her into unconsciousness, Lucinda had regained her senses, and she felt a great weight on her back—Giles, squatting gargoyle fashion over her. "I think you're a snake person, Lucy. I'll sculpt snakes all about your feet as if they come to you for advice and succor. You damned witch. You slither in here and get my hopes up and now this. I even trusted you for a brief moment."

She felt the first incision, and she screamed. The incision ran from the base of the cranium to the tailbone, coursing down and through the center of her back. She screamed murder. Giles stopped cutting long enough to stuff an oily rag in her mouth. Moments later, she felt the artist's scalpel continue on its way. "I'm sure you have a backbone in there somewhere" were his last words to her.

Now she was neatly packed away, as were all his sculptures, including the dogs, horses, birds, figures and all the vertebrae, including Lucinda's own in separate crates.

Giles lifted another pine wood lid top and covered over the crate of carefully packed spinal columns, which he'd thought safest if packed all together, even the one he'd so arduously glued back into one piece with super glue and a bevy of C-clamps. He'd done this work while Lucinda looked on through dead eyes.

It never failed to surprise him how quickly he could, when he put his mind to it, bug out, even though encumbered with artists tools, instruments, the life-size sculptures, all his various colors and elixirs, cleaning fluids, brushes, scrapers, scalpels, oils, easels, papers, pens, clips, clamps, scaffolding, as well as his clothing and personal belongings. As he worked to place everything in boxes, bags, suitcases and crates, he half wanted to forget the box beneath his bed. Part of him said, "Incinerate the damnable thing." Perhaps if flames consumed it, he might forget it, but he couldn't forget it, now could he? It had been pushed into his hands by his dying mother.

"Go on, take it, you little bastard . . . spitting image of

your father, you are. Sonofabitch that he was. You're just like him . . . just like him. Long line of sonsofbitches all the way back to the origins. Might as well know all about him now. I spent all these years protecting you from the truth, but it's in you—that same *evil fucking seed*, his malicious *being*, his hatred of the world that short-changed him, and his absolute instinct for blood. I've seen you, Giles, out there in the backyard, killing animals. You've got the same disease as your father, exactly. You can only feel when you're inflicting pain. So go on, *take* the box! *Take it and open it after I'm dead, and maybe, just maybe you'll come away with me.*"

He now held in his hands the hefty but ornate leather-covered box she had handpicked for him, thinking it a beautiful box, yet fearful of what it contained. *"When I'm gone. Not before. I don't want to see the results of it,"* she had insisted.

She had taught him to make love to her, had lain with him since infancy till her illness had devoured her, the cancer eating her up from the inside out. She had beaten, raped and tortured him. He had prayed for her death for years, and then finally it came, all in an instant, with him standing before her, the strange box purporting to be his legacy in his hands, searing his hand along with his mind.

He asked the same question today as he had at his mother's deathbed. "What have I inherited? Who is my father? You say he's dead, killed after having gone on some mad murder spree, but you refuse me any details."

"Details? You want details? Open the box. I've kept it in a vault until now just for you, Giles."

There was something awkward inside, loose and bounding from side to side. Something heavy like a cast-iron loose cannonball. Giles to this day wondered what the hefty item might be.

Her lawyer had brought the sealed box to her hospital bed. When Giles had left his dead mother's side, he carried home the box with the noisy bouncing object inside. He shakily took the box to the kitchen table and placed it there, squarely at the center, pushing aside the salt and pepper cellars.

Fourteen years old at the time, Giles had sat before the box, alone in the world, staring at that cursed box for fifteen minutes, his hands going to it, tentatively touching it, pulling away as if snakebitten by the lifeless thing, knowing that an evil beyond anything he had ever felt or experienced lived a kind of palpable life within this dust-laden old box of crap his mother had collected. All of it kept just to one day prove to him that she was right about him. To show that her summary of his character, his core traits, those at rock-bottom, unchangeable, indelible were gathered together inside this hideously fascinating box that, if opened, would speak volumes, would open his soul to the truth about himself, would define him, *be him*, reflect him, and cut through to his most secret self, the self that knew what was in the box, and feared it all the more for this knowledge.

His curious but shaking boy's fingers had reached out and toyed with the leather ribbons and ties, and in a moment they'd come undone, as if of their own accord. *I hardly touched 'em*, he had thought at the time.

He gritted his teeth and took hold of the oxblood colored lid and slowly inched it open. Microscopic dust bunnies filled the air as the lid was disturbed, making the boy's nose itch and his eyes water. An odor of mildew rose along with the dust. Still, he had to go on. His dead mother's shrill words cheered him on, filling his ears. Higher, higher, closer he came to unleashing what was inside. He caught a glint of glassine tubing and steel bands, as on a coffeepot with a snaked tube end, and a strange flick switch along its center, all wrapped half-assed in a yellowed sheath of newspaper. Another piece of newspaper clung to the roof of the lid until it came away and slithered into his peripheral vision. Giles made out only half of the words in the bold headline: *Torture Level . . . Blood Addict.* Then he slammed the lid shut, tied it tight and rushed from it, leaving it on the table. It had traveled with him to his foster home in Millbrook, Minnesota, and later it had traveled with him to Portland, Oregon, and later it had come back across the country when he moved from Portland to Milwaukee after he'd taken Sarah Towne's spine. Since he had been in Milwaukee, almost a year now, the box had resided beneath his bed. Giles had at times forgotten of its existence, and now here it was, again begging him, pulling him toward it, pleading to be opened, to be completely explored and fully digested.

On hands and knees now, staring below the bed at the dirty old brown box left him by his birthmother, Giles again felt like the child in the kitchen, afraid to touch the damn thing, for as evil as he felt, something far more sinister than Giles Gahran resided inside the box gifted over to him by his mother.

Open the damn box! he heard his mother's dead wail reverberate though the coils of his inner ear, bouncing off the walls of his brain, echoing down the corridors of his cerebellum. *You cheated me long enough! Open the damned box!* It was always strongest—this insistence—after he had claimed someone's spine.

A part of him wanted to tear it open, spill out all of its contents, spend hours pouring over all that she had planned to rub in his face—all that she had horded all those years for his eyes only. But another part of Giles screamed to burn the damnable parcel from hell.

He reached beneath the bed and pulled the box toward his eyes. Dust flew. He held his breath, felt it catching as if he might be somehow cutting off his own air supply. "Fuck this. It's just a box of crap, old papers, shit, nonsense. I'm a man now. I don't need this shit." Even as he said it, he felt the beads of perspiration that'd formed on his forehead and hands, and he felt his stomach churning and lurching as if some phantom bitch was rhythmically suctioning his insides like butter in a bucket.

You don't have to open it, Son, came a voice, a male voice, one he had no recollection of save as the one he'd made up as a child—the voice of his loving father, the one his mother had lied about all those years. *The box is just a pack of lies, Son. Burn the fucking thing, Son. Burn it all. She's with Lucifer now and can't ever hurt you again. Send the box back to hell, back to that cunt who dared call herself a mother!*

He sat Indian fashion just staring at the box between his legs for a long time. Minutes passed. The trash chute out in the hallway was mere feet from his door, a straight shot to the incinerator. *Why not burn the fucking box and send it back to Hades?* asked his loving father. *Why not get shed of it forever. Why not take some action, my helpless Hamlet?* came the soothing father's voice.

He grabbed hold with both hands and rushed to the door, tore it open. Eyes wide, he rushed toward the trash chute, but Mrs. Parsons, the eighty-year-old hag from down the hall was standing there with three trash bags, working each in one at a time.

"Hello, Giles!" she called out.

"Mrs. Parsons."

"Nice weather we're enjoying."

"Yes ma'am indeed."

"Whatcha-got-there-inyer-hand?"

"Ahhh . . . this? This old box? Nothing . . . nothing, really."

"Interesting box. Can't get boxes like that anymore. Find it in an antique shop? Seen some file boxes with ties wrapped round them, but they were just cardboard. That's a fine box."

"Hell of a box."

"Wanna part with it? My granddaughter would love it. How much would you want for a thing like that?"

"I'm . . . ahhh . . . afraid . . . you see, if it wasn't a gift maybe . . ."

"Oh, really? An heirloom! How enchanting."

"Ahhh . . . you could say so. It was gifted to me by . . . by Mother . . . upon her death."

The landlady's hands shot instantly up in a mock gesture of surrender. "Oh, dear, I'm so sorry for your loss. You can't possibly part with a thing like that, and I certainly understand."

"Thank you."

"Just that last time I saw one like that, it was in a library, housing important papers."

"Yes . . . I keep all my important papers close," he lied. "I've got to finish packing now, Mrs. Parsons. I gotta go." He began disappearing from the hallway as he spoke, inching spiderlike back into his apartment.

"You sure created a ruckus in there last night!" she called after him. "Making that art of yours. My, but it must take a lot of perspiration indeed, all that banging! Makes a body go loco to hear all that incessant hammering."

But Giles had safely returned to his apartment and closed the door on the woman's ranting. He dropped the box into one of the crates. He'd move it again, put it away at the new place, and perhaps one day he'd have the guts to open it and look on every word, every item collected by his mother.

He stared around at his studio and slid down the side of the crate, exhausted. He pulled the phone to him and called UPS to come get the boxes and crates he'd be shipping.

"Chicago, City of Blues and Dirty Politics, here comes Giles Gahran, and as for professor of art, Keith Orion, get ready *Dr. O*, for a visit from an old flame."

He looked across the wood floor of his studio apartment and saw a fleck of blood he'd missed with his cleaning fluids, and while on the phone with UPS, ordering them to pick up his crates as soon as possible, he saw a trail of other specks he'd overlooked, mocking him. Lucinda's blood. He lifted a jar filled with red fluid, already labeled *LW*. He remained on the line, on hold, listening to "Sweet Lorraine" in its original Nat King Cole version. Annoyed by the culmination of these circumstances, he located his concoction of ammonia, bleach, Mr. Clean, and that muriatic acid the Ace hardware man had assured him could clean a gravestone of a hundred years of accumulated mold, and he sprayed the powerful, nose-pinching, eye-gouging concoction over the last remnants of Lucinda's blood.

WHEN Jessica lifted her ringing cell phone from where she had left it beside the bed, she stood shower refreshed and staring out at the terrace where Darwin Reynolds had wandered to stretch and to lift his face into the early morning rain.

She opened the phone, careful not to allow the camera to see anything but herself. When she pressed to receive Richard's incoming call, the first noise she heard was the sound of a working backhoe.

"Richard? Is it you?" She could hardly hear him over the backhoe's grunting and bawling hue. "What the hell's that noise?"

"Backhoe!" he shouted.

"Are you in the middle of a construction zone?"

"Exhumation-in-progress zone!" he shouted back.

"What're you talking about, Richard? And what time is it? And what kind of a gin mill're you in?"

"Six-fifty . . . ahhh . . . no, seven here now . . . Minnesota time. What is it there? Same time zone, isn't it? Sorry to wake you, but wanted you to know . . ." The backhoe won out over several of his words, but she caught the single-most important one: *exhumation*.

"How did you get . . . embroiled . . . in an exhumation?"

"Hold on! Hold on!" He stepped away from the rhino-bellowing machine and found a quiet distance beneath a tree. There he informed Jessica of events at the Milwaukee M.E.'s office that led to the exhumation. She took the bad news about the lack of DNA evidence on file with Krue-shach's office in relative stride, but Richard could not hold back. He took a moment to get his ire off against Millbrook authorities.

She shook her head as his camera phone revealed a grimace. "But it sounds—from the backhoe—as though they are fully cooperating with you now?"

"Well, yes, but only after I threatened them with more FBI descending on them. 'Fraid I woke up Eriq before you. Still, at least the lead investigator—Brannan—is onboard with us, entertaining the thought that Towne could possibly be innocent of the murder in Oregon."

"God, an exhumation. Difficult task. How're you holding up, sweetheart?"

He sighed heavily into the phone. "I'm standing in a drizzle the middle of a rank old cemetery since before 6 A.M. and have been up all night . . . Now I'm amid people with whom I wouldn't share a pint and don't particularly like, and I am missing hell out of you, but otherwise . . . You know very well that I am managing."

"Like the professional, I know."

"Yes, and here digging up the sad remains of one Louisa Childe."

"I'm so sorry you're being put through this, Richard, really I am. An exhumation, Richard? I could never have predicted you'd have reason for—"

Sharpe ordered her to stop. "I'm fine, really. I'm a big boy. I got myself here where I stand all on my own, dear, sad details of law enforcement in Millbrook notwithstanding." He finished with a good Christian curse against ineptness that ended with "and may your Herefords sire no calves nor give milk nor sustenance to you and yours, Dr. Krueshach!"

This made her laugh. She asked that he keep her apprised.

In Millbrook, he replied, "I'm switching off now, and I'll be letting you know what, if anything, comes of this horrible morning's effort by we resurrection men."

"Richard, you've gone above and beyond for me again. Thank you, dear, so much."

"Not at all. A man's life is at stake. I begin to believe with each moment ticking away that this fellow in Oregon is innocent."

"Proving it may be impossible, Richard. I'll tell you what I told Darwin. Don't build your hopes up so high that when they are dashed that you can't ever hope again."

"Kind advice . . . The kind I might expect from an angel."

"You're so sweet, Richard. I so miss you."

"And I you." Richard again said good-bye and put away his cell phone.

Jessica hung up, breathing a sigh of relief that Richard had seen nothing and heard nothing of Agent Reynolds in her room at this hour.

ALTHOUGH Sharpe had presided over a number of exhumations in Great Britain, it was never an easy process nor easy on the nerves. Still, it had been his call, and he felt he had to remain aloof. He tried to show some élan by nonchalantly leaning against a large headstone marked curiously enough with the bold name of Churchill 1893–1933, about the average lifespan of the day, when the headstone moved under his weight. "Shit," he muttered, quickly readjusting his stance, taking his weight off the stone.

Overhead, flapping in increasing anger or parody, the banner strung across the ancient wrought iron whipped in the breeze, distorting the good name of The Henry Knox Memorial Cemetery. The place looked to be a sad patch of earth far from the center of Millbrook on a winding country road that multiplied the rural-ness of this Minnesota haven just west of the Twin Cities tenfold. Brannan had explained that the cemetery had been the old settlers' plot, but when the town was at a loss for things the city council might do with funds found leftover from the various bake sales, the city fathers had ceremoniously renamed the weed patch in honor of President George Washington's Secretary of War, General Henry Knox, commander of the first American Artillery placed in the field against the British. The tale of the Boston Siege of 1775 was postscripted with the heroic story of how Knox made the arduous overland journey that brought the guns of Fort Ticonderoga, New York, to bear on the British at the Siege of Boston in dead of winter. The entire story seemed a reminder to Richard that he was a guest in this Land of Nod, and that his host was an Irishman whose ancestors enjoyed killing British soldiers. No love lost there. The surreal circumstances only enhanced the notion that the differences dividing Americans and the Crown remained intact after nearly 230 years.

Brannan told the story of Knox with a boastful pride, but Richard knew it was to also cover his nervousness in this place, doing this work, to help pass the time while the backhoe desecrated the ancient earth they stood on so many miles from Boston and Washington, D.C., hallowed as it was by the local citizenry and given sanctity as result.

"Why was Louisa Childe buried here?" Richard asked. "I mean, rather than in the large cemetery in Millbrook? Was she D-A-R?"

"D-A-R?" Krueshach then asked.

"Daughters of the American Revolution, Herman," explained Brannan.

"Oh, far from it I'd say," replied Krueshach, his arms tightly wound about his shoulders. "No ties really to any organization. Rather a recluse, wasn't she, Dan?"

"Then why the burial in Fort Knox here if you're all so proud of this . . . ahhh . . . cemetery?"

Brannan glared for a moment at the aspersion to the cemetery. Pointing to one side of the field, he said, "This section is the old settlers' graveyard." Then wheeling, continuing to point to where the deafening backhoe continued its work, he added, "While this other section is a potter's field."

"Potter's field, as in a place for John and Jane Does—called A.N. Others in England."

"If you mean by that the anonymous John or Jane Doe, yes."

"But you knew her identity."

"Louisa Childe had no burial insurance, nothing other than a health insurance policy, and no one came to claim the body. City couldn't house her indefinitely in Hotel Krueshach's refrigerated suite, so the city paid the freight. She had a great huge turnout at the church service at the Unitarian chapel though, didn't she, Herman?"

Krueshach nodded successively. "Folks from every county within a fifty mile radius came to show their respects."

"I'm sure they did." Richard wondered how many came out of curiosity to see the woman whose spine had been ripped from her by a brutal monster. He was reminded of stories he'd read of the old American West where outlaws were not only hung, but as in early English history, their bodies put on display. The display tickets paid the local undertaker's wage, and sometimes he sold the display, body and all, to a traveling carnival. Ironically, the criminal made more "honest" money as a dead man than he had earned in a life of crime, but it was his reputation as a criminal that got people to pay. The larger the reputation (often created for the show), the larger the take.

Knowing human nature and the criminal tendencies of the mind, Sharpe felt instant skepticism as he tried to imagine the motives of the fifty-mile-radius people who'd ostensibly come out of genuine concern or pity. Had that been the case, why had they not raised enough money to give Louisa Childe a decent burial? Still, he knew that in rural areas of England, say Bury St. Edmonds, such a death would be equally poorly handled and made the more curious by the local authorities and press. Little difference at all. Rural was rural and parochial parochial the world over, Richard just hadn't been braced for it in America, not even in Minnesota, not in the year 2004.

Rather than be contentious and ask more pointed questions surrounding the woman's burial, Richard, turning to his military training, decided to allow Brannan's small-town-cop illusions about human nature to remain intact, as he saw no tactical advantage to stripping them away.

Sharpe thought briefly of Jessica, wishing he could be with her now, in her bed, rather than here with the gloom and grim wail of the backhoe. The unnatural noise amid all the surrounding trees and foliage felt so like a desecration. To push off the chill, Sharpe again ruminated about Jessica and the warmth of her body close to his; he recalled how they had first met: how he had approached her for help, hat in hand, and how from the moment he saw her that he'd been struck by the need to have her, and how he tried to resist, and how futile was the attempt.

Sharpe glanced now from Dan Brannan's red-splotched drinker's face to the sullen Dr. Herman Krueshach's raw-boned German features. Both Millbrook men had agreed that the matter should stay in their jurisdiction after all. Still, a nervous agitation wound around the predawn light as thick as the cemetery fog.

Sharpe hated the damp earthy smell of cemeteries. He tried to focus on the work of the backhoe as it systematically uncovered Louisa Childe's crypt. The workmen then got atop it and removed the concrete lid with pulleys. Then they climbed atop the coffin, working like hunched-over gargoyles to inchworm thick old world hemp ropes beneath it. Then the coffin was lifted and gently placed on level ground.

The workmen pried open the lid, and inside they found the skull's empty eye sockets staring back. The corpse still had swaths of skin here and there, and some strands of wispy hair went fluttering as the wind dove into the coffin and sifted through it. Sharpe felt a pang of sympathy for the woman, and he was suddenly struck with why Krueshach wanted the fingertips returned to her—after all, she'd gone to eternity without her vertebrae. The least Krueshach could do to restore some dignity to the corpse was to return her fingertips—all but one that was never recovered.

Now they had dishonored her grave. Violated its below-ground sanctity. No one was happy about this, least of all Richard Sharpe.

Sharpe now watched Krueshach lift the bony hand and pry it open, first from the sketch that Lieutenant Dan Brannan had returned to her, and then from its three-year position of a hard fist. Sharpe lifted the bloodstained sketch of the woman in her lifelike pose feeding the birds. Strangely, save for some splotches of now-brown blood and insect activity about the edges, the charcoal drawing appeared as fresh as the day it had been rendered. Sharpe thought it the most peaceful scene he'd ever laid eyes on, not unlike a Hogarth portrait.

Her right-hand nails remained barely intact, coming away with Dr. Krueshach's tweezers. The sun had come up while the backhoe had completed its work, and the light—made to dance through the flurry of leaves—caused each fingernail to wink like mother-of-pearl. Krueshach bottled each nail separately, and for good measure, he took scrapings of the area below each nail, all bone now, and each of these scrapings he bottled, labeled, and capped. Sharpe, no longer able to stare at the corpse, saw the sad, small evidence bag filled with fingertips that had been placed alongside the body. Krueshach offered up a silent prayer, his lips barely moving. When he was finished and back on his feet, the little M.E. in wire rims shouted, "Place Miss Childe back into her earthly chamber!"

Before the workmen could do so, a small swarm of chirping meadowlarks appeared, flew about the scene in a circle and as quickly disappeared, all but one. The straggler landed on a low-hanging tree limb overlooking the coffin, silently staring down at Louisa Childe, as curious as a Minnesota farmer, rubber-necking, tweeting as if a lone voice in the desert, wailing a cosmic complaint that Richard Sharpe himself felt like making.

TEN

Just a line to let you know I love my work.

— JACK THE RIPPER

Apartment of Giles Gahran, Milwaukee

THE apartment smelled so strongly now of bleach and ammonia and muriatic acid that it'd gotten into the air ducts and visited apartments throughout the building. People began pouring past Giles Gahran's door, exiting the building, fearful some sort of terrorist attack had been accomplished, fearful their lungs were already in advance stages of collapse and decay. Even Mrs. Parsons was ambling past his door, and seeing him peeking out, shouted, "Giles! Get out of the building! It's awful. Some sort of airborne poison has been let loose in the building. Get out! Get out now!"

More people filed past as firefighters in protective gear rushed in, searching for the source of the disturbance. Giles slammed his door, gritting his teeth. He cursed himself for having overdone it with the cleaning fluids.

"Fuck me! Damn! All right . . . just have to remain calm. Guy's got a right to clean his place, even if he is moving out. Just tell 'em it's a compulsion, one of those anxiety things, a phobia of germs, microbes, dust mites. A personal war. They'll buy it. Hell, it's partially true. Hell, it's entirely true."

A thundering pounding against the door through which Lucinda had attempted escape the night before now filled the room along with the pungent odors of the cleaning fluids and rags he'd used. Giles lifted the cleaning rags and the mop to the door and cracked it open. He stared out through the crevice at a huge, imposing fireman whose flat, black visor looked like the face of death, like Giles's dead, faceless father come to visit. Amadeus in a Milwaukee firefighter's biohazard suit.

Through a mechanical speaker below the visor, the man inside the suit, sounding like Darth Vader said, "Sir, we've traced an odor emanating from this unit that has disturbed all the inhabitants, most of them aged and now on the street awaiting our clearance. Can you give an explanation of what that odor is, sir?"

Giles smiled and chuckled.

"Something funny about all this, son?"

"No, no, of course not . . . Sorry, it's just that some old fool in the building called you guys out on a wild goose chase, I'm afraid, and it's . . . well . . . it's silly."

"The odometers are registering high, son. So no one's thinking this silly, least of all the Milwaukee Fire Department."

"But it's just my fucking cleaning fluids is all." He pulled the door wider, showing off the mop, a bucket of water at the center of the room near all the crates, boxes, bags and luggage. Giles held out a handful of dirty rags toward the black-visored, tall man, now being joined by his fellow firefighters, curious and staring past the door and into the apartment.

Inwardly, Giles quaked. They stood only feet from Lucinda's body, all his collection of spines and jars of blood-paint, all his sculptures. In a matter of minutes, if they chose to barge in and do a thorough inspection, Giles could be found out, more authorities called in, his crates ordered opened by a search warrant. In his mind's eye, Giles saw it all happening, a complete, total end to his quest to one day display all of his work in a glorious opening of his own choosing, his own time and place.

The big man with the dark visor finally removed his protective helmet, his ruddy good looks rivaling anything Giles had ever seen in the way of a magazine model. "We're just going to take these soaked rags with us, if you don't mind, Mr. . . . ahhh?"

"Gahran . . . Giles Gahran."

"Yes, Mr. Gahran, and if you don't mind, would you remove the mop head, and we'll remove that as well. It'll speed up the process of the odors dissipating in the building."

"Oh, sure . . . absolutely . . . and I'm so sorry about all this. Really had no idea—"

A second, older fireman with gray-black hair pushed past the younger man, taking everything in, his uncovered nose sniffing. "You using some form of marine pool deck cleaner in here, young man?"

"Ahhh . . . yes, sir. Muriatic acid. Guy at the hardware said it'd get off any mildew on the planet and the moon. That's the way he put it. Said it'd clean a gravestone with a century's worth of mildew on it. So I got it."

"Smell bleach, too," replied the man.

"Yes, sir. I . . . I didn't entirely trust the hardware guy and the acid, so . . ."

"Sonofabitch . . . you mixed muriatic acid and bleach? What the fuck else did you throw into this cocktail? No wonder the odor don't bother you, boy. You've burned out your olfactory instruments, scudded out the lining of your nose, blown it out your ass. Fucking fool. Getting us all out here with all this gear and equipment, sending everybody in the fucking building into a panic. Christ, don't you watch the news, kid?"

"I don't, sir. No TV. Come in and have a look!" Giles stepped aside, inviting the man into the apartment, pointing to the interior. "A war could be going on and I wouldn't know. It's all negative vibes I just don't allow into my life."

"There *is* a goddamn war going on! We're sitting on a terror alert stage orange, fella! Get this out to the media, Tom," said the older firefighter to the younger fireman, "and round up everybody."

"Code thirteen, sir?"

"What the fuck else? We're done here! Christ, this is going to bite the budget."

"Yes, sir, Chief. Right away, Chief." The younger firefighter rushed off with the rags in hand. Giles heard him on the landing, shouting to other firefighters up and down the stairwell, "All's clear! That's a Code thirteen. We're outta here!"

The older man did a quick walk through of Giles's apartment, cursorially looking here and there. He noticed the ornate box on the kitchen table, commented on what a nice-looking box it was, and continued on. Giles popped open one of his crates and told him to have a look at one of his sculptures. The big fireman leaned in over the crate almost as tall as he, and stared down at the statue of a woman. "Looks inter-estin'," was his comment.

"Oh, it is, sir. And fulfilling, very fulfilling if you don't mind not eating that is."

"The mop head, young man."

Giles had been carrying the mop around with him, and now he stood with it and stared at the chief. "What?"

"Remove it and hand it over."

"Oh, yes . . . absolutely . . . and I truly am sorry about this."

"You might wanna get yourself to a hospital, kid."

"Sir? I'm fine, really, but thank you for your concern."

"Concern? Damn you, fella, I'm talking about when my boot goes up your ass. We're both going to need a medical professional to get my foot out your hole! Now give me the fucking mop head."

Giles pushed the entire mop, handle and all, into the

fire chief's hands. "Take it. I'm moving out anyway. Won't need it."

"Weird is what you are, kid. Who cleans up a dump like this while moving out?" He started away, in his huge boots, white biohazard suit, holding his visor in his right hand like the helmet of a knight, and the mop head flowing over his enormous gloved left hand as a scepter. If all of this incident hadn't so terrified Giles, he thought it would be laughable.

"Just my own concoction of cleaning fluids," Giles said to yet another passing fireman.

"Some concoction, son."

"My cleaning cocktail, I call it."

This fireman also carried his helmet in his gloved hands, perspiration dripping from his face. "Enough kick in it to knock over a horse," the stranger replied.

Giles closed his door on the retreating army. He took a whiff. It didn't seem so bad to him. Maybe the fire chief was right. Maybe he had blown out his olfactory senses.

The other side of the door remained noisy as more men filed out and the first brave souls of those who lived in the building began to trickle back. Giles pictured Mrs. Parsons as she'd looked going down those stairs. He'd never known the woman to move so fast. The image made him smirk and shake his head.

UPS would be here soon.

He still had as yet to clean out his bathroom medicine cabinet. As he did so, he breathed a sigh of relief. Things could have gone badly, but it seemed fate remained his friend.

Later the same morning in Milwaukee

Exhausted but so over tired he could not readily sleep, still pumped up from the excitement of discovery at the cemetery, Richard Sharpe telephoned from the privacy of his room at the best motel in Millbrook, the Minnesota Motor-lodge. He stood staring out at the flat terrain overlooking a calm stretch of water the shape of an hourglass here in the land of ten thousand lakes, wondering what the locals had named the hourglass lake, or if they were in the habit of re-naming their lakes like they did their cemeteries. What a spin they had put on the potter's field.

No answer at Jessica's end. Where the hell was she? Already out, at the crime lab in Milwaukee, he assumed. Still she should have her phone with her, and if so, on vibrate in her pocket.

Richard continued to stare out at the calming water, his thoughts going back to the lone meadowlark on the branch overlooking Louisa Childe's remains. How ironic, given her predilection for feeding birds. The exhumation and "theft" from the body concluded, he had an insistent urge to contact Jessica, to let her know of his progress, but mostly just to hear her voice.

The phone rang a fourth and a fifth time. The thing must be out of Jess's ear shot, ringing incessantly somewhere. Perhaps she was in the shower or otherwise indisposed. He flashed on the notion of seeing her in the shower via her cam-phone.

Finally the ringing ended and she was on, sounding a little winded as if she had just finished climbing stairs. Clearing her throat, getting her bearings. Another noise he could not place, an incessant knocking on a door, and then a sound like a grunting animal.

"Richard, it's you again!"

"Surprise, yes. Just got into my room here," he replied. "Why is your cam off? I want to see you."

"Ahhh . . . food is . . . room service just arrived."

"That's a good thing normally."

"And I'm running late. Lots to do at the lab. Lots to process, and I want to go over the evidence gathered and the body once again."

"I'm going to sack out for a few hours, catch up, but I wanted to see you again before doing so. A funny thing . . ."

Something crashed to the floor at Jessica's end like silverware hitting one another.

"Please! Keep it down," he heard Jessica say.

"Busy place you have there," he commented. "Want me to call back?"

"No, no, dear. Just my breakfast, room service. I must have laid back down. Fell asleep after your last call . . . showered . . . almost missed your call."

"Great to hear you, love. Strangest thing happened on my way to an exhumation today."

"Can you hold that thought a moment, darling?" she said. "Didn't eat much last night," she lied, "and—and I am so famished."

"Switch on your camera, so I can see what you're having."

Jessica feared him finding Darwin in her room at this early hour—despite her innocence, she told herself—but then she knew that her thoughts hadn't been entirely guilt free, and that this was making her sound erratic. Finally, she said, "Oh . . . ahhh . . . appears Darwin is here, too. He's brought over autopsy files on the Millbrook and Portland cases for me."

"Then it does sound as if you are busy there. I'll just bugger off then and get some much-needed sleep."

"No, no, Richard, hold on just a moment."

Her camera came on. She panned around the room, showing the breakfast cart and cutting quickly to the table where folders lay stacked neatly. It panned to Agent Darwin Reynolds who smiled at Richard and lifted a tentative hand.

"Say hello to Agent Reynolds, dear. He wants to personally thank you for doing what you can from there."

The two men exchanged pleasantries.

She had just moments before shushed Darwin after he had barreled past her to exchange their dinner dishes for breakfast, resulting in a lot of clanking noise. He had taken the hint. Darwin now grimaced and, like a bad actor, woodenly said to Richard via the cam-phone, "I brought Dr. Coran the latest toxin and serology reports over from Dr. Sands. He says basically there was nothing whatsoever in the woman's system. The bastard didn't even give her the benefit of a sedative."

Jessica returned the camera focus to herself and smiling, said, "Why don't you get that well-earned sleep, Richard. I'll call you later before we fly out to Portland."

"To Portland? Both of you?"

"To talk to the governor . . . bring him up to date on what we have, our suspicions, all of it."

"No way they're going to have DNA tests completed by then. Last I heard the earliest is forty-eight hours even on a rush job."

"I'm aware of that, sweetheart. But we've got to go with what we have. Try to stall the governor until these DNA tests in Minnesota are done."

"Right . . . sure. Agreed."

"So, what were you saying about the exhumation?"

"Ahhh . . . just a strange Jungian serendipitous thing having to do with a . . . a bird. Seems silly now. Nothing really."

"This Dr. Krueshach, he did put your request at the head of the line didn't he?"

"In Millbrook, Minnesota, dear, even if you are at the head of the line, let me tell you, life moves slow here. I built as big a fire under their asses as I thought prudent without pissing them off. On second thought, I guess I did piss Krueshach off, but he's now moving as fast as he can, I assure you."

"Then you did find enough tissue under her nails to have tests performed?"

On hearing her question, Darwin inched closer in an attempt to hear the answer. Richard saw a cup in one hand, a pastry in another.

"Affirmative, and I'm assured that a DNA fingerprint for Childe's murderer will come of it."

"How can you be so sure?"

"Call it intuition, instinct, whatever. I sense the killer reasoned wrong, thinking his DNA was under only her left-hand nails."

"You sound fairly certain of it."

"You see, he didn't bother with the hand clutching the charcoal drawing. I see it this way: She tears at him with the one hand, and he grabs both her wrists, one hand clutching the drawing. He forces her to her knees and brings down the hammer. She was struck twice with it according to Krueshach. Once while standing, once while on the ground."

"I see . . . on her knees, bending to his will."

"Yes, he sees the drawing and *draws* the conclusion from it, that her scratching him had been done with the free hand, but—"

"—but somewhere in the struggle, she's exchanged the drawing from left to right, the actual hand she attacked with."

"Precisely . . . perhaps. All hinges on these tests."

"We don't have the luxury of time, Richard, so have them run a test for blood type in the interim. It's quick and easy. If the blood type fails to match Robert Towne's at least we'll have that to add to our arsenal of items that don't add up!"

"Good thinking."

"Meantime, Reynolds and I will fly up to Portland, meet you there. We'll need time to locate Towne's DNA fingerprint."

"Are you certain he has one on file in Portland?"

"Reynolds assures me he does. Nowadays, Portland, like

a lot of cities, does a DNA fingerprint for anyone arrested on a class-A felony."

Just then Reynolds knocked over a lamp on the table. "Zeus, what was that?" asked Richard.

"Sorry, Darwin's like a bull in a china shop."

"Big man, I could see that much. And handsome."

"I hadn't noticed." she said, waving the silverware in her hand to cover the lie. Off camera, she gritted her teeth and glared at Darwin. He mouthed, *Sorry*.

"Darwin is leaving now. We are both late for Dr. Sands, who has been extremely cooperative, Richard. A delight to work with."

She felt an unreasonable guilt over the lie of omission already, the failure to tell Richard that Darwin had in fact spent the entire night in her hotel room, regardless of its having been in a perfectly innocent fashion. "He's had his coffee and roll now and is out the door."

She panned the camera on a willing subject now as the Milwaukee agent, coffee cup in hand, waved good-bye while disappearing through the door, closing it behind him.

"The privilege of your company," began Richard, "I should think, is uppermost on that young fellow's mind. Wants to learn from you, doesn't he?"

"He wants to use me, if that's what you mean. It was a set-up from the get-go. Darwin didn't want us here to solve the Olsen woman's case but to prove his theory about the connection between Louisa Childe and Sarah Towne, and that this guy Towne is innocent. He's had a hard-on for it long before I got here."

"And he wants your backing."

"Exactly."

"And he's won it?"

"Up to a point, but I'm not entirely convinced that Towne could not have killed his wife in copycat fashion, thinking authorities would be looking for the Minnesota murderer instead of him."

"But you're getting on a plane with this kid tomorrow for Portland and—"

"Today sometime, not tomorrow, because I am convinced Oregon needs to slow this down and give a hard look at the inconsistencies. Why not wait for the DNA test now that we have one in the offing?"

"Yes, of course. To be rational. But perhaps people in Oregon are not being particularly rational at this point."

"Towne certainly has managed to engender hatred and blood-lust. Interesting that he refused any appeal."

"You're a softy, Jessica."

"Me? What about you, my sweet Richard of Millbrook?"

"Keep me apprised when you get to Portland, what *goes down* as you Yanks say."

"Reynolds says he can get a chopper or a jet assigned to us from the local FBI pool."

"Sounds like a plan."

She tried to gauge the amount of sarcasm in his voice. He wouldn't ordinarily use such an American expression if he wasn't being sarcastic. "That's the plan, after I have one final look at Joyce Olsen's body. I pretty much left the initial autopsy to Dr. Sands. He's quite capable, and I want to be in Portland as early as possible, before official offices close down. Still, questions linger that I hope Olsen's body can answer."

"I'm sure she'll sit right up and speak volumes to you, Jess. If anyone can get the dead to talk, it's you."

"Oh, I much prefer the way the Dead Can Dance ensemble talks. And by the way, Richard, I'm so proud of you."

"Oh? And where is that coming from?"

"The way you created DNA evidence where there was none before. You're some magician. Millbrook won't soon forget you."

"Gary Cooper come to rescue the foolish from the more foolish?"

"Sleight-of-hand artist, that's what you are."

"I am more the trick cyclist, but let's not count our black doves before their curtain call. Thus far, all I've got are some additional nails and scrapings being analyzed at the local lab, which by the way has limited capability."

"So now we go to Portland, take our trick cycling show on the road."

"You can get their attention and stall them, Jess. I know you can."

"I'll do my best."

"That's quite the best. You lured me across an ocean."

"Right, I did indeed."

"Thief of my heart."

She laughed lightly. "As if you had nothing to do with a like theft."

Richard laughed his full, rich laugh. The sound filled her with warmth.

"You're leaving Millbrook a bit more on their toes than before your visit. Taught the yokels something about investigating, Agent Sharpe."

"Good chaps actually, but much of the evidence was bungled from the gate. I dread to think if they had a child abduction here. It'd be the JonBenet Ramsey case all over again."

"I love you, Richard, and I'll hopefully see you in Portland tomorrow with the DNA fingerprint?"

"Tomorrow midnight perhaps, and that's a big maybe. Operative words being *maybe perhaps*, understood? I've built a fire under authorities here, but I can't rebuild their lab overnight. You know very well how long it takes to get DNA tests accomplished."

"It can be done if they work day and night."

"They don't have our Quantico facilities, resources or manpower, Jess."

"Then they should farm it out to a private lab in Minneapolis."

"Not sure there's time. And I'm working with one proud, stubborn German here."

"Herman Krueshach, yes. Has he learned anything from all this?"

"Proud man like him? 'Fraid he's been—"

"Embarrassed? Shit, Richard, a man's life is at stake and he's worried about saving face?"

"And saving his ass along with his job."

"Damned small-town M.E.s are all alike."

"Bottom line is, we don't get instant DNA fingerprints. I'm not even sure we'll discover any DNA other than the victim's own in the sample."

"Go for the blood type in the meantime."

"I'll see to it before I nod off. *You* are now sounding far too hopeful, my sweet. Perhaps I can be there in time with some extenuating new actual DNA evidence, but as you warned me earlier, careful of flying too near the sun, my lady Icarus."

"All right. I'll watch my wings don't get singed, but we can't afford even forty-eight hours, Richard, that's—"

"The space between eyelashes, I know."

"—cutting things awfully close."

"As shy as the horse to the saddle, I know," he lamented. "Still, if I were to leave here any earlier, it would be empty-handed."

She allowed his complaint time to settle. "I understand."

"In meantime, you can play it up with the governor that we *do* have some new evidence being examined here. Perhaps that will cut some teeth."

"Ice," she corrected. "Cut some ice."

"Very little ice, I fear."

She smiled at him and waved to the camera lens. "All right, dear one, hurry as you can to Portland with the goods."

"You know, Jess, it could turn out to be Towne's DNA we have here in Minnesota."

"Let the evidence fall where it may, but there's no record of Towne's ever being in northern Minnesota."

"When last did you meet a serial killer who kept flight records?"

"There was a guy who kept meticulous travel records for the IRS even as he murdered people all along his route, writing off mileage, food and lodging. He'd created a self-employment situation, a sole proprietorship—subcontracting out to medical supply companies as an independent contractor."

"Christ . . . in a sense he wrote off murder to his business."

"In the best tradition of the IRS, even after Matisak was long in prison, they sent him a bill for back taxes."

"Ahhh, yes, that awful Matisak again."

"Yes, Mad Matthew Matisak."

"Who also had his murder weapon, that spigot he jammed into his victims's jugular vein to 'tap' into his supply patented with your U.S. Government Patent Office, correct?"

"That was Matisak all right, but he had help, a money-man, a lawyer-entrepreneur in the lucrative medical supply field. Lowenthal was only one of many Matisak dupes."

"Well, then, I shall find you in Portland."

"With the fingerprint, yes. And I love you as well, dear one."

When Jessica closed her television phone, she turned to see Darwin peeking in to see if she were off the phone yet. He had used a coat hanger to keep the door from latching. "Reynolds. Damn it, Darwin, are you deliberately trying to make trouble for me?"

DARWIN Reynolds had stood out in the hall, awaiting Jessica, assuming she'd want a ride to the crime lab. He patiently now awaited her last-minute primping, as he stared out over his growing metropolis. The midweek traffic jammed West Allis Boulevard for downtown Milwaukee, the skyscrapers of the business district standing sentinel to the influx of the Wednesday morning rush hour. He turned now, gritted his teeth and shrugged apologetically. "I'm sorry, Dr. Coran about earlier, if I caused you any embarrassment or a moment's awkwardness with your husband."

She called back as she tied back her hair. "Richard is not my husband, not yet anyway."

"Sorry again," he said almost as if to himself, grimacing. "I'm just naturally clumsy." He went to the tray and grabbed a doughnut and poured himself another cup of steaming coffee. "I really wouldn't—*wouldn't*—want anyone to get the wrong impression, and most certainly not your man or my wife, trust me."

"Really? Well, it may be too late for that." She wasn't about to let him off the mat.

Reynolds poured her coffee, shaking his head. He handed the black liquid to her. "I'll see what I can do to arrange for the jet."

"Why aren't you gone and taking care of that?" she asked. "I can get a cab or walk to the morgue from here, Darwin."

"Ahhh . . . I just . . . well, are you sure?"

"Sure, yes."

"All right, then. I'll catch up with you there." Feeling her ire, sensing her coolness, Reynolds took his doughnut and coffee out the door.

Jessica frowned after him, sat down and uncovered the hot plate of hash browns and scrambled eggs he'd ordered for her. "Carbs're going to kill that kid," she muttered, "if I don't first."

After reviewing the preliminary autopsy report, a thumbnail sketch of the final autopsy on Joyce Olsen—put off thanks to her having to focus on Oregon's Sarah Towne and Millbrook's Louisa Childe—Jessica realized that Ira Sands must know that it provided nothing new. Reynolds

had somehow managed to get this early-stage report out of
Sands sometime the night before, during that period when
he had disappeared and suddenly appeared with last evening's room-service cart, she guessed.

She wondered if he were hiding something, some more
personal stake in all this. Had he known one of the victims?
Did he know Towne personally? Perhaps before becoming
FBI? Had Towne somehow reached out to Darwin from behind prison walls for one man's sympathy or letters threatening blackmail?

Perhaps, perhaps not. Perhaps her unflattering suspicious
nature, part of her job and makeup, was at work overtime.
None of it made much sense except to excuse him on the
grounds of having become a crusader, and yet she had
learned long ago to trust her fears, to accept fear as a gift, a
gift of innate intelligence that sounded certain bells within,
and the ringing of said bells saved her life on more than one
occasion. Not that she feared Darwin, but she wondered at
the depth of his motives in all this. Then she chided herself,
recalling the depth of her own feelings and motivation in
many cases she had worked as a younger woman, and she realized why she liked X. Darwin Reynolds so much. His enthusiasm was contagious. So much so that even Richard
must have felt it over the phone. And that enthusiasm reminded her why she did what she did, reminded her who
she was, what the culmination of years of FBI work meant
to her.

"Guess I could use some of that kid's zeal about now."
She sipped at the hot coffee. Still a tweaking, annoying
doubt hung in the air, suspicion lurking in the corners of
her mind, some twinge of intuition that questioned Darwin's reasoning and actions. She caught a glimpse of herself
in the hotel mirror, her long auburn hair tied in the businesswoman's bun. It normally trailed to her shoulders these
days, playfully ribboning a frame for her emerald eyes, and

she knew she looked good in the virgin-white of the hotel terry-cloth robe. Did Darwin have designs on her?

No . . . just a wrong instinct this time, she assured herself. The guy is desperate to help an innocent man, believes in Towne's innocence. Likely has allowed the case to consume him . . . obviously so. Likely hasn't slept a full night's sleep since beginning his quest to save Towne.

Jessica quickly finished breakfast, finished dressing, located her shoes and medical bag, and walked the few blocks to the morgue. When she arrived, she found Ira Sands already at work, having clocked several hours on the autopsy the day before, and being a thorough scientist like herself, taking enough time to be rested and coming back at it. He'd become obsessed in his effort to run down any miniscule medical lead in the Olsen matter. Perhaps to show her up . . . perhaps to beat out the most famous M.E. in America, so that he could tell the tale at the next annual meeting of the AMEA—the American Medical Examiners Association.

Jessica suited up and joined Sands for the second go-round.

Seeing the Olsen woman's body again shook Jessica to her core. Again the stark horror of the crime clawed at Jessica's own spine. It slithered upward and curled around her brain stem on its way to her innermost psyche.

With Sands closely watching her reaction, she shook off the paralyzing feeling and went to work. Several hours later, she and Sands finally gave up the ghost. There was nothing further that Joyce Olsen could tell them. Nothing further that Jessica and Ira could do beyond feeling absolute frustration. As in the Minnesota case, they had scant little to go on. The toxicology reports had come back absolutely negative. Serum and blood tests demonstrated there was no one's blood or saliva present other than the victim's. No evidence of rape, no DNA evidence, no fingerprints, no bite marks on the body. The only thing they could say for certain was that she, like the other two victims, had been struck by a blow to the head with a hammer.

Using the mop, which tested negative for prints, the killer had even robbed them of bloody shoe prints. The two M.E.'s hated to call any murder a perfect crime. To do so meant admitting failure. Still, this one had all the markings of a flawless crime.

She shared with Sands the one bit of good news about Richard's scavenger hunt through the Millbrook evidence lockup, morgue and cemetery, and the hope that Richard's investigation there held out.

"You're telling me our mastermind cut off the wrong fucking fingers?" Ira Sands's laughter filled the silent autopsy room. "That's rich. That does give us hope."

"Still," cautioned Jessica, "the DNA found in the exhumation is more likely to free a death-row inmate than to capture a murderer."

"Unless someone's charged with the crime and his DNA is in the system and we gain a match."

"A lot of *ifs*. Look, I have to get out of here, now," she confided and marched off for the lockers.

Jessica felt a gnawing, clawing, claustrophobia creeping in, one she recognized as the frustration and stress monster her shrink had so often warned her to get as far from as possible when she felt the onset. "Go out and feed your inner child immediately. Go to a zoo, a museum, a park to watch the dogs frolic and kids laugh, anything but your grim reality, your fucked-up work ethic, and your current case files."

"But I'm twenty-four-seven an M.E.," she'd argued at first.

"Then you gotta reclaim that time. No one else can do it for you, not even Richard."

So she knew now, after the night she had spent and the day's autopsy, that she must release the little kid inside. "Gotta at the very least get the fuck out of the lab," she swore aloud as she pushed through the doors leading into the locker room area for female medical personnel. She tore off her protective wear, showered and dressed a second time today. Grabbing her things, she went past Sands's office.

"Join me for coffee?" Ira held up a pot and a cup, a smile stretching his mustache.

"No thanks, Ira," she responded to the offer. "I really have to get myself some air, get out of the building, you know. The kind of day you've had, Dr. Sands, you should play hooky with me."

"A tempting, tempting offer, Jessica. Ahhh, yes, space and air . . . things I am denied for the time being. Go, yes! Go for the rest of us, and when you return, tell us what is out there in the land of the free, but no . . . can't break away just now. Too many people would have my scalp, but I quite understand the impulse, my dear. Go . . . go for both of us, Dr. Coran."

"As quickly as possible, but you must come along, Dr. Sands. We've had not a moment to simply catch our breaths and talk," she persisted, but there appeared no budging the man. He seemed in a marathon of his own making.

SHE easily found the local Caribou coffee house, where she sat in an enormous overstuffed chair by the window looking out on the avenue. She felt a need to control the sheer amount of aggravated, discouraged and stymied anger rising up in her as a result of this mad phantom who sketched his victims before killing them. And after a time of silent meditation and forced relaxation, she felt annoyed with Darwin Reynolds. To a far less degree than she did toward the "Butcher of West Allis," as one paper's headline called the spine thief, but annoyed with Darwin nonetheless. She had time to think about the tall, handsome, broad-shouldered man who had popped up at times when she didn't need to hear from him. But now, when she wanted to hear news of their departure time, where the hell was he?

She wanted to get out of Milwaukee, to put some distance between herself and the failed investigation, and the growing cancer of what appeared from the get-go as an unsolvable crime, a futile investigation—one that would never go away but remain on the open books forever.

Although fearing it a fantasy, perhaps some distance from the Olsen case might give her more perspective, the logic or illogic rather being that the farther she was from Milwaukee, Wisconsin, the more insightful, intuitive and clearheaded she'd become.

She struggled to clear her mind now, but try as she might, Jessica couldn't get the case out of her head. She tried concentrating on thoughts of Richard, tried thinking of their plans for the house, and for their bright future. She thought about her stable of horses back in Quantico, Virginia. She missed *so* much. She also fantasized a great fear as well, that some madman who made soups and stews of murdered women's bones lurked about Millbrook, Minnesota, and learning of the newly arrived FBI agent with a British accent and mild manner, hatched a plan of assassination borne of fear. She struggled to kill such thoughts at their inception. It was like living with the 9/11 fears of a terrorist on every street corner—simply an impossible ordeal for anyone. She forced herself to think instead of that sixteen-year-old furnished apartment of hers and how she'd had to give up all those comforting old furnishings so that she and Richard could find common furnishings they both could live with.

She stirred her coffee, listened to the light strain of New-Age music here, and gave her mind over to a great deal of decorating in the newly acquired old ranch house and stable that remained undone, given their competing schedules.

She next began to people watch both inside the shop and through the window, when her eyes lit on a large banner advertising a major new exhibit at the Hamilton Museum's Fine Arts Center. The exhibit featured some artist she had never heard of, a fellow by the name of Keith Orion, who billed himself as the "Professor of Shock Art."

"Sounds more like a rock star than a painter, wouldn't you say?"

She saw Darwin's enormous shadow creep over her table, knowing it was him even before he'd spoken a word. Still, her look of surprise must have registered, as he hurled explanations at her.

"Sands told me at the morgue you'd gone out for air and coffee. Caribou is the only coffee shop on the block. I am, after all, a detective."

"Obviously a regular bloodhound. I thought you said you'd call."

"I did."

"You didn't."

"I mean I *said* that I would, but since I had to come over to the morgue anyway . . . and I assumed you'd be there." He sat across from her on an ancient-looking recently reupholstered paisley-patterned ottoman.

"Have we got clearance to use that FBI jet?"

"We do, but not until three-thirty."

"But our meeting with the governor's at six, right? That's cutting things close, isn't it?"

"It's the best I could do. A commercial flight won't get us there any sooner," he said, fingering the sandwich and desert menu.

The waitress came and he ordered a chicken salad sandwich and coffee. Alone again, he broke the silence. "Hey, I want to apologize again for this morning. I certainly don't want to cause trouble for you and yours."

"No need to apologize, no problem."

They sat in silence for an awkward moment. "So, since we have time to kill, why don't we walk across to the arts center and have a look at the new exhibit?" he suggested. "I live here and I never get to the museums."

She considered this a moment, looked into his eyes and said, "No, I don't think so."

"Come on, this is my town. Let me show you the finer side."

She shook her head and then stared into his eyes again. "Reynolds, Detective Reynolds, our relationship has to remain on a—"

"—a professional level, I know that, but like I said, we've got two hours to kill. Trust me, Jessica, while I do find you attractive and intelligent, I have an Italian wife and three little girls."

"Really? Photographs, let's see 'em."

He pulled forth charming pictures of three girls ranging in age from four to seven. "Keep me hopping."

"I'll bet." She noticed he showed no photo of the wife.

"Children'll keep you running on the one hand, grounded on the other, and all four of my *girlfriends* would bust my balls if I so much as looked at another woman."

This made her laugh, and he joined in. "Sounds like you've got your hands full."

"Oh, I do, I do!" *His infectious smile is the irresistible part of him, that and his eyes,* she thought, but she said, "What would she do to you if she knew you slept in my room the other night?" asked Jessica. "This Italian woman of yours?"

"Let's just say she wouldn't be as understanding as your friend Richard. Now that that's out of the way, how about we go see the Orion exhibit?"

"As soon as you finish your sandwich and coffee. I'll just go freshen up, Darwin. I like your name, Darwin."

"Given to me by my adoptive parents," he replied. "My adoptive parents were great people who happened to be black like me. I had a good childhood once I got hooked up with them. Prior to that . . . not so good."

She dared not ask about the not so good, at least not here and now.

"So you like 'Darwin'?" he asked.

"Yeah, interesting choice your parents made."

"You mean it beats 'Thomas,' " he joked. "I'll put a stop to the proposed name change proceedings." Something jammed with sadness flitted across his eyes. The big black man sitting before her dropped his gaze. She thought she might see a tear fall into his coffee if she watched long enough.

She changed the subject. "I think an art museum opening would be just the thing to feed my child. It's a ritual I must go through so I have something positive to report to my therapist."

"I hear you."

"I suppose we both could use a break from this case."

He nodded, looking up again at her, having regained himself, in control. "I'm with you."

"But nature calls first. Be right back."

He waved her off, dabbing at his eye with a napkin.

Inside the restroom, she stared at herself in the mirror for the second time today and said, "You damn sure still know how to make a fucking fool of yourself, *Doctor* Jessica 'Sensitive' Coran."

But for the life of her, she could not decipher what had made Reynolds tear up.

ELEVEN

The body snatchers they have come
And made a snatch at me . . .
Don't go to weep upon my grave.
And think that there I be;
They haven't left an atom there
Of my anatomy!

— Thomas Hood

ON the train to Chicago, Giles slept sitting up. He hadn't had much sleep since killing Lucinda, and fatigue now washed over him in waves. Drowsy, his eyes glazed over and his mind went numb with the steady sound and vibration underfoot of the train as it wended its way along the tracks toward downtown Chicago. As the train picked up speed and stormed toward the Windy City, he replayed the way things had unfolded, how he had killed Lucinda, his own benefactress.

He had thought her knocked unconscious with the hammer blow, but when he'd relaxed his vigilance, believing her completely subdued, she'd pulled free and rushed to his workbench, frantically searching for a weapon among his tools, knocking over an array of knives and sculpting tools. She screamed amid the panting, but she couldn't get enough breath to do a good scream justice. In fact, it sounded like the scream of a woman in the throes of love. Maybe she did love him. She swiped at him, grimacing, hissing catlike, an animal ferocity that screamed her desire to live in her eyes.

He backed momentarily away, studying her contorted features. They were like those of a young nurse he'd seen once in a photograph hidden away among his foster mother's things, a photo of Mother at about Lucinda's current age. "You're not doing yourself any good this way, Loose. Only prolonging the inevitable."

As he backed off, she came at him, the raised sharp end of the triangled spade coming at his eyes. A dodge and a grab, and he had her arm in a viselike grip, all the while she screamed, "I'm not going to die like this! Like some victim in a goddamn horror movie! Damn you, Giles, may God damn you!"

His weakened arm could not hold her as she pulled free and brought the glinting spade down at his chest, but he grabbed her arm and locked it, wresting the weapon from her grasp and tossing it aside. She found the air and screamed at the top of her lungs for help.

She felt the stun to her temples as he brought a fist to her head. Lucinda Wellingham fell to the floor a second time amid the rubble of art supplies and tools there. It had all happened so fast, Giles could hardly recall the exact linear thread of events, but he recalled how she fought for her life. Desperate, dazed, she again managed to wrap a hand around the pointed spade, the one he used for special line effects—perfectly aged skin, like parchment, on the late-forties figures of the women depicted in his sculptures, likenesses of Louisa Childe, Sarah Towne and Joyce Olsen in his final plastering on of the last layer of "skin"—the epidermal layer. They all looked, after a fashion, like Mother, even Lucinda's general features matched Nurse Gahran from the photos of Mother when she was Lucinda's age. Mother and Loose . . . Mother *was* loose, Loose *was* a mother.

Yes, Lucinda had fallen beside the spade and grabbed it up again, jabbing at him with it.

Giles tried to wrench the spade from her a second time, Lucinda now on her back, pointing it menacingly up at him. He stood over her with a hammer in his hand, and then he kneeled down to administer the blow.

She stabbed out at him in an attempt to put the spade into his heart. He somehow grabbed her wrist as the shining spade came barreling forward, and she screamed at the pain he caused her wrist, twisting it until the stubborn fingers popped free of the handle, and it fell away with a clanging complaint.

Giles instantly choked off her screams with one hand over her mouth, and he fought for control of her struggling body by strangling her. Blood—his blood—dripped down over her from a flesh wound she'd inflicted in her repeated jabs at him. His arm had been seriously cut. In the excitement of the moment, he hadn't felt a thing, but Lucinda had nicked him badly. The bleeding bothered him. He didn't do well seeing his own blood spilled. It made him feel heady, giddy, filled him with nausea and threatened to send him into a shiver leading to a possible blackout. He fought this. Fought it hard as he held her down, kicking and attempting to scream, his hands cutting off her air supply at two points.

He finally squeezed off her air supply altogether, so tightly that her eyes rolled back in her head, her tongue lolled out. She had passed out.

It gave Giles some respite. He rushed to the bathroom and cleaned off the stinging, bleeding wound to his forearm. This left Lucinda's unconscious form lying nude amid the debris field and ruin of his tools. He glanced over at her and in that moment of seeing her nude, silent, looking dead amid the scattered bones against the now slick, wet wooden floor like a crocodile out of its element, he thought how beautiful the sight, that it would be in this fashion he would pose her sculpted form alongside her backbone as if it had leapt from her evil body to disown her. It was then that he noticed water leaking through the floorboards, seeping through grooves and cracks. He rushed to throw towels over the epicenter of the spill, attempting to dry up the damnable swimming pool she'd made of his living room. He feared it might seep through to the apartment below, and lead to bad consequences involving others below. He didn't want unwelcome visitors anytime.

His arm continued bleeding into the one towel he'd wrapped about himself. He returned to the bathroom and turned on the shower to run cold water over his arm. The blood and water meshed in a swirl of ribbons, intermingling and washing down the drain, the blood of his mother and father and himself, but only God alone knew what Father was, Father all wrapped up in that box below his bed, tied tightly and held at bay, yet always asking to be introduced to his son. *Family ties . . . blood ties . . . everybody has 'em. The blood of the fathers shall be upon the sons*, he thought, watching it flow from him.

Dropping the bloodied towel into the bathtub, Giles had grabbed a fresh one, dabbing as the blood flow lessened. He found a first-aid kit he kept for whenever he nicked himself while working, and he plastered the wound with salve and covered it with gauze and bandage.

He thought he heard Lucinda moan, and he heard her scratching along the floor in an attempt to move once more toward freedom and life. He returned to stand over her, watching her crawl. It brought to mind an old fantasy of his: seeing Mother in the same position, crawling, mewing, begging his forgiveness, pleading for her life.

Giles then lifted a handheld mirror up to his features.

Dark circles blotted his eyes. That old pallor, white and pasty, had crept back into his epidermis. What the hell was that all about? He felt lethargic. More and more, the sunlight of day became intolerable.

"Maybe I should just sculpt my own backbone. Put an end to this aberrant behavior. I could do it if I put my mind to it. It's not like I need to do this to feed myself. But then again . . . perhaps it does feed me . . . in ways I don't even understand."

Then he saw his form in the mirror retreat backward until it was sitting in the lotus position, bent over the broken vertebral rack that once belonged to Joyce Olsen, struggling to get the glue down in the joints, struggling to get the C-clamps on just right, when an army of Milwaukee firemen stormed in and attacked him with untold fire axes, screaming obscenities at him as they hacked him to pieces, shouting, *"Die monster, die!"*

He came awake with a start, finding himself on the outskirts of Chicago, Illinois, the train having slowed, the rhythm of its bounce along the rails having dramatically changed. In the near distance, he saw the mammoth John Hancock Center, and beyond this the even taller Sears Tower. "A new home," he muttered.

"Say what, son?" asked a passing conductor.

"Chicago, sir, . . . my new home."

"Well, welcome home, son. City of Big Shoulders and Wide Arms, I always say. Greatest city on the planet. You'll love it here."

"I'm sure I will get acclimated."

"Well, son, . . . I don't know nothing 'bout where you'd begin to find anything like that!" the conductor joked. "Who is this ac-climb-ated, huh?" The conductor moved on, laughing at his own lame joke, a man singularly in love with his work, and shouting now, "Chicago downtown! Union Station! All Out!"

* * *

THE monotonous *thrum* of the public-trust FBI jet, a state-
of-the-art Beechcraft had put Jessica at such ease that she
began to doze as they sped toward Portland, Oregon, at
sixty thousand feet. The much-needed nap had crept over
her without warning. Leaving Milwaukee for their scheduled meeting with Governor James Jason "J.J." Hughes in
Portland had been difficult after what she and Darwin had
found in the darkened corridors of the Orion showing at the
Fine Arts Center. She had had to convince Darwin to take
no immediate action against Keith Orion. Darwin, bent on
arresting him on obscenity laws dating back to the 1800s
was too willing to tip their hand. They compromised, and
so Darwin instead set in motion a surveillance of Orion and
a full background check in an effort to gain enough information to warrant going to a federal judge for a search-and-
seizure order.

Meantime, she got him on the plane for Portland as
planned. Slumbering now, Jessica revisited Keith Orion's
showing, her mind playing over the dark and sinister images created by the artist, some of which had startled them
both into suspecting Orion of being the Spine Thief.

Orion's work was created for one purpose only, to shock
and chase people from the gallery, his underlying theme the
humiliation of women. His work depicted women in all
manner of degradation, all poses of disgust. So ugly and distasteful was the work that Jessica had to force herself
through the motions alongside Darwin.

Orion's palate ran to stark blood-orange, an array of red,
deep ochre, shades of black and gloomy grays. Special-
effects lighting, lasers and strobes shattered the otherwise
utter blackness of the cave created for the showing. Blaring
heavy metal music further attacked the senses.

Darwin, too, had felt uneasy. "You want to skip this?"

he'd asked early on, seeing that the exhibit was not much different than viewing an array of crime-scene photos.

"I can see this on the job," she had replied. "Let's give it a little more time. Maybe there's something redeeming just down from the next painting or sculpture."

But soon they had agreed that there simply was nothing redeeming in Orion's work, and they were on their way out when she was stunned by a small painting that'd been left un-illuminated, alone in a corner. What had caught her eye had also immediately caught Darwin's as well. The painting depicted a woman lying facedown, a huge black abyss of a gash, bloody along the edges, taken out of her back from shoulders to backside.

They continued to stare, examining the strange oil on dry wallboard. It was dated 2001, the same year Louisa Childe had been murdered.

"My old grandfather would call this coincidence paaaartic-cularly peculiar," Darwin said as they stood before the painting.

"Certainly bears looking into. Can it be this serendipitous? We come in to see an art exhibit and we discover our murderer is this close, this public?"

"Nobody's that lucky. Still . . . damned eerie isn't it?"

Jessica cautioned, "Could be a thousand explanations. Could just be representational, symbolic to Orion alone and meaningless to anyone else, and so it's a very personal expression that has nothing whatever to do with our case, Darwin."

"Sure . . . of course . . ." But Darwin was ready to put the cuffs on Orion.

Jessica had simply continued to stare long at the strange painting, seeing a child in the gloomy darkness of the backdrop at what appeared at once the distance and up close in a kind of optical illusion. The child stood as a ghostly shadow over the body of the woman with the huge gaping blackness running up and down her spine. "You see the kid standing in the gloom? Staring down the length of the dead woman?"

Darwin squinted. "Now that you point it out, yeah. I could've easily missed it."

"Self-portrait you think?"

"You think?"

"Could be . . . could also be homage to Dali."

"Dolly? You talking about the cloned sheep?"

"No, the artist, Salvador Dali. He put himself into each of his paintings as an observant child."

"I see."

"I think we need to learn a great deal more about this so-called artist, Orion."

"Sounds like a stage name, Orion."

"We'll find out."

"Agreed."

She checked her watch. "Getting close to takeoff time. We've got to grab a cab, but before we do, let's talk to the museum people, find out what we might about this character. On our way to the airport, I'll make a call, order an FBI background check."

"To hell with that. I can put a surveillance team on his ass."

"Sure, okay, but Darwin, we don't want to tip our hand to him. We want to—"

"See what kind of snakes come crawling out from under this rock. Like I said, I'll put my people on a twenty-four-hour surveillance of Mr. Orion."

"That's good."

"While we're in Oregon, he won't be disappearing anywhere, and from his MO, we know he doesn't kill again for a long time," Darwin thoughtfully reminded her.

"*If* our guy sticks to pattern."

"He will. He has so far," Darwin assured her as they found the museum curator's office.

After finding out all they could about Orion from museum authorities, they were referred to a woman named Lucinda Wellingham. "Daughter of a major contributor to the museum," said Karen Quinelson, the curator. "Lucy . . . Lucinda runs her own art gallery at this address and number," she finished with a flourish by ripping off a notepad with Lucinda Wellingham's logo, address, E-mail address and fax number. Get in touch with Lucy if you want to know more about Orion. Trust me, the rest of us had very little to do with Mr. Keith Orion—nor would he be showing here in this life if her father hadn't made a sizeable donation."

Jessica and Darwin had next rushed out for a cab to make the airport, stopping only to pick up his bag at FBI headquarters and hers at the hotel.

They had made their respective calls from the cab on the way to the airport. Keith Orion's life was about to become an open book.

Now, her eyes closed, her head resting against a pillow, Jessica's mind filled with the vile shapes, forms and splatterings of lurid color and oils of Orion, the trash some dared call art, Keith Orion's most outrageous splatter-punk paintings. And while some of his work appeared less bloody and vile and disgusting, even these depicted rape, sodomy and torture against women. In one painting not one but three women were hanging as if crucified, their toes just touching pedestals, and all three appeared to be in the final stages of life, all three having been "simultaneously" tortured by electric shock, and an array of horrid instruments laying about on tables and on the floor, including a pressure washer. The caption on the painting read *Homage to Author Joe Curtin*.

It could not be called disturbing in the Clive Barker fashion of disturbing literature that ripped at the core of being human. Disturbing was too high a word for it. Disturbing art at least had purpose, meaning, depth, a reason for being, a spine. Ironically enough, Orion's work lacked backbone, along with artistic worth. No, it did not even rise to the *level* of disturbing due to its own level of disgusting filth and hatred of the world and women in particular. In panel after panel of work that was meant to be episodic, each painting adding more to the story, Orion depicted women in various frescos of being slashed to pieces. The total effect was one of a mural of horror, thus the name of the exhibit: *Horror's Raw Mural—The Downside of Being Dead.*

Jessica normally enjoyed dreaming while cruising at sixty thousand feet, but she didn't care for the lingering imagery of Orion's exhibit impacting her nap, insinuating itself on her in its tastelessness, its sheer crudity. She awoke to Darwin's shaking her and saying in her ear, "Heads up. We're landing. Get your seat belt on."

"I dreamed bad things about that Orion guy, Darwin. If he isn't the killer we're looking for, he's sure doing a hell of an imitation."

"Thank God we can't convict a man on our dreams. Still, I like him for the murders, too."

"Yeah . . . spectral evidence was thrown out in 1693 with the end of the Salem witch-hunt. Still, sometimes your gut knows what you instincts are talking about long before there's a dialogue between the two."

"We've got good people on Orion. They're not going to lose sight of him. Right now, I want your mind focused on getting a new trial for Robert."

"Sure . . . you're right, of course. Don't worry."

The plane began its descent.

"Local field ops're set to meet us and run us out to the governor's mansion."

"We've got our ducks all in a row. We're ready for Hughes and anything he can throw at us, Darwin. Rational thought will prevail."

"I wish I were as confident as you. Forty-eight hours. We've got a lousy forty-eight, Jess." Again his eyes glazed over with glistening wetness, threatening to tear.

She placed a hand over his, recognizing his distress. "It's going to be all right, Darwin."

"Sure . . . sure it is."

"The cavalry has arrived. Your friend, Towne, is not alone anymore."

"Friend? I never said the man was my—my friend. He's a wrongly accused black man, who . . . who deserves better . . . a better shake. That's all he is to me, Dr. Coran."

"No. No, he's much more to you than that. Darwin, are you *related* to Robert Towne?"

His gaze met hers, and he swallowed hard. "You can't let anyone else know."

"I understand. I also understand why you wouldn't want Govenor Hughes to know that."

"Press gets hold of it . . . that Robert's my half brother . . . and what credibility does that leave for my fight to free him? None, not a *scintilla*. Everyone would simply believe I had no evidence, only a blood tie."

"You could have trusted me. You might've given me the benefit of a doubt." She felt betrayed, hurt.

"Don't take it personally, Doctor, but if I'd have told you on our first meeting, would you have worked so hard on Robert's behalf? Would you have sent Richard Sharpe to Minnesota? Would you even be here now?"

"I'd feel better if Sharpe had something concrete in Minnesota."

"He's on it, you said."

"Best man we could have put on it. Think Gary Cooper, *High Noon*, who else could've played the part?"

FBI Agent Richard Sharpe felt he might go mad in Millbrook. Nothing had gone well. The lab had not completed even the preliminary work on the scrapings taken from Louisa Childe's nails, cellular tissue almost invisible to the naked eye with an infinitesimal amount of dried, degenerated blood clinging to it.

In Dr. Herman Krueshach, he had a real winner. Krueshach had shopped out the work to Minneapolis, only now telling Sharpe that Millbrook wasn't big enough to handle the process, not without taking chances, not with the limited and limiting equipment, and not with the limited amount of material taken from Louisa Childe that they had to work with. Much of the substance they'd scraped had been compromised and broken down over time due to the poor quality of the coffin, allowing dampness and water to seep in.

"That's what the bird on the overhanging branch wanted," Richard had decided, stating it aloud now. "The water she . . . the corpse . . . had been lying in." To Krueshach he added, "So everything has been transferred already to a lab in Minneapolis?"

"Ahhh, St. Paul to be exact."

"Christ, you might have consulted me."

"This decision is mine."

"Give me the information. What's the name of the lab?"

"Cellmark of St. Paul. They're quite reputable. Do a lot of work for the Mayo Clinic."

"And they have a backlog and Mayo's at the top of their list of clients. Shit, gaw-blimey for a fool!"

"No, Agent Sharpe, they promised to put it at the head of the line."

"And can you trust that? I'm going there to await results. To sit on them."

"Suit yourself, Agent."

"I damn well will." He stormed from Krueshach's lab and shoved past Brannan as he was entering. Brannan threw up his hands and asked Krueshach, "What gives?"

After Krueshach explained, Brannan rushed after Sharpe, catching him on the steps of the police station. "I'll arrange to drive you to St. Paul," he offered.

"Don't do me any favors."

"Goddamn it man, I'm not doing shit for you. I want this freak that killed Louisa Childe more than anyone, and if it's not the guy in Portland, then by God, I want his execution set aside, so we can search for the real motherfucker!"

The two men glared at one another, their eyes boring in, twisting and turning before they mutually pulled back. Finally, Richard said, "Then it would appear we both want the same thing."

"Exactly."

"All right then . . . all right, I accept your offer to drive me to St. Paul."

"We'll sit on their doorstep until we get results."

"That's my plan, that and a call from the director of the FBI."

"That oughta cut some ice."

"We can only hope so. Where's your car?"

"Whoa up there, Sharpe. I've got to clear all this with my superior. Even in Millbrook, there's such a thing as protocol and channels."

"And how long has that been the case?"

Brannan glared, but then he burst into a hearty laugh. "It won't take long. In and out, especially if you're 'longside me with that mug of yours. My boss is a sucker for higher-authority types like you. Come on."

DARWIN and Jessica disembarked and stood on the runway with bags in hand, no one to greet them. Darwin looked off into the distance at a row of other hangars, searching for the FBI car that was to take them to the governor's mansion. Jessica looked at her Citizen watch. "Time's running low. If we miss the meeting, there might not be another shot, at least not today."

"Damn it, I was told the local field guys would be here to greet us."

She handed him her cellular. "Get on the phone and call them," she urged. "Tell 'em to haul ass."

Darwin pushed her phone back into her hands, and pulled out his own. He got right through to someone, but in a moment Jessica saw Darwin's brow crease, first in confusion and then anger. "I don't give a damn about your motor pool problems or your mother's gallbladder, Agent Riley. Get us transport and do it now!" He swore under his breath and shook his head and stepped about in a tight little circle of indignation and rage. "Fucking bastard says they didn't expect us for another two hours, some shit about logging it in as A.M. instead of P.M., so a car was waiting at 4 A.M., and some shit about since *we* did not show, *blah-blah-blah*."

"A car was waiting for us? At four this morning?"

"*Was* being the operative word. It obviously didn't wait for us." His attempt to lighten the situation didn't improve either of their moods. Darwin's mood had darkened to the hue of his skin, and he sent a fist into a sign on a chain-link fence, rattling the entire fence and denting the sign that read: *No Loitering on Runway*.

"There's a cab stand the other side of the fence. We can grab a cab, Darwin."

"No, the car's on the way. It's on the way."

Ten minutes passed.

Sitting on her bags, Jessica finally said, "Let's catch a damn cab, Darwin."

"There, there it is!" he pointed to a car pulling out onto the runway. It carefully made its way toward them, two agents inside. These two appeared pissed off at pulling this duty; they looked deeply glum, deadly serious and terribly unfriendly.

"These boys look unhappy in their work," she said in gross understatement.

"They're going to be a lot unhappier when I get through with them."

The car halted, the trunk popped open and the two men climbed out.

"Let's just get to the wedding on time, Darwin," Jessica cautioned. "Let it go for now."

"All right, agreed, *for now*." He hefted their bags and tossed them into the trunk as the two Portland field agents flashed their badges and offered their halfhearted clichés about being at their disposal while in the Portland area, while at the same time offering no help with the bags.

"Save it. We've wasted enough time here, gentlemen," Jessica said, fearful of losing her own control at their attitude. "We're only here to save an innocent man's life."

Darwin added nothing but an approving look.

Jessica quickly climbed into the rear of the luxurious Lincoln Town Car, not wishing to be witness to Darwin's rage at the two should he decide to unleash it. But while she heard him use the term *jag-offs* moments before he climbed into the rear himself to sit alongside her, she was proud that he'd held himself in check.

"You know what's going on?" he asked her as the Portland agents climbed into the front. "These men don't want us here. They're perfectly happy to let Robert Towne die. In fact, they think the way he's going to be executed by the state is weak and flimsy final justice for the man. Isn't that right, gentlemen."

She said quietly in his ear, "Sounds like the entire state has him down as guilty."

"Why not?" he shouted, his booming voice taking off the lid of the car, startling the two agents in the front seat. "Robert's been judged guilty by twelve of his 'betters,' not to mention all of law enforcement in Oregon! Including the FBI."

One of the agents turned and shouted back, "Look, man, some of us saw what that bastard did to his wife."

"You mean that *white* woman, don't you?" Darwin shot back. "Might as well be in fucking Alabama or goddamn

Mississippi in the fucking forties as be out here. Goddamn no-man's-land between prejudice and racial hatred."

"Whoa up, Agent Reynolds! Nobody's talking race here but you," said the driver.

"You play that race card, you play it alone," added the other.

"Fuck you both. Just drive."

"Yes, sir."

Jessica realized only now that Darwin was right, that Towne, in large measure, had been found guilty by these field ops largely on the basis of his race. "Take it easy, Darwin. We've just got to get to the governor. He's got to have more on the ball than these yahoos."

"Take the fastest route you know, Agent Barnes," ordered Darwin.

"Right on it." Barnes eyed Jessica in his rearview, almost striking an oncoming mail truck.

"Look out there, Barney!" shouted his partner. "We don't want to delay Agent Reynolds and Dr. Corman any further."

"It's Coran, Dr. Coran," she corrected the agent in the passenger seat. Jessica read between the lines that the two had engineered this delay, and each felt quite good about himself as a result. A glance at her watch told her they were already late.

The car sped toward the governor's mansion.

TWELVE

The next of kin may also donate a body.

—Uniform Anatomical Gift Act

Governor Hughes only needed the least provocation and excuse to disappear before they could get to him. He'd gotten clear of his office the moment it appeared the FBI agents from Quantico and Milwaukee were running late. He was off to his next appointment, and his appointment was in the next county.

Mrs. Agnes Dornan, the governor's appointment secretary, a thin, tall, big bird of a woman with pinched features and a stern glare, dressed them down for having wasted her boss's precious time. She then spewed forth noises from her gritted teeth as she searched and scanned her book for a moment of the governor's time. "Now . . . let's see . . . mmmm . . . a suitable time when the governor can see a pair of FBI agents from the East bent on discussing a reprieve for a convicted murderer . . . mmm . . . One who has been determined guilty of mutilating his wife by the great state of Oregon."

"Listen, lady!" began Darwin, but Jessica placed both hands against his massive chest and moved him off from the frightened secretary.

"Damn it, Darwin, let me handle this. You're too person-ally involved. Sit it out."

She turned back to the secretary while Darwin retreated to a corner and leaned against a window, looking out on the well-manicured lawns of the mansion and muttering under his breath, "Fucking place . . . fucking governor."

The secretary looked relieved that she had only to deal with Jessica at this point, and not the brutish black giant in the corner.

"Now . . . Mrs. . . . Dornan, is it?"

"Yes, dear."

"I'm going to get on the phone now to call the *Director* of the FBI. You know, the one who answers only to the *President* of the United States and the State Department, and I'm go-ing to turn him over to you, and you can tell *him* when we can see the fucking governor of Oregon. Is that understood?"

Mrs. Dornan's icy silence and stare clearly meant she would call Jessica's bluff if it were up to her.

Jessica dialed the number. Darwin looked on with inter-est. Mrs. Dornan's chin rose still higher in the air.

Jessica called out, "William Fischer, please. No, this is an emergency. Do not put me on hold. Do you recognize this number? Yes, Dr. Jessica Coran, and I am calling on urgent business from the great state of Oregon. Now put me through to Will wherever the director is at, and I mean now."

She silently hummed "What I Did for Love." Mrs. Dor-nan's chin had fallen slightly off.

Then Jessica said into the phone, "Will? is that you? Good! You sound like you're inside a drum. Bad connec-tion? What? You're in the can? Oh, shit. Sorry . . . I mean sorry to catch you there, but this is extremely important, Will. What? Oh, really? I-I suppose, yes . . . if I can get back in time. Sure . . . I'd love to see Mercedes, too, and how is Tricia? Uh-uh . . . yeah, that's so cute. Uh-uh. Look, Will, I need you to set someone here straight."

Jessica paused a moment, her eyes going to Mrs. Dornan.

Then Jessica yelled into the phone for emphasis. "Straight, straight! I want you to set the governor's personal secretary straight."

Mrs. Dornan swallowed hard.

Jessica continued her phone conversation. "Yes, it's what we talked about, and it appears you were right about Governor Hughes—strictly a nine to fiver. Yeah, skipped out on us. Yes. Everyone here is so very ready and excited about the prospect of executing Robert Towne day after tomorrow, seems almost like a preternatural hatred for Towne here, and the sonofa . . . The man won't even see us, and his secretary doesn't think she can fit us in before the bloody execution!" She laughed aloud at this. "Yeah, lotta good it'll do to see the man about a reprieve *after* the execution. *Macabre* is right. Whole thing here is surreal." Jessica laughed more, and the voice on the other end laughed with her.

Darwin's lips curled into a grin. Mrs. Dornan crossed her arms in defiance.

Jessica held out the phone to her. "He wants to speak to you."

"Me?" Mrs. Dornan hesitated taking the phone. "William Fischer wants to talk to me?

"Yes, the FBI director wishes to speak to you. Seems he's on a fact-finding mission in Minnesota, St. Paul, to be exact, but they patched me through, and the director wants to say hello to you, Mrs. Dornan."

"I-I . . . me? Talk to William Fischer?"

Jessica shook the cell phone at her. "Yes, please take the phone."

Mrs. Dornan took the phone in hand and placed it to her ear only to shove it off her ear as Richard Sharpe shouted on the other end, "You will accommodate my people, young lady, or your boss will hear directly from me! Do you understand?"

"Ahhh . . . yes, sir . . . of course, sir. There's just been a little misunderstanding here. That's all. We'll rectify the situation, I am sure."

"Today. Rectify it today."

Mrs. Dornan stared at the phone, now gone dead.

Darwin and Jessica stood united before her. "So, when can we see Governor Hughes?" Jessica asked.

Mrs. Dornan had gotten on the phone, located Governor James Hughes, and promised him it was in his best interest to cut the fund-raiser short and get back to the mansion to see Dr. Coran and Special Agent Reynolds. When she'd gotten off the line, she informed them that it could be upwards of two hours before Hughes might return, but that he did want to speak to them *today*, knowing that time was drawing short for Robert W. Towne.

"We'll call in, keep tabs, and be back," Jessica said. "Can you get us a cab? We're both famished."

"I recommend the Capitol House Inn," she said, all smiles now. "It's not too far, and there's a lovely view of the lake, and they have the very best seafood if you like seafood, and no one does steaks better."

"That sounds positively lovely indeed," Jessica replied.

Once in a cab leaving the mansion, Darwin asked, "You had Richard Sharpe on the line the whole time?" Reynolds laughed. It was good to see him relax enough to do so.

Jessica joined him in laughter. "Saw a statistic the other day, says we laugh an average thirteen times a day. Not hardly enough."

"Gotta hand it to you. You played Mrs. Dornan like a fiddle." He laughed again. His handsome good looks reminded her of Sidney Poitier.

"I think she's otherwise known as Agnes of Oregon."

Again Darwin's laughter filled the cab.

"The bad news is that Richard really is in St. Paul."

"Not Millbrook?" asked Darwin.

"Trying to hurry along the DNA testing on the sample taken from Louisa Childe's corpse. It's at Cellmark of St. Paul."

"Man, I hope they don't take as much time as Millbrook has on this case—two years."

"Yeah, in two years, Argentina will likely see six more presidents if the past few years are any indication." she joked. She then explained what little she'd actually understood from Richard's cryptic and frustrated remarks at their last conversation. But now Sharpe had lived up to his name in playing along with her sudden, out-of-the-blue call asking him to impersonate Fischer, the FBI's top cop. His ranting had covered his British accent well enough for the likes of Mrs. Agnes Dornan, and he'd wisely not turned on the camera component of his phone.

Jessica and Darwin were soon seated across from one another in a clean, well-lit mountainside restaurant overlooking a bay filled with rental boats and pleasure craft. Life floating by. People enjoying a leisure that Jessica had begun to wonder more and more about. She couldn't recall the day when she had not carried the badge of FBI M.E., even on holiday.

"See why Robert ran here from Milwaukee. Came as far away as the continent would take him. Beautiful place. All this open country, fresh air, clean water, fishing, hiking, hunting. He taught himself all those things, you know?"

"Now he's imprisoned on death row."

"Yeah . . ." Darwin dropped his gaze. "Yeah . . . could've just as easily have stayed in goddamn Milwaukee for all that he's accomplished." He laughed only dully.

She tried to cheer him. "We'll convince the governor. We have to."

"Yeah, what choice otherwise? Break Robert out of a maximum-security prison?"

"Hope it doesn't come to that."

They ordered salmon steaks. When in Rome, she joked. "This is salmon country."

She lifted her glass, toasting to their successful mission and then sipped her white merlot while Darwin lifted and drank his Guinness beer.

"I don't like this waiting."

"I know. It's hard for me, so it must be excruciating for you."

"It's like all the time is bleeding out, like Robert's blood is being drained with each second. People want his blood, Jess. My blood."

"We're going to beat this thing, Darwin. Trust me."

"Geez, all this time, and I haven't so much as thanked you . . . all the trouble you've gone to, you and Sharpe."

"Not at all . . . not at all. Why don't you tell me more about Robert?"

The waiter arrived with their meals. After the clatter of dishware and a few bites, Darwin said, "My brother, Robert and I, we had things rough for the first few years of our lives. He's older than me by almost two years. His mother left him to get away from our father. Our father takes up with another woman, *my mother*. She follows suit. My father was a compulsive gambler and an alcoholic and not a happy-go-lucky one, I can tell you, but a *mean* drunk."

"I'm sorry to hear that."

Darwin dropped his gaze. "It was like living with a Satanic Incredible Hulk, who might come through the door anytime. Now Robert . . . he did what he could to protect me all those years, and then when something really major happened, we were taken off by Family and Child Welfare Services."

"This was where?"

"Chicago. South Side. I was soon adopted by the people who raised me as their own, but Robert stayed in the system until he was sixteen, bouncing in and out of foster homes only to return. He disappeared after that—got on a bus . . . ran."

"And you lost touch?"

"Years went by, yeah. Then I read about him in the FBI bulletins, and I see him on CNN for *murdering* his wife."

"But if you haven't seen or heard from him in all those years, how could you know he was innocent?"

"I didn't, not until I visited him in jail. Since we had different names, I arranged it by claiming to be investigating the Louisa Childe killing in Millbrook. I'd done my homework before seeing him. Oregon authorities bought my story, and I had clearance to see and interview Towne on the basis of my FBI status. They thought—"

"You were doing research . . . behavioral-science aspect of his case."

"Exactly. Then I get back home to Milwaukee, and damned if a third woman hasn't been killed in a like manner."

"Weird coincidence all right."

"It was so close to home this time, I thought anyone looking at it from the outside might conclude that I had something to do with Joyce Olsen's killing just to clear my brother's name. You know, throw up a red herring, a flare."

"To make it appear the killer's still on the loose."

"That's when I got a notion. You see, I had read your book, so I decided to get you to come and take a look at what the police had in Milwaukee."

She ate from her salmon dinner. She drank more wine, not knowing what to say.

"Tomorrow we can go out to the prison and see Rob. I know when you meet him, you'll know he's incapable of what they're wanting to execute him for. He's just too gentle."

"Even though your father has a history of violence and Robert didn't have the stable home you had, Darwin? Can you be so sure?"

"Yes, I have an absolute faith in Robert."

"You just remember the older brother who threw himself between you and an abusive father."

"No . . . no. I've gotten to know him. I tell you, he's innocent."

She breathed deeply and nodded. "I trust your instincts, Darwin. I'm working under the assumption you are *right on* and keenly attuned to the facts here."

"Will you come with me to the prison tomorrow? Regardless of how it goes with the governor tonight? Will you meet Robert?"

"Yes, I will, but don't we have to make petition to see him at this late date?"

"We're FBI. Besides, tomorrow I go see him as his only living relative."

"I see." She lifted her wineglass to him, and he lifted his beer in toast. "To success with the governor tonight."

"To success."

With dinner completed, they pushed from the table in the restaurant and bags in hand, they walked across the room. It felt as if every eye in the place followed them, curious and wondering if one or both had stepped from the pages of some tabloid or Hollywood gossip magazine. They checked in and located their rooms, wanting to settle in for the calm before the storm, before meeting J. J. Hughes, the single-most important man of the hour.

"I'm going to attempt a brief nap," Jessica told Darwin as they reached her room.

"Jet lag kicking in?"

"That and ordinary fatigue. Wake me when it's time."

"Will do. I'm not likely to sleep."

"Perhaps you ought to. We need to be clearheaded when we see the man. Now that he's given us the slip the first go-round, I suspect he really doesn't want to talk to anyone about Towne's pending execution."

"I know you're right, but still . . . don't think I can sleep. Catch the news . . . see what's what on CNN."

Jessica unlocked her door and tossed her bags inside. They had booked adjoining rooms for the duration. "I have a feeling this could drag on."

As Darwin followed suit, unlocking his door, he asked,

"So, when's Sharpe going to get on a plane for here with some physical evidence?"

"I'll let you know the minute I know. I imagine he's about ready to shoot someone in Minnesota by now."

A couple passed by staring unabashedly at them. The eyes of the couple were as large as plate-glass windows, and desperate to follow their movements.

"You get the sense we've stepped back in time?" she asked. "To a kind of puritanical period?"

"Welcome to Portland, Dr. Coran. I tell you it's a major cause why Robert was so quickly condemned, she being a white woman."

"Get some rest, Darwin," she pleaded. "Call the desk for a wake-up call. And I'll do the same."

"All right . . . I will," he assured her with the lie.

In St. Paul, Minnesota, Richard Sharpe paced the Cellmark laboratory waiting room when finally a young lady, looking as if she'd just stepped off a college campus, came toward him. "Agent Sharpe?"

"Yes, and you?"

"Amanda Howland. I'm night supervisor of the lab here."

"Really? And so young. Congratulations. Now, have you good news for me?"

"I'm afraid not."

"What?"

"It's just impossible to run the kinds of tests you require in so short a time. I'm not sure who led you to believe we could do it in a few short hours, but that's just not going to happen without a court order."

"A man's life is at stake."

"I understand that, but there's no physical way we can rush such sophisticated tests within such a brief span. You say you're here on behalf of a medical examiner, a Dr. Jessica Coran . . . Well, sir, she should know—"

"We all know how much time it takes to do DNA tests, but in the case of the Lanark boy—the one believed to be a missing and exploited child, your offices did the DNA work in twenty four hours."

"Not without a court order. I'm sorry."

"God of the heavens, I can get a federal court order across town. I'll be back with it within an hour, an hour and a half at the most. In the meantime, you get your people on this full time front burner, Dr. ahhh . . . ahhh . . . Dr.—"

"Howland, Amanda Howland. I can only tell you that the blood analysis done on the nail scrapings proved conclusively to be AB-neg. So, it is not the victim's blood type, it belongs to someone she obviously scratched."

"Her killer's blood . . . all this time buried with her due to some . . . some inanity perpetrated by the very people who are charged with speaking for the victim. Now you look here, Dr. Howland, someone . . . some one of you Minnesotans has to make amends . . . to make up for the gross inadequacy uncovered here. Is Cellmark going to step up to the plate and take its best swing at this thing or not?"

"Baseball metaphors notwithstanding, sir, we can only do what time permits, but if you are sure you can get the federal court order, then I will see to it that Cellmark bats it out of the park."

"All the same, we need a game clincher here if we're to save a man from being executed for a crime he may well not have committed."

"You just get me the order as quickly as you can. My superiors see the discrepancy between when we began on this project and when we got the order . . . Well, it's my job, sir."

"All right, but promise me you'll go out on that limb and waste no more precious time."

"I've already started the ball rolling, but I'll stay myself to oversee until it gets done. Now get me the paper."

"I'll send word to Oregon that the Millbrook killer is AB-negative. That may be enough to clear Towne."

"Unless he, too, is AB-neg. In which case . . ."

"Yes, well, apparently authorities in Oregon are so entirely convinced of this man's guilt that such a match could get him the chamber a day earlier, I suppose."

Amanda Howland's eyes and forehead narrowed at this, creasing as she mulled it over, and then her eyes went wide. "Ahhh, one of those subtle English deliveries is what you have. That was a joke, right?"

Even as he rushed away from Dr. Howland, Sharpe pulled out his cellular phone to call Jessica, waking her with the news that at least they had a blood typing on the killer, that he was AB-negative. "So, what is Robert Towne's blood type?"

"I don't . . . I don't know, actually. Let me get Darwin on that. He can find out more readily than I can. He has had access to Towne. In fact, we go to see him tomorrow on death row. Turns out that Darwin is Towne's biological half brother, Richard."

"What?"

"You heard me right."

"This puts another complexion on things altogether."

"It changes nothing and explains much about Darwin and his behavior, that's all."

"And if Robert Towne proves to be AB-negative? What then, Jess?"

"What then? Millions of people are AB-negative. If he is AB-neg, then it proves nothing, but if he is not AB-neg, then it proves him innocent just as surely as any DNA evidence."

"I don't think the governor or the people of Oregon are going to see that as clearly as you, darling. And in the meantime, the DNA tests here are slow going yet. I'm on my way to gather up a federal court order and rush it through as we speak."

"I'll let you go then. I have to get freshened up for our belated meeting with Governor Hughes."

They said their good-byes and Jessica was left with the knowledge of the killer's having an AB-negative blood type. She wondered if it were a trump card or a discard, and she wondered how she would feel if it turned out to be the later.

She went to the washbasin and threw water on her face and toweled off. She then banged on the wall for Darwin, going to the adjoining door and throwing open her side, continuing to bang.

No answer.

"Where the hell'd he get off to?"

JESSICA found Darwin in the hotel lobby bar downing whiskey shooters with beer chasers. She instantly grabbed him and pulled him from the bar. "Are you nuts?"

"What's up? What's sa-matta? You never see a black man get loaded before?"

"Don't wimp out on me now, Darwin. Damn you, be a man a little longer. We're off to see the fucking wizard and you're getting plastered? Shit."

"For all the good it'll do, hell." He staggered with her to a darkened booth. "I'm not going to be able to help Rob. I just know it. He's going down like the prover-pro-ver-bial . . . yeah, proverbial stone down the fucking well and no matter what kind of song and dance we do for Hughes, it isn't going to mean one damn fucking thing on account . . . on account've the guv like *veryone* else. Did I say 'veryone' else?" He laughed.

He was smashed. She motioned a waiter over and ordered two pots of black coffee be brought to their table. Once she had plied him with coffee and prescription uppers she'd found at the bottom of her purse, she got him on the elevator and back to his room. There she ordered him to strip and get into a cold shower.

He smiled at the notion but did as told while she turned her back. He came to her and placed his powerful arms around her while standing there naked.

"Damn it to hell, Darwin, get your hands off me and get into the goddamn shower now!" She almost melted under his touch, and for that she was angry at him, angry at the situation he had created, and most of all angry at herself for having such feelings for the younger man, for thinking even for a moment of betraying Richard's trust.

Darwin turned her around and kissed her full on the lips, his hands going everywhere. She pushed away and slapped him hard across the face, so hard he got the point in no uncertain terms.

To stave off her feelings, she blurted out the news from Richard about the AB-negative blood. He only stood there, his enormous manhood hard and throbbing. He grabbed a towel and the white cloth against his black body created a stark contrast. He stepped into the bathroom and into the shower without a word.

When he had finished showering, Darwin silently dressed in the clothes and suit she'd laid out for him. She joked lightly about having to do his laundry for him next. He muttered a preference for another tie. They said nothing about what had passed between then.

"The blood test'll prove it. Robert's got AB blood. But the motherfuckers over at the prison are not going to let us in till tomorrow to conduct any medical test. Some nonsense atop their nonsense. Warden Gwingault's orders."

"That's great news, Darwin, but Oregon authorities appear to have lost your brother's medical records, and they roll-up-the-streets-at-nine, so we'll get in there first thing in the morning. A test for blood type we can get results on in a matter of hours, but I fear now that the DNA test is going to take more time than we have. So . . . we have to convince Hughes it's worth waiting for."

"Rob's most likely got the same blood type as me, right?" he asked as he dressed.

She shook her head and threw the tie he wanted across the bed. "Wish I could say it works that way but unfortunately, Darwin, it doesn't."

"But when we were kids, I gave him my blood once, a transfusion. Our father'd hit him over the head with a half empty Jim Beam bottle. He bled something fierce and I couldn't get it to stop, and he'd gone unconscious, so I called nine-one-one. It was after that they took us into custody."

"And you were how old at the time?"

"Five, six . . . going on. Rob two years older."

She shook her head at this. "Didn't happen."

"What didn't happen?"

"The hospital personnel may have gone through some sleight-of-hand with you, Darwin, allowing you to think they had taken your blood, but they don't take blood from kids so young. Quite possibly they used plasma packs stored for such emergencies."

"Using his blood type."

"Exactly."

"Then there's no knowing how the Minnesota blood type will work out for Rob . . ."

"We'll get it done."

"And if it's a match, Jess? What then? What is it, a one-in-four, one-in-five chance?"

"Odds aren't that simple. Many more AB-negs out there than any other type. But we can get lucky. Even if it is the same blood type, we can also determine if the blood comes from a white male, black male, Asian, or other nationality."

He raised his hands. "If it ain't his blood, we'll know it."

"The problem comes in making Governor Hughes and

everyone in Oregon believe the blood evidence was not manufactured."

"No one can question that. Sharpe did the gathering from the exhumation. An unbiased and independent—"

"Yes, but a two-year-old degenerated scraping from fingers turned to bone, Darwin. You've got to brace yourself for the possibility that the DNA tests could, after all this time—"

"Prove inconclusive, I know, but hell, I read where they did it with Columbus, Abraham Lincoln, some Egyptian pharaoh's bones. What's two damn years?"

"Those are extremely time-and-labor intensive, sophisticated tests, Darwin, conducted by experts in DNA matching and topology. Besides, few people outside law enforcement even understand the significance of that sample even if it does go our way."

"We just have to educate people then."

"Yeah, stomp out ignorance like the brushfire it is. It's why I need your big, ugly feet sober."

Darwin bit his lip. "I do apologize. I just lost it there for a time."

"You're under a hell of a lot of stress keeping your relationship with Towne a secret all this time. People could, you know, misconstrue your intentions in doing that as well."

"I'm coming clean with it tomorrow at the prison. Everyone is going to know then. But I do it on my own terms, in my own way."

"All right. Your secret is safe with me. Now let's go take down the governor."

"I'm with you."

THIRTEEN

Don't go looking for airborne, fire-breathing dragons, until you run out of grounded 'gators and crocks.

—GOVERNOR J. J. HUGHES

Portland, Oregon
8 P.M.

THE Honorable Governor James Jason Hughes proved to be an expansive man, exuding the dignified air of a man above the common fold who might have regaled people in another time, a man for whom the old European designation for those in power, highness—as in your high-ness—was turned into high-ass, as he physically and metaphorically carried his overweight ass on his shoulder. He indeed proved expansive, both in size and generosity, filling the room with his pancake griddle–sized face and frying-pan hands in welcome, smiling wide all the while. Jessica immediately decided it was all for show. "J. J.," he repeatedly said, "just J. J. to anyone who knows me!"

Hughes offered them coffee, pastries, a seat, and sent Mrs. Dornan chasing after his needs even as Darwin and Jessica declined any refreshments. When Mrs. Dornan had gone, Hughes offered cigars and brandy, California wine if Jessica preferred.

"We are here, Governor Hughes, on a very important matter," Jessica began.

"Of course, you are. Everyone who comes through that door comes with the most important matter on Earth troubling them, I can assure you, and I have heard tales . . . well, stories that would curl that Dante Inferno guy's hair."

Jessica started to correct him on Dante Alighieri, but she immediately squelched the notion. Darwin exchanged a troubled look with her as Hughes continued on about Oregonian politics and the economy, the war over timber and proposed offshore drilling rights, tree lovers, beetle lovers, the recent find in the state of a boy who had been abducted from his mother twelve years before by an estranged husband now living in a cabin on a mountain in the deep woods.

"Yes, sir." He slowed to take a breath, but before Jessica could get a word in, he added, "Why else? Why indeed come through that door . . . Why else come to me?" The big, wide-shouldered man sat back in his Corinthian leather chair and guffawed at some mental image. "I've had heads of state come in here with their hands out, and I've had clowns and acrobats parade in here from the Barnum & Bailey Circus. This office is ripe for *Ripley's Believe It or Not*, I can tell you stories, Dr. Coran—Jessica. May I call you Jessica?"

Not replying, Jessica noted that J. J. spoke exclusively to her and not to Darwin. Darwin must have noticed, too. He jumped right in. "This is a man's life, we're talking about." Darwin sat on edge. "An innocent man. This isn't an episode of *Ripley's* and it sure isn't any circus."

Jovial Hughes rankled at this. He sternly and firmly replied, punctuating his every word from behind his desk with his lit cigar. "Young man, Agent Reynolds, believe me when I tell you this, I certainly meant no offense by sharing with you and Dr. Coran here the absurdities that come across my desk. I did not in the least mean to imply that your brother's case has anything smacking of that nature to it, but rather—"

"My brother? Towne is—"

"We have investigators working for us night and day, Agent Reynolds. And as I was curious about your . . . Let's say profound interest in a case so many miles from your territory, I began to ask discreet questions."

"You had me investigated. Then you know I'm Towne's *half* brother."

"Half or whole, it will only play one way in the press and in the hearts and minds of my constituency."

"You can't really sit there and play politics as usual, Governor," Jessica said, rising to her feet to put a hand on Darwin's shoulder and ease him back into his own chair.

"I have seen nothing to prove this man's innocence, but I have seen—"

"He was assumed guilty from the moment of arrest," shouted Darwin, losing control again, "and he has never been given a fair trial! That alone is grounds for a stay."

"As I was about to say, I have seen nothing to persuade me to act against the wishes of the state or the people of Oregon, or in fact, the wishes of Robert W. Towne."

"Let me apologize for my colleague, Governor," said Jessica, ushering Darwin to the door. "Wait outside!" she told him.

"What? I didn't come all this way to be put out on the doorstep like some errant cat."

"Just do as I say, or we're going to get nowhere with this man. Darwin, the man's a covert racist anxious to see your brother die. Now damn it, step outside."

"What good can I do from outside?"

"If he sees you are taking orders from me, a white woman, he's going to take me more seriously. Trust me. I know the type. He won't deal with a black man, and he doesn't like dealing with women, either."

Darwin got it. "Two strikes against us going in."

Mrs. Dornan fought past them with doughnuts and coffee for her boss.

"In this man's mind, women are subservient as well. Watch how Dornan acts around him. She knows how to play him to keep her job. Now let me do mine."

Darwin stared at the doting personal secretary and read her body language around the governor. Jessica continued in Darwin's ear, "You were right all along about this being about race."

"How is my acting as your *boy* going to help?"

"He's already heard your pleas for your brother. He's not responded well to them yet, has he? And your ranting at him is only going to solidify his feelings against Robert. Now leave. Do it for Robert."

Darwin clenched his teeth and glared past her at Governor Hughes, now putting down a doughnut and coffee while simultaneously puffing away on one of his Cuban cigars. "All right . . . for Robert."

Now back with the governor, Jessica asked that he indulge her.

"A very nice word, 'indulge.' All right, Dr. Coran, indulge away. . Whatever you like, Doctor, after all, I rushed back here to bend over backward for the FBI and your boss. I turned this time over *just* for you."

"Good. I'm glad those field operatives who were late picking us up at the airport weren't getting signals from you or your staff to do so. That takes a great deal off my mind and the director's."

"I hope you will convey my apologies to Mr. Fischer . . . ahhh . . . that is when you next speak to him. I had no idea such . . . games were being played. But you hafta understand how high emotions are running here on the eve of Towne's execution."

"Can we cut to the chase, Governor?"

"Absolutely." He sipped at his brandy, took a long pull on his cigar, and stood, coming around his desk. There he leaned his considerable behind into the sharp apex of the edge where two sides met. She thought him a water buffalo scratching an itch where the sun had never shone. He rubbed at the itch through his tailor-made pants. From his new position, he towered over her where she sat. "Indulge more, Dr. Coran," he said with undisguised abandon now that Dornan had again left the room and he found himself completely alone with Jessica.

She shook loose from her head the awful picture of him nude. She got up and paced the room, putting some distance between them.

Jessica, huddled near the window, keeping her distance. Using a conference table, she spilled out autopsy photos, including those of the two victims from Minnesota and Wisconsin as if in error. It effectively stopped his advance.

"What's the matter, Governor? Can't you handle the truth? Go ahead, look at them." She held up Sarah Towne's autopsy photo. "All three women are victims of the same brutal monster, the single Spine Thief. In all three cases neither the killer nor the backbones have been dragged into the light, no recoveries. Only questions."

"Exactly, all you have are questions. I see no new evidence laid before me."

"Your own prosecutors never found the goods to positively link Towne with his wife's murder. Now we will have compelling new DNA evidence coming out of the two-year-old Minnesota case, and we are building a case in Milwaukee against the real culprit."

He pointed to the clock on the wall over his shoulder. "You're telling me nothing that will stop time, Dr. Coran. That's not going to happen unless I see some real proof. While I don't doubt your sincerity, emotion alone cannot sway me from my duty."

"All right, we have a match on the killer's blood type, and further tests will reveal the killer is not even a black man, and soon after we will have the real killer's precise

DNA fingerprint, sir, and that, combined with the vigilantism obvious in the court transcript that proves Towne could not get a fair trial here is all the more reason to warrant a stay of—"

"A few days while you run tests. Will you remain here during that time?" he asked.

"If that's what it takes. Until we get the results from Cellmark on the DNA."

"Quite a speech, Doctor. Perhaps you can sell it to the press, but I remain unmoved."

"But the blood type found at the scene of the crime in Millbrook, it . . ."

"It what, Dr. Coran?"

"It does not match Robert Towne's blood type!" she lied.

"Really? I'm flabbergasted."

"So you can't possibly contemplate going ahead with this execution knowing that?"

"Like the *Titanic*, this ship is set on a course, and it will take an iceberg to keep it from its destination, Doctor, and your little fib about the blood test isn't quite a big enough chunk of ice, nor do I see two-year-old blood scrapings suddenly uncovered in a lab in St. Paul—quite possibly engineered by the brother out there in the hallway—"

"Christ," she muttered. "The blood was scraped from the dead woman's nails during a formal, on-the-record exhumation overseen by a competent M.E. and one of our top agents."

"Yes, your live-in lover, I am given to understand."

She rankled at this. She knew any moment now she would so lose it as to be escorted out of the building. The man was infuriating. "You had me investigated, too, then."

"I like to know with whom I am conducting business, and it appears from the casual observer that you Eastern FBI folk have some sort of pool going as to whether or not you can come clear across the country and tell us what to do in Oregon."

"*Geez*, how did you ever get elected governor?"

"Good old-fashioned politicking, dear. Want that brandy now? I know from your dossier, Dr. Coran, you tend to drink a little heavy in times of stress." He poured her a large tumbler with the emblem of state on it. "The three of you, Sharpe, Towne's brother, and yourself, Doctor, to any outsider, you look like a crusading clique *het up* out of some misguided notion gotten up at a liberal prayer meeting, like one of those Baptist revival meetings. Now take the g'damn brandy and drink."

"Are you going to look at these other bodies, Hughes?"

He stood holding the brandy out to her, his eyebrows rising and lowering as if suggesting they get a great deal closer before he consider anything further she had to say on the subject. "Toast gets buttered on both sides in Oregon, Dr. Coran . . . Jessica. May I call you 'Jessica'?" he asked again.

"No, you may not"—she registered his shock at this—"and I'm not here to butter your toast. I believe you have Dornan to do all the buttering up you require. Now it's time for you to recognize the extraordinary detective work on the part of the accused's brother, Agent Darwin Reynolds and Agent Richard Sharpe. You vile man. All this time you've strung this out, entertaining Darwin's calls, his letters, seeing him tonight, all just a fucking game with you, all just to watch him squirm for Towne's life while you never once considered the man's innocence, not once!"

"Of course, I have! Who in his right mind . . . in this position . . . Look here, all has changed. Knowing what motivates Reynolds is *blood*! The man's prejudiced in the extreme. He's family. His brotherly affection for Towne is what drives him. Even Hitler had a mother someplace who likely kept saying, 'My boy couldn't possibly do such awful things.'"

"No doubt, but Towne is no Hitler, and Agent Reynolds

has compiled an impressive list of items that surely must give you pause."

"Pause is one thing, a reprieve is quite another. This state has a long-standing history of punishing the guilty, Dr. Coran, and that means carrying through with jury decisions. And who am I, one man, to overturn a jury decision?"

He let the unspoken *unless* hang in the air.

"You're not simply one man, sir. You represent the pinnacle of law in your state. You are governor."

"I am quite aware of my office!"

"Then exercise it for a change!"

They glared across the crime-scene photos at one another. She finally broke the icy stare and silence, saying, "Suppose, just suppose in the next few weeks or months we can prove beyond a shadow of a DNA-fingerprinted doubt that Robert W. Towne is indeed innocent of murdering his wife in this hideous fashion, at a time when your execution machine here has already rolled on Towne? If he is summarily killed by you, by your jury, by your great state of Oregon, and the world learns of his innocence, what then? How will that play out on national TV? Do you think the sympathy vote will swing your way or to an opponent who will be only too willing to also play politics with this execution?"

"Nice speech, Doctor, but conversely, if I don't allow that switch to be pulled on time, and Towne is proved guilty once more by your precious DNA print?"

"Then what will it have hurt?"

"The integrity of this office and state! Besides, my political enemies will play that card just as quickly."

"Do you hear yourself, Governor? You are playing politics with a man's life."

"A confessed killer who is deemed guilty by the system. A man who refused his own defense appeal."

"A system we know is flawed."

"What in life isn't flawed?" He touched her, his hand going to her breast.

Jessica flinched and pulled away. "I assure you, Governor Hughes, I am not sleeping with you so that you can hold the power of your position over me. You can forget whatever cesspool notions are swimming round in your—"

Darwin pushed open the door. "You need help in here, Jess?"

"No, no Darwin. We're just getting a little heated on the debate here. Wait outside now, go!"

She watched Hughes watch Darwin go quietly back outside. "You've certainly got him well trained. You could *train* me, Jess, and afterward, we can talk about this Towne affair in more . . . shall we say depth."

"We have a DNA comparison . . . from blood found in Minnesota during the exhumation, blood not the victim's, blood that proves it could not have been Towne who—"

"Killed some woman in Minnesota. We are in Oregon, darling. It does not sway me. Too many variables. The so-called evidence has passed through too many hands, too many opportunities to taint it, and one too many relatives involved in gathering this evidence."

"No way, this comes directly from Cellmark of St.—"

"Do you have any idea what kind of crucifixion I would have to endure if Towne is shown mercy?"

"Just postpone it. Just do it. Do the right thing."

His response was to again attempt to put his hands on her. She backed along the table, lifting the autopsy photos and files she'd dumped there. "I think we're through here."

He placed a hand over hers. "Of course, I will look at any new and compelling evidence you bring me, Dr. Coran, the operative words being 'new' and 'compelling'. And I will entertain your suggestions, but I cannot promise you or Agent Reynolds anything. Is that understood?"

"Be open to the new evidence that is on the way from Minnesota as we speak," she calmly replied. "That is all I ask."

He pressed in against her when suddenly Mrs. Dornan stepped in. "It's your wife, Governor, on line one. She's insistent, sir."

Hughes had backed off with a calm born of practice when Dornan had broken the silence in the room. Hughes loudly said to Jessica, "So far, I see nothing in my possession that warrant's a stay of execution. I'm sorry." To Dornan he added, "I'll get it, Agnes."

"I was just leaving," Jessica said, joining Dornan for the exit.

"When your Agent Sharpe arrives from Minnesota, I will gladly look over any new information that warrants my attention, Dr. Coran."

She thanked him from the safety of the door.

When they were on the other side of the door, Dornan said to Jessica, "It can't be easy on James . . . ahhh . . . the governor. It's so troubling, this whole matter of holding a man's life in one's palm."

Yeah, unless you get a kick out of it, Jessica thought but only said, "Some phantom killer running loose over the moors doesn't seem to bother him in the least. What about you, Mrs. Dornan?"

"Sometimes the facts don't make for good copy for any of us. The idea that a man can do such a thing to a woman with impunity and . . . and remain free to roam, but somewhere in all of it . . . someone must pay."

"But we must not execute Towne for the actions of this fiend or our failure to recognize our shortcomings."

Mrs. Dornan bridled at this as if it were a personal attack on her. "I'm sure Governor Hughes will see your Agent Sharpe and the two of you again when and if you come bearing something in the nature of new and compelling evidence. What other step can he take?"

Jessica nodded and took in a deep breath. "Agreed, and thank you, Mrs. Dornan. Do keep the light burning for us."

"You make a persuasive opponent, Doctor. Most persuasive. Debate society?"

"When in college, yes."

"Impressive. Perhaps you ought to teach young Reynolds a thing or two about negotiations."

"Yes, I will do that."

Jessica left the governor's personal assistant, not believing she'd made any headway with either her or Hughes. She found Darwin pacing the outer hallway like an expectant father.

"What'd he say? What's the upshot of it all? Tell me."

"He's going to give Richard Sharpe a hearing as soon as he arrives."

"What about all that we brought him, the theory, the pattern, the blood type?"

"He's not interested in theories and patterns, Darwin, or tests not yet performed. He wants—"

"But it's a pattern crime, and it's going to be repeated as sure as we're standing here."

"He needs hard, irrefutable evidence, Darwin. And we've got to pray Richard's found it."

"We still need to compare whatever Sharpe finds in Millbrook with Robert's DNA strand, and we're running out of fucking time, Jess."

"I know that, Darwin. I know."

"Get on the phone with Sharpe. Find out where the hell he's at. Get—"

She raised up both hands to him. "Whoa up, Darwin. Calm down! We're going to get Richard here in time. We have to."

"Call him."

"When we are back at the inn, I'll call him, and I'll let you know when we can expect to get out to the airport to greet him. Meanwhile, we'll have the local FBI lab prepped and ready to do the blood typing and the DNA match, so it does not look like the fix is in."

Darwin visibly calmed, nodding. "OK . . . OK . . ."

"We've got the governor to agree to this step. We're batting a thousand, Darwin," she lied.

"That'd be great if this was a fucking baseball game."

Darwin stormed off ahead of her, going out the huge doors and into the Oregon night. She dropped her head and sighed. In a moment, she found him on the mansion steps, seated, head in hands, slumped and quietly holding back tears. Jessica allowed him a peaceful moment before sitting alongside and placing an arm over his shoulder.

He muttered, "Robert doesn't deserve this . . . doesn't deserve any of this."

"I know . . . I know . . . He's his own worst enemy, Darwin. If he'd gone for appeal, we'd have had months to prove him innocent."

"The blood test'll prove it. Hell, I know it will. Then they've gotta listen."

She allowed him this, his final illusion. Secretly, she prayed Richard would somehow miraculously be waiting for them at the inn with the DNA strand they so needed.

Later the same night at the Minneapolis Airport

"I can't believe I missed the fucking plane out of here," Richard Sharpe complained to Brannan.

"Hey, there's another one in a couple of hours. At least you've got the goods from the lab, right?"

"Not exactly, no."

"Whataya mean, 'no'?" Brannan replied with a short inward gasp that spoke of a developing ulcer.

"They're going to hot-wire the results over the Internet to the FBI lab in Portland. It's the best I could do under the circumstances. Just hope it's not too late."

"I'll stay behind . . . sit on 'em for you."

"That might help. Thanks, Brannan."

"Hey, this was my case first."

Sharpe nodded. "Dr. Howland says they simply need more time and can't perform miracles."

"What exactly can they hot-wire over the Net that will be useful to create a match—or hopefully a mismatch—with the DNA sample here?"

"Basic results. A replica of the DNA strand. Definitely something they can match up with what Oregon has on our man on death row."

"OK, all right . . . good . . . You did well, here, Sharpe. Don't berate yourself. Go on to Portland with the blood-type confirmation, and don't worry. I'll stay on Howland and her people."

"Buy you dinner?"

"Nah, better get back. No decent food in the whole damn airport, and besides I'm off fast foods—fries, soft drinks. Doc's orders."

They shook hands again.

"Sorry you gotta fly commercial, that your field office couldn't get you a lift."

"It'll be all right. I just have to fly to San Francisco and make a connecting flight to Portland. Seems crazy, but there you have it." Sharpe waved him off.

"I miss my days of the red-eye flights," Brannan shouted over his shoulder.

"Not me," muttered Sharpe.

Even though Brannan looked to be earnestly shuffling off, the Millbrook detective turned and held up a thoughtful index finger to his temple. "Hey, pal. You mean to tell me that you informed the Minneapolis field office what this is all about, and still they couldn't get you out on something?"

" 'Fraid so."

"I used to be a detective in Houston, Texas, you know. Did a lot of extradition work, flying all over for the job. You think to try Flying Tigers?"

"The cargo-transport people?"

"I've used them on occasion. They can be quite cooperative with law enforcement. Most of 'em are gung-ho retired military."

"I'll give it a go."

Sharpe, with time to kill, went in search of the Flying Tigers hangar. As he made his way through the terminal and out on the tarmac, guided by a security guard, he telephoned Jessica in Portland.

Jessica brought Richard up to date with the bad news about the stubborn *idiocy* of Governor Hughes. She did not want to tell him about the man's leering advances. She didn't want either Darwin or Richard to go rushing at Hughes like an angry pair of bulls. They hadn't as yet played every card, and they might need J. J.'s dubious help somewhere down the line.

"Just pray the lab has the DNA map done and forwarded by time you get here," she told him, putting a finger to his image on the phone screen.

"I take it you've softened up the governor for our presentation."

"You have no idea."

"You mean he's at least willing to entertain the idea we may have uncovered new evidence and to give us a fair hearing?"

"Let's just say he's willing to listen."

"I see. Everything hinges on the outcome of tests here. I wish we had more time."

"*Mean* time this waiting period."

"I know it's hard on you, Jess."

"Swore I wouldn't get this emotionally involved but it's so easy to fall into it, you know?"

"Of course I do. And what's the alternative for people who do what we do, love? I certainly don't wish to return to the jaded, cold, unfeeling person I was before . . . well, before we met."

"Nor I . . . Nor I."

"How's Darwin holding up?"

"Convinced him to take a couple of my sleeping pills. He's out for now. It's particularly hard on him." Jessica again brought up that Towne was in fact Darwin's half brother.

She watched as Richard stepped into a hangar and waved down someone.

"Have you given any thought, Jess, to what happens if the tests match Robert Towne's DNA? Putting his DNA under Louisa Childe's nails in that coffin all this time?"

"While I've given that possibility little air time in my brain, I admit it has floated in and out, yes. But damn it, I've come to trust Darwin's instincts, his knowledge of his brother."

"I love you, Jess, and will see you when I get in tomorrow late, unless I can get help here from the Flying Tigers freight people. If you don't hear from me, assume around six-thirty tomorrow night."

"God, Richard, why so late?"

"Can't get a flight out for hours, and even then, it takes me to San Francisco for a connecting flight to Portland. It's all that's flying."

"Let's hope the Tigers can help you out then. I have so missed you, Richard. I'll be at the airport to greet you."

"I'll call you from wherever I am. Let you know. How has Portland treated you so far?"

"I think if Christ came to Portland under present circumstances, they'd inject him with a death cocktail, too."

"That bad?"

"That bad. Public sentiment against Towne has been whipped up to a frenzy here."

"Watch yourself then. Take all precautions."

"Not to worry."

"G'night then, dear. I love you."

"After this is over, we're going to reassess our lives, you

and me, Richard. I'm considering alternatives."

"That offer I made you? Or are you talking about the offer from D.C., to return to the M.E.'s office there, or the Virginia state lab?"

"Carte blanche I'm told. I would have total, complete control at Virginia. Don't think I could go back to D.C., not comfortably, and certainly not with what Virginia's offering."

"Certainly, you of all people, have earned retirement from the FBI, but what about my proposal?"

"I survived the FBI for over a decade, survived the horrors and what it's done to me, what it's made of me. As for marriage, darling Richard, I-I'm just not sure we're either of us ready just yet. You still have issues with your former wife, and you've got your children to think of, and I . . . I still have this fear we will break what we have if we change anything."

"You are an intelligent, articulate, giving, beautiful soul, Jessica Coran, but in this you are wrong."

"I'm also a chicken, a fearful chicken."

"I know of no one braver."

"Not when it comes to relationships and getting my heart broken."

"Sounds like perhaps you are the one with the issues."

"Emotional baggage, it's called, and it's why I can't marry you, Richard, at least not now, not until I deal with it all. It'd only drag you down into my emotional—"

"We can work through any problems together. I can be your support, Jess."

"Sweet . . . you are so sweet, Richard. I am so lucky to have you. Please be patient with me."

"My name before I changed it was Patience," he joked. "And you really are lucky to have me, you know."

"Ohhh, I do know that."

"And that you are blinded by your devotion to me? Did you know that?"

"I confess it! I confess it all!" She then closed her eyes and blew him a kiss through the miracle of the cam phone.

He sent it back to her.

She thoughtfully said, "Back into private sector. No more of this screwy FBI crap for me. Sounds like peace and paradise."

"Whatever you decide, you know I will support you, Jess."

FOURTEEN

Curious about evil since they had never known evil, the gods produced evil by interacting with mankind, usually a woman who was soon impregnated with a misfit child.

—DR. ABRAHAM STROUD, ARCHAEOLOGIST

The following day in Portland

JESSICA was awakened by a pounding on her door, but it turned out to be the adjoining room's door—Darwin, shouting something unintelligible on the other side. While she threw on her terry-cloth robe, she worked out in her head what she was hearing. Darwin continued shouting, "We've gotten a terrific break in our case, Jess. On the tube, now!"

She tore open the door and he barged past her, searching for her remote. Finding it, he snapped on the television set.

"What is it?" she asked, following him into her room. "Darwin?"

"Watch! CNN, MSNBC, Fox, they all have the breaking story, and it's going to blow that fucking smug Governor Hughes outta his pants. They gotta give Robert a reprieve now. They won't have a choice."

Jessica sat on the very edge of her bed facing the TV

screen as it filled with images of a police raid, a box crate the size of a small pool table confiscated, shots of a man in handcuffs, his long hair and clothing looking like that of a rock star. Jessica tried to put it all together, wondering what it had to do with their case.

"It's Chicago, and the guy they're snatching around and forcing into the squad car, that's Orion, Keith Orion. Seems an old girlfriend's corpse turned up."

"You mean Orion pulled an Ira Einhorn?"

"Yeah, and in similar fashion. Crated up a murder victim—someone my team in Milwaukee believes we've heard about before."

"My God, who?"

"Lucinda Wellingham."

"The art gallery girl, the one who backed Orion's exhibit in Milwaukee? This could be our trump card to get your brother off death row."

"Yeah, but it gets even better. Listen." Darwin pointed to the tube, and her gaze followed.

CNN newswoman Paula Zahn was reporting.

"I thought Zahn went to night-time television," Jessica said.

"She's back to daytime. Will you just listen?"

With a look of frightened consternation creasing her forehead, Paula Zahn read the TelePrompTer. ". . . following a breaking story out of Chicago . . . just in . . . just gruesome . . . something out of an Evan Kingsbury novel." Zahn took a moment to compose and gather her assaulted sensibilities, obviously shaken. "In a bizarre and gruesome find, Chicago UPS workers, sorting mail at their Grace-Ravenswood-Lakeview facility, discovered a large, leaking container. With terror alerts still at *orange*, UPS management immediately notified officials, and the leaking container remained a mystery for the better part of the day as seven hundred eighty employees were evacuated and Chicago biohazard team and the EPA went in."

Coanchor Bill Zimmer cut in with, "After initial tests, chemists on hand at the UPS facility discovered the fluid staining the container and floor to be the result of human decomposition—fluids from a decaying body."

"How could she be decaying so quickly," asked Jessica, "if no one even knew she'd disappeared until now? Unless . . ."

"Yeah," said Darwin, "unless. Keep listening, Jess."

Paula Zahn, through gnashed teeth and frown, continued. "The crate was ordered opened, and within was found a nude young woman in mid-twenties who's back had been so completely splayed open that her killer had actually . . . Oh, dear God . . ."

Zimmer had to pick up the story from here. "The killer had actually removed the victim's entire backbone, which remains missing! Paula."

Paula looked as if she wanted to storm off. Again Zimmer took up the slack. "Investigators suspect there might be a connection between this and three previous murders in three other states involving the taking of spinal columns— for what grisly purpose no one yet knows."

Zahn finally recovered and turned to her coanchor and mock-gagged, repeating, " 'Backbones'? A killer interested in backbones? Uggghhh . . . whatever for?"

"Well, Paula," replied Zimmer, "police aren't saying for certain that they have the murderer in custody, but they do have what CNN sources are calling a person of interest in custody."

Paula shook off any thoughts of hyperventilating and interjected, "And given UPS's penchant for a lot of paperwork, they strongly suspect the man to whom the box was being shipped, as Keith Orion is believed to have sent the crate to Chicago from Milwaukee—where he was having a showing of his artwork."

Zimmer picked up the story there. "We're not likely to hear anything definite on the identity of the lady in the crate anytime soon from authorities, but there is rampant speculation at this hour as to her identity. Some saying that it is this woman."

They flashed a photo of Lucinda Wellingham, smiling, bright, cheerful, eyes alive with excited enthusiasm. "We are told," began Paula, "at this time that while police won't speculate on the identity of the victim, CNN has obtained a second photo for comparison."

They flashed the second photo, this one a morgue mug shot of the victim. "Geez," complained Jessica, "how do these parasites do it? How do they get photos from an M.E.'s office?"

"Big bucks change hands," was all that Darwin replied, glued to the set.

Zahn continued speaking now. "Many speculate it may be Lucinda Wellingham" again they put up the vivacious photo of Lucinda, but this time side by side with the morgue shot. "Friends knew her as Lucy, and she was last seen in Orion's company at an opening in Hamilton Museum's Fine Arts Center in downtown Milwaukee. Eyewitnesses said the couple quarreled and got into a shouting match during the largest opening in Orion's career."

Jack Cafferty, the third wheel on the show, piped up now off-camera, saying, "I thought we couldn't release the name of the victim until police have notified the next of kin."

"That's easier said than done if you are so well known in the arts community," replied Zimmer quickly and calmly.

"Just hope we can take the heat when her parents come at us with a lawsuit." Cafferty's chuckle could be heard off camera.

Paula Zahn added, "Many in the art world in and around Milwaukee and Chicago will likely recognize her photo and we will soon have a positive ID."

"We will keep you posted on this developing story," added Zimmer moments before breaking for an Altoids commercial.

Darwin looked as if he might jump on the bed and

bounce to the ceiling. "It's what we've been waiting for, Jess, a break in the case! Evidence the real killer is indeed still out there, still operating and not some copycat killer. Two such mutilations involving backbone theft in a matter of weeks in Milwaukee."

"Certainly, it's gotta cut some ice with the governor."

"Cut some ice? Wake up, Dr. Coran. Hell, it'll free Robert. Damn fine morning for Robert, this news."

"Not so fine for the young victim."

"We gotta call Chicago authorities and get the details."

Paula Zahn's image came back on screen. Unaware she was on, she was saying again to Jack Cafferty, "Backbones? What the hell's he doing with the backbones?" Then she shivered as if something like rough sandpaper had scratched across her spine.

Cafferty indicated the camera was rolling, and he replied to her question, "He must've wanted to be certain she couldn't stand up and come back to haunt him maybe?"

Zimmer shook his head as in mourning. "Each time we hear someone at CNN say, 'And I thought I'd heard it all,' we know better. There's always more at CNN, America's number-one choice for up-to-the-minute, unbiased news reporting."

Paula waved a new sheet of copy over her head, announcing, "Now we turn to lighter fare, the New York City's Bronx Zoo's ninetieth anniversary fair."

Zimmer cut in. "Paula, sorry but we have more news on that horrible story coming out of Chicago. Our sources tell us that the box's origin was indeed Milwaukee, its destination the controversial artist and sculptor, Keith Orion, care of Chicago PropWorks Inc., a company owned by Orion that sets up and breaks down theatrical, educational and cultural events, including but not limited to plays, music concerts, film production needs and art showings."

Again Paula read from the TelePrompTer. "Keith Orion has never been without controversy as he creates shock-value artwork calculated to get a reaction from viewers of his art. Called the Marilyn Manson of the arts community in and around Chicago, his notoriety has followed him across the states, wherever he has shown."

Smirking to suppress a laugh, Zimmer added, "His record for art show shutdowns stands alone. His last showing in Milwaukee, while sold out, saw people leaving in droves before promoters had time to uncork the champagne bottles and serve the cheese."

"Do we have film on some of Orion's more shocking pieces?" asked Paula of an off-camera producer.

"Sorry," she apologized to the public, "but perhaps later, we will bring you an example of Mr. Orion's decidedly shocking work. I am told he has gone so far as to hang crucified cats, dogs, and other small animals in relief against his paintings."

"He calls it odorous art," commented Zimmer. "Wait till Bill O'Reilly gets wind of this."

Cafferty joined the other two coanchors in a belly laugh, adding, "Indeed."

Jessica switched it off to an elated Darwin who looked ready to bounce off the walls. "If we can say we have someone in custody in Chicago, and new evidence has surfaced now in Chicago as well as Minnesota with DNA matching, *and* we can show a connection between Orion and Millbrook then—"

Jessica put up both hands to him and cautioned, "You're reaching way ahead of yourself, Darwin."

"But this is good! Great!"

"You're reacting, creating rationalization to arrest Orion on the basis of a news story that has him connected in some way to this recent body, but he's a long way from replacing your brother in the death chamber."

"I tell you there's something sick about that motherfucker. You saw his art. Hell, you smelled it—roadkill on the canvas, and he's guilty as hell of . . . of . . ."

"Of what? Rodent murder? Call in animal control. What's he done beside be a prick? Where's the evidence he's actually killed anyone? You and I can't work on suppositions, Darwin."

"He's the Spine Thief. I just know it."

"Sure he's despicable and distasteful and has a hate on for women, but that does not prove he's the killer we seek, and I don't have a good feeling about him suddenly falling into our laps like this."

"Regardless, Hughes has to listen to reason now. I know . . . we'll confiscate all Orion's art."

"That crap'll go through the roof in value. Become the hottest collectors' items on the market thanks to this notoriety. Look, hell, we don't even know who the victim in that crate is, not for sure, and it could all prove to be an elaborate hoax for attention, part of the bastard's public-relations effort—got a body from a morgue or a funeral home, some sick shit like that. Hell, I can imagine someone even wanting to set Orion up—possibly the real killer."

"What're you saying?"

"It's all just too pat is what I'm saying."

Darwin gritted his teeth, paced the room and wound up at the window, staring out over the expanse of gardens and trees of a nursery across the street. "We still gotta find out. We gotta know what Chicago knows. I have Agents Amanda Petersaul and Jared Cates teaming on it."

Jessica blew out a long breath of air, a signal of exasperation. "Who's Cates?"

"A five-year man with our field office. He's good and thorough."

"I'm glad you have an experienced agent with Pete."

"Pete's a fine agent. She's sharp as a tack, and she is dogged about getting the facts."

"Now you're talking. Let's get some details and facts. The Devil is in the details as they say."

"That's my intention."

"Your people need a little paving of the way in Chicago, I know some of the agents in our field office there. Worked a couple of cases with them."

"What about the M.E. there?"

"As a matter of fact, I know the Chicago M.E. well. Keene, Horace Keene. Runs a fine crime lab and morgue. Fact is, we both studied under Holcraft, just not at the same time."

"That's good. You two'll be on the same wavelength."

"Keene is quick and efficient. By now he'll have any facts ascertainable from the crate, and maybe he can verify that the body is in fact Lucinda Wellingham's."

"And if it is?"

"Then we learn what evidence they have against Orion, circumstantial or overwhelming."

"And then?"

"Then we go at the governor with all the facts, and we shove it down his fat face."

"Now *you're* talking."

Still, something nagged at Jessica and she was not ready to celebrate. "But what troubles me is that from what we know of Lucy Wellingham, she does not fit the victim profile."

"So Orion changed the pattern. It happens. I've read about it happening in your own book."

"Still, we can't ignore the facts. All the others were matronly, in their late forties. They were all shut-ins or self-imposed introverts who related better and more to animals than to people. While Lucinda appears their opposite."

"Hardly reclusive with a business of her own," he agreed.

"A large, prominent family. Busy businesswoman. Bet she had no animals, at least not in the city, at her place."

"From her photos, she appears to be a classy dresser, quite up on fashion."

Jessica agreed. "Beautiful from her photo, in step with the young and hip crowd in Milwaukee, *and* in her mid-twenties. Not the killer's victim of choice."

"OK, so Orion changed his pattern *drastically*."

Jessica paced the room, her chin in her hand. "It could mean that she somehow found out about his extracurricular activities and . . . so she was killed out of expediency, not like the others who were targeted, stalked, massaged through the drawings and then murdered."

"By now every scrap of his artwork and supplies and instruments are confiscated, and the techs are searching for blood evidence on his art scalpels."

"Yeah, and maybe they found the bone cutter still fresh with Lucinda's blood on it," she sarcastically replied. "Let's stay grounded, Darwin. In a few hours we're going to be meeting Richard at the airport and all we've got in hand is the blood typing. So, let's go as planned."

"Penitentiary for the blood test."

"Right. And to meet your brother."

"It's all set for two this afternoon."

"And Richard's plane is due in at six. We see the governor again at seven. Now get outta my room and let me get dressed for the day."

"I'll keep you apprised of any and all I learn as Petersaul is going down to Chicago to find out all she can. Meantime, our people in Milwaukee have raided the place where Orion stayed while in Milwaukee, the downtown Marriott, for anything he may have left behind."

"Anything breaks in the investigation, let me know. Otherwise, I need some peace and quiet, and to put on my foundations, Darwin. Out, out, and Darwin, don't get me wrong, I am as pleased as you at this new development. I just think, given what we know now about J. J. Hughes that nothing 'back East' is going to persuade him *unless* it is absolutely overwhelming."

"By end of business day, I am hoping to make it overwhelming," Reynolds countered.

"I do hope you can, Darwin. I do hope so."

CAFE Avanti sat flush below a four-story brownstone on Southport within shouting distance of the Music Box Theater's marquee, just as Lucinda had described it to Giles. The doors to Cafe Avanti opened inward and a lilting bell sounded, announcing yet another customer. The place appeared as quaint and curious as Lucinda had told him it would be over pillow talk just before he'd fallen asleep, just before he'd had to kill her.

He stood at the center of the room, staring down a narrow corridor leading to the rear where he'd been told the cafe housed a small galleria-styled maze of nooks and crannies. Standing before the stenciled windows, Giles Gahran, his ornate box tucked under one arm, his huge artist's portfolio dangling from his other hand, drew the attention of the Spanish woman behind the counter.

"Good morning. Can I be helping you, sir?"

"Lucinda sent me."

"Who?"

He replied, "Art dealer in Milwaukee, Lucinda Wellingham."

"Ahhh . . . jes, jes. She sends you here to me? Ahhh . . . that is good then. Let me see your work."

"Said you'd show my stuff on her recommendation. I have a note to that effect with her signature."

"That's perfect timing. I just got the rooms cleared out again. Get tired of seeing the same things too long . . . not good for business. New exhibit is. Show me what you got."

"Lucinda said Cafe Avanti is the premier place for a first showing in Chicago, and from there word will spread."

"Right, spread like spilled India ink on a white satin tablecloth. Lucinda told you that, sweetheart . . . good how she help us . . . good to us . . . and now they are showing her picture in the paper and saying she has been killed, do you know?" She handed him the *Sun-Times* lying on a nearby table. "Horrible . . . so horrible what that black-hearted bastard Orion done to her, and look how he goes walking free!"

Giles read the headlines and scanned for details. "Imagine letting a monster like that just walk away," he muttered in response.

"God, so awful about her death—murdered, horribly disfigured."

"Terrible, I agree."

"I'd only seen her jus' last week in Milwaukee to preview Orion's work, too."

"Oh, really? What'd you think of it?"

"The man is a pig. A murdering pig now. Such evil in him to horribly disfigure my beautiful Lucinda."

"Yes," he agreed. "It turns my stomach, the whole thing." Giles pretended innocence for the part owner of the Cafe Avanti.

"It must've been so shocking for you. Oh, where are my manners. Coffee? Juice? Something stronger?"

"Coffee, yes, thank you. Yes, I . . . I just saw her a few days ago myself. How could such a thing happen?"

"Well, how well do you know that arrogant ass Orion?" she asked. "I can just imagine if a girl were to cross him. It's been all over the news. Hated that man before, but now I really hate him."

"I didn't know until recently. Been too busy moving in, you know. I rarely look at the papers, and I don't own a TV."

"The bastard wasn't even arrested or arraigned! No jail time, no bail, nothing, but if he dares show his face here again, I'll make him wish they had kept him behind bars.

I'll personally scratch his eyes out, you know, for my poor, sweet Lucinda."

She'd gone back around the counter and handed him an Irish coffee with whipped cream. "On the house."

"Imagine, Keith Orion, *theeeee* Keith Orion, a killer."

"He's finished in the art world, especially in the Chicago arts community." She teared up. "When I saw her face on the tube . . . and then they flashed her death photo . . . Oh my God, I thought I'd throw up and faint. I called the authorities immediately, you know, to, you know, identify her as exactly who they thought she might be, but I think I . . . my word put a cap on it for them."

She took a moment to compose herself. "Now tell me, Mr. Gahran, why should we display your art, your paintings, your sculptures at Avanti? I've got to fill out a flyer, get the word around, plaster it on some windows that original artwork is on display at Avanti. Got to have good reason, other than the fact Lucy sent you to us just before she died. In other words, defend your work."

He spread out his show photos and several sketches and a few paintings to give her a broad range of the kind of work he was doing at the moment.

She tried to curb her immediate positive reaction to the unusual work.

Giles began speaking as she glanced over each painting and sketch slowly, carefully sizing each up, one at a time.

"Kinda reminds me of Goya, your style anyway, and maybe Picasso's *Guernica* like the way their bones are out of their bodies."

"In occult physiology the most important bone in the body is the sacrum and—"

"What's a sacrum?" asked Conchita Raold, interrupting Giles's spiel.

"Ahhh . . . sacrum . . . it's not what you think," he said with a little smirk.

"Oh, and what am I thinking?"

"It's got nothing to do with the male member. It refers to the ancient *sacer*, meaning the sacred, so it's called . . . *was* called the sacred or holy bone—the—"

"Spinal cord."

"Backbone to be exact—cord refers to the nerves. You mean spinal column."

"Holy bone but not holy boner then. OK, so your show is about this holy bone."

"You see in ancient civilizations it had a role to play . . . a role of like special—"

"Significance?"

Giles hated the way this woman finished all his sentences for him. "Yeah, significance in many systems of divination by the bones of the body, in religious rites, in sacrificial—"

"Ceremonies?"

"Ahhh . . . right again. It was commonly believed to contain the immortal part of the body and to be directly connected with the spirit realm. In the Western tradition this was the bone kissed at the *witch sabbat*."

"Man, really? Wow. I didn't know that. I love Wicca stuff like they got next door in the candle and card shop. How many people would know that. That's kinda amazing. Man, Giles, you are going to fit right in around here. People coming to Avanti, they love shit like this."

"It means different things to different people, still does," he continued. "Semitic peoples have a tradition that there exists in every man a tiny bone that cannot be seen or felt, cannot be burned or otherwise destroyed, never rots or perishes, and is lodged in the sacrum."

"You're shitting me?"

"No, really. I've studied it. At death this indestructible, incombustible, imponderable, impalpable, atomic bone particle will remain incorrupt in the earth, and when the time of resurrection comes—*and it will*—it will form the 'seed' around which a new body will be built, the body that will proceed to the last judgment and to its final destiny in heaven or hell."

She had been silenced, awed by all this strange talk.

Finally, Conchita stammered, "Damn, I gotta get you a showing, and I mean immediately. Just start carting your stuff over. I love it . . . love it, fucking love it."

"Formerly, Jews believed that when they died this bone, which they called *luz* or *luez*, would find a resting place in the Holy Land, and that if a Jew was buried far away, the luz would travel underground or find some means of getting to the sacred soil. If the bone was eaten en route by say a bird or an animal, it would not be absorbed into the system but passed out while using the bird or animal to transport itself."

Wide-eyed at this, Conchita muttered, "That's some *creepa-zoid* shit, Giles. OK, I call you by your first name?"

He nodded, but kept on explaining about the luz bone. "Muslims, too, believe in the existence of this bone, which they call *al ajb*."

"Al-a-jib? What's that mean?"

"The curious bone, a tiny fragment around which the resurrection-body will take shape."

"The resurrection-body? Yes . . . I see . . . I think."

"In medieval Europe a number of popular beliefs were associated with the spine. I mean a man possessed of an unusually large spine, such as a hunchback or an Abe Lincoln was thought to be endowed with almost talismanic power."

"Fucking cool man. I'm pretty tall myself."

"Didja know that an old form of address for a hunchback was 'My Lord'?"

"No way. Amazing."

"To touch a hunchback brought good luck, and to touch and wish at the same time ensured that the wish would come true. The expression 'to have a hunch,' implying—"

"Get out, no way."

"Implied prescience."

"Pre-what?"

"Knowing about something before it happens, like in pre—"

"I know! Precognition!"

"A belief in the precognitive faculty inherent in the hunch of a hunchbacked person actually."

"Damn, you oughta write all this up for a program guide on the gallery showing."

"And explain why a gnarly little hunchback psychic is trusted far more than a good-looking, straight-backed person claiming such powers, huh?"

"You mean like the little sawed off psychic in *Poltergeist*! I get it. Right. Look, Giles, I really want you to show here at the Avanti, and I swear to you that I'll get all my contacts in the art world here in Chicago to be here for the opening show. You're going to be a smash with them, and soon it'll lead to larger shows, larger venues for your work. Is it a deal?"

"It's wonderful. I understand you've showcased a lot of talented artists here over the years."

"Since eighty-two, yes, we have—my husband, Arnie, and me . . . We worked hard to build a reputation for the place as being a refuge for struggling young artists of all sorts, from artists like yourself to cabbies working on screenplays. We encourage all creative-like-stuff here." She frowned and added, "Orion got his start here, I'm ashamed to say now."

"You have my undying gratitude." He shook her hand vigorously.

"Can you arrange to have the sculptures here tomorrow?"

"Tonight if you like."

"Then it's settled."

They shook on it again.

"You don't have to get your husband's OK?"

"Hey baby, this is 2004, and I'm a liberated Spanish Gypsy Queen. I didn't even take on his name when we got married. He's Irish. What the fuck am I going to look like to people with a face like this, and a name like Conchita Murphy? Huh? Hey? It's got no whatayma-callit?"

"Cadence?"

"What's that?"

"Like music, rhythm."

"Ahhh . . ." She gave it some thought. "Nah, I was thinking something else, not about the sound but if people would believe it or not. You know, like I was some kind of liar. Me!"

"*Credence*, it doesn't feel like it has credence."

"Yeah, right, credence, cadence . . . like that, yeah. You're right, Giles. You're smart, aren't you? Hey, you know what, you oughta talk to the cops, too, since you knew Lucy and you think Orion was trying to set you up."

"I have! I did."

"And they still let him go?"

"They're keeping an eye on him. They let the fox out of the cage for good reason, to lead them to where the evidence is buried."

"You think so?"

"Remember how the cops did things in the Laci Peterson case? They didn't arrest the guy right away, remember?"

"Oh, yeah . . . that's right."

She contemplated this for a long moment. "Hey, Giles, don't you find it a little ironic that the bastard ripped out her spine and here you got sculptures with spines floating up above people's heads?"

"That's just it. Orion was jealous of my art. Jealous of Lucy and me. I think he thinks the cops'll think I killed her 'cause my art is like it is."

"Wow, how diabolic is that?" She laughed raucously and he struggled to join in her mirth. "You're not worried the cops're looking for you?"

"Nahhh . . . I got nothing to hide."

"Good . . . good, Giles."

Later that same day, Giles was erecting his various sculptures in the dark back rooms of Cafe Avanti.

* * *

IN the muted light of the dimly lit old world cellblock look of the back rooms of Cafe Avanti no one could see the strings, and Lucinda was right again about leaving one of the spines in its natural state, unpainted.

The curious sweet smell of blood on the three painted vertebrae, comingling with the damp, earthy odors of the ancient sweating brick walls, proved the perfect olfactory effect, one that would never be captured in an aerosol can. The colored lights of this palace of old Chicago history reflected magically off the myriad multifaceted surfaces of the other three vertebrae. The life-size sculptures could not simply be walked around but required care in negotiating their way into the back rooms as they filled the closed in little nooks and crannies made available to them. There remained hardly elbow space in the rooms featuring each of his three women and four spines.

Looking on the work, once set up, Giles again felt a sense of pride come over him. He wondered what Father would say if he were here; he knew Mother would not understand any of it as art. Still, he'd never felt so certain and self-confident of himself than at this moment of his unveiling, his coming out, toasted by Conchita and all her patrons, wine flowing and cheese balls abounding. Across the doorway to his showing, Conchita had surprised him with a banner reading: *Sweet Marrow of Life*.

Delighted at causing grief and bad publicity for Keith Orion, Giles felt even more delighted at having learned that Orion had been picked up for questioning a second time now. Although allowed to roam free again, no doubt suspicions surrounded him wherever he went now, and no doubt police officials were hounding his every step, while they knew nothing of a Giles Gahran.

Orion's balloon had burst, while Giles's future could only be up-up and away!

If he could keep from acting on a great urge to rip out the energetic spinal column of one Conchita Raold.

Conchita called to him now and in tow she had her partner and husband, Arnold Murphy, an enormously powerful looking black man—hardly Irish. "Go ahead, tell him, Giles . . . Tell Arnie all that stuff you told me about how the shamans of old used the backbones of their victims, you know, how 'waste not, want not' meant something to these people, and they even used bones in their everyday lives— bone jewelry, bone implements, dishes, even bone utensils—bone forks." She yanked at her husband and asked, "Isn't that fascinating, Arnie?"

Arnie only stared, his mouth going slack at the four spinal columns floating one after another through the rooms in places usually preserved for darts and pool cues.

"Giles, you gotta tell Arnie about the luz bone." She made the two men sit down. "Arnie, you're not going to believe this shit."

FIFTEEN

*In the psychopathic mind no common law exists.
Without law, there is no injustice or moral
wrongs. Only a Hobbsian state of nature wherein
power, rape, torture, mutilation is the order of
things—natural selection, for in this parallel
universe inside a psycho's head every man has the
rights of nature, including the right to another
person's body.*

—JESSICA CORAN, FBI M.E.

AGENTS Amanda Petersaul and Jared Cates had learned
that Lucinda Wellingham had showed up at Keith
Orion's art opening on the arm of some no-account, down-
and-out artist whose work no one had ever seen, a guy
named Giles Gahran whom Lucinda was talking about all
night long, a guy she threatened to replace Orion with, and
she made these comments loudly and often during the
night. It had something to do with putting Keith Orion in
his place, seeing to it that if he didn't behave and do exactly
as she wanted, that she would back another horse. Petersaul
and Cates had gotten this information before leaving Milwaukee for Chicago.

Petersaul had gone from the museum gallery people to

locate the mysterious other artist, Gahran. They failed to locate Gahran, who had left Milwaukee in what appeared a sudden flurry of activity. This they had learned from his landlady who'd been surprised when he paid up all his back rent.

"Did he say where he was going?" asked Petersaul, mulling over this news.

"He only said he would soon be a household name. I took it to mean due to his art, nothing like being wanted by the FBI."

"We only want to question him, ma'am," Cates had said.

"You ought've been here last night then when the fire department was called out and they traced an odor in the vents to the man's apartment."

"Fire department?"

"A whole truckload of firemen tearing around the building in gas masks, yes. We all thought it was some sorta terrorist thing, you know."

The agents telephoned the nearest firehouse and asked if anyone there had cited Giles Gahran for causing undue alarm at his apartment building.

A Captain Edward Lee was put on. "Damn," he muttered when he learned who they were and who they were interested in. "Stay put. I'll come to you!"

Lee was soon filling their ears with information and his regrets at not having looked closer at their guy, Giles Gahran. Cates and Petersaul learned that the fire marshal, Captain Lee, had left Gahran without giving him a citation for causing the choking odors that had permeated the building.

"Ah-ha, odors of decay and death?" asked Cates.

"Filthy odors like purification?" Petersaul eagerly added.

Fire Marshal Ed Lee shook his head while chanting "No." "It was really just the opposite, cleaning fluids . . . lots of cleaning fluids, including muriatic acid, enough to burn out the lining of your nostrils and throat, but this guy seemed oblivious to the odors escaping the place and working into the vents."

"Muriatic acid," repeated Cates.

"Did he offer up any explanations as to why he was so bent on cleaning house?" Petersaul asked.

Ed Lee gritted his teeth hard, obviously angry with himself. Petersaul thought Lee looked like an even wilder wild-eyed version of the actor Billy Bob Thornton.

The Billy Bob look-a-like, thin and angular of face, rubbed his day-old stubble and said, "Something to do with a final pa . . . pa . . . patina? I think it was something he'd had to put over his sculptures. Keep 'em from breaking in transit. The guy talked like nonstop."

"Sculptures? Transit?"

"Yeah, he was crating up, preparing to leave. Back of my head, I thought just for a couple seconds of calling in the cops. Cops get real interested in this kinda quick exit, don't they? But everything seemed to check out. Crates were carrying his stone sculptures. Soapstone I think it was, but don't quote me."

"Crates? He was crating up stuff . . ." Petersaul shared an astonished look with Jared Cates.

"Yeah, but it was just his artwork. He even pried open one of the boxes to give me a look inside. Not my type art, but it was you know, different."

Petersaul replied rapid-fire fashion. "Different? Just how different? Give me some detail here, Captain."

"Weird shit, you know. A lady holding out her hand, a bird sitting on her finger. Couldn't see much else, you know, looking downward from overhead and the statue was lying on its side, stuffing all round it like exploded bedding."

"But why do you say it was weird?" pressed Petersaul, while Cates rolled his eyes.

"No eyes."

"No eyes?" she repeated.

"You know, only blank indications of eyes, and no features really, just like a blank face, like it wasn't yet finished is how I took it to be. Or like it was 'spose to represent all mankind, some shit like that you know, so it had to be kinda blank to be . . . whataya call it . . . representational, symbolic?"

"I see . . . blank features."

Captain Lee muttered, "Certainly not my cup of tea. I mean I wouldn't go outta my way to see it. Like something my wife would drag me to."

"And what kind of art do you like, Captain?" asked Cates.

"Oh, I ain't much for any art, but if I gotta have it, give me dogs 'round a poker table or pool table and I'm happy. The wife, she likes canopy trees over a road leading to a light in the distance, but not me."

"You only looked into the one crate then?" Petersaul tried to get the conversation back on track.

But Lee was off track and seemed only too happy to remain that way. "I saw that unbelievable damn Picasso they got in Chicago once. Not my cup a tea neither. I says to the wife on our way to the Sears Tower—observation deck, you know—I says to Maddy, 'And they paid big freakin' dollars for that pile of rusting metal shit to sit out here on the plaza!' Hadda-be the fix was in, the politicians getting their cut, you know?"

"So, where did Gahran say he was moving his crates to?"

"He didn't say."

"And you didn't ask?"

"I didn't ask. Saw no point in it."

"You confiscate anything from the apartment when you wrote up the citation?"

"Sure."

"What?"

"Old rags he was using . . . for the patina, he said."

"Where are they now?"

"Dumpster behind the station house. Smelled to high heaven. We confiscated his fuckin' acid mop, too—stuff they use for cleaning pools."

"Anything else?"

"Nah, just the rags and the acid. Left him his bleach and Tide. Damn fool had mixed 'em all together. Amazing he didn't faint dead away, but he just seemed oblivious to everything going on."

"And you saw no sign of any bones?" asked Cates.

"Bones? Oh, wait a minute. Has this got to do with what they found at that UPS place in Chicago? Holy shit! Is he the guy . . . that Orion guy?"

"It could have something to do with the Chicago business, yes, but Gahran and Orion, we believe, are two separate people."

"Did you see any evidence of bones about the place?"

"No . . . no bones."

"Anything else? Anything you want to add to your statement?" asked Petersaul who'd jotted down notes on a pad.

"Yeah . . . come to think of it. He had this strange box."

"Box?"

"A beautiful leather-bound thing tied with velvety sash and all."

"That seem even a little weird to you, Captain?"

"Seemed a lot weird, but in my line you see it all, so I shrugged it off, you know. But he also had this huge, long shoulder bag. Figured it was an easel bag for carrying his easel, but I noticed that even though the elongated bag appeared stuffed full, bulging, an easel stood in the corner. Didn't really pay it much mind. Figured it was a second, old easel he meant to leave behind. Now . . . I don't know."

Petersaul handed Lee her card, saying, "Anything else comes to mind—anything at all about this guy—you call, understood, Captain?"

They said good-bye to the fleeing fire marshal who seemed now to want to put distance between himself and the FBI agents. Lee was muttering angrily to himself the entire way out of the building, paying no heed to the landlady's calling after him in search of some answers to questions of her own.

Petersaul returned to combing through the immaculately cleaned apartment. It appeared absolutely empty, save for the silent furniture left behind in the furnished one-bedroom, oversized living room, bath and kitchenette.

"We need blue lights and Luminol spray on every inch of this place," she said. "All I smell is blood here."

"No way you can smell it over the cleaning odors."

"I feel it then. Will you make the call?"

"Sure." Cates got on his cell phone and dialed Sands's office.

"I'm going to check out the kitchen cabinets and the bathroom cabinet, see if he left any prescription bottles or anything useful behind."

He didn't answer, as he was speaking to Sands directly. "Yeah, Dr. Sands. We got what might turn out to be a lair here."

Petersaul dialed for Darwin but Darwin wasn't answering his phone. In fact, it failed to ring. It'd been deactivated, the carrier said in a mechanical voice.

Frustrated, Petersaul attempted to get hold of Dr. Coran and only after eleven rings did someone answer. It was a gruff male voice announcing, "Oregon State Pen. Dr. Coran is inside death-row lockup. Call back later. This phone has been confiscated."

"Tell her Pete called!" she shouted to the sound of a *click*. "Fuck! Now what?"

Petersaul rejoined Cates in the living room. They stood in silence for a long several seconds until Cates finally burst out, "Well? What'd he think of our findings?"

"Couldn't get him. Couldn't get anyone."

"No one?"

"I believe Darwin and Dr. Coran are on death row with Towne. Darwin told me they had a two o'clock appointment there, but apparently, it was pushed back."

"Then we call the fucking governor."

"Yeah . . . yeah, we call Hughes."

"Let's go to the Chicago field office, set it up as a three-way with the governor. That'd be easier for all concerned and you can help me get all the details in," she told Cates.

"It's your show. Darwin did leave you in charge."

"He trusts me. Look, Cates, Darwin has . . . well, he has a personal reason for stopping this execution. I can't give you any details as he promised me to secrecy, but I . . . trust me . . . he has good reason, and Robert Towne is unjustly accused. He believes that. And if he believes it so strongly, then I do as well."

"Kinda like on faith, huh? All right. I'll follow your lead with the governor. We'll see if we can't sway him."

They rushed to Chicago to go to the FBI field office there, a good hour and a half even with the siren at full blast.

AGENTS Cates and Petersaul stepped from Police Plaza One where they had gone to see the body of Lucinda Wellingham and had met Chicago's top M.E., Horace Keene, who graciously and earnestly shared all that he and his team had learned about Lucinda's death and the awful coffin she'd been found in at UPS. The agents stepped out into a Chicago downpour and into a blackened sky, the clock tower across the street at the LaSalle Bank read 5:48 P.M.

"Time's running out for that guy up in Portland," Cates commented, fighting with the wind to light a cigarette from where they stood beneath the canopy outside Police Plaza One. "What is it, tomorrow midnight? Nothing we got here is going to change a lotta minds in Oregon."

"We need to compare our notes," she replied. "There's a Bennigan's across the street. Let's go have a meal and we can decide what to pass along to Darwin that's going to help out there in Portland."

"Tell me, Pete, you sleeping with our young boss?"

"What a goddamn question to pose to me in the rain in

the midst of an investigation with a wind howling so loud I can't hear myself think!"

"Don't call it the Windy City for nothing," short and stubby Cates replied.

"I always heard that Windy City referred to the politicians here," she said, stalling.

He just stared at her, his silence a kind of friendly fire-acid bath.

"Fuck, Jared." She stared long into Cates's steely gray, unflinching eyes. "Does everybody know it?"

"Everybody knows it."

"Fuck . . . and we've been so cautious. Never anything in the office, never so much as a glance."

"That was the giveaway. You two never make eye contact, and *never* check each other out. It's unnatural, like an ignored instinct. Sore thumb, Pete. Besides, you are working in the middle of an office full of detectives. Pete, I know it's none of my business but—"

"It'd destroy his marriage and screw with his kids' heads, Jared, if it ever got out."

"Then cut it off. End it."

"I will. I will."

"You sound like a junky or a gambler now."

"I fucking will!"

"That's sounding a little more convincing."

They dodged cabs and traffic for the restaurant. Once sitting inside, along with ordering a meal, they exchanged notepads and discussed the case and its most salient aspects, creating a list of items to share with Darwin in Portland.

"I'll call him," Cates volunteered. "I'm senior here, partner, and he doesn't have a hard-on for me."

"No, he's expecting to hear from me."

"Christ, Pete, do you hear yourself? You sound like a high-school girl on a prom date. This is an FBI investigation, not a sock hop."

"They don't do sock hops anymore, they do raves and hazings, Cates. Get with the times."

Cates pulled out his cell phone and began to dial. She put a finger over his phone and said, "*I* will call him, and it will be a professional call. That's the end of it, Cates. No more." She left the table for a quiet corner of the room, pulled out her own cell phone and speed dialed Darwin's private cell number.

REPEATEDLY Jessica and Darwin had been put off by the Oregon state penal authorities, who cited a litany of reasons why they could not visit Towne until after four in the afternoon. But finally they were in, after they had undergone frisking and scanning, their telephones confiscated along with their guns.

Darwin introduced Jessica to Robert Towne who looked so much like his brother that Jessica did a double take. "I thought you guys were half brothers, different moms. You look like twins."

"To authorities, we *are* twins in here," replied Darwin, going to his brother and hugging him. "Rob, Dr. Jessica Coran has helped me tremendously."

"Little Brother has told me all about you, and how hard you've worked for my reprieve and in gathering evidence for a new trial. But like I've told this knucklehead, I'm done for and prepared to meet my Maker."

Jessica shook the hand Towne offered. She took an instant liking to him. He was Darwin all over again, the spitting image. "I swear Darwin didn't tell me how closely you two resemble one another."

"Not for long," joked Towne.

"Not if things keep hurtling 'long downhill," added Darwin.

"We are doing all we can to free you, Mr. Towne, to prove your innocence."

"How can you know I am innocent? We only just met."

"I've come to trust my instincts over the years, and I trust my faith in Darwin and all that he's uncovered. Besides, all the holes in the case lead to one conclusion. The evidence in your case has to be viewed side by side with Millbrook, Minnesota, Milwaukee and now Chicago."

"Yeah, I heard about Chicago." A brief moment of hopeful light entered his eyes. "Heard through the prison grapevine."

They were in a sealed, locked room with cameras panning, monitored by guards at a video station outside. They were within six feet of Towne's cell, within fifty feet of the chamber were he was scheduled to die.

"We've got people all over the thing in Chicago, Rob, doing everything possible to pull a rabbit outta the hat."

Jessica added, "Not to mention our agent who's lit a fire under Minnesota authorities. He sent us the blood type found under the victim's nails."

"All the way from a two-year-old corpse in a cemetery in Millbrook, Bro," added Darwin.

"So we need to take your blood type and match it against the findings there. I've brought my medical bag in order to conduct the test. All I need is your OK to go ahead."

"What's the use? It won't change any minds, no matter the outcome of any damn tests you got, Doctor."

Darwin fell into a chair, stunned. "This makes no sense, Rob, just giving up, like . . . like a whipped dog."

Jessica noted Darwin with his brother, how alike they were in mannerism and speech pattern if Darwin chose to use the easygoing language of his youth.

"Got no reason, Darwin, to trust on anything no more. I've made peace with going over. I can't take another false hope that's going to die on the vine. Told my lawyers that already. Told 'em I didn't wanna see you but one time more and then I'm done, Bro . . . Done and over with and you can get back to your life, your kids, man, that woman of yours. No more wasting your life over me, Darwin."

Darwin shot to his feet and got in his brother's face. On profile, they really did look the part of twins, Jessica thought. "Damn you, Rob! Damn it, if your blood type is anything other than AB-negative, then that cell door has got to swing open for you, man! Now give the doc here some blood and do it now. With this, the governor's got to listen to reason."

"Only one problem with that, Little Brother . . ."

"What problem?"

"Already know my blood type . . . and it's AB-negative all the way."

"Jesus . . . God . . . why?" Darwin moaned.

"Are you simply saying this because you've made up your mind to die, Mr. Towne?" asked Jessica.

"I asked the doc here to give me the test moment I heard what you had got from that dead woman in Minnesota. Talk to the prison doc, Old Doc Waters, if you don't believe me."

"Is that why you didn't want to see us earlier, Mr. Towne? Because you want no more false hopes?" asked Jessica.

He turned to Darwin. "I told 'em I didn't want to see you, Little Brother. Sorry but that's the way it is. I want you to give it up now, Darwin."

Jessica met Darwin's gaze. Darwin asked, "When the hell are we going to get those DNA results from Cellmark?"

"I'm going to get on the phone to them personally, and I'll see if I can get the real Fischer to get on their asses, too."

"I appreciate all you've both done for me," said Towne, "really, I do. But I have to be reasonable now, practical. I know there's no way I'm getting outta this business alive . . . not in this life, not now. I've got to let it go. Else I can't make my peace, Darwin, with God, you know."

"You do that, Robert," Darwin angrily replied. "Make your goddamn peace with God! Meanwhile, we're going to find a way to get you outta this fix. I swear it."

"Your family is missing you, boy. You're going to lose

that pretty wife and those kids. Now you just get on back to Wisconsin where you belong, Little Brother, and forget about me!"

"Ain't gonna let you go like that, Robert."

They glared like two bulls now, each in the other's face, prompting a guard to rush in and cuff Towne.

"That's not necessary!" shouted his brother.

"We're OK here," Jessica shouted, waving her hands at the guard. But this only brought on more guards and they wrestled Towne from the room, threatening Darwin with a clubbing if he interfered.

As they left the facility, having regained their belongings, Jessica finally broke the silence. "Well, that went well."

"Same fucking blood type. Wouldn't you know it? Hughes'll make hay with that. All the excuse they need to execute Robert now."

"We don't know that."

"The hell we don't."

"We don't know that Robert was telling us the truth."

"What? Why would he lie?"

"You heard him. He wants no more false hopes, dead ends. He's got to come to terms with dying, and you and I . . . we represent something that's pulling him away from that, so . . . so maybe . . ."

"So perhaps he's lying about the blood test?"

She nodded. "I got the number to this Dr. Albert Earl Waters. You and Towne certainly have one thing in common besides your good looks."

"What's that?"

"You can both lie with a straight face."

"Call it survival tactics learned at an early age."

"Given your brother's state of mind, I suppose I can understand him . . . if he was making it up."

"You really think there's a chance the blood type is still in question?"

"I think we need to verify his blood type one way or another and not simply take the word of a depressed man facing execution."

"Hell yeah . . . his emotions hafta be going yo-yo, sure." Darwin grasped at the straw, happy to have it to hold on to.

They now stood under the waning sky, clouds rolling in, outside the Oregon State Penitentiary, the sunny day was turning to dusk with threat of rain in the air. "I was told Albert Waters is not here but that we can catch him at a clinic in Portland. I have the address and number."

"In the meantime, we've gotta get on Cellmark's ass. Can you really get Director Fischer on them?" Darwin urged.

"I'm going to do my damnedest."

They climbed into the rental car Darwin called an investment, not wishing to rely on local law enforcement and FBI for anything. They drove off the dismal grounds, having to get clearance at three checkpoints. Once outside the gates, before getting on the road to Portland, they still had to drive through the protesters on either side of the car, slowing their progress. Pro-lifers and those wanting to have the execution televised shouted slogans at one another. Jessica could never understand the mentality that had people who were for execution picketing prisons on the eve of an execution. They were getting what they wanted. What else could they possibly hope to accomplish?

Finally, they were past all the checkpoints and the mob. With Darwin driving, Jessica telephoned FBI headquarters in D.C., hoping to catch Director William Fischer, her mental fingers crossed. She announced herself and asked to be put through to the FBI director.

Darwin meanwhile dialed for Dr. Waters.

A pleasant sounding woman's voice came over for Jessica, one she recognized as Fischer's personal secretary, Madeline. "Why Jessica Coran, how nice to hear from you. What can we do for you, Doctor?"

"I need the director. I need his help."

"I'm afraid he's en route to Africa."

"Africa?"

"South Africa to be accurate."

"Then find a way to put me through to him. I need him to call in a rush order at Cellmark in St. Paul." She gave Madeline the phone number to the DNA test labs. "It's a matter of life and death."

"Yes, the Towne affair in Oregon, we know."

"You do?"

"Director Fischer has heard all about it, and your part in it, Dr. Coran." She sounded icy.

"What do you mean he's heard all about what? Eriq Santiva always keeps him informed of my movements."

"Well . . . when the governor of Oregon calls and learns that you falsely used the director, well then that puts a less than desirable light on things, Dr. Coran."

"That bastard Hughes. No telling what that mashing SOB said to Mr. Fischer."

"Whatever it was, Director Fischer left word for you that he'd deal with you, dear, when he returned from Africa."

The woman had such economy of words. She could write a book on how to be brief. "Put me through to him wherever he is, Madeline, now."

"He won't be inclined to talk to you just now, dear, and I suspect—"

"I'll take my chances, Maddy!"

"—and I suspect a little cooling off period might do you both good." She hung up on Jessica.

Jessica stared at the phone and thought about Hughes's personal secretary calling Fischer's personal secretary, comparing notes and putting the governor on with Fischer, who told his side of things. It all seemed like the world hinged upon the predispositions of bitties like Mrs. Dornan and Madeline Camden.

"What just happened?" asked Darwin, his eyes reading the strange look on her face.

"Fischer's out of the office."

"So?"

"Way out—somewhere on his way to South Africa."

"But you can still reach him."

"I'll send him an E-mail. That bitch Dornan must have given Madeline an earful, and she's not sympathetic. In fact, she's always been a bit hostile toward me . . . and just waiting for an opportunity to do something about it."

Dr. Waters came on the line for Darwin. Darwin introduced himself and asked about his brother's blood type. "Did you give him a blood test today at the prison? And what were the results?"

"I have a blood sample on file, one taken over a year ago. During his preliminary incarceration, while awaiting trial. I would have no need of taking blood from him in his cell today. You must've been misinformed."

"And the blood type, Dr. Waters?"

"AB-negative."

"Are you staring at the results as we speak?"

"Don't need to. I remember because you're not the only one interested."

"What're you saying, Dr. Waters?"

"I got a call from Donald Gwingault, the warden, asking the very same question only a few hours ago. Said he and the governor wanted to know."

"I see," replied Darwin.

Waters continued, "As I understood it, the governor himself requested it, and I'd hoped Towne's test would have come out anything but AB-negative. He's a good man, Rob Towne, and God, for the life of me, I can't see this man falling so far into depravity as to open his wife up and rip her apart that way. Unless I am a complete idiot in judging character, but I have had over thirty years working in the penal system as well as my private practice."

"Thank you, Doctor, for that. And you are sure there can be no mistake about the blood test?"

"None whatever. I am sorry."

He hung up, saying to Jessica, "No point in going to Waters's clinic now." Darwin appeared defeated, all his earlier enthusiasm drained.

"The prison doctor confirms a test was done and Robert was right about it being AB-neg?"

"Yeah, but the test was done long before today, so you were half right about Robert's not being completely honest with us. No wonder Robert's so discouraged. His own blood is accusing him now."

"Bad luck, sheer bad luck."

"It always followed him, and even now with him going nowhere, it still hangs over his head."

"Keep your eyes on the road," she said, and he got the double entendre.

"Will do." Though he said it with little conviction.

"Look, we've gotta get to Fischer. Find a computer and contact him, have him call me. If I can put everything in proper light for him, I know he'll do all he can to save an innocent man from execution."

"By now the governor knows the blood test went bad for Rob," said Darwin as they sped down the interstate.

"Same blood type. So what?" she announced.

"So what?"

"It proves nothing! There are millions of people walking around this country with AB-negative."

"So what the hell're we going to do now? The rabbit is dead."

"We go after those DNA results more aggressively, and we get all the might of the FBI behind doing so."

SIXTEEN

The band is out, the society is out,
Watch out Mother who made me,
The band's out, the society's out
Mothers of Children
Tie up your stomachs.

—HAITIAN VOODOO SONG

JESSICA and Darwin had little difficulty finding a computer. They were everywhere these days, and so they located a computer cafe on the outskirts of Portland, wishing to stay close to the airport, the governor's mansion and the prison.

Jessica telephoned and roped Eriq Santiva in on their side, Eriq promising to pressure Cellmark. "As much as possible." But the savvy Cuban also added, "But I gotta agree with you, Jess. Getting Fischer onto their heads at this Minnesota testing facility . . . that would far outweigh anything I can say or do to move them along."

"There's gotta be a way."

"I've already talked to Sharpe about this, Jess, and he—"

"Richard? When?"

"Less than an hour ago, maybe forty minutes. He called from a flight to Oregon out of San Francisco."

"What was his request?"

"I sent men from our Minnesota field office to camp on them. He said a Millbrook detective wasn't enough of a presence."

"And you complied with the request?"

"It's a favor to Richard. He seemed adamant, and I'm going to need him soon. Things may be popping with that China deal we've been brokering, and as always the State Department's first priority is to international cooperation among crime-fighting organizations worldwide."

"So you want Richard back at Quantico for a briefing."

"Very good, Jess. Go to the head of the—"

"Thanks, Eriq, for your help."

"Tell me, Jess."

"Yes?"

"You've met this guy Towne now. What do you think? What does your gut tell you about him?"

"Innocent, railroaded," she shot back, "and sadly broken."

"I gotta tell you I was shocked . . . well, truly surprised . . . to learn you'd taken up the cause of a death-row inmate. You of all people."

"I had a good guide to this one, Eriq."

"And this thing in Chicago? It certainly smacks of a connection. Is it connected?"

"Too soon to be absolutely certain, but yeah, we have people working on connecting the dots there."

They said their good-byes and he wished her luck and foolishly reminded her that time was running out fast now.

Darwin's pained face met hers when she got off the line with Eriq. He looked stricken.

"What is it? Your brother? What?"

"Damn fools Petersaul and Cates."

"What about them?"

"They gave all their findings to Hughes's office, and it was . . . *was* good stuff."

"Christ, it won't be, not by time Hughes and his people have poked holes in it, and put their spin on it."

"Damn fool Amanda!"

"What's with Petersaul?"

"Said she couldn't get hold of either of us or Sharpe. Called while we were without our phones in with Robert. Damn!"

"Why didn't she just leave a message?"

"She did on my voice mail. It's why I called her back but too late. She thought she was doing right."

"No way she could know the governor's as big an ass as . . . as . . . as the governor's ass."

Darwin laughed at this.

"I've got my plea in now to Fischer. All we can do now is pray that he puts on the needed pressure, and that Cellmark gets the DNA mapping done for the signature of the killer, and then we match it to Rob's, and we'll have the conclusive proof we need to free him."

Jessica pressed *send* on the E-mail, a detailed *needs* list directed at her boss's boss.

"What if he doesn't get it?"

"The E-mail?"

"The E-mail, its contents, the reason for all of this?"

"We have to hope he does."

"Hope is become a shredded, unraveling cord, Jess, or haven't you noticed? Damn that blood type. Why couldn't it have gone in our favor?" he asked.

"Because God is enjoying the drama a little too much, maybe? But wait a minute. Just hold on a minute."

He stared at her, trying to fathom her thoughts. "What? What're we holding on for?"

"We need to . . . I mean what if . . . could it possibly work?"

Still confused, Darwin placed both hands on her shoulders and amid the cafe crowd gripped her strongly and said, "Spit it out."

"No . . . not here. In the car on the way to pick up Richard at the airport. I've got to think this through."

He plunked down enough bills to cover the coffee and pastries they'd nibbled on along with the usage fee for the computer. "If you've got a new direction, I want to hear about it. Come on."

THEY sat out on the airport taxi strip, having flashed their FBI badges out the windows of the rented LeSabre. Now they watched as the jumbo jet arriving from San Francisco, and carrying Richard Sharpe, touched down with a bark of burning tires, calmed, slowed and came to a stop to make a forty-five-degree turn for the terminal. Jessica anxiously awaited Richard as the jet lazily taxied toward the terminal.

Sharpe, traveling light with only a carry-on, found them and he and Jessica hugged and kissed for a long, warm reunion.

Darwin hung back, standing at the open driver's side door. In a moment, Jessica put the two men together to shake hands.

A deepening dusk had fallen over Portland. By midnight tomorrow night, Robert Towne would be executed. Time seemed now to be pouring through the hourglass like a flash flood through a baked dry, thirsty ravine. Unstoppable, unless Jessica's plan could be made to work. She feared letting Richard know of it, feared he would on the one hand oppose it as too dangerously criminal, outside the bounds of the law and their duty, and on the other hand he might agree to it almost as quickly as Darwin had, which would make him another accomplice in the act, another culpable party.

They would have to broach the subject carefully with Richard or attempt it without his knowledge. The decision was hers entirely. Darwin had made it clear that, with or without Richard's assistance, he would break his unlawfully prosecuted, unlawfully convicted brother out of prison if only for a few days, until they could prove conclusively via DNA evidence out of Minnesota that Robert Towne was indeed *not* the Spine Thief.

"Why don't you two just hug as well as shake one another's arms off," she said of the two men greeting one another with mutual admiration and a kind of benevolent pissing contest as to which would stop shaking the other's hand first. To end it, Jessica pushed them into one another for a hug, saying, "After all we've been through, we could all use a group hug."

"I just got off the phone with Howland at Cellmark, and they're unsure," Sharpe told them. "I've bugged this Dr. Howland there repeatedly, and Eriq has stationed men on their doorstep."

"What's taking so damn long?" pleaded Darwin.

"Dr. Howland refuses to let anything out until she is satisfied, and apparently, it takes a great deal to satisfy her."

Jessica gave him a glare. "I hope you don't mean she came at you the way the governor of the great state of Oregon came at me."

"What's that supposed to mean?" he asked. "Did that man lay a hand on you?"

She groaned. "No . . . no, but not for lack of trying. He is a sexual predator, it would seem, not above selling his principles for a cause, if a girl is willing. He likely seldom gets turned down, and it didn't please him any."

Darwin got in her face. "Why the hell didn't you tell me about this, Jessica?"

"I don't want either of you two going into this meeting with Hughes like a pair of raging, insulted bulls, damn it. Just forget about that crap for now. Richard, we've worked out something that will spare Towne should the governor rebuke us again, and should the DNA evidence not materialize by tomorrow afternoon."

"What sort of duplicity are you planning, Jess?"

"You know me and authority figures, and particularly assholes in authority . . . like Hughes and his lackey, Warden Donald Gwingault. Also a real charmer."

"I want to hear all about it."

When she and Richard climbed into the rear of the car, Darwin behind the wheel, Jessica's eyes met Darwin's in the rearview mirror, and she shrugged and said, "I could never keep a secret from Richard." She then launched into her and Darwin's plan.

"Stalling the execution isn't in the cards anymore, so far as I can see. No reprieve. Not with the way these people twist reality and facts, like they've done with news coming out of Chicago," she told Richard.

Richard's phone rang. He opened it. "Oh, good, Dr. Howland from Cellmark," he announced for the others. "Tell me you have good news for us."

Silence as Richard listened to the voice at the other end.

"What? A lab mishap . . . spoiled test . . . had to start over? When did this all occur?"

Again he listened, fuming. "So this is what you told Agent Santiva? And all along you've been stalling for time. Well now, Doctor, time is fast, fast running out here in Oregon."

He cut her off, afraid of what he might say next, afraid it might jeopardize any further attempt to get the DNA to them at the last.

"More bad news," commented Darwin.

"Pour it on," she agreed.

"Some idiot in Howland's lab has, she fears, destroyed what little sample they had to work with, and she—heroically, she feels—has salvaged a minuscule microscopic spec of it from the bottom of the vial it had been transported in."

"Some fool photographed the sample on an electron microscope, no doubt," said Jessica, trying to understand this lab "accident." "That process will destroy any sample for further analysis."

"What does that mean for Robert?" asked Darwin, certainly knowing the answer.

"It means that they lost another day," said Richard. He then nervously cleared his throat and added, "It means you've got a hell of a lawsuit when . . . I mean if . . ."

"We've still got the news out of Chicago for help," said Jessica, "but I fear it is not going to be enough to dissuade this governor."

"As it turns out, Chicago authorities let Keith Orion walk, not having enough evidence on him," Richard informed them.

"Damn, you've got to be kidding," said Darwin. "Didn't anyone look at his artwork? And he's got a crate with his name on it with a dead girl inside minus her spine, and . . . and shit!"

"We've been so busy setting up meetings and getting shunted off," Jessica said to Richard, "that we didn't hear this latest."

"Orion showed off to the crowd when released, and he gave a series of 'exclusive' press interviews."

"God, I hate that about our media. This has all been a boon to the sonofabitch's career," Jessica complained through gtitted teeth.

Placing a hand in hers, Richard replied, "No doubt about his reveling in the attention. People are buying his work now as never before. Amazing but true. Kill somebody and you're fifteen minutes of fame is assured in the U.S. of A."

"Power of the press," said Darwin.

"Power of the tube," added Jessica.

"Orion did prove he's not as stupid as first glance. He did not send the crated body to himself. The paperwork was forged by another hand, someone slick enough to get a UPS clerk to attach Orion's corporate number to make it look like Orion sent the crate to himself from his Milwaukee show."

"You learned all this in airports while between flights?" she asked.

"CNN nonstop at the airports, yes, along with what I learned from Eriq. He's been closely monitoring Chicago."

They drove to the governor's mansion, the thrum of the car the only sound for some time. The darkening country-side pressed in around them. A shrieking hawk sounded in the distance.

Richard broke the silence. "Eriq tells me that question-ing of the Milwaukee-based UPS clerk has led to a compos-ite drawing of a man who bears no resemblance to Orion. The sketch is in all the newspapers and the search is on in earnest for Lucinda Wellingham's killer. There is a real dis-parity here. Earlier victims, save for Sarah Towne in Port-land, were hardly noticed by media and the public, while Lucinda has been made the darling of the dead victims, a poster child for them by CNN, MSNBC, Fox News and the print media as well. Lucinda's rich father has put up a quar-ter million dollars for information leading to the arrest and conviction of his daughter's slayer."

Darwin turned into the driveway for the mansion. They were waved through by guards at the gate after a show of badges.

"We spent some time today with Towne's lawyers," Jes-sica said. "They've tried to make the case that while he is of sound mind, he is driven by depression in turning down an appeal defense. At this point, I believe in strength in numbers."

"At trial he only had a court appointed lawyer. There they are . . . the defense team, waiting for us," said Darwin, pointing as he pulled to a stop.

After introductions and handshakes, the large delegation filed into the mansion and down the corridor to the end of the hall, there to pressure Governor Hughes to allow Towne's defense team to arrange for a DNA test, requiring a postponement of the execution—a governor's reprieve.

On entering, Jessica saw that J. J. Hughes had gathered his own team of lawyers.

The FBI agents had agreed to allow the lawyers to talk to the lawyers, and Hughes seemed happy with this, asking the others to retire with him for brandy and cigars. Richard played the underpaid, overtaxed, easily impressed civil servant to the hilt, ingratiating himself with Hughes, smoking his cigar, drinking his brandy and agreeing that it was a good thing to let the lawyers hash it out. Darwin fumed in a corner. Jessica remained silent, sipping at her brandy from a Waterford Crystal snifter. Jessica gravitated to Darwin and quietly asked him to remain calm, to allow Richard to do his thing.

Raucous laughter broke out between Hughes and Sharpe, Richard telling a dirty joke about a monk on a camel at a Los Angeles brothel. Even Jessica was beginning to wonder if Richard were acting or not with his Hugh Grant imitation.

Finally, Richard subtly brought the subject around to Towne and the stay of execution. The words *amnesty*, *pardon*, *acquittal* came through and Hughes was no longer laughing.

"Without definitive new and compelling evidence, I will tell you the same as I have told your cohorts here, a stay of execution is out of the question and will not be granted for Robert Towne."

"Why you fat, pompous, racist windbag!" Richard exploded as if Hughes had attacked the queen or the Union Jack, his true colors now unfurled. "All that we've done in the past few days, all the holes large enough to drive your limousine through, and you can't see past your bloody pride and the ignorance of your constituents?"

"Out! All of you, out of my house now!"

Jessica tried to smooth it over, hoping the lawyers in the other room—*heated discussion also coming from that quarter*—might have made better inroads. She tried to calm the governor when Mrs. Dornan pushed through a back door and entered. She announced like a parrot on cue, "The governor wishes for you to leave now. I should not wish to be forced into the position of having to call security."

"Who needs security when they have a bitch like you?" shouted Jessica. To the others, she announced, "Come on. This is an absolute waste of our time."

When they got to the steps outside, Jessica punched Richard hard in the arm. "You," she began. "I was worried Darwin was going to lose his temper, and what do you do? Get into a shouting match with Hughes, a bloody pissing contest."

"You were right about the man. He's infuriating."

"And we all handled him badly," Jessica glumly replied. "We ought to know how to get what we want from a small-time politician, people of our experience."

Darwin leapt to Richard's defense. "But Richard didn't say or do anything I didn't want to say or do, and besides, he was dead on."

She gritted her teeth. "Darwin, while Richard is right, it does no good for your brother's situation."

The lawyers now joined them, all three looking dejected. The lone female of the group, a Marilyn Stuttgart told them as her colleagues walked ahead of them to their cars, "Governor Hughes points to the release of Orion in Chicago and the discrepancies between the victims of Towne, ranging in age only from forty-eight to Sarah Towne who would have been fifty days after her murder. As tight a margin as anyone has ever seen, while this Lucinda Wellingham person was only in her mid-twenties."

"He and his lawyers think the Chicago connection is only a copycat killer also working Milwaukee. Is that what you mean to say?" asked Jessica.

"That's right. Afraid so. Wish you people hadn't given so much ammunition and guns to the enemy before we got here."

"Our first lover's spat, hey, Ms. Stuttgart?"

"I'm afraid my partners are taking a nosedive. They're

talking of getting roaring drunk until the execution is over and done with. Can you blame them?"

"No . . . no I can't."

"The governor's twisted the Chicago find entirely to suit his preconceived notions and racism, and he's had all day to perfect his arguments. Everything we came here tonight to argue had long before been decided."

"Set in stone," one of the male partners shouted over his shoulder ahead of them where they all walked to the cars. Ms. Stuttgart continued, "I can also tell you, he hates your guts, Dr. Coran. Whatever you did to him to piss him off . . . well, it sealed Towne's fate I'm afraid."

She rushed off in tears now, unable to hold the emotional flood back a moment longer.

Darwin caught up to Stuttgart and rammed his face close to hers. "Then try new strategies, go drastic, do *something* even if it's wrong."

"Like what? We've exhausted every avenue."

"File papers against the fuck-king governor," Darwin fired back.

This stopped her from climbing into the car alongside her partners. She called into the car's black interior, "Shanley, Ayers, did you hear that? Take Governor James Hughes to court in his own state. You guys wanna put up drywall the rest of your lives?"

The lawyers screeched off and out of sight down the tree-lined sandy red earth path and out onto the highway in the distance.

"So much for pinning hope on a gaggle of lawyers," Jessica said. "No need to rip out a few spines there."

"What do you call a thousand lawyers without a single spine among them?" asked Richard.

When no one could find the answer other than stuttering, Richard delivered the punch line. "A snafu . . . Situation Normal, All Fucked Up."

"Richard has had run-ins with divorce lawyers," Jessica

explained to Darwin as she and Sharpe again climbed into the rear seat.

"Oh, yeah . . . I see," Darwin replied, getting behind the wheel and starting up the engine. He peeled out, leaving smoking rubber behind them.

As they found the highway for the hotel, Richard remarked to Darwin, "I'm afraid only Cellmark in St. Paul can save your brother now."

"Not if we work together on our last-straw plan," said Jessica.

"It's madness," protested Richard, "and it could get Darwin killed in his brother's stead, even if you could get Towne into full agreement."

Darwin shouted over his shoulder, "If I can manage to take his place, I will not for a moment hesitate, Sharpe."

"If we could bait and switch this prisoner free," mused Jessica, "I mean since you two look so startlingly alike, and with his guards all being white . . ."

The others stared at her. "Well, it's a known fact that cross-cultural and cross-race eyewitness testimony have been proved notoriously wrong in accurately identifying people."

"But are you sure they look enough alike, Jess?"

"We're like a pair of twins," Darwin assured him.

"It's still too damned risky."

Jessica ignored Richard's negativism. "We could get you inside and him out," she said to Darwin.

"Then what?" asked Richard. "We all become fugitives except for Darwin who is executed in his brother's stead?"

"No, we videotape Towne, hold him someplace, and we stick it to Hughes. We get him to grant the stay of execution on the grounds that it is the wrong man—*literally* the wrong man now—that he has on death row."

Richard vigorously shook his head. "That's blackmail of a high-ranking public official, isn't it?"

"So our combined list of criminal activity grows?" she

asked. "And at this point, what other recourse have we? What help or support has been offered? Even from our own FBI field offices here?"

"So we go to death row and we break a man out as if it's to be as easy as . . . as changing out a roll of toilet paper." Richard remained skeptical.

"It's our only recourse, Richard! The only one the system's left us. I didn't wake up this morning and say, 'Why don't I break the law, today?' but you went your rounds with Hughes, you know what we're up against."

"Whoa, I didn't say it lacked *nobility*, just common sense, Jess."

She suggested, "I say we use the media."

"Leak the story at the crucial right moment, ingenious," replied Darwin. I can see the governor choking on the headlines now: *11th Hour Stay for Towne in STRANGE TWIST As Towne's Twin Surrogate Laughs in Governor's Face.* Hey my fifteen minutes of fame!"

"Will the real Robert W. Towne please stand up?" joked Jessica.

"How can you two be so cavalier about this?" asked Richard. "A thousand things could go wrong with this so-called plan, one of them horribly wrong."

Darwin only replied, "Here's another headline: *Officials Unsure When and for How Long the Amazing Switch Took Place.*"

"*Dramatic Desperate Act to Save a Brother from Execution,*" added Jessica.

Sharpe gave up, joining in the speculation about headlines. "*Towne's Whereabouts Still Unknown While Brother Is Executed.*"

"It's the only fucking way we're ever going to get a stop-execution order," said Darwin.

"And Big Jim Hughes will get his well-deserved hefty dose of the *Geraldo* moment coming to him," Jessica added.

Laughter filled the car. Sharpe added, "It may well be worth it to be handed our walking papers just to see Hughes brought down."

"And if we all go to jail for it?" asked Jessica. "For a conspiracy to save an innocent man from execution by the state . . . Gentlemen, sometimes morality is more important than the law."

"Ask Huck Finn," said Darwin.

Sharpe replied, "Here here. I like it."

"If it is the only way to stop this gross injustice," said Jessica, wrapping her arm around Richard's, "then it is the only way, and if it means our jobs—"

"Then may God blind me . . . ahhh . . . *us* if we don't act."

"Just do it. Trust me, *Nike* will be calling us to do an ad."

Darwin didn't hesitate. "I'm in."

"If you harbor any doubts, Richard, you go . . . fly back to Quantico before it goes down," Jessica said to Richard.

"You mean no point in our losing both incomes?" he asked, patted her hand, and added, "No, dear one, I'm like Darwin put it . . . in. *I'm in*. I'll stay and see it through, Jess."

"Then we do the bait and switch."

SEVENTEEN

Dancing in the lion's jaw.

— FROM A HAITIAN VOODOO SONG

GILES Gahran made for a strange sight standing at the concrete barrier wall created by the Chicago Parks Authority, dressed in black with a long coat flapping around him in the breeze—Keanu Reeves in *The Matrix*, minus the cool elán. But he carried with him an interesting-looking, curiously irregular shaped, ornately ribboned leather-bound box. Where he stood staring out at the oceanlike enormity of Lake Michigan. Dusk had come on. He'd hoped for darkness by now as a blackening sky had rolled in from the lake to cover Chicago in a blanket of metal-gray turning to onyx.

His knuckles had gone white holding so tightly to his father-in-a-box, as he fully intended to do away with the parasitic mind-leeching holdover from his childhood. Mother's final gift to him.

He had come to the enormous great lake of the Great Lakes here in Chicago, with a wind whipping so treacherously up at him from the stone barriers erected along this section of Lincoln Park that he felt as if the Devil of the wind wanted the box, that it meant to rip it from his hands and do with the box what it willed rather than see him throw it into the pounding waves. He imagined the contents spilling out and flying in all directions, flyers to the world here disseminating who he was—the sins of the father making tomorrow's *Tribune* and *Sun-Times*. He clutched the box against the wind even tighter. If he pitched it whole into the water, it might float for hours, and some fool might fish it out. But if he dared open it, the wind would stab at its contents with its draconian fingers and lift out whole sections of loose news clippings, photos, documents and send them off like blind birds in a fit of flapping and squawking.

A true Chicago storm was brewing overhead. A darkness like night had crept like evil itself over the city as if to hold it ransom to darkness, Chicago turning from daylight to midnight within the hour owned now by the power of the storm edge.

It seemed to Giles that all the forces of nature had aligned with him to be in agreement, in sync, chanting in the powerful wind and the threatening lightning streaks out over the water, and in the rolling thunder, all as if to say, *Do it! Do it! Do it now, Giles! Fuck the consequences, just rid yourself of Mother's nasty little legacy box, bequeathed from so enormous a hatred as to set your backbone to quivering.*

The voice in the wind now pounded his psyche and inner ear. It sounded like his dream father's voice from the far off other side, telling him to go ahead and hurl any and all knowledge locked away in the box into the raging waters to be swallowed whole there in the pounding waves, that it wouldn't float, that no one would ever find the box buried below the lake.

He lifted the box overhead, preparing to do as all of nature and all of his instincts told him; an absolute instinct it was to destroy any vestige of the carefully guarded, carefully accumulated, carefully passed on reams of information detailing the man who had fathered and abandoned him.

"Sonofabitch . . . son of one motherfucking bitch is what you are!" he shouted at the box as a female jogger hastened her speed to get past the strange figure in black with the box held overhead, talking to himself.

A second jogger along the lake path stopped and stared. The man faintly asked against the wind, "Hey, buddy, you all right? Not thinking of jumping, are you?"

Barely hearing this, Giles turned to the sound, half expecting to see his dead mother or his living father. His mother had told him that his father would live on forever. Somewhere in the box. Also somewhere in the cumbersome box—no doubt—she had left Father's last known address here in Chicago. Mother had said he'd once lived in Chicago, and that he was killed under strange circumstances in New Orleans, but that could all have been fabricated, he imagined. Perhaps Father was as alive as Giles and living right here in the city? Perhaps his address lay just beneath Giles's fingers, in the box. He imagined a large house filled with rooms, his father coming to the door and welcoming him in with open arms.

Subconsciously, he supposed it a reason underlying all others for his coming to the Windy City. To finally face his father. To see if he was the monster Mother portrayed after all, and to ask him why he had left Giles with so vile a creature.

She'd said his father liked hurting people, that he had even killed some people and was thrown into a prison for the mentally insane. "That's why I say, boy, you're just like him, killing my goddamn cat, my innocent cat, and for what? So you could suck out its spinal fluid and its bone marrow! My dear God you are born an evil spawn of Satan, evil incarnate, and I can't stand the thought of your having once occupied space and time in my womb! Like some fucking real-life Rosemary's baby is what you are."

He reached out to her, trying to calm her in her last moments, but she spat in his face.

"Just like your father," she repeated the endless mantra of his childhood. "Gives me the dry heaves just to think he had his *thing* in me even once, much less a dozen times before he could impregnate me. And then he runs off. All because he got a little ill in the head and began to think he had some sort of cancer or disease 'cause some asshole doctor tells him he's losing red blood cells or some such shit, and then in the end, he checks outta reality altogether . . . becomes a total fucking murderous maniac and winds up in the loony bin in of all places Philadelphia, from where he escaped in a blood bath and—"

"I don't wanna hear no more, Mother!" he'd shouted at her. "Just go die of your own foul disease!"

She didn't miss a beat. "—and you, you know what they say about the acorn not falling far from the tree, and if you want to look up your genetic freak of a father, you only have to look, in the box, boy."

She finished with another coughing jag, blood coming up. So apropos to her cursing Giles.

That had been years ago, the year of Mother's death that somber November day and night while he kept vigil at her bedside, not to ease her mind or as the obedient son but to be sure she was really dead when she finally took her last breath. He'd so wanted to open her up, remove her spine and feed on it as he'd done her cat, but he never got the chance.

Afraid of him, afraid of what he might do to her after death, she had ordered up her own cremation and the funeral home placed in charge, a place called French and Parker's back in Millbrook. The funeral boys rushed in like ghouls on automatic pilot and whisked her off straightaway on the basis of a court order she had made out in the event of her death to be cremated. French and Parker did not disappoint Mother. They did the cremation within hours according to her wishes, no wake, no fanfare, no candle burning, nothing. Mother's lawyer worked in close conjunction with the funeral home, overriding

Giles's wishes for an old-fashioned, closed coffin wake, thinking he might get at the body sometime between its being embalmed and put out on the floor, thinking the spinal fluid and bone marrow from the backbone ought rightly to be his.

The thoughts most certainly frightened him, galled him even, but worst of all, the thoughts of doing this to Mother, extracting her essence, her *luz*, her *al abj*, her strength and her power to make it his own made him wonder even more deeply than ever about his father's identity, his insanity, his urges and actions. Only hinted at all these years by Mother but now handed over to him all wrapped in ribbon as a fucking nasty awful joke of a gift. Like handing someone a gun used by a suicide victim and calling it a gift that potentially "keeps on giving." But that was Mother.

How much of his ill thoughts, his satanic and draconian urges had he in fact inherited from her and not Father? Why hadn't she bequeathed two boxes? One filled with dear old invisible Father and one filled with dear old venomous and quite visible Mother?

Giles had been given only a moment with her after she died there at the hospital, and he knew he had no chance given the openness and busyness of the place to take what every fiber in him craved. And the strict record kept of who was in and who was out of the rooms at any given time discouraged the violence he wanted to do. And with security just down the hall, he struggled mightily to restrain himself, thinking he'd have his chance to break into the crematorium at Frenchy's, as it was called in the neighborhood, and attack the old crone, dead at forty-eight, that night. But the damnable partners at the funeral home acted quickly, paid well to do so.

Even in death she had cheated Giles of all he needed or ever really wanted.

No matter now. He had killed Mother many times over now, and even Lucinda, in her way, was more like Mother than she was unlike Mother. And now all of his many *Mothers* dangled over his sculptures like long sleek egrets at full wing gliding over the mores of a strange sanctuary.

Unlike his other victims, he had only an opportunity to sketch Lucinda in death, never alive like the others. Sketches he had thrown into his own box along with news clippings and stories and materials and journal entries about his own exploits to rival those of dear old Dad.

Mother he had sketched many times over both alive and dead, depositing her into the box many times over, feeding birds in a park, petting a dog, walking a horse.

"Perhaps Father is here someplace in Chicago," he said aloud to Mother on the wind over the lake. "But so long as I don't know who the fuck he is, I really don't have to know, now do I?"

A voice from behind Giles interrupted his audible thoughts. "Whatcha doing with that box?" asked the nosey male jogger who'd stopped to tie his shoe as if an undercover cop. He was clean cut and bulked up from lifting barbells. He looked like a cop.

Giles lowered the box. "It's my fucking box. I'll do whatever the hell I want with it."

The jogger nodded successively and rushed off.

"Not a cop after all," Giles told himself.

He then tucked the box under his arm as the first raindrops fell. He walked across the great expanse of the park, the grass growing wetter and wetter as he passed until his pant cuffs soaked through, even though the drizzle had remained light. The wind at his back pushed him hard as if a pissed off Satan were shoving, angry that he had failed to carry through on what he'd thought was a firm, final decision, one he *would* act on. The thunder overhead roared again and while his back was turned to Lake Michigan, he saw the flashes of lightning reflected in the thousands of blinking windowpanes ahead of him along Michigan Avenue. Cars whizzed past on the Outer Lake Shore Drive. When he finally arrived at the overhead bypass and the traffic at the terminus of Fullerton Avenue, the mild drizzle had become a steady beat like insistent pellets fired angrily into him. All of nature had agreed with him moments before, but now all of nature disagreed vehemently and the downpour felt like a power pressing in on him, all the divine and all the satanic at once mad with anger at his inability to follow through on a simple decision.

He'd made the decision only after arranging for a debut showing of his artwork at Cafe Avanti, where he had already set up his "unique and ingenious" sculptures—words of praise from the owners of the premiere artist cafe and art gallery across from the Music Box Theater.

He found a bus going west that would take him to Southport where he could exchange for a bus running to the 3000 block and Cafe Avanti. As he rode the bus, his pant legs dripping a puddle where he sat, he thought of Cafe Avanti, how fortunate he was to be showing his work there in the shadow of art history in the city and in the cafe's somewhat cramped and stuffy, dungeonlike rear rooms that formed a kind of myriad labyrinth that art patrons, and the curious numbers floating in and out of Avanti could wander through to Giles's delight. In a sense all of them, Mother, Sarah, Joyce, Louisa, and Lucinda Wellingham as well, must be seeing at this moment the fruition of Giles's work.

The bus arrived at the stop nearest Cafe Avanti, and Giles, his box safely in hand, deboarded the bus and walked proudly into the cafe, wondering if anyone viewing his showing with the brief descript and his photo would recognize him, and if his work would be rewarded with accolades from men and women who mattered, those in a position to help his career along.

Oregon State Penitentiary
November 12, 2004

The video cameras were disengaged by the bogus actors wearing uniforms of the power company that served the penitentiary and most of Portland, The Yakima Valley Power and Light Company. They'd come in on the heels of Sharpe, Reynolds, and Dr. Coran, all here for what appeared to be Robert Towne's last good-bye to his brother.

Inside the visitation room, Jessica, Sharpe and Darwin went into immediate action as soon as the cameras went down. Darwin began to strip off his clothes and throw them at his brother. Richard kept vigil at the door. Jessica explained to Towne what was going on.

"Oh, no! No way! You going to get Darwin killed. No matter what, they're going to put a man to death here tonight at midnight. It ain't going to be Darwin."

"It ain't gonna be anyone, Bro. We've got it planned out. News that I am in and you are out is going nationwide today, long after you've been stashed."

"Strip off that prison jumpsuit, Mr. Towne," Jessica ordered drill-sergeant fashion. "We only have minutes before the cameras are up and running again."

Towne stared around the room at the still cameras, their lenses closed. "You're all crazy. You'll all be thrown into jail."

"Just do it, Robert!" Darwin's angry face was within inches of his big brother's. Jessica thought it like pressing one's face against a mirror. Their profiles perfectly matched, and Darwin had found a pair of glasses to match those his brother wore.

"I can't let you do this, Darwin."

"Get the fuck outta those clothes, man. Now!"

Darwin stood in his underwear, his fists clenched, his chest heaving. "Let me do something just this once for you!"

A long moment of silence passed between the brothers.

"They're getting damned restless outside," warned Sharpe from the window in the door.

"Please, Mr. Towne," Jessica pleaded.

Towne raised a huge finger to the two-way mirror. "The screws are probably watching this whole damn foolish scheme right now, so just back off, Little Brother."

"We disconnected the two-way before we entered," Jessica assured him. "Along with the cameras, all save that one." She pointed to a single camera still operating. "We want to tape this, to insure Darwin's life."

"We'll get the tape," Richard assured Towne.

"They think it's the power company," explained Jessica.

"Now please, Robert, just do as we say," began Darwin.

Jessica pleaded, "Put yourself . . . your life in our hands."

Towne continued to stare at them all as if they were lunatics.

"We've exhausted every other avenue, Rob. Let us . . . let *me* do this thing."

"It'll mean an end to your career, Darwin. You know that?"

Darwin slapped him hard across the face, drawing blood from his lip. Robert Towne hardly flinched, standing his ground, glaring into his brother's eyes, searching them for something. "I guess I had that coming for letting you down, Dar—"

"What the hell're you talking about? Letting me down?"

"I couldn't hold us together. They split us up, and I couldn't stop them. Couldn't never find you all those years I tried, and then I gave up hope of our ever being a family ever again."

"I never once felt you betrayed me, Robert, or gave up or did anything to hurt me, not once."

Robert Towne hugged his brother to him. Darwin pushed away after a moment and said, "Now give me those goddamn prison clothes."

They exchanged clothes and dressed quickly, still buttoning up when the cameras began to pan around the room again.

Darwin went immediately into character, picking up a chair and hurling it at his brother, who was now in a three-piece Brooks Brothers suit.

Towne, as Reynolds, deflected the chair and charged at Darwin, now in the orange jumpsuit. Richard grabbed the false Darwin's arm before he could land a punch and shoved him hard against the two-way mirror. "Stand down, Agent Reynolds! This isn't Dodge City, and you're not Wyatt Fucking Earp!"

"We're outta here," Jessica announced, knowing the audio and video equipment in the room was again operational. Two guards pushed through the door and ushered Darwin, in jumpsuit, out.

"Stay in character," Jessica said in Towne's ear.

"Let's get the fuck outta here. He don't wanna talk to me, then fuck Robert Towne."

They leap-frogged the power and light workmen who busily cleaned up after themselves. The party of three apparent FBI agents stopped at the last inside checkpoint where their telephones and guns were returned to them.

Jessica exchanged a look with Richard as Robert Towne hefted his brother's weighty .43 Smith & Wesson, a half smile creased the giant man's features.

The power and light people passed them now carrying out their cables and tools. The three FBI agents signed out and marched down the corridor, falling in behind the men wearing the brown uniforms of the local power company, each carrying cables and strange handheld gadgets. Jessica had earlier found these willing activists among the mob at the gates, wooing them away and striking a deal with them. They not only wanted to help but to film as much as possible of the event. Death-penalty opponents, they were also film students and actors who had grown up with computers and media.

"Don't get complacent, Towne. We still have three checkpoints to get past," said Sharpe.

"Yeah," replied Towne, "but I got my FBI badge and gun."

"Under no circumstances, Towne, do you use that gun," warned Sharpe. "It would only destroy our chances of making this work."

"Besides," added Jessica, watching his fingers itch over the bulge of the holstered gun, "it's not loaded."

He broke into an enormous laugh which he suddenly stifled. "Figures . . . goddamn just figures."

A couple of guards stared in reaction to Towne's outburst.

"The way he deals with grief," said Jessica aloud. "Who can figure how a man's going to deal with the death of a loved one?"

Sharpe whispered to Towne, "A little grief for your brother's plight, Darwin, might be in order here."

"He dies in this fucked up place from listening to you two, and I'll fucking show you grief, Agent Sharpe, you and Agent Coran both."

In the car, Towne breathed the air as if he'd never had the experience before, but his deep inhalations became near gasps as they began to make the first hurdle past the first outside checkpoint and he heard and saw the enormous crowd gathered outside the prison—90 percent screaming for his blood while waving homemade signs that called him filthy names and asked that he burn in Hades. A small contingent of others waved the signs of those opposed to any sort of capital punishment.

"What the fuck have you people got my little brother into. Turn this car around and take me back! I won't abandon him like this. I can't!"

"Shut up and see this thing through!" shouted Jessica over the noise of the protesters and the blood-for-blood revenge crowd that mistook vigilantism for justice.

"Play it out, Towne," shouted Sharpe sternly, his face livid. "Damn it, man, we have a foolproof plan to keep Darwin from any harm. You've got to trust us and trust Darwin."

Towne calmed and fell silent in the back seat. "One more checkpoint and it's a hotel room with a meal and TV and freedom, Mr. Towne," Jessica assured him.

"Tell me how you plan to keep Darwin from becoming a dead man at midnight?"

"We've sent the truth to all the news agencies and newspapers, marked to be opened at 10 P.M. The shit will hit the fan and everyone in Oregon and the country will know that J. J. Hughes literally has the wrong man in custody. This he'll be forced to deal with; this will force an end to the execution. It's a perfect plan."

"Foolproof, huh? Have you considered the fact that James Hughes is a fool?"

"Of course we've taken that into consideration."

"But you can't predict what a fool will do! Besides, why should he . . . how can he be persuaded that Darwin is Darwin, and that a switch was made?"

"Two pieces of evidence will convince the press and Hughes," she fired back.

"You are dealing with Dr. Jessica Coran, Mr. Towne," said Sharpe. "She has thought of everything, every contingency."

Towne flashed on the power and light men. "They have a tape of the switch as it went down, the power and light guys working for you?"

"That's right. Walked right out with it."

"Will that be enough?"

"There's one other exhibit for the jury."

"His blood type . . . of course. You've got *his* blood type on the record."

"Courtesy of your friend Dr. Waters, who will attest to it as a disinterested party, who, in giving Towne a routine blood exam discovered it could not be Towne's blood, thus staying the execution of Darwin as well."

"This state means to kill somebody. I'm still not going to rest till we get Darwin outta here."

They got past the last checkpoint and Towne's deep inhalations grew even greater as they pulled out onto the highway leading away from the prison.

"We have one more tape to make, Mr. Towne," said Richard.

"A tape of you, *dated*, showing that you are in federal custody, Mr. Towne."

"I think you two have earned the right to call me Rob," he replied. "And even though it's belated and sounds pretty pitiful . . . thanks . . . thanks a whole . . . a whole heap. But I still won't rest till I see Darwin again outta that hellhole and off death row."

"Then you have a crusade, Rob. Something to live for," said Sharpe.

"And we have it on good authority that the lab in Minnesota will have a DNA string to match against yours within twenty-four hours."

"Lotta good it'd have done me tonight at midnight."

Jessica replied, "Precisely why we have put everything on the line."

"Where're we going now . . . I mean to hide out?" he asked.

"Taking a flight out," said Richard, "all arranged."

"Getting you out of Oregon altogether." Jessica looked over her shoulder and watched the power and light van following them to the airport. She dialed a number for the van. "Are you all set back there?"

On the other end she heard cheers and put the phone up to Towne's ear. "Not everyone in Oregon hates your guts, Rob."

"That's a comfort. Now where're we going?"

"Chicago."

"Chicago?"

"Everything is pointing to Chicago, yes. We have agents on the trail of a man believed to have killed a woman in Milwaukee and—"

"But the cops in Chicago released the guy!" protested Towne. "Said he had proof he didn't kill that girl."

"Darwin had a long talk with Agents Petersaul and Cates just before we came to see you, Rob," countered Jessica.

"Petersaul and her partner are closing in on another suspect," added Richard.

Towne looked hopefully into her eyes. "Who is this guy?"

"A kind of shadowy second to Orion with whom Lucinda Wellingham had spent a little time close to the end of her life. Likely grooming him for his own showing."

"Another artist . . . fits in with the sketches. I tried to tell these fools here I haven't a lick of artistic talent but—"

Bouncing through a bit of turbulent roadwork, Jessica added, "We suspect this guy reacts badly to major events happening in his life."

Richard told him, "We suspect that his mother's death rather unleashed him on the world. His chance at a showing in Milwaukee, perhaps out of some sudden incident that set him on a rage, perhaps fear of success—who knows—precipitated his killing of his benefactress. Perhaps your wife and Louisa Childe in Millbrook were in a sense benefactors."

"We've uncovered an unsolved case connected to him as well, years ago in Millbrook, the disappearance of an art dealer–agent type who had some dealings with Gahran. Male this one."

"Most of his victims," added Richard, "we again suspect were fill-ins . . . ahhh . . . stand-ins for Mommy Dearest, Nurse Ratched, the Evil Queen or whoever he hates most in this life."

"And a study of the victims not only shows how close in age they were but in matronly appearance, all save Lucinda Wellingham, and this other art dealer, of course, but these two also represented power, authority figures who held his future in their hands, like his mother, we surmise."

"Big events set him off?"

"One reason he takes months, sometimes years to strike

again," she said. "He lives a quiet, patient, long-suffering lifestyle between in which he buries his urges in his artistic endeavors—puts them in his work, so to speak."

Clearing his throat, Richard smirked. "He literally puts the 'objects' of his rage into his work."

"Sounds better and better for this, doesn't he?" asked Towne, a half-satisfied smile creasing his stern features. "How . . . what else you got on him?" pressed Towne.

"Not to get your hopes up too high," Jessica said, sipping hot coffee from a Thermos, "but this guy was born in 1980 to a single mother, Larina Gahran. Ring any bells?"

"Gahran . . . Larina . . . son named Giles? No, none."

"Didn't mean a thing to us, either. You see, he's remained under the radar. Never been arrested, so he shows up on no one's screen. Certainly not the FBI's Violent Criminal Apprehension Program—VICAP."

Outside the tinted car windows the black landscape of Oregon turned to lighted strip malls, gas stations, fast-food restaurants and the debris of urban sprawl as they neared the airport.

In the darkness of the cab, Richard again broke the stillness. "Guy's mother is said to have berated him all his life, or so school records show a distinct psychosis involving his relationship with her—was a disability check recipient, former nurse, in of all places, Millbrook, Minnesota."

"How do you know all this now and not before?" asked a frustrated Towne, accepting a cup of the hot coffee from Jessica.

"Once Petersaul and Cates got on his trail, it led back to Millbrook," began Richard, "so I called my contact there, Brannan, and he dug up all he could find on Giles Gahran and faxed it to Petersaul, who in turn, contacted Jessica on her cell just before we arrived at your address, Mr. Towne."

"Then it's all good, solid information, right? All to the good, right?"

"You tell me. Born and raised in Millbrook with a history of medical problems, yes." Richard held a smug look of assurance. "Everything points to Giles Gahran."

"That's his name, Giles Gahran," repeated Towne.

"Now Darwin's got to play out his hand first, and as soon as possible, we will bring him home, too," Jessica assured him.

Sharpe continued with, "Records show that Gahran attended Millbrook schools, and Brannan's got hold of a yearbook photo he's forwarded to Chicago PD and FBI."

"Our first victim, Louisa Childe was killed only blocks from where this kid went to high school. He has no college record other than a Portland arts school—"

"Wait . . . whoa up there. You have him in Portland? at the time of Sarah's murder?" asked Towne.

"We do," replied Sharpe.

"And this only after his mother died and Childe was killed," added Jessica. "His tuition in Portland was seeded by money coming out of her estate, the house sale."

"Sold out and moved to Portland soon after the Childe killing," Richard said, his hands like fluttering birds, insistent of the truth. "Only weeks after Giles Gahran's mother dies, two years ago, Louisa Childe's mutilated body is discovered in late November, determined to have been killed in mid-November."

"Your wife was murdered in mid-November too," added Jessica. "Joyce Olsen murdered in Milwaukee in the same manner in mid-November."

"Records also show his having attended Portland's prestigious Kanar Institute of the Arts. While in attendance there, your wife is killed."

"Damn . . . Sarah was taking classes there . . ."

"Gahran next shows up in Milwaukee, having not quite completed his studies in Portland, and now we have not one but two killings using the same MO in Milwaukee."

"Sounds like you're all over this guy now like he fell outta the sky. Where they hell was all this when I was locked up all this time?"

"He's disappeared into oblivion each time," Jessica's tone turned from excited to apologetic, "and he allowed so much time between his killings."

Sharpe said, "Now he's become part of the Chicago cityscape. Still very much at large, but he *will* surface."

"It's only a matter of time and credit-card use," Jessica assured Towne, "a registration record, signing a lease, a lot of interviewing and footwork in the arts community on our part."

"Besides, Chicago's as good a place to stash you as any," added Sharpe.

"When do we make the tape?" he asked.

"At the airport, back of the van. It's all set up. Plan is to keep you mobile."

"You musta paid those boys good."

"Yeah, we did pay them well," replied Jessica, "using my FBI MasterCard, but they are also anti–death penalty advocates."

They pulled into a Flying Tigers airport hangar, the van following. The hangar door came down on cue, just as Richard had promised it would. "That credit card's going to be maxed out anytime now."

EIGHTEEN

Evil is easy and has infinite forms.

—BLAISE PASCAL

WITH the exhibit up and already looking like a hit among cafe patrons at Avanti, Giles wandered outside to gaze at the cityscape and found himself and his box parked on a bench at the terminus of Oak Street overlooking the lake again. He kept staring up at the enormous, lovely, revolving, lit-by-a-million bulbs Ferris wheel at Navy Pier. The lights and sounds wafting across the lake from the joyous time people—*normal people*—were having there seemed so close, so within his touch. And yet so far from it.

A well of sadness balled up inside Giles for all the harm he had done in this world, in this life given him by some deity somewhere who must have known . . . had to have known what he would do with it, how he would ruin it, given all that he was even before exiting his mother's womb, and all that she molded him into; after all, such a deity did play with people's lives. He put Louisa Childe in harm's way, in Giles's path. He put Sarah Towne at that right juncture along that riding path in the park in Portland within miles of the Kanar Institute. He had placed Joyce Olsen at that park just as Giles had passed by, and he had molded the faces and bodies of these women to look and move just like Mother. After all was said and done, God had placed all the others within Giles's reach as well, Lucinda and that fool in Millbrook, the one who would never be found. His spine, along with all else, had been dug up by roaming animals, quarry dogs most likely, and dragged, he supposed into some deep cave or burrow to rot there—a waste of a good spinal column, but at least no one had ever discovered Cameron Lincoln's body. Not even Giles. By the time he'd gotten nerve enough to go back to where he'd hurriedly buried the art exhibitor, below a scattering of twigs and leaves, the dead man had disappeared into the deep Minnesota woods.

Giles stared up into the heavens at the night stars, the constellations winking in a clear, bright sky. "You planned all this right, God? You got those mysterious ways for us not to question, so whatever else, You—You're at back of all of it, invisible strings attached to our spines, manipulating all of it. Used to think it was Satan pulling my chain."

He stood and lifted the opened box, the one with all the news clippings and the letter Mother had carefully typed out and lain across the pile of horror stories that explained who his father was. The one with the heavy metal and glass object lumbering about inside it.

The ribbons lay limp at each side, and Giles had read Mother's parting words at last. She, too, was created by God, and she and his father, were in their way both evil incarnate. While Mother had never killed anyone, she had destroyed a spirit—the spirit Giles might once have had a chance at being or at least at becoming—the shadowy other self who might have eschewed all that his father was, and fought off the ravages of his mother's assaults on that spirit, and overcome the genetic mark left on his soul by a monster seed.

All gone now . . . any flickering hope of chance for that other self to survive extinguished long ago with his first murder. Too damn much stacked too high against him, borne of man and woman, a creature carrying both the mark of Satan in his very makeup, in the soup of his mother's womb, and the mark created of her doing, of his upbringing and environment. God could not have found a way to save him from Mother when an infant? Why not? Why in God's name not?

Giles stood and looked down from what seemed a far away place at the damnable, cursed box, realizing that it had been a blight on his soul from the moment Mother had handed it to him from her deathbed. She had had a lawyer bring it to her there in the hospital. It had been sealed for years until she herself broke a thick wax seal she had applied to it when the box had been placed into a bank vault for this day.

"You have a right to know precisely who and what you are, Giles. That is why I gift this to you. It is the gift of self-awareness and fear . . . Yes, the gift of fear. You rightly ought to fear the thing you are and until now you have had no idea *what* you are, not really. You only think you do. Ever wonder where you get the urge to kill a living creature and to feed on its . . . its spinal fluid and marrow?"

Now Giles knew what she had meant. For the first time everything fit, each puzzle piece in his brain, psyche and in his soul . . . it all fit. Finally, he understood precisely what Mother had had to live with, why she was so bitter, and why Mother, on bended knee, so often asked God why He had spared her for this—while pointing at Giles. Asking God why she had not been killed by his father.

Giles wanted to run from the box.

All these years since Mother's death, he had fixated on its contents—both fascinated with it and terrified of it at once. Drawn to its contents, closer and closer, until his fingers would inch inside it, fearful of the snakebite of its contents. At once wanting to bathe in it, to luxuriate in the sheer knowledge and power within the box, and to run in terror from it.

Finally, steeling himself, Giles reached in and snatched out a handful of the news clippings, snatching them from below the dead weight of the strange metal and glass tube device lying atop all. His eyes registered a kind of garden tool device like a hose attachment perhaps. He could not fathom its meaning, but he quaked at touching it. Then he abruptly closed the lid on the thing. Now he began to bravely, courageously read the bizarre stories in the clippings.

Tales of Father . . .

"I could just walk away from it. Leave it right here. Never see it again," Giles spoke to time, space, the stars and God as he stared down over the box, standing beside the park bench he'd been occupying as he'd read the accounts Mother had gathered over the years for his keepsake.

He took tentative steps away. "When they catch me, they'll think I'm monster enough without knowing who my father was. Least now I know he's long dead. Mother didn't lie about that. They'll think me a common unfeeling sociopath, a psychotic fucking horror to make a blood splatterrama film about, like they did about Father. They'll think me a thing worse than all the other horrors combined, a thing without an ent of humanity—all granite and nerve and unleashed animal instinct like a starved wolf escaped from an ancient cave, as guileless and without pity as Jack the Ripper or Father . . . dear well-remembered Father. The man everyone on the planet *knew* about but forgot about with his death, everyone except me. I didn't even have the luxury of forgetting about him, having never known."

He halted, hearing a rustle behind him. A homeless man with a bundle of *StreetWise* newspapers to sell under his arm was now admiring the box, poking about its contents, curious as an overgrown cat.

Giles reacted instinctively. "Get away from that, old man! It's mine! I . . . I just forgot it there."

"I found it! It's mine," argued the half-demented fellow.

"Here, here is for your newspapers!" Giles handed him a ten dollar bill.

The shaky hand extended toward Giles to brush his cheek in a moment of need for human touch. Giles felt the scratchy, rough fingers caress his cheek. "You remind me of someone . . . someone who loved me once," said the old man in a sandpaper and gravel voice.

Giles pulled away after a moment. "You can keep the papers, re-sell them. Double your profits, old man," he said as he lifted the ugly gift from Mother, her twisted homage to Father—every detail of his every crime against humanity. According to the news reports, the work of a man who lived a heartless, unfeeling double-life and killed wantonly like an animal by night while selling medical supplies by day. A man who had designed and patented his own medical device for extracting blood from the jugular artery as the hearts of his victims pumped blood to his waiting mason jars, each carefully labeled and packed into a cooler. Mother always said that Giles was neat to a fault, meticulous about his art supplies. Now he knew where he'd gotten the trait.

Father was a blood drinker, a man convinced of his own need for blood, a vampire named Matisak—Mad Matthew Matisak, the newspapers proclaimed him.

In the news stories, Father was characterized again and again as a weak little man suffering a debilitating disease who'd come to think of himself as a parasitic vampire who had to feed on the blood of other human beings to save himself from the disease that threatened to overtake him. One reporter wrote that his mental state had deteriorated far more quickly than had his physical condition, his physical state seemingly taking power from his each kill, and that he could be counted among the truly insane but masterful and ingenious murderers in murderer's row going back through all time. Another reporter claimed that Mad Matthew Matisak had established a strange bond with FBI Agent and Medical Examiner Dr. Jessica Coran.

Giles wondered what this woman could tell him about his father. He wondered how he might best his father's reputation and in doing so possibly meet this Dr. Jessica Coran. Father had wanted her to go into an eternal bliss with him, and he apparently damn near got his way in a warehouse in New Orleans many years ago.

Giles wondered if this FBI doctor were still alive, still working for the FBI, and if so, he wondered if she would feel any kinship—as strange as such a kith and kin might be— to the son of Matthew Matisak. He made his way toward the array of lights and the sounds of gaiety spilling from the ongoing Navy Pier fair. He felt an overwhelming need to be among people even knowing he would never fit in among people.

Unsure why the lights of the Ferris wheel pulled him, Giles began a brisk walk for the pier.

The homeless man looked after him until certain the young man had no intention of returning. He then unfolded the white sheath of paper with the sketch of the suspect in the Lucinda Wellingham–UPS murder case, with a strong possible connection to the Spine Thief mutilation murders.

The cop's excited hands revealed shaking manicured, painted nails below the gloves as the detective tore them away, finally able to open the tightly folded paper on the likeness. There seemed a definite rough similarity between the man with the box and the man in the sketch. But undercover police detective Tanith Chen, peeling away a layer of her stifling makeup that created the rough texture and manly appearance she was known for, as it was the opposite of her feminine beauty, remained unsure. This kid parked so long on a park bench and talking to himself was new to the area, else he'd have known about her and her nightly collars of degenerates and drug dealers using her territory for all manner of perversions in the park, perversions now on the decline thanks to her collaring so many who dared "do their thing" on her watch. She'd kept one eye on the suspect in the distance now, his back to her. She began to slowly, cautiously follow the stranger, curious as to what he'd been up to. She'd watched earlier from a safe distance, watched him intentionally leave the package like it was some ransom demand or something. Certainly, her blue sense told her not everything in this picture was kosher.

She found a park lamppost, one of those almost useless ones put up for decoration in the park by the pork-barrel politicians and Daley. Make Chicago beautiful . . . keep Chicago beautiful . . . the park is for the people . . . all a lot of crap, a moneymaking boondoggle the whole thing, as dripping of political favoritism and corruption as the deal with the tow-truck companies in this town. She laughed lightly to herself, recalling what her partner, Gene Kelley said just the night before at the Red Lion Inn where they mingled with other cops and writers and cops who wanted to be writers and writers who wanted to be cops. In a Faux baritone voice, he declared, "If Christ came to Chicago, his fucking donkey would be ticketed at the curb and more'n likely towed to boot by the Lincoln Park pirates. And where in the love of God is Christ going to come up with that kind of cash?"

Under the weak glow of the old-world styled lamppost, Detective Chen pulled forth the stolen note she'd palmed from the box, a cryptic note from mother to son as it turned out, but an eerie, even chilling note at the same time. As Chen read it, she felt the hairs on the back of her neck stand on end. She felt her skin crawl as if a sudden cold rash of creeping satanic fingertips scraped over her soul. She gasped, glanced all around, over her shoulder, half certain that the son of the infamous Matthew Matisak must have the eyes and instincts of a tiger, that he could not only pierce the night with his vision but her very mind, to know what she held in her hand, and to kill her for it.

"My God . . . it's him . . . gotta be the one the APB's out on, the creep that rips people's backs open for their spines, and he and I are the only two people on the planet who know who . . . who he is."

Tanith Chen had never felt so vulnerable or so absolutely alone in her territory before. She feared, even as good as she was, she'd be no match for this cunning madman.

Still he'd kept going, moving north toward the lights of Michigan Avenue, Saks, Neiman Marcus, Lord & Taylor, Water Tower Place. He'd be swallowed up in the crowds. She had to follow, to again catch sight of him, and she had to get backup. She folded and put away the note and the police sketch, noticing that her hands shook. Her fingers struggled with the keypad on her cell phone. As she called for help, she began tearing away her baggy, oversized clothing, dropping it as she went to rid herself of the disguise he would spot. At the same time, her feet moved her fluidly toward Michigan Avenue in the direction the son of Matisak had taken. She'd lost sight of him, and having to pass by hedges, she feared he knew what she was thinking and who she was, and that he might, at any moment, dart out at her. Fleeting thoughts of how great it would be to have the Spine Thief collared by an Asian Chicago policewoman flitted through her mind as well.

And the note she had plucked from the box and folded away. What about that? This was hardcore evidence. It must not be lost or damaged or ruined by her fingerprints or perspiration any further. It needed to be under glass and studied by the experts chasing this guy. It needed FBI attention. This whole damn night needed FBI attention.

Her call to her partner for help went through. Looking now like a jogger, all her makeup peeled away, wearing only sweatpants and T-shirt—a bit chilled by the mix of cool air and stumbling onto the biggest case of her career, Tanith

Chen tried consciously to slow both her mind and her breathing. It didn't work. She breathlessly told her partner what she had, standing now at the perimeter of the park in the shadow of the Drake Hotel, traffic noise causing her to shout into the mouthpiece.

"Where is he now?" asked her partner, Gene Kelley.

She looked all round her. He was nowhere in sight. She had to admit this to Gene. As she did so, she wondered if the killer had somehow doubled-back and faded into the green blackness of the park foliage. Or had he stepped up his pace, going north on the Magnificent Mile?

Gene promised a shitload of backup, so they could cordon off the entire area for six blocks. But Tanith cautioned any sirens, and any big show of force. "You'd just alert him to the fact we're on to him."

"How can you be on to him if you don't know where the fuck he is?" countered Kelley.

"Given the nature of the beast, innocent lives could be put at risk if you come rushing in like the cavalry, Gene. Look, I think he went south on Michigan. I'm going to do what I can to get and keep a visual on him. But no helicopters or guys rappelling down on the avenue unless they can stay out of his sight."

"You go cautiously, Slick."

"I talked to him, Gene. He's a cool customer. Didn't spook, but then he was convinced I was Barney the *Street-Wise* salesman. He had no idea who I was."

"We've all got his likeness now. You were out when it was disseminated. We all know what the guy looks like."

"So do I . . . now." She spotted him in the crowd ahead. She'd jogged, stopping only to talk to Gene. "My God, I got a visual on him!"

"Where's he headed?"

"I dunno. The *Tribune* tower maybe?"

"What, to give himself up?"

"Could be."

"Keep your eyes on him."

"Wait . . . where'd he go? Shit . . . disappeared like smoke. Stepped into a shop doorway or down a side street."

"He may be on to you. Don't take another step. We're on our way."

Two squad cars converged on her location, followed by Gene's unmarked sedan used in backing her up in the park. All the uniformed cops spread out with the caveat to locate Giles Gahran, each with a photo in hand. Gene put a big arm around Tanith. "How's my lady love, Slick?" He'd begun using the nickname shortly after their first partnering.

"Slick is just fine, but damn I really wanted this guy." She carefully pulled out the note she'd lifted from the unattended box. "You think the way I got hold of this it'll stand up in a court of law?" She held it out between thumb and forefinger, gingerly, when a Chicago gust stole it away, sending her chasing after it.

"Fuck!" The document seemed as elusive as Gahran. It took Gene stomping on it, dirtying it badly, to stop it from completely blowing off.

"You got hold of the FBI?" she asked.

"They got word, yeah. All nine yards of it. Couple of their agents from Milwaukee've been canvassing and scouring the city for Gahran. Imagine it, Slick, this freak that rips out people's goddamn spines."

"So you tell 'em about the note?"

"Yeah."

"And the news that this guy is . . . or may be related to Mad Matthew Matisak, the creep caught here in Chicago like a decade ago and put away and escaped and finally brought down in New Orleans?"

"I relayed all of it, Slick, all of it."

"Then why in hell aren't they all over this? Where the fuck are they?"

"Apparently, they've run down an apartment house where he's staying. They're sitting on it."

"A stakeout?"

"Waiting, yeah, for a damn warrant for search and seizure, all ready to make an arrest if and when he shows."

Another unmarked car arrived, and a tall, broad-shouldered, handsome FBI agent who introduced himself as Laughlin made long eye contact with Chen in her sweats. "You're the one with the weird story of having run into Giles Gahran, and is that the document you found?"

She looked down at the soiled note, the stains now smeared across the ink lettering. Agent Laughlin said, "Looks like an old Underwood style typewriter. But our boys and girls at the lab'll know soon enough. They're trained on this kind of thing."

"Sorry about the mess we made of it," she apologized.

"Don't worry. We've managed around a lot worse." He read the note and his face went ashen, two shades lighter.

"You all right, Agent Laughlin?" she asked.

"This is what I call the true nature of evil."

"A real Mommie Dearest story in it, that's for sure."

"Look . . . it appears you all have lost sight of him, and our best chance now is to catch him at the rental, and Petersaul and Cates have that covered, so . . . how 'bout if . . ."

Gene instinctively read her body language that told him to disappear.

"Yes, Agent?"

"Well, I mean . . . have you had a bite? There's a great restaurant—Joe's Chicago just a couple blocks up back of the Marriott. Best of Chicago."

"Oh, yeah, great place across from the . . . yeah . . . I am famished after all that's happened."

"I'll get your stuff outta the park if none of the real bums have stolen it already," Gene called to her. Gene signaled to the uniforms moving from storefront to storefront on the most protected mile of real estate in the city that they were done here.

The police presence disappeared as quickly as it had materialized.

GILES Gahran had insisted he be allowed to take his box up on the enormous shining Ferris wheel with him. The operator argued that he'd be happy to set it aside and hold it in a safe place until his return. It took an additional twenty to show the man how seriously Giles wanted to take the box on the ride.

"Look man, I got no metal detectors here. I can't know what the fuck is in that box. And never in life ever seeing a box like that. You say it's just photos and papers, stuff important only to you, but how am I to know you ain't got something, you know, sinister in the box. And even if you don't got something, you know, like that in there, I got people I gotta answer to and I need this job. You got no idea."

"Look," Giles directed his eyes to the box. Giles shuffled his hand through all the papers. Just paper. Feel how light."

The operator waved him off. "Yeah . . . OK . . . I can see it ain't nothing but paper, but still the rule is nothing carried on, not even a friggin' umbrella even, not even if it looks like rain, you know, 'cause if something fell off, it's a damn instant projectile, you see my drift?"

Giles slipped in another forty atop the twenty.

The operator glanced around. Finally, he nodded, a cigar bobbing in his mouth. "OK, but you gotta promise to keep that thing from falling. It falls out, you could hurt somebody at such heights, you know. Don't matter how light it is."

Giles got aboard the car with the box. He'd had to again untie it to demonstrate its harmlessness to the fool, and now he could not place it on his lap because of the bar placed across his front. From his coat pocket, he pulled forth the

Spigot—his father's blood-draining device—and replaced it in the box.

"The wheel's so damn big, it only goes around once, you know? Don't want any complaints," the operator said in a monotone that spoke of an eternal boredom. And so the ride began.

The operator moved Giles and his cargo by increments as he let off others who had already made the trip to the top, carefully monitoring weight and balance as he did so. Giles's trip to the stars was stop-start, stop-start, not the smooth ride he'd expected, and it didn't allow for any sensation of flight to occur. Rather for Giles, the box of the gondola gave him the sensation of being inside the box he carried on with him.

Finally, he arrived near the top of the mammoth arc. Held here as the operator far below now continued his endless quest of balance, counterweight, balance, counterweight, working now with people at Giles's extreme opposite as new arrivals boarded.

Then the gondola lurched, and Giles's box slid from the seat beside him, spilling onto the footrest, clippings and photos threatening to spill over the side, along with the glass-and-metal contraption his father's patent papers had referred to as the Spigot.

Giles knee-jerk response had him reach for the box, and in lurching forward, the gondola swung wildly beneath him, and one of the news clippings scuttled over the side. Unable to grab the box, the Spigot or the papers, his arm and body held in check by the bar, Giles watched the devilish wind whip in and dance around the papers, flirting with the papers as they continued to move snakelike from the spilled box. "Fuck, fuck, fucking hell! Is this how you want it, Mother? Is this what we've been waiting for?"

People below began to see small newspaper clippings floating down to the midway at Navy Pier. People in the cars below him caught a few of the clippings in their cars, and they heard his swearing, although they could not see him. One man yelled up at him, "Shut your dirty mouth! I have little kids down here!"

Giles finally pried loose the restraining bar but his foot kicked the box as if guided there by Mother, and the entire box, along with the Spigot, slid incrementally along the floorboard of the car. Giles went to his knees for the box, but the foot area refused to accommodate his size. As a result, his bulk shook the gondola badly. The operator had begun cursing sailor fashion at Giles to remain seated and to calm himself. People on the ground feared a suicide attempt in the making.

Then he realized the note written by Mother to him overlaying the pictures and the clippings that told of the history of Mad Matthew Matisak was *gone*. He knew it had not been swept out of the gondola, but he could not see it anywhere with the paperwork.

He finally got a firm hold of the box and the Spigot and returned to his seat, clutching both in his lap, rifling through the dense pile for any sign of Mother's departing note to him. It had simply vanished. But he had not seen it go out over the side.

"The bum in the park. That old bastard . . . like some kind of prophet. It had to be him."

The wheel lurched forward and down, stopping at each gondola now as the operator began pulling people off as quickly as possible. Those pulled off began to form a small crowd at the base of the Ferris wheel, some angry, most confused, all of them looking up to where Giles sat waiting his turn to be removed from the wheel.

"Lovely up here, isn't it, Mother? Just beautiful. Wonder what it would be like to end it all right here. To take the one-hundred-fifty-foot leap. You, me, Father here. What a spectacular splash we'd make. Surely, it will make my artwork go through the roof at Cafe Avanti, if they sell it before the cops can confiscate it."

He stood in the gondola, rocking it as he prepared to

jump. But a dizziness from having had nothing to eat for more than twenty-four hours and the height conspired against any resolve he may have had. He plopped back onto the seat and, in a fit of rage at having lost his resolve to end this misery called life, began filling his hands with words of Father and tossing all the photos, clippings, sketches, court documents, paperback books and magazine articles and bubble-gum cards devoted to Matthew Matisak out over the side of his sinking ship.

The papers floated down the length and breadth of the Ferris wheel like confetti now, growing larger as they meandered down and down. The first snowflake-like sheets and half sheets were now within grasp of the adults standing guard about their children below. In a moment, the midway floor around the wheel was littered with the debris of the box.

Save for the Spigot, the box sat empty now, and it lay sad beside Giles as the operator pulled him roughly out of the gondola, angry and snatching at his clothes, whipping him to the ground and throwing the box at him, shouting, "And don't fucking ever come back!"

The curious who could read stood about looking at the clippings and pictures they'd gathered up, and they stared from the newspaper stories and other stuff to Giles. He felt no pity or concern from this crowd, only confusion and fear and perhaps, if they guessed the truth, loathing.

Giles handed the ornate box with its now rattling contents to a small smiling boy standing closest to him, his mother's arms draped about him in protective stance.

"What's your name?" he asked the boy.

Perhaps five or six, the handsome, happy little boy proudly shouted, "Kevin!"

"Go ahead. You like the box? You keep it."

Little big-eyed Kevin looked up to his mother on high, craning his neck, for the OK. She nodded her approval.

"Put your frogs and your play toys in it for me, Kevin. All the things that make you happy."

"I will . . . I will."

Giles got to his feet and shambled off, muttering, "The box'll like that, having a new owner with new stuff."

Giles heard the sound of sirens. Someone had called the cops.

He must get away. Must blend into the crowd and rush, get some rest, try to clear his head now that he had divested himself, finally, of Father. What to do next? Where to go? What of his showing at the cafe? All seemed lost and confused now. But after a good night's rest . . . perhaps he could think clearly enough to find a way out, one that didn't involve a Ferris wheel and a failed attempt at leaping off it.

"Maybe I can find the nerve to use this," he said aloud to himself, fingering the .22-caliber gun he'd purchased earlier on the street. "A shoot-out with the cops. They're bound to kill me. They gotta fire on a man who opens up on a crowd like this."

He saw a small army of uniforms coming at him, and a number of plainclothes detectives as well. A door marked GARAGE opened on the enormous parking facility at Navy Pier. Giles weaved in and out of the aisles as police rushed the Ferris wheel, responding to a call about some nutcase dropping newspaper clippings from atop the wheel, all of which related to Mad Matthew Matisak.

Giles held firm to the gun in his pocket, at the ready if he had a moment's opportunity to take advantage of the cops, to use them one final time. To go out under his own terms. But he waltzed from the garage unimpeded and down the darkened little street running alongside the inlet to the Chicago River where boats sat silent, some idling, waiting to board passengers.

He grabbed on to a rope and climbed aboard one of the many cruise boats plying up and down the water, asking if he might exit at Irving Park.

"Absolutely," said the captain's mate who welcomed him

aboard. "What sort of ruckus is going on at the midway?"

"Not sure . . . some damn fool caused a big disturbance at the Ferris wheel, I think."

Giles found a seat on the boat and stared across the water. A waitress came to his table and asked what he'd like to drink.

"Spinal fluid," he said.

She laughed a giggling, tinkling, feminine laugh. She had a southern accent. "Ho-whoa, now *you* are a funnin' me ain't-cha now? I been waitressin' from Georgia to here for six years, but I never heard that one. Bartender's gonna hafta dig out his drink manual for a Spinal Tap. Is it some new kinda Chicago drink?"

"Yeah, tell your bartender to mix Johnnie Walker Red in equal parts with a tumbler of Absolut Vodka, J&B Scotch, gin, vermouth and three inches of white grape juice—and you got Spinal Fluid."

"I better write that down!" she joked back.

The boat began to move away from the dock, the pull of the current wanting to take it opposite of its engines, but the engines revved and they were off to follow the coast of the lake first south toward the museums to see the magnificent multicolored Buckingham Fountain and the skyline of Chicago, for the photo-obsessed tourists, and then they would turn and do the shuttle run north.

The city lights twinkled as if alive in the distance. Beautiful beneath a warming breeze. *How Lucinda would have loved this boat ride*, Giles thought.

NINETEEN

We must be still and still moving
Into another intensity
For a further union, a deeper communion,
through the dark cold and empty desolation.

— T. S. ELIOT

SURVEILLANCE of Giles Gahran's rented apartment in Chicago continued. Watching for any sign of him, Petersaul and Cates spent the time discussing and arguing their next step.

Petersaul shook her head from behind the wheel of the unmarked sedan. "No way we collar him without a warrant or provocation."

"We approach him, he runs, you got provocation."

"Yeah, but suppose he never comes out?"

"We don't know that he's even inside there, Pete. If the local PD has him at Michigan Avenue!"

"Do you really think they actually spotted him, or someone who looks like him? Our collaring this bastard will make up for our screw up with the governor in Oregon, Cates."

"Wait a minute! We didn't screw up. How'er we to know the governor of Oregon is a prick? When Darwin didn't give us a heads up on the guy, Pete? All we did was report the facts. Hell . . . people sure can distort the facts."

"We get a collar that turns out to be this brutal guy who's ripped out the spines now of four women in four separate venues . . ."

"Three venues. Two were killed on our watch in our town, Olsen and Wellingham, and let's not forget the reward for the arrest and conviction. Honey, with that kind of money I might even begin to look good to you, and we could retire to Acapulco until we got our heads straight and want to surface. I hear the diving there's great. You scuba? Snorkel? Have any desire to see me in a bathing suit?"

She exaggeratedly shook her head and pulled at her ears and hair. "God let me get that image outta my mind."

They laughed at the good-natured ribbing.

"I'm serious about you getting interested in a nice guy who is unattached, though, Petie girl. I mean——"

"Will you stop mothering . . . I mean fathering me! You keep it up, I'm going to put in for a new partner."

He raised his hands in mock surrender. "Hey, God forbid someone tell you what's good for you, and all 'bout the pain of forbidden fruit from one who knows. Experience, baby, nothing like it, along with adversity in human relationships."

"Adversity? You?"

"Adversity—father of invention I say, and damn sure the invention of the lie, and the biggest of all lies, the one we tell oursel——"

"Shut up! There he is! It's got to be him. He fits Gahran's description and he's carrying an oversized bag."

"The easel bag. He's got it on his back."

"You reckon it's chock-full with another spinal rack?"

"That'd give us all the evidence we need," replied Cates, "unless he's carrying art books."

"How do you want to approach? You front, me back or vice versa?"

"All the evidence we need could be sitting up there in his apartment. Maybe we should let him go in, knock on the door."

"We need that fucking warrant!"

"A warrant can take hours if we get a liberal judge, and even then it won't give us the latitude we need. Better to get him to *invite* us in," advised the senior agent, Cates. "Then anything in plain sight is fair game."

"But he's not likely to do that." She whipped out her .9mm automatic and taped it to her leg. "Here's my invitation, and besides, who can resist a long-legged, young, impressionable, shapely art groupie? I'll tell him Lucinda Wellingham sent me. He'll be so freaked by that—"

"—that he'll kill you, Pete!"

"—that he'll invite me in to see his etchings. He makes one wrong move, and that's when I drop his ass, cuff him and call you in to help me search."

"Sounds fuckin' risk free, sure. No, Pete . . . can't let you do that. I let you do that, and you get even a scratch on your pretty little derrière, and Darwin'll have *my* ass."

"It'll just require a little undercover work. It's legal. It won't come back to haunt us. I follow him to the local bar, get him to pick me up. What could be simpler?"

"All right . . . if you're sure, but the moment I think you're in danger, I come crashing in with guns blazing, you got that?"

"You're on."

"Gotta treat this guy like the snake he is," began Cates. "And dead or alive, I don't care how we do it, Pete, but I do say *we* nab this guy, take the glory ourselves."

They sat huddled in the chilly sedan outside the apartment rented to their quarry, a cold wind whipping around the car, fingers of cold drafting up through every vent. "You ready to go knock at the door of the supposed son of Mad Matthew Matisak?"

"Yeah, sure . . . but we call Darwin first. We let him know our every step, just as he ordered."

"Come on with that shit," Cates complained, his curmudgeon features pinched in consternation. "He ain't here to blow your nose, Pete."

Amanda Petersaul frowned, ignored Cates, and dialed Darwin's number as the suspect, one Giles Gahran, went through his front door without noticing them, straight up to his room where a light came on.

THE phone rang in Robert Towne's pocket inside the van, inside the hangar as the filming of his brief statement was underway.

Towne raised his hands in a gesture of confusion as the phone continued to ring.

"Shit! Cut! Cut!" shouted the serious young man directing the tape who had played one of the power and light decoys at the prison. "Can't work like this, people," he kiddingly said.

"Answer the call," Jessica said. "It could be Petersaul in Chicago with good news."

"Maybe you should answer it," countered Towne. "She's not going to recognize my voice."

"Are you kidding? You sound just like Darwin." Still, Jessica took the ringing phone he extended. She announced herself to the caller, adding, "What can I do for you?"

"This is Petersaul. Where's Darwin? I've an update for him. It's urg—"

"He's somewhat indisposed at the moment."

"Indisposed? How so?"

Petersaul's tone gave her away in the slight twinge of building anger. "This is urgent," she repeated. "Put him on, Dr. Coran."

"I'd have to smuggle the phone into the Oregon state pen to do that."

"What? What are you talking about?"

"He's exchanged places with his look-a-like brother, Robert—"

"—Towne, I know . . . I know they are brothers. Now please explain to me whose brilliant idea it was to put Darwin on death row! Are you people all as crazy as . . . as . . ."

"As Darwin? It was my idea, but Darwin is loving it, and we have everything under control. He's not going to be executed, and neither is his brother."

"So you're all now fugitives?"

"One way to look at it. So, what have you got for us, and how soon can we take this guy Gahran into custody and start sweating out a confession?"

"We're sitting outside his apartment."

"Really! Excellent! How did you locate him?"

"Followed the trail of a train ticket to a taxicab that brought him here. It helped that we had the composite drawing got up from the fire marshal and the landlady in Milwaukee."

"Do you have a warrant for search and seizure?"

"Not yet, but we've been here less than an hour, trying to determine if he's in or out. Now we know he's in. Meanwhile, the field office is working on a search warrant, yes."

"Don't move on him without the warrant and backup. We don't want this creep slipping through any legal loopholes later, and you certainly don't want him giving you the slip."

"Don't worry. Like I said we're all over this guy and he doesn't even know we're parked on his—"

Two gunshots rang out along with the sound of shattered glass and a scream—Petersaul's scream, then silence.

Jessica shouted into the phone, calling Petersaul repeatedly but to no avail, when suddenly a male voice with a slightly familiar, irritating motorboat-like gravelly sound behind it said, "Is it you, my might've-been Mother? Dr. Jessica Coran?"

"Gahran?"

"The one who killed my father?"

"Listen to me, Giles."

"Giles is it? Do you have any idea how much I hate you? Be wise. Don't come looking for me, or you will lose a major portion of your skeletal makeup like these two when I'm finished with them."

"Giles, you need help."

"Help? I've done quite well without anyone's help. Or do you mean to say that you wish to help me debone these two?"

"Giles, I know why you hurt, how deeply you hurt. I know how awful your mother—"

"Do you now understand me—you—Father's obsession?"

"I do, more than anyone on the planet, I do."

She struggled to keep him engaged, her mind doing cartwheels. She wrote out a note telling Richard to call Chicago PD to get a car immediately to the address where Petersaul and Cates had staked out the apartment. Richard was immediately on it.

Giles said over the phone, "Have I become your obsession, Jessica? You keep coming at me like it's so, like you're looking for Father in me. If so, there's no stopping the inevitable, is there, and you become my obsession, and together, we are both mad."

"Giles, there's a name for what you have, a mental disorder, and there are drugs and therapies, and we will get you the best doctors in the—"

"Only doctor I want is you, Jessica. You'd make a wonderful gift for dear old Dad."

"It does not have to come to that, life or death for either of us."

"They say history repeats itself. It happens all over again like New Orleans in that Mardi Gras graveyard where you almost died. We'll just have to find the proper time and place, you and me. But I won't take just your blood like Father."

"You don't have to be like him, Giles!"

"But I am . . . just like Father. And I will take all of you. I'm going to cut out"—she heard him rummaging through Petersaul's wallet—"to cut out Agent Petersaul's spine like the others, you can be sure, along with this fat man, Cates."

Jessica heard the sound of the car's ignition, and then Giles Gahran came back on. "I know you've been chasing me just as you chased my father before me, as you've chased all the truly brilliant and ingenious monsters, all the heirs to Jack the Ripper, all of us. But if you come after me, I will debone you, do you understand? Debone you." His laughter was the last thing she heard before the phone went dead.

"Christ! I don't even know the address." Jessica was rattled, but she knew she had to remain calm.

"Chicago field office agents are racing to the scene now," Richard told her. "They're on it, Jess. Nothing we can do but pray they cut off his escape and that our agents are not dead."

"Not sure I want to wish them alive in his hands," she replied.

Robert Towne listened closely to the terrible turn of events.

"We've got to get to Chicago without any further delay!" she announced once off the line with Chicago FBI, who were on the lookout now for the car, the apartment at 3010 North Sheffield, the Hermitage Apartments, in the Wrigley Field ballpark area known locally as Wrigleyville.

"They're going to treat the apartment as a crime scene. We'll see it as is, untouched. They hope to have word on the missing field vehicle, Agents Petersaul and Cates, and the suspect by time we get there."

"What're we waiting for?" asked Sharpe. "The jet is juiced up."

"What about our video?" asked the young director. "This is going to go to CNN, Fox, MSNBC, all of 'em. It's going to put Scorp-Ion Productions on the fucking map, man."

"Perhaps more than you know. How dramatic will it be to do a live feed from a jet plane to the networks? And can you do it? Do you have the equipment for it?"

"Are you kidding? We've got state-of-the-art, same as reporters had during the Iraqi war. Sure . . ."

"Terrific, but there's to be no information going out about our destination."

The young man, Darren Callahan, turned to his technicians and fellow actors. "So, who's up for a trip to Chicago?"

"Cool!"

"Way cool!"

"I'm in, man."

"Hey, bud, this is going to rock!"

The others looked at Jessica with large, expectant eyes. She replied, "Why the hell not? My expense account is blown anyway."

"BEFORE we send this out to every major network in America—"

"This is going worldwide, Dr. Coran," Callahan corrected. "The final take, after we're OK with the last edit and audio, is going to hit a number of satellites at once, and it's going via laser-beam feed to the world."

"All the better. But we give Governor Hughes one last chance to call the warden for a stay."

"Damn, can't we just run it?" asked Callahan. "It's great stuff."

Sharpe replied, "The kid's right. Hughes had his chance. Fuck him."

"No, Richard. We lay it all out for Hughes. Give him fair warning."

"He's not going to believe you, Jess. It's just a waste of time."

"All the same, we warn him."

"Prick doesn't deserve any warning," said Towne, "but go ahead, Dr. Coran."

Jess contacted Hughes's office, getting Mrs. Dornan, who began making excuses for her boss, saying he couldn't be disturbed.

"You mean he's sleeping through the execution?"

"Not at all. He's simply washed his hands of your . . . you crusaders."

"Mrs. Dornan, I called to give him fair warning. The man sitting in the cell on your death row is not Robert Towne but his brother, Darwin Reynolds."

"What? I've never heard of such . . . such a bold ploy in all my life. The very idea."

"We have a tape of the exchange between the brothers, and a blood test performed by Dr. Waters only an hour ago will prove you have Agent Darwin Reynolds on death row and not Towne. Towne is here with me, on a jet plane, thirty thousand feet over D.C.," she lied. "Now, would you care to wake the governor or not? Your call, dearie. Oh, and by the way, within fifteen minutes, the story is going to break on every network in the U.S. and abroad."

"I-I-I will get the governor on the line. Hold on. Hold on."

It took several minutes but finally Hughes, his voice thick with sleep, came on, asking, "What is this nonsense, Dr. Coran? Do you know how upset you have made Mrs. Dornan, my personal—"

"You don't have Towne on death row."

"What're you saying?"

"The FBI has Towne. *I* have Towne. *You* have Reynolds. Take a lot closer look at the man you intend on executing while you sleep."

"This is preposterous, a lie."

"Ask Warden Gwingault why Dr. Waters gave your phony Towne a last-minute blood test tonight, and it will prove what I say. Or call Dr. Waters directly and put it to him. He is expecting your call, and he expects to lose his contract with the state over this." She gave him Waters's phone number. "He is waiting for your call."

"You're bluffing, and if you aren't . . . if there is anything to this . . . if you *have* broken a man out of a maximum-security prison, you will pay, all of you to the fullest extent of Oregon law, you will—"

"Five minutes!" Jessica hung up on him.

The pilot informed them that he would start his descent for Chicago in ten minutes. "We gave the governor five minutes to call off the execution. If we don't hear back, then it's a go."

The film production company hoped for a go. She could see it in their anxious eyes. Richard's eyes told her he held out no hope for the governor's coming around, and Towne voiced what was on everyone's mind. "Even if he does call the warden now, you people ought to air that tape."

GILES had driven the two dead cops, whom he had since discovered to be Milwaukee-based FBI, to the castlelike Gothic-gated Rosehill Cemetery at 5800 North Ravenswood where he drove the car into the enclosed courtyard just beyond the open mouth of the castle. Ever interested in the "permanent" residents of a city, ever the cemetery buff and headstone reader, Giles had gotten a book called *The Graveyards of Chicago*. He'd earlier visited Rosehill with his box, thinking he might buy a plot and have the damn thing buried along-side some of Chicago's most famous scoundrels and get-rich quick artists, schemers, dreamers and real-estate investors whose final investment had been plots here at Rosehill.

He pulled the car to a stop and one by one, he groped and tugged and dropped the dead weight onto the paved court-yard, an enormous foyer leading up to the final gate, locked against him at this hour.

When he had slipped through the apartment building

after seeing the two cops, and had sneaked around the back of their vehicle where they seemed in argument over their next step, he had brought his bag with him, filled with his tools, and the gun he had purchased as a precaution walking Chicago city streets. But now the hefty little .22-caliber proved extremely fortuitous.

He had fired a single shot into each of their craniums. The male never knew what hit him, but glass and his brain matter had embedded in the woman's cheek, sending up a shriek of shock and pain, and then he put one in her head. She didn't suffer long.

He now cut away the clothing from each body and began cutting away at each back from top to bottom, determined to take their spinal cords off with him. He had just finished work over the man, lifting out his cord when he heard a noise, someone with a huge flashlight, the beam raking over them where they were, Giles and his two new friends.

He knew the car could not be missed, that the watchman would come to investigate, even if he didn't know what he was looking at. Giles slipped just the other side of the car, realizing only now that he'd left his bone saw and bag out in plain view with the two mutilated bodies. Cates's spine, too, lay alongside him.

The watchman at first ambled over, yelling as if he'd discovered some pesky repeat offenders, teens out to test their metal against the neighborhood superstitions. "Get yourselves and that car outta here! This time o'night! Go home!"

Gaining no response, he found his cell phone and made a call. "Something strange out here, Milos. Think maybe I ought to call the cops again? OK . . . You're on your way. I'll wait till you get here."

The watchman put down his phone, stuffing it into his overalls, the nametag sewn into them reading Liam. Raising his light overhead, he cautiously approached the two bodies lying alongside the deserted car. "Fun's over, you two! Time to get home to your—"

The watchman stopped as if hit by a wall of horror, the light from his Bic Torchlight wavering and wildly illuminating the tops of nearby trees. Visibly shaken, he again grabbed for his phone, this time dialing 911. The watchman looked energized somehow, animated, his mannerisms and moves exaggerated. Turning wildly leaflike in the blustering Chicago wind. Finally, the man found his legs and ran to put distance between himself and the awful mutilations not twenty yards from him.

Giles fired a single bullet and it sank a tiny hole through the back of the man's spine, making him fall, twitching on the way down, and crying out, sniveling, he continued in fits like a wind-up toy lying on its side.

He wasn't dead when Giles turned his face away, and facedown, began tearing away his clothes with the titanium scalpel he used. Once the twitching man's back was exposed, he dug into him with the scalpel and carved out the now familiar long coffin-shaped box of flesh from his back as the screaming subsided and finally died with his victim going into blood-loss trauma.

Holding a spinal column in each hand, Giles felt an overwhelming sense of power course through his veins. He turned his eyes back on the woman, Agent Petersaul. "Not to be greedy, but I want yours, too," he said to the dead woman. "This will make Chicago headlines and serial killer history. Three spines in one night. Maybe I'll get my own bubble-gum card, like Dad."

Giles went to the female whose back he had earlier bared. Stuffing each of the already stolen treasures into his easel bag, and setting this aside, its Wirtz Art Supplies logo shiny in the half light of sodium vapor lamps peeking over the castle walls, Giles made a move toward Petersaul. She had a lovely, long back, graceful, gazellelike. *It must contain a beautiful spine,* he thought. Brushing off the leaves and debris that had fallen on her, Giles felt her still-warm body, when suddenly beneath his hand, she *moved.*

Independent of his touch, she had moved.

She was alive.

She moaned in utter distress, the sound of a keening animal in pain.

"Hellllllllllpa-pa-meee!" she cried, unable to be loud about it.

Giles leaned back on his haunches and watched her and listened to her pain like a perched gargoyle or gremlin, fascinated by the hand of death as it pressed in upon this stranger who did not resemble Mother in the least, but whose spine more readily would.

The lights of a cruising police car alerted Giles. The Chicago city cruiser's side panel spotlight scanned on-off as its beam cleared the .castle entrance, but it didn't quite make the distance from street to the furthermost inner courtyard where Petersaul's car stood and her body lay alongside the other two. The police squad car moved slowly by and continued like a grazing animal.

"Either way, Hughes can forget about reelection," Sharpe said as they watched the young production team polish the final take, finish the final splice, and add audio onto the computer feed beamed to satellites spread across the cosmos.

Everyone on the plane held a collective breath as the feed was beamed to the world. Richard grasped Jessica's hands and clasped them in both his. "Whatever happens, we have the knowledge of having done the right thing. Perhaps not the wise thing, perhaps not the prudent thing and perhaps not the legal thing, but the morally correct thing."

"Rare nowadays," muttered Robert Towne. "Rare to see justice and good old-fashioned revenge prevail, too. Hughes's political future is in the shitlands now."

They all laughed at this.

"All the same, I think I'd better call Warden Gwingault," suggested Jessica.

Robert asked, "Just to be on the safe side?"

"Make sure he's looking at the late-night news."

She made the call to alert Warden Donald Gwingault, telling him to turn on the news.

"What channel?"

"Any channel."

In a moment, she heard the warden gasp and say, "Oh, my God."

"Have you heard from the governor yet to put an end to this?"

"No, not a word. Does Hughes *know* about this?"

"He does by now."

"I hardly believe my eyes. How did you manage to make a switch like that with my guards on hand, and with cameras running, and damn it, how'd you get that tape out of our library and past our checkpoints?"

"Will you call me, Mr. Gwingault, at my cell phone number the moment you hear from Hughes?"

"I don't have to hear from Hughes if this is true. If this is true, we have an innocent man on our Green Mile who's had his shoes replaced by booties, his head shaven, his spiritual needs met and his last supper."

"Mr. Gwingault, you always did have an innocent man on your row."

"I'm putting an end to this right now."

"Excellent."

"And just where is Towne now?"

"Catch us if you can, Warden." She hung up, knowing that any forward movement toward an execution in Oregon was at an end. She informed the others of Warden Gwingault's action.

Cheers filled the airplane.

"Darwin's under arrest now," said Towne sadly once the

euphoria had died away. "Gone from an FBI field chief to a common criminal in lockup."

"Darwin knew that going in," Richard assured him.

The pilot announced that they were on descent for the runway at O'Hare, and he asked everyone to buckle in.

The news of what they had done spread wildfire fashion, and FBI headquarters was abuzz with the story.

One of the young techs on board the plane had a hand-held Sony television and he silenced everyone as an excited Wolf Blitzer shared the story with his viewers. "News networks across America are now carrying this incredible breaking story. A party of anti-capital punishment conspirators, including a number of FBI personnel, have successfully helped convicted killer Robert W. Towne in a secretive escape from death row in Portland, Oregon, and the man now sitting on death row in his stead is his brother, FBI Agent Xavier Darwin Reynolds."

The news would be all over Chicago even before they landed. Towne, still worried, erupted with, "What if Hughes convinces Gwingault and the rest that it's all a hoax, what we say we did? What if he goes through with the goddamn execution?"

"It won't happen. Gwingault won't let it happen," she assured Towne.

Richard came to her support. "It can't happen now with so many eyes trained on him."

"And J. J.'s precious state," Jessica assured Towne as she buckled into her seat for landing, the last to do so.

"Not till we get that call from Darwin am I going to be satisfied," Towne replied.

TWENTY

AT the apartment rented by Gahran, Jessica took control, her FBI badge extended as she passed local authorities. "Any word on Petersaul or Cates?" she asked Harry Laughlin, the Chicago FBI field office chief.

"Not a word. The car's not been found, either."

"And no sightings of Gahran?"

"Perhaps in time. We just got the sketch around, and it missed the evening papers. It'll have to wait until tomorrow."

"What about the apartment? Anything of interest?" asked Sharpe, displaying his badge.

"Nothing of consequence. Lotta charcoal sketches but no blood, no bones, no souvenirs."

"How soon were your guys on the scene here after your last communication with Petersaul? After she requested the warrant for the place?"

"An hour, maybe an hour-ten."

"He may've had time to clean out anything incriminating."

"Found something!" shouted one of the men going through the artists tools, instruments, paint cases and boxes. He held up a box. "Scalpels—thirteen artists quality scalpels."

"Bag 'em. We'll run tests for blood residue," Jessica assured everyone in the room.

"Take a look at what's on the guy's bookshelf," came another tech, holding several old yellowed volumes in his hands, one shiny with beautiful binding, green with foil-like green lettering.

Jessica and Richard began to closely examine the reading material of one Giles Gahran. "Gahran's taste in reading," Richard muttered, noting how dog-eared and marked up and highlighted portions of one volume were.

"A strange collection of bizarre materials. Books I've not come across before."

Jessica looked over each spine and cover. She and Sharpe passed each to the other as they examined the killer's bedtime reading.

"What the hell is this?" asked Sharpe of her. "*The Grand Symbol?*"

She took the volume and read the title aloud, "*Man As Grand Symbol of the Mysteries* by Manly Palmer Hall. Philosophical Research Society, 5th edition, Los Angeles, 1947." She glanced quickly through it. "A book on the symbolic power of the spinal column."

"Here's one simply titled *The Body*," said Sharpe. "By an Anthony Smith. Oh, a London publisher, Allen and Unwin, 1968—a little more current, but not by much."

She read a third title. "C.A.S. Williams's *Encyclopedia of Chinese Symbolism and Art Motifs*, 1960. You got me beat. Oh, look . . . a chapter in here on the backbone as an artistic construct."

"Damn, tell me what is a 'luz bone'?" he asked, handing her yet another book to peruse.

"*The Bone Called Luz* by F.H. Garrison," she read the spine of the green book. Opening it to the title page, she continued. "New York Medical Journal, 1910. Pages marked here." She flipped through to the marked pages, muttering, "Ninety-two . . . and 149 to 152."

"What're they on?"

"Both sections on the backbone."

Agent Harry Laughlin greeted someone at the door, a sharply dressed, shapely Asian black-haired officer he introduced as Tanith Chen. She shook hands with Sharpe and Jessica as she held an ornate leather box tied with ribbon into a comical bow. "What's in the box?" asked Jessica.

Chen and Laughlin exchanged a glance. "You want to break the news?" asked Chen.

"She's already had an inkling that this guy thinks he's somehow related to Matisak," Laughlin explained, bringing Chen up to date. "But I think she needs to know the extent of this guy's psychosis and possible fixation on her." Laughlin called another agent to get him the duplicate made of the letter now in an FBI lab.

"This overlaid all the clippings and articles in the box," he told Jessica and Richard who still stood with one of Gahran's books in his hands.

Sharpe lobbed the book onto the small bed and looked at the copy of the document. He read it with a shiver going down his spine. "Jess, I don't think you need see any more of this or the box it came from. Let's get out of here for some air."

She frowned at him and snatched the letter out of his grasp, quickly reading it, finding it hard to swallow. "This woman . . . she was likely mad herself . . . no proof of her being with Matisak. At no time in the course of our investigation or during his trial, or in all those years he spent in prison did she ever surface, and now this? It's got to be bullshit."

"We'll know if we can find some DNA on the silverware and glasses left in the sink, match it up to what's on file about Matisak," said Sharpe, taking a deep breath.

"Seems Gahran went up to the top of the Ferris wheel out at Navy Pier," said Chen. "He'd gone there from the

park. I was tailing him in fact, when he disappeared on
Michigan Ave."

"Witnesses say he emptied this box and its contents over
the side," added Laughlin, dropping the box with a heavy
thud on a table between them now. "And while he appeared
interested in killing himself, our Quasimodo failed to follow the box down."

"You saying he's a hunchback, too?" asked Jessica.

"Only in spirit, I mean . . . way his mother meted it out
to him," Laughlin softly replied.

Chen added, "Gahran handed the empty box to a little
boy at the amusement ride, and we made the boy cry . . .
confiscated it, along with as much of its contents as we
could recover. Some jerk wanted to sell us a fistful of clippings he had confiscated!"

"So the box is stuffed with what Matisak memorabilia?"
Jessica asked. "A lot of Goth heads and weirdos buy all
kinds of crappy serial killer paraphernalia. They can buy it
on fucking eBay."

"This is no collector at work. This woman got hold of
some of the original crime-scene photos—and I don't mean
copies downloaded from AutopsiesRus.com or ME.org.
These are straight outta the case files, some from the actual
Matisak autopsy."

"The one that cleared me of any wrongdoing in his
death, you mean?" she replied.

"How the woman got them I haven't a clue, but you can
bet money or goods of some sort passed hands. There's stuff
here you'll never see on a website, not even that sick fuck
Michael Slade's web page has stuff like this."

"See for yourself," added Chen.

Jessica untied the bow and carefully lifted the lid, and
she gasped at its contents. She turned and buried her head
in Richard's chest, heaving a sigh and quietly sobbing. The
picture laying atop the jumbled mess was a coroner's shot of
a candy striper hanging from a rafter in an old shack in

Wekosha, Wisconsin. Jessica recalled her vividly as the first victim to lead them to Matisak. Jessica turned the photo over as she didn't want to see it anymore only to find scribbled on back the name of the victim and the price Larina Gahran had paid for it from some creep named Scarborough. "Bastard boyfriend of hers pimped her out in life, and sold her in death as well," she muttered. "Like to know what rung in hell is waiting for him."

"Him and the guy that sold it to him," agreed Laughlin.

"I think you're going to want to see this, Dr. Coran." Chen handed her a shot of an aged woman and man hanging from their heels in a barn by tenderhooks, chains and pulleys, an old horse carriage overhead in the barn with them where they died.

"The Red Birds, a lovely old couple living on an Oklahoma Indian reservation soil who had made the terrible mistake of allowing Matisak to dine with them," said Jessica as she stared at the picture. "He dined on their blood."

"Is that it with the coroner's photos? Are there any more like this?" asked Sharpe, a tincture of concern in his voice. Jessica knew the concern was for her.

"Ahhh, no, just newspaper photos but nothing like this except . . ." Chen hesitated.

"There's one picture we thought it best to remove," added Laughlin.

"What picture is that?"

"Otto Boutine."

"Otto?" Boutine had died trying to save Jessica from Matisak.

"His autopsy photos, several of them. That autopsy was done right here in Chicago, we are investigating how those photos got into Larina Gahran's possession."

Sharpe and Jessica turned their attention on the box. "Thanks for your . . . your sensitivity, Chen, Laughlin," she said, showing her old steel. "What else have we got here?"

"It's not going to help your disposition or help you sleep

at night, Dr. Coran, but it may help lead us to this guy and to understand him a little better."

Larina Gahran had squirreled away in this box every word ever written on Matisak, including a paperback version of Jessica's own book about murderer's row that included a chapter on him, and including copies of her FBI research findings on Matisak, all the years of studying him—all material any of the FBI public relations people or her publisher in New York might have. All of it entombed in this ornate Devil's box with its own diablo spinata— devil's spine that read *Mementoes of Father*.

The box had the obvious feel of a one of a kind, as if created specifically for her purpose, and Jessica began to imagine the depth of evil that Larina had perpetrated on her son. While he might have Matisak's DNA, while he might even have a real inclination toward violence, a predisposition to cut open living things to find out what was inside, still if he had had any chance whatsoever at a normal life, his mother had absolutely destroyed any chance of that happening.

No one needed say it. The silence as Jessica rummaged through the remaining heap said it all.

"The woman bequeathed the box to her son," said Sharpe, trying to wrap his mind around the idea.

"Cruel bitch," Jessica muttered. "She's managed to create another Matisak, rather than protect him from this terrible knowledge. It's how he knew about me. He read the stories . . . read all about his mad, blood-drinking father."

"The son of Matisak," muttered Sharpe, who had heard so much about the infamous madman that he had finally gone back into the records and read all of the material on Matisak. How Jessica had been maimed by him in his Chicago lair; how he had killed Jessica's first love, behavioral science pioneer Otto Boutine of the FBI, the man who had recruited Jessica from a D.C. coroner's position after observing her coolheaded professionalism at a horrendous plane crash site. He'd heard all about how Matisak was put into a federal facility for the criminally insane in Pennsylvania, and his subsequent bloody as hell escape, followed by a new wave of terror across the nation, as he fed on others in his maniacal urge to stalk and corner Jessica a second time in a Mardi Gras warehouse. That time with a plan to bleed both her and himself to death by use of a dialysis machine working to empty each of them of blood, their blood and spirits to commingle there in New Orleans and in the netherworld of eternity.

"It would figure that this young man must be related by blood to the most notorious serial killer of our time," she said. "Why the fuck didn't I see it? It was staring me in the face the whole time."

"He has an entirely idiosyncratic MO, nothing like Matisak's. Matisak was a blood drinker. We don't know what Gahran does with the bones, what kind of rituals he might have come up with in all these books, but it bears no resemblance to that bloodsucker's goal . . . unless . . ."

"Unless he's feeding on the bone marrow deep within the spine."

"And to get at it, he's got to empty the spinal fluid."

"Maybe the books can tell us more. If he's drinking the spinal fluid and consuming the bone marrow . . . maybe it's because he believes in some of the esoteric rituals found in these books about ancient cultures and bone use."

"Meanwhile, where are Petersaul and Cates?"

"And are their spines intact?"

"Right now only God and Giles Gahran know."

"There's one other horror we think you should see, Dr. Coran," said Laughlin, his eyes apologetic. He gave a nod to Chen.

Chen lifted a large, sealed Tupperware dish from Gile's box. Through the plastic, at eye level, Jessica saw Matisak's awful blood tap, the Spigot, or one of several that had, long years before, been confiscated on his capture. "It was also in the box," said Chen.

"Part of Mother's gift," finished Laughlin.

Jessica held it up, staring at it, the light filtering through, touching it. "Voodoo bitch. Truly evil . . ."

"Indelible evil," agreed Richard. "Insidious evil, that woman."

"And so is her offspring with Matisak."

Rosehill Cemetery
November 13, 2004

Milos Drivdnios, the morning caretaker at Rosehill Cemetery, felt a slight discomfort of acid reflex well up, and so he again popped two anti-acid pills prescribed by his doctor, and earlier he had taken a coated aspirin. He had a heart condition. Carrying too much weight at 226 pounds, standing only at 5'6", he had difficulty just climbing from bed in the morning to spell Liam Rielsen from the nightshift at Rosehill. Climbing into and out of his car, going up a flight of steps, any exertion, even as simple as raking leaves put a great strain on his body and heart. As for shoveling snow, he had strict orders to never pick up a shovel, but Enid, his wife, believed it all nonsense, that Milos needed *more* exertion, *more* exercise, not less. He'd had to make Dr. Stephanik write it on his letterhead for Enid to see, and even then she thought it a bought-and-paid-for agreement between men. That's when Milos told her that Dr. Stephanik was a woman, and Enid went crazy on learning this, that some other woman was seeing him half naked, her hands on Milos, checking him out.

"What happened to Dr. Weagley?" she'd shouted. "You were supposed to see Dr. Weagley!"

"He died two weeks ago. Lung cancer I'm told. I told him that Greek cigarettes would kill him, and they did."

Milos played over the scene in his mind as he drove to work in the dark twilight of predawn. He asked the empty cab of the car, "What does the woman want? Does she want me dead? Weagley, the man was in worst health than me. Ha!"

Milos arrived at the outer facade of Rosehill, the building created by the same architect who had created the famous Chicago Water Tower. As with each morning, Milos superstitiously rolled down his window and reached out and rubbed the brass placard on the cornerstone here. It read *Est. 1859*. History. The place exuded it. The old things. The old days. That was what Milos liked about Chicago, her history.

"At least with the young lady doctor the medical facility assigned me," he continued to muse aloud, enjoying the sound of his own rich voice that helped to keep his eyes open, "at least she is fucking easy to look at. What harm . . . what harm in a look? You tell me that, Enid. May God strike me down if I have had any evil thought about Dr. Stephanik. Although in that lab coat . . . with those legs . . . that wavy red hair and—"

He saw something like a shadow squeeze through the brick wall at gate's end, a flaw in the design of the enclosure, one routinely taken advantage of by neighborhood brats and hoodlums who, for some sick reason felt an attraction for graveyards after hours, and to do harm to headstones. It was a maddening routine, especially before, during and after Halloween, but now it was November. Such should not be the case.

Milos realized the moment he drove into the inner courtyard where he routinely parked in one corner, that something awful had happened here. A strange car squatting there at the gate, and three odd shapes scattered about it. Lumps of debris of some sort also scattered about.

They weren't homeless. They had a car. Some sort of drug for money exchange gone bad? They looked dead. But one was moving, the tall womanly form, nude from the waist up.

Milos rushed from his car to the woman, seeing that she had suffered a terrible knifing to the back, a huge scar in the shape of a rectangle running the length of her back. The two male forms, also stripped to buttocks had not been so lucky. In each case, the bastards who did this awful thing had removed whole chunks of rectangular flesh from the men, the flesh boats cut from them dirty and lying on the cement and field stone block floor of the courtyard.

Milos averted his eyes, but not before they registered the fact that one of the men lying dead was his friend, watchman Liam Rielsen. Milos moaned his name and crossed himself and looked over his shoulder in fear all in one fluid motion.

"Gotta get help . . . nine-one-one . . . hold on, lady . . . hold on!"

Milos rushed back to his car and grabbed his cellular phone and with his large fingers desperately punched the tiny numbers on the keypad, cursing the small pads as never before.

Finally someone came on and breathless, Milos shouted for help.

"Slow down, sir. Can you give me your location, your name, the nature of your emergency."

"Nature of emergency! It's an emergency! Need an ambulance here for the live one, the woman. Need authorities."

"Your name, sir."

"Milos."

"OK, Milos . . . is that your last name?"

"My God, woman! I am . . . my name . . . Milos Drivdnios. I am caretaker at Rosehill Cemetery."

"The address, Milos?"

"*Everydamnbody* knows where Rosehill is! Ahhh Ravenswood . . . ahhh . . . fifty-eight-hundred block Ravenswood. Hurry!"

"Nature of the emergency, sir?"

"Murder! Two people murdered, a third badly hurt!"

"Please stay at this location and on the line, Milos."

"At the gates of Rosehill . . . need ambulance. Help."

"Help is on the way. Police assistance in three minutes dispatched to your location, Milos. Milos, take a deep breath. Help is on its way."

"An ambulance for the girl."

"On its way, I assure you."

"Thank you, thank you." Milos held tight to the phone as if it were a lifeline, his knuckles white. His lovely Rosehill, always a haven away from the world, from his problems, from Enid, from the traffic and the horrors of the street, even ironically a haven from the fear of a heart attack, as everything in the cemetery conspired to make you relax and feel the breeze and listen to the birds and see the life amid all the gravestones insisting on continuing no matter. Now his safe little haven had suddenly and violently again asserted itself as a place of death, and Milos felt the violation, and that deep within he no longer felt at ease here in his Rosehill. It had become a place of disquiet, not out at the graves but here, in his chest, inside him. His Rosehill that he had cared for for so long now, thirty-three years of his life, now harbored something evil that had come this way out of the world beyond the gates, and still it lurked in every shadow and in Milos's fear.

He must assume that the monster capable of ripping out backbones did not climb from the cemetery earth as some subterranean monster, but had driven that car in here, had the hands and legs and torso and brain of a man. A worst-case scenario indeed.

Another part of his mind disagreed. The thing that could do this was still nearby, staring from the darkness just out of his sight, its hunger for blood burning within it as strong as ever. Even though his mind admonished him that whoever did this thing used a precision cutting instrument or one hell of a sharp butcher's knife, and so must be human, still a part of his old-world genes believed it must be a wild animal somehow loose in the city, a wolf or tiger or lion escaped from Lincoln Park Zoo, however improbable that sounded, due to the precision carving this monster managed.

Milos came around, his ears filling with an angry honking horn and a screech of tires. Morning traffic passed within twenty yards of the castle facade, and now the rush-hour traffic had picked up, workers at nearby factories along Ravenswood or the enormous neighborhood employer Miseriacordia—the Catholic charitable organization and school for the handicapped where the mercy and goodness of mankind evidenced itself every day.

Evil and goodness side by side, Milos thought.

Then his chest pains began.

But he couldn't think of his heart now. He must do what he could for the woman in so much pain. He rushed back to her as the 911 operator introduced herself as Gina.

"Gina, I may need help too before this is over. I got a bad heart, and this . . . this ain't doing me no good, neither."

"I understand, Milos. Try to remain as calm as possible. I will alert the medic team about your condition. They'll know what to do."

"Easy to say," the man muttered in return, looking again on the nasty wound to the woman's back. Realizing now what the wound actually represented. "The shadow I saw . . . must've been him."

"What is that, Milos?" asked Gina over the line.

"He was here, hunched over her when he saw my headlights. He panicked and ran off. I saw him the way you see a deer dash from sight, only a shadow. He was doing to her what he did to poor Liam and the other man when I frightened him off. Her wound is bad . . . but it could've been worse."

"Thank God you arrived when you did, Milos. You're a hero."

"I don't feel like no hero. I feel sick and . . . and helpless. How do you help someone you can't touch for fear of causing her pain?"

Finally, the sound of a siren, and in a moment, Milos saw

the squad car pulling in beside his own. The spotlight was welcomed but the guns pointed at him were not.

"Hands up!" shouted one of the cops.

Milos also heard the metallic voice of a female dispatcher over the radio car's airwaves saying, "See the man, Milos . . . See the man, Milos, at the scene."

"You fools! I am Milos!" he shouted back. "Do you wish me to have a heart attack now?"

The sound of an ambulance siren came thundering toward Rosehill. Milos handed the first cop his phone. "Nine-one-one—I call nine-one-one for you guys. I am caretaker here!"

The cops holstered their weapons, one of them joking, "Damn Dean-o-boy, 'nough lights and sirens to wake the dead."

Laughing, the second cop replied, "You the man, Stan. I think you oughta seriously consider doing that stand-up comedy club open-mic night deal."

"Who the hell's got rehearsal time?"

"Hell with that! You think Andy Kaufman rehearsed? Jim Carrey?"

"Look! Here . . . come with me! Look!" Milos, holding his hands crossed in a supplicating gesture against the chest wall, a kind of unconscious prayer to reduce the pain now shooting through his chest and shoulder and down his left arm. He guided them to the bodies and the woman in pain.

"Holy Mother of God," said the one called Stan, crossing himself.

"Jesus, Stan," said Dean, "we've lucked out here, buddy. You know what we've got here? Those two missing feds! Victims now of that crazy sonofabitch the feds chased here from Milwaukee."

"Geez, you think, Dean?"

"Their fucking backs are cut open like deer kill, Stan. Yeah, now this is stand-up comedy material for sure, Stan."

"Shut up, Dean."

"Catching this case . . . This could mean a rank up, pal. Luck of the draw."

"Will you fucking shut up, Dean?"

"I tell you it's that Spine Thief killer, the one all over the tube, the one in the composite we got today that—"

"The bastard's cut out their spines, and he was working on the woman but didn't finish."

"I think . . . I interrupt . . . him," said Milos. "She needs hospital . . . doctors."

"You don't look so good yourself, Mister."

"Milos . . . know other man . . . caretaker."

"Grab him, Stan!"

Milos went over in a dead faint. "Christ but we got our hands full here, Dean," said Stan, his arms full with the big Greek. "You think we ought to administer mouth to mouth?"

"I-I'll see to the woman." Dean left Milos in Stan's care, going for the woman. He bent over the helpless form, afraid to touch her, unsure if he should not wait for the experts. "We're here now, Agent . . . ahhh . . . Agent Petersaul? Are you Petersaul?"

"Cates? Is he . . . is he dead?"

"I-I think he may just make it, Agent," Dean lied to keep her spirits up as much as possible. "Ambulance is on its way."

The ambulance pulled in alongside them as he said this, the lumbering thing like a panting pachyderm where it sat idling and bouncing at once.

"Take care of Cates first. I-I got him into this," Petersaul said before passing out again.

The paramedics pushed in, taking over, shouting for Dean to get out of the way. Another team worked on Milos with a defibrillator and a hypodermic filled with something they called "eppie" and then the man closely examining Petersaul's back said to Dean Rodriquez, "Man, thank God you didn't move this one. Had you rolled her over, this entire block of her flesh would've fallen away."

Dean breathed deeply, fighting back an unfamiliar feeling of nausea. He hadn't wanted to throw up on the job in years.

"Tom, we've got a real problem here," shouted the paramedic to his partner. "She needs massive injections of antibiotics. This wound's gotta already be infected."

"Gotcha, yeah." The paramedic named Tom kneeled beside Petersaul. "*Jesusgodalmighty*, Bill, what the fuck did this?"

"All I know's we can't put her on her back, but we have to keep her flat and still."

"She's in need of major, major help at the ER."

"Let's get her evac'ed then as soon as possible."

"But she'll die at Hope General. We need to airlift her to Northwestern. She won't make it anywhere else. Trust me."

"All right, Bill. You know best. I'll call for the chopper."

"And you, Officer!" he shouted to Dean. "Clear this whole courtyard of cars to make plenty of room for the chopper."

"All right but we can't move the suspect vehicle. It's a crime scene within a crime scene for now."

"Understood."

"And as for the two dead, they gotta stay put, too. They're also the crime scene."

"Do you mind our taking this one to the ER, or is she part of your fucking crime scene, too?" Bill Waldron shot back, not expecting an answer.

"I'll just clear the way for the MedEvac chopper."

Just then another car tore into the courtyard. The police ban airwaves were abuzz with the discovery. Emerging from this unmarked car, stepped Jessica Coran, Richard Sharpe and Chief Laughlin.

Jessica rushed in to see about Petersaul, and to determine the extent of her wounds. The bloody matted hair spoke of a gunshot wound to the head, but when Jessica probed with her gloved fingers, she announced, "The wound to the head is superficial. No penetration."

She next examined the wound to the back, withholding a sense of rage and tears and stomach wrenching sickness. She wondered if Gahran had done these killings just to seed her interest in putting an end to him, just to taunt her and as a warning. If so, his mother had been right about one thing— it'd be his father's way. Just like Matisak.

Paramedic Bill Waldron brought her up to date as he and his partner placed Petersaul on a stretcher. As they did so, Jessica watched the boat of cutaway flesh down her back shake like Jell-O.

"She's in good hands, Jess," said Sharpe, placing his strong arm around her as the helicopter descended.

Dean and Stan had by now gotten all the various vehicles out of the chopper's way.

"Caretaker's had a heart attack. The second guy cut open was a pal of his, I gather," said Dean to the feds. "We've already thrown up a perimeter search, a ten-block grid. The old man"—he indicated Milos, where he was being placed in an ambulance—"says he thinks he saw someone slinking off as he drove up. Says maybe some guy squeezed through the gate end where a thin man or boy could fit."

"How's the old-timer doing?" asked Sharpe.

"He's regained consciousness. That shot to the heart hit him good."

"Epinephrine," Jessica said. "Did he say it was Gahran when you showed him the composite?"

"Said he was just a shadow. Said he wasn't even sure at first he'd really seen anything, just a trick of light, until he saw the bodies. Nice old guy. Only wants to know if the girl will live. No thought to himself except to call the wife."

"I want this cemetery combed, men and dogs, the works," said Jessica. "He's at home in such places, just like his father."

She recalled the games Mad Matthew Matisak had

played in New Orleans, how he had had her canvassing a Metairie Cemetery at midnight on the promise he would be there for her, a ruse as it turned out, another dead end. This could also end in a dead end in a cemetery, or another death if not the arrest of Mad Matisak's crazed kid.

"Sun'll be up soon," said Stan, the uniformed cop. "If he's within these walls, or tries to climb over them, we'll get him."

Dean added, "We've got squad cars encircling the place from here to Petersen and Western. Got the North Side wall covered, too."

She stared in through the bars where the sonofabitch of all sonsofbitches had possibly escaped. Already they had given him too much time. She disbelieved he'd be foolish enough to still be in the area. However, he'd obviously lost the usual disciplinary controls he had maintained over himself all the years since Millbrook. His newfound madness, likely a response to his having learned who his father was, may have triggered the belief that he was invincible. If Gahran thought for a moment of coming back to finish his carving and raising of Petersaul's spine—the thing he apparently, madly and wantonly had to have in numbers now—the flood of need beyond any control he had once exercised—he might have hesitated long enough to find himself surrounded by the quick response of the Chicago Police Department.

Else he was smoke again . . . gone.

TWENTY-ONE

May your own blood rise against you . . .
and may the hearthstones of hell
be your best bed forever

— FROM A TRADITIONAL WEXFORD CURSE

WITH nowhere else to go, Giles found himself at Cafe Avanti, ringing the doorbell belonging to his two benefactors who lived overhead. At four in the morning, Giles had arrived carrying two spines in his blue easel bag slung over his shoulder, the bones rattling against one another, sometimes noticeably. He'd been wandering the streets of Chicago since his escape from the cemetery. He'd located the old homestead where his demonic father had lived once, but it was occupied, turned into a loft-styled duplex. Warm lights, pleasant to view from the street, trees all about. No one would ever guess that a serial killer had once lived there. Then he saw the unmarked FBI car cruising near. Jessica, no doubt, had sent some of her legions to keep an eye on Matisak's old place, just in case he should show up, and he had. The M.E. was sharp. He'd ducked into shadow, made his way off through alleyways and was gone.

Now Conchita Raold came to the upstairs window and

called down, asking, "Is that you, Murphy? Who the fuck's ringing my bell? Is it you, Murph? You Fuck! We're through! So over! Get it?"

Giles backed away from the cafe doorway to stare up at the woman in the window. "It's me, Giles! I need a place to stay. I was thrown out of my apartment. Too much noise making my sculptures! I . . . I have to get some rest, and I have to see my sculptures."

"We have the big-big opening tonight! You'll need to be alert to talk to visitors to the exhibit! Help me sell more coffee. You can't be hungover or nothing. It is tonight, isn't it? We agreed to the showing, tonight!"

"All right . . . OK, but I have to *add* something." He held up the easel bag.

She could faintly hear the rattle of bones. "What is it?" she asked.

"More bones. The showing needs *more* bones."

"All right. I'll come down and open up for you."

Giles felt a great wave of relief come over him. It was a place where he was welcomed in, a place where he could hide, a place where they didn't turn him away, a place where they knew his name and it didn't frighten them.

It reminded him of the story he had read about how his father had killed two Cherokee Indian people, a man and his wife, living on a farm on a desolate section of a reservation in Oklahoma. How Matisak had been welcomed, fed, given a place to sleep the night, only to turn on the old couple like a viper, taking their lives for their blood, and for a long moment, he hesitated now at the door, fearful of something similar happening here, that he would wind up killing these people who had so fallen in love with his sculptures. At least Conchita had; Murphy reserved judgment, remaining aloof, cool. Giles didn't want what had happened with Lucinda to happen here. He hadn't wanted to harm Lucinda, either, but she'd really given him no choice.

Why had she been so wakeful that night? Why had she been such a snoop? Why did she have to pry and pry until he could no longer have her walk freely out his door?

Conchita stood in the doorway in her untied robe, inviting him in, telling him in no uncertain terms that she was alone and she could use a man.

"Where's Murphy, your husband?" he asked.

"We had another big fight. Whole thing . . . the marriage, the cafe, all of it's shot to hell. We really aren't what you'd call compatible. It just took us six years to find that out. Conchita's out of the box, Giles, out of the box."

He thought of his box at the reference.

She continued nonstop, "And for the first time in a long time I can breathe."

"You two seemed so . . . so . . . ."

"Together?"

"Like really in love, yeah."

"Front we put on for all our friends and the clientele, you know? You know how it is. In private we make war like fucking Indians on a tear! Damn that Murphy!" She laughed. "Only man who can make me see red. Didja know we both have some Native American in us?"

"No, I didn't know that."

"That big black Murphy's a mutt. He's got some Blackfoot and Crow. Me, I'm Eastern—a touch of Pottawatomie—Blackhawk's people—aside from Mexican! And proud of it. You ever . . . ahhh . . . you know, make it with a Native American–Mex mix before, baby?"

"Ahhh . . . no, can't say as I have."

She grabbed hold of Giles by his shirt and hauled him through the door. "Then you ain't really lived yet, white boy. Come with me." She led him up to her bed, saying, "I liked you the moment I saw you."

"My mother told me I had a little Cherokee in me . . . on my father's side. Told me how he got the blood and everything."

"Cool . . . you'll have to tell me all about it sometime. But for now, I need your mouth on me, not flapping anywhere else. Come on!"

Giles saw not a single television in the place, and he asked about it.

"Fuck I want with that white man's opiate, sweetheart? Don't read his papers, don't listen to his bullshit radio, not even Rush Limp-baugh."

She pushed him onto the bed, stripping him. Giles, fatigued, only marginally awake, laid back and enjoyed it, falling into a deep slumber even as he came in her.

GILES Gahran had vanished. It seemed he had again disappeared off the face of the earth. Jessica and Sharpe had been to see Petersaul to tell her that Darwin was safe, that Warden Gwingault had acted on the evidence twenty minutes before the scheduled execution, ten minutes before he got the call from Governor Hughes, who apparently had thought that he'd make FBI Agent Reynolds sweat out the end as if he would surely die. From what Darwin told Jessica, a major rift had resulted between Gwingault and Hughes, and the entire state was in an uproar and many residents wanted to see Darwin hung or drawn and quartered, or at least thrown into a cactus bed for his part in the hoax.

Darwin had been released pending any charges. It seemed no one knew exactly what the charges would be or how many would be leveled.

Jessica gave Darwin the number where he could talk to his brother, still in hiding.

"Then I'm on my way to Chicago. I want in on the kill."

Harry Laughlin showed up at Petersaul's bedside as well. She had lost a lot of blood, and while weak and doped up, doctors had been able to repair the damage Gahran's scalpel had done her. It would take a long recuperation and some skin grafts, and even now she could not lie on her back, but they must all be thankful she was alive and in one piece.

"Get this bastard for Cates and for all *his* victims, Jessica," Petersaul said, her voice quivering with pain, despite the drugs.

Laughlin took Jessica and Sharpe aside and said, "I've got bad news."

"Now what?"

"Orders from Quantico passed along from D.C., you and Sharpe are off this case, ordered off. I'm to see to it you two get on a plane for HQ. Seems they're taking a dim view of the fun you had with Oregon Governor Hughes . . . that stunt you pulled, and the fact you are holding Towne in an undisclosed location believed to be somewhere along the O'Hare Airport hotel strip."

"You don't think we'd have him anywhere within a thousand miles of Chicago, do you, Harry?"

"Don't play me for one of them. I applaud what you people did, but you did break the law, regardless."

"To save an innocent man from certain execution!" countered Sharpe.

"I'm on your side, just not officially. You don't need to drag any more asses down with you. Now, you gotta turn Towne over to me, and you two have to be standing before Eriq Santiva and his boss, Hemmings, and maybe even Fischer this afternoon. Santiva said, 'No ifs, ands, or buts.' I guess you've been cornered."

"We'll have to make arrangements to get Towne here to turn him over to your custody."

"After all," continued Laughlin, "he's got to be returned to Oregon."

"Sure . . . I expected as much," she said.

"Meantime, there's been some buzz on the street about our guy. People have his face now in their homes, on the tube and on the front pages of the papers. He was spotted early this morning on Southport in the Lakeview *and* Wrigleyville area at the same time."

"So reliable."

"More than one source. One a newspaper delivery kid, another a shopkeeper, bakery guy just opening up. They each reported a man looking like Gahran with an oversized, stuffed blue bag slung over his shoulder."

"That's good. Give us the location. Hell, run us there."

"But you're off the case."

"Not until we get on the plane."

"Guy at the Greyhound terminal also spotted someone fitting our yearbook photo from the *Tribune*'s page one. Again a guy with an oversized blue bag using a locker there last night, stowed the blue bag there and picked it up early this A.M."

"Traveling light," commented Sharpe.

"But where are his sculptures? The crates?" she asked.

Sharpe began musing aloud. "Maybe in storage or . . . If . . . just suppose Wellingham had gotten him a gig here? Introduced him to someone in Chicago for a showing? That would explain where all his stuff might be."

"If he's rented space, he'd have stowed the blue bag somewhere other than the bus station," Jessica said.

"I can tell you none of the major galleries would touch his stuff if it's anything like Orion's," Laughlin assured them.

"But a medium-sized gallery, a small one . . . and there are countless other venues where art or so-called art is displayed."

"No way to cover them all," said Laughlin. "Certainly not before you guys have to board that plane."

"We can start with all the papers, including the neighborhood papers, especially those covering Wrigleyville and this Lakeview area you mentioned."

"That'd be one way. If his stuff has been advertised or given a freebie mention in a 'Who's Who' or 'What's Happening' column."

"Even so . . . he'd never be so foolish as to stick around for a showing of his art, would he?" asked Petersaul from her stomach at the bed, having overheard everything. "I still have twenty/twenty vision and my ears ain't bad, either," she joked.

They returned to Petersaul and included her in the remainder of the discussion. Laughlin said, "This guy hasn't exactly kept a low profile. Hell, he's at damn Navy Pier tossing Matisak memorabilia off the Ferris wheel. Made one hell of a big show. Yeah, he's just wacko enough—"

"Or arrogant enough—" interjected Sharpe.

"—to stick around to see how his showing goes. He has to know it will be his first and last."

"I'll make a deal with you, Harry," said Jessica. "Towne for all the help you can put on the street for this dragnet."

"You gotta turn Towne over regardless. You've got no bargaining chips, but be assured, I'll put every available man on the hunt, and we'll enlist every agent and detective in the city on it. We canvass the near North Side neighborhoods for any sign, any flyer, any word of mouth at the coffee shops about this guy's debut Chicago showing."

"If it's not advertised in any of the papers," muttered Petersaul wincing in pain, "then whoever's got Gahran's stuff to show, the stuff that Lucinda Wellingham supposedly threatened Orion with, Harry? It's going to be a small, small gallery with no ad budget."

"Hang in, Pete," Jessica said to her as they left to continue the search for Gahran.

"What else am I going to do?"

The word on Milos was that he was working toward a recovery, but that he'd be away from his job for at least a month, perhaps more.

Agent Cates and Liam Rielsen lay in the morgue in the basement, the body of each man eerily divested of their backbones.

TWENTY-TWO

Scream like the Devil's baby.

—ANONYMOUS

CPD and FBI agents fanned out all over Chicago's near North Side. Every art gallery and bar and coffeehouse that ever exhibited a stick of artwork, particularly those known for "outer limits" artwork, were paid a visit and even if they never heard of Giles Gahran or his artwork, they were questioned about anyone new in the neighborhood, any new buzz in the area about a hot new artist with whom Orion could not hold a candle.

Nothing came of the initial canvass.

Other operatives combed the newspapers, from the most prestigious to the smallest and avant-garde or the unusual like *The Art of the Onion.*

Three o'clock came and went. Laughlin had chosen to ignore his orders, to claim he had seen them off at the airport and that had been the last he had seen of them, and that they had given him a false lead on the whereabouts of Towne.

The list of coffeehouses, bars and meeting places in the enclaves and tightly knit neighborhoods in and around Wrigleyville, Lincoln Park, Lakeview and others was astounding. Jessica knew they would need a miracle to find this needle in the haystack, and even if they did, there was no guarantee that Giles Gahran would be foolish enough to expose himself again as he had at Navy Pier. That he would be foolish enough to show up at his own gallery showing.

But then where was he?

Every exit from the city had been closed off to him. Both airports. Trains at Union and Northwestern, the Greyhound and Metra stations. Everyone had his picture. Still, he could have hitchhiked out or rented a private vehicle, using a stolen card. There were simply too many highways leading out of this hub to throw up roadblocks and shut them all down. Besides, they'd acted too late for such action to be effective.

"He's hiding here somewhere . . . someplace close," Jessica said to Richard. They sat in a coffee shop called BeBo's having Irish coffees. Neither of them had had much sleep in the past twenty-four hours, and each struggled with fatigue.

Time had grown late as the clock neared 6 P.M. "If he does have a showing, it could be tomorrow or the following day and not tonight at all," suggested Richard.

"True enough, and we're extremely late in not complying with HQ. In fact, they'll be sending U.S. marshals after us if we don't soon turn ourselves in."

"On the FBI's most-wanted list, heh?"

"We are out of time, Richard."

"I know now why Darwin hasn't gotten here yet from Portland, Jess."

"Tell me why."

"I did some discreet checking. The reason Oregon didn't hold Darwin on charges."

"Spit it out, Richard."

"The State Department is conducting the investigation into the matter, into the part we all played in it."

"That's why we've been ordered back to D.C."

"And apparently Darwin's flight on an Oregon field office jet was ordered directly to D.C."

"Explains why Santiva wants us in D.C."

"Towne's expecting Darwin to join us here."

"Yeah, he's going to be disappointed."

"Oregon really must have Towne back and soon. It's all a great embarrassment to them."

The couple smiled across at one another. Jessica said, "We pulled off the bait and switch of the decade, I think."

"I dare say so."

Jessica's phone rang and she opened the cover and answered. "Yes, right," she began, "hello." There only came an eerie silence. "Is anyone there?"

"Dr. Coran?"

She recognized the chilling voice.

"It's me again, Jessica."

He even sounds like Matisak now, she thought, *now that I know the truth.*

"I'm sorry . . . who is it?" she stalled for time.

"Your favorite prey. By now you and everyone else chasing me knows who I am."

"Giles? Gahran is it you?" She waved and pointed her finger at the phone to indicate to Richard that she had him on the line. Richard was already on his phone calling their carrier for a trace. A satellite trace was difficult and took time, but Jessica had anticipated this possibility, knowing he still had Agent Amanda Petersaul's cell phone. Jessica had alerted her carrier to the possibility, too, and they were on speed dial on Richard's companion phone.

"Where are you calling from, Giles?"

"Wouldn't you like to know. And you may call me Mr. Matisak now, Giles Matisak. Really, it's a good righteous fit, my new skin. Shedding the old one has been liberating. Feels right in this skin. It suits me."

She took a stab at a hunch, picturing him atop of the Navy Pier Ferris wheel. She discussed it openly, asking him what he thought he was doing tossing out all those news clippings and serial killer playing cards, autopsy photos and police reports. "Liberating yourself from that damnable box and its contents? Why don't you go beyond the box, really liberate yourself, Giles?"

"Too late for that. I am born in my father's image. I look like him, even think like him."

"No, Giles, it isn't you. It's only your mother's inculcations you're acting on, as you always have, and Giles, get this."

"What, Dr. J.?"

"We ran a DNA match and—"

"I know, saved that poor Devil on death row. I heard on CNN. His life was courageously won."

"You don't understand. We ran a scan on Matisak's DNA and compared it to yours, and guess what, Giles?"

"You're lying."

"What possible reason would I have to lie about such a thing, Giles?"

"I don't know . . . going to have to figure that one. Pretty sneaky of you . . . to throw a curve like that at me. Likely your way to keep me on the line while your partner runs a trace."

"No, I just wanted to know the truth. How about you? You interested at all in the truth of your lineage?"

"Bullshit. You're bullshitting me."

"Well, look, if you're not going to get to the point, Giles, and just run up Petersaul's minutes, I'm hanging up."

"Agent Petersaul? Amanda need not worry about Cingular now."

"You talk like Amanda's dead."

"And you want me to believe Amanda's still alive?" He laughed. "Let the games begin."

"She is quite alive and recuperating. Took all you could dish out and still survived. Oughta build a new reality TV show around this woman."

"Survived?"

"Yes."

"The first ever to survive my interest in a spinal cord."

Jessica replied through gritted teeth. "What do you think? That she's going to die just because you want her to?"

"I think she did die. I had gotten too far on her when I was interrupted by headlights I thought belonged to you."

"Petersaul survived. Now, Giles, let's talk about how you want to give yourself up so that no one else gets hurt—including you—since every cop and FBI agent in Chicago is gunning for you."

"No, Dr. Coran, let's talk about you coming to my showing."

"Really? You want me to come to see your art?"

"It's good . . . very good."

"I'm sure it is. You forget, I've seen your sketches."

"My worst day, my worst piece of art is far better than that prick Orion's junk. My art does not rely on smoke'n mirrors, special effects'n strobe lights'n all that shit. My work has character . . . backbone, you might say."

Jessica immediately realized now what he was doing with the stolen racks of bones. "Your art . . . is . . . it is built upon the bones of your victims?"

"The centerpiece of each sculpture, yes. A must-see."

"Then I must see it. When and where?"

"Not so fast. First off, you come alone."

"That flies in the face of all my training and experience, Giles."

"You want the son of Matisak, don't you?"

"There's no scientific proof, Giles, that Matthew Matisak was your father."

"What're you saying?" This had not once occurred to him ever. Getting the showing at Cafe Avanti might not seem like much of a showing, not to an Orion perhaps, but it had given him the courage to open and digest all that Mother had left him by way of his father. "Why would Mother lie about . . . about a thing like that, Dr. Coran. One good reason. Give me one good reason."

"Your mother might've had it all wrong, despite what she convinced you and herself of."

"That's truly insane, Dr. Coran. Are you simply afraid to face the facts?"

"Like you?" she softly taunted. "Tell me where to be and when, Giles, and I promise you, I will come alone."

"Our little rendezvous . . . a kind of reunion. Old Dad picked you over Mom, didn't he? Gee-whiz, Pop wanted to go off into eternity with you and leave us to fend for ourselves. I read about his fixation and how he cornered you in New Orleans, how the roof caved in on him, and you got the upper hand, or rather fate in the shape of one big-assed nasty hook took care of Poppa."

"That's right, and I watched him squirm on that hook."

"Are we *on*, Doctor?"

"Will you tell me where you are, Giles?"

"No . . . No . . . I gotta think this thing through."

"Your showing, Giles. Where is it happening? I want to see your work and to finally meet you."

He hung up.

She cursed. "Bastard."

"Appropriate word in this case," replied Sharpe, snapping his own phone shut. "But Jess, we've got his signal location via satellite. Hurry!"

She followed him out to a waiting car. From the car, they radioed Laughlin that they had a fix on Gahran's location.

Twenty cars silently converged on Cafe Avanti, covering front and back. Men poured into the cafe, making it crowded, frightening and disturbing the usual customers and others who'd come to enjoy the evening with laptop computers opened, notepads busy, books propped beside large helpings of exotic coffee drinks and pastries. Other people milled about in the rear, *ohs* and *ahs* spilling out as they literally *walked* through the mind of a killer, examining Giles Gahran's artwork, commenting on the realism of even the blood odor along with the sight of the spines.

Police and FBI agents secured every exit. The owner rushed at them, calling them pigs and demanding to know the meaning of this outrage, saying, "You think this is Guatemala or something you can just bust into my place like fucking Nazi storm troopers? You got a warrant?"

Laughlin dealt with her as other agents swarmed upstairs and cleared each room one by one. Jessica, with Richard at her side, took the gruesome tour through Giles Gahran's mind, going from a dark little room down even darker little corridors to another adjacent room and another larger one partitioned off. She recognized the featureless, eyeless creations as those of each victim. The park bench and birds in one, the playful dog in another, the extremely cramped horse with Sarah Towne's form, and dangling above all as if lifting out of the backs of women flew the backbones—so lifelike and amazingly startling and eerie in their levitation above the human forms frozen in time. Because, as Jess determined now by touch, they were real. Made even the more eerie as Jessica confirmed her worst fear, that the sculpted bones were sculpted not by Giles but by God.

Onlookers were being ushered out of the gallery created here to display Giles's twisted idea of art. Laughlin joined them, the owner still on him, bitching at him, when he announced there was no sign of Gahran. "We've hit every nook and cranny from basement to third floor and the roof. He's not here, and the owner isn't cooperating."

"This is a crime scene now. We don't need her cooperation to process this place," Jessica replied. Jessica stepped up to Conchita Raold and glared at her with such intensity that Raold averted her eyes.

"Ms. Raold. You could be prosecuted for harboring a murderer, and we could tie you up so many ways legally and illegally that you will lose this cafe and everything else you hold dear. You will cooperate with us. Where is he?"

"I don't know. He came down here during the day and began working in the very back room, and I tried to bring him something to eat and drink, but he wouldn't let me go in there. Then he came out all exhausted. He never got no sleep the whole time we were . . . I tried to get him to sleep, you know. He'd been up all night. But he came with more bones I . . . I thought he made them outta his own head, you know. I . . . I can't believe what they are telling me."

Jessica took her aside and sat her down. Calmly, Jessica asked, "He worked all day and then what?"

"He wasn't too clearheaded. I tried to get him to go back up to bed, you know. He looked mad when he got off the phone, just five minutes before you all come bustin' into my place. I thought Chicago was part of America, but I guess not."

"Hear that, Laughlin? He's possibly still in the area!"

"Unless he grabbed a cab, hopped a bus or the nearby elevated," replied Laughlin, "but we'll get on it, canvass the neighborhood and paper his face everywhere."

"Did you see this, Conchita?" Jessica asked, showing her the photo of Gahran as a high-school student on the front page of the *Sun-Times*. "You *had* to've seen this. *He* had to've seen this."

"He told me you were all trying to frame him for something Keith Orion did, that you released Orion because you didn't have enough to hold him, so now you were making up stuff against Giles."

"And you believed that?" asked Sharpe, straight-faced.

She glanced up at him but said nothing. Jessica asked, "What was he working on all day? Show me."

"It's a back room."

"Is that supposed to be humorous?"

"No, it's just for empty boxes and shit."

"An ordinary back room."

"Giles said he made up something special for me in here, but I didn't get no chance to go in there since it got so busy and then you all busted in. So I locked it up, not wanting

no one to see it until I did, you know. He said it was special
to me."

"I think we need to see it now, Conchita."

She led them back past all the sculptures of the three victims when Jessica noticed a fourth rack of backbones free-
floating alone, newly draped with black sheets as backdrop
canvass for Giles's special brand of black art.

"Lucinda Wellingham," said Sharpe. "Read the placard."

On the doorjamb Giles had created a placard naming
each of his works. Where the three more elderly women had
been depicted, he had simply used November 1, November
2, and November 3. This one read: *Essence d'Lucious.*

Conchita unlocked a door to the very back storage room
in this maze behind her cafe. "All right," Jessica said, brac-
ing herself. "He could still be in here . . . in the shadows."

"Better let us go in first," suggested Sharpe.

"No way—I won't lose you, Richard, not to this fiend,
not as I did Otto."

Sharpe pushed past her, taking the lead, throwing the
door wide on a blackened room, a soft, diffused, muted light
striking an object at the center of the room, and the strobe
light slowly revolved about the thing at the center.

Jessica and Laughlin followed Sharpe, with Conchita
peeking around them, watching as the light source picked
up yet another backbone, then another, and finally a third.
They hung high in the air here where the ceiling was a good
fourteen feet high.

"Three . . . I count three more spinal columns," said
Richard.

"But whose is the third? We've got one unaccounted for
victim," said Jessica. "Bones will tell us something about
him or her."

Dangling and eerily turning in a draft, the spinal
columns looked like flying dragons and the strobe light
gave them the illusion of flight. "Flying bones," Jessica
muttered.

Then a second light source on a timer set to go on at intervals came on and raked quickly as a knife stroke across a nude male body, its back splayed open, bloody yet, dripping still from the mangling it'd endured at the hands of Matisak's son. Then the light raced off.

"What in hell was that?" asked Laughlin.

"Is it Gahran?" asked Sharpe. "But how?"

"No," she countered, "looks like an African male. But who?"

The light source no longer on the body in the dark, no one could say, but Conchita managed words. "It almost looked like Murphy, my husband, but he hasn't much been around. We had a bad . . . really nasty fight."

The lights again raked over the set of three flying spinal columns overhead. In a beautiful blue artistic setting, one could construe the bones as birds in formation flight, in perfect sync, and then they realized another light source was directed on yet another scene in the far back of the room. The new light source directed attention to a sculpture of a child holding a small rack of bones—an animal spine—overhead, and from it, flowed a sickly yellowish fluid raining down and dripping over the lips of the boy.

"That's Gahran," Jessica declared. "As a child."

"Who's the other guy supposed to be?"

"Where're the lights?" Jessica asked.

Conchita found the switch but Giles had removed the bulb. The alternating light hit the strange unnamed man in the puzzle again, the lifelike nude body posed in the manner of Christ being removed from the cross, the dead body held by unseen moorings, bent in an arch of death throes.

"Oh my God, it is Murphy! Murphy! It's my husband!"

"It might have been you, Conchita," muttered Laughlin.

"I can't believe this."

Jessica grabbed her and guided her away from the sight, and back through Giles's colorful show, noting the tincture of blood odor in the air even here and she imagined the bloodred bones in the exhibit had been painted with the blood of Gahran's victims.

"Get a light generator set up in that back room, Richard, and call in the local M.E., Horace Keene, and his team to process all of this. I'm not up to it."

"He kept saying, 'the lovely bones, the lovely bones . . . I gotta go see the lovely bones exhibit,'" Conchita was saying over and over. "When he left here, he said that's where he was going to go . . . to see the lovely bones."

"'To see the lovely bones'?" Jessica repeated. "What the hell's that?"

Patrons still held at bay by police began to kick this over as if it were a puzzle. "That book . . . the bestseller . . . on the *New York Times* list for a long time a while back . . . *The Lovely Bones* by . . . by . . ."

Some took stabs at the author's name, but no one could dredge it up.

"There's a bookstore around the corner," said Laughlin.

"Several," said another cafe patron. He rattled them off, names and addresses, "Booked Up, In and Out Books and there's Afterword Books."

"Could mean the elevated," said another. "Slang for the elevated is the bone rattler. Rattles your bones. You get off and your bones are still moving," he joked.

"No, man . . . it's that exhibit," said a young, shy-eyed Latino girl.

"Exhibit?" asked Jessica at this.

"Downtown at the Field," she replied.

"Yeah, that's right, dinosaur bones," added another patron, coffee in hand. "Some famous archeologist named Stroud . . . dug up some new kinda dinosaur bones. Claims they're like supernatural—at least to the Indians they are."

"Field Museum," the shy girl added.

Laughlin had already left, dispatching radio cars throughout the area and to each of the nearest bookstore locations. Richard had gone back to the storage room with a police photographer.

Jessica sat across from a young woman with exotic features who lifted an ad from the newspaper for the Chicago Field Museum. Bold letters overlaying a fade in of Chicago's famous dinosaurs of the Field Museum, a corner shot of scientists working a recent dig, and a third shot of lab-coated men and women with recent bone acquisitions, said: "Come See Our Lovely Bones!"

"He's gone on holiday," Jessica murmured to herself.

The dark-skinned woman with the ad only smiled and said, "Can I buy you a cup of coffee?"

That's where he wants me to meet him, she told herself.

Everyone was busy now. The Chicago M.E.'s people had arrived, and patrons of the cafe were ushered out.

While shaking hands and saying hello to Jessica as an old friend, Horace Keene, Chicago's top M.E. said in his stentorian voice, "Cafe is closed until further notice, people. Everyone out!"

Sharpe guided Keene and the evidence techs back to the body in the dark. With them, they carried all the instruments and light-generating equipment they would need.

Jessica quietly slipped out, located the car she had come in, found the keys dangling in the ignition, got in and drove for Chicago's Lake Shore Drive and the Museum Campus.

Along the way her phone rang. She looked at the signal to determine if it were Richard. He'd be angry and fuming by now if he had discovered her gone. But she recognized the signal as coming from Amanda Petersaul's phone. It was Giles calling.

"It's a special night," he said. "By now, you've seen my work. What do you think, Dr. Coran?"

"It's . . . It was unique . . . Yes, very different from anything I have ever seen before, I must say."

"And coming from you, that's saying a hell of a lot."

"An amazing display of bravado on your part. Are you wanting to be put down like a dog, Giles?"

"I think I've surpassed the master! Dear old Dad?"

"Yes, in a manner of speaking, absolutely."

"In a manner of speaking?" he said, clearly annoyed that she hadn't agreed wholeheartedly.

"In some ways, yes."

"In all ways."

"If you say so, Giles."

"No, bullshit. If you say so, Dr. Coran, and I know you feel it, too. Wish we had time to delve into this more, time to just sit over coffee there at the Avanti and just talk about it."

"We do, Giles. We have the rest of your life."

He exploded with laughter at this, and then he hesitated. "You mean, Dr. Coran, you'd come to see me? Visit at the asylum? Have tea with the freak, the criminally insane, Satan's son, heir to Jack the Ripper? Did you know that Jack, too, was an artist?"

"I believe any tea we might have, Giles, would be shared on death row, in the shadow of the execution chamber."

"Society's monster killer. You know very well I'd get the asylum, like Father. Come now! My crimes are too insane to not offer up an insanity defense."

Silence followed as her car sped along the faerie tale lit outer drive past the gaiety of Navy Pier with its array of colors and giant, lit-up Ferris wheel, a beacon in the night. She wondered why he had not leapt off the wheel after overturning the box of clippings on his father. She now asked him point-blank.

He replied, "You think you know me, don't you, Jessica? But if you really knew me, you'd never ask such a question."

Something chilling in his remark told her that he meant to do as his father had attempted, to take Jessica with him into eternity, be it heaven or hell.

Given the full-page ad for the Field Museum's night opening of the bone show, Jessica assumed the place would be overrun by people. Capturing or killing Giles Gahran, or dying in the process herself as Otto before her, one way or another, this life and death struggle between them was going to happen here and now. It would end at the Field Museum, his chosen venue.

She felt the bulge of her holster and gun below her armpit as she drove. She felt the heft of her second weapon on her ankle. If Matisak was indeed his father, she'd need both weapons.

"Well, Doctor? Which is it to be? Execution tonight or the asylum? You think there's an asylum that can hold a Matisak?"

"No . . . on that we agree."

"How lovely a spine you must possess, Jessica. Come alone."

TWENTY-THREE

The blood of the moon
steeps through me,
but you cannot find me,
as I have disappeared
into your darkness.

—STEPHEN R. WALKER, POET

THE Chicago Field Museum had a long and distinguished history as one of the original buildings of the famous White City of 1893, created for the Chicago World's Fair Columbian Exposition of that year. It had stood sentinel at 1400 S. Lake Shore ever since, and millions annually flocked to its doors to see the wonders of the natural world.

Ironic, Jessica thought, that her chasing down Giles Gahran, the son of her worst nightmare, should end here in this palace devoted to all things *natural*—its other name being the Museum of Natural History. But then there actually was something *natural* about the development of the criminally insane, too . . . How natural it all was, despite what people wanted to believe to the contrary. The criminal mind was as old as man himself, and like an ancient, persistent, resistant virus, it resided—sometimes dormant, sometimes active, but always present—within every developing human brain, the paterfamilias of evil. Like a new layer or patina over an old deck, the rotted original boards remained.

Still, a part of Jessica recognized the role that Larina Gahran had played in creating the monster Giles. No matter his genetic makeup, no matter the mark of Cain on his soul, no matter his predisposition toward blood and violence and that which could not be predicted, his sick fascination with spinal fluid, bone marrow and bone, fed as it were by the rare esoteric volumes he'd collected over the years. Despite all of it. Despite what he may or may not have done as a child to make Larina believe him the spawn of Satan himself, Mother Gahran could have gotten him help, she could have shown an inch of compassion, she could have shown a modicum of love at least for that part of the child that was good and innocent, but she chose instead to pour poison over poison.

It reminded Jessica of a story of child abuse written decades before it became commonplace news and TV and radio talk fare. The tale entitled *Born of Man and Woman* was penned by the master storyteller Richard Matheson. Matheson's monster, too, was created of poor parental attitudes and behaviors as much as the boy's birth defects.

These thoughts swam about in Jessica's mind even as she keenly and warily watched her every step now that she'd entered the museum. She was suddenly barred from going farther by a hefty black woman in security guard uniform. When she flashed her badge, the woman didn't budge from her path. "Everybody pays same here, cops, no different."

"I'm on the job here, in pursuit of a fugitive."

"How do I know that?"

"Fucking . . . Christ lady look . . ." She read the woman's nameplate, "America? Is that your name?"

"That's right. Mama was a marine, first lieutenant."

"Well, listen, America, I need your help on this case."

"My help?"

"That's right." Jessica pulled forth a folded sheath of paper. "Wanted poster," she added.

"This looks like just a kid," she replied.

"His high-school photo. It's all we've got to go on. Look, America, I want you to make copies of this picture on your museum copier and get it out to every security guard in the place for me. Can you do that? And can you let me have your radio in order to keep in touch with all your personnel?" Jessica pointed to the state-of-the-art earphones and mouthpiece.

America nodded and handed over the radio and said, "Does it rain in a rainforest? I'm a law-and-order woman."

"But no one is to go near this guy. He's armed and dangerous."

"No way he got through our screening with a gun," she countered.

"Perhaps not, but he is a multiple murderer."

"I see."

"Point me in the direcon of the Lovely Bones exhibit. I'll start there."

"Straight ahead. That big mess, you ain't gonna miss."

Jessica started out alone save for the headphone hookup. She wondered how quickly and efficiently America might act or fail to act. She entered the huge, marbled concourse of the Field Museum, the lights turned down for effect over the simulated dinosaur boneyard created for the exhibit at the center of the concourse rear. Instead of a museum, she had walked into the Mojave Desert. Leading up to the bone yard itself a simulated dusky red earth trail. On all sides, an impressive illusion, created masterfully with Hollywood effects and lights made Jessica feel herself in a strange desert filled with people in black tie and evening gowns toasting the museum's latest major opening, celebrating an enormous find in the Mojave. From what she gathered, the find had come of a vision. This vision had led the chief archeologist in charge, a millionaire named Abraham Stroud, to the exact spot and layer below the surface, and aside from the dinosaur find, it had also uncovered evidence of an early race of forgotten people, the Mojaves, Stroud named them.

Jessica meandered through the desert on the Field Museum marble floor, and she wondered what the effect had had on Giles, and where he might be at this moment. Certainly, he hadn't donned white shirt, coat and tie. He should, like herself, stick out in this crowd. But she could not find him.

Her phone rang, annoying people closest to her, milling about the complex recreation of the dig.

It must be him. Still playing games.

She let it ring until other patrons showed their annoyance. The man of the hour, Abraham Stroud—a bifocaled elderly Kirk Douglas look-alike, in need of a good tailor—looked ill at ease with unkempt hair and a scraggly beard at odds with his baggy tuxedo. He addressed the crowd in a warm and unpretentious manner, folksy in his approach, befitting the string tie, Navajo jewelry and western boots he wore with the tux.

"The find at Mojave is perhaps the most important single . . ."

Jessica answered the phone and heard Richard's voice, angry at her sudden disappearance. He did not disguise his anxiety. "Are you mad? You've gone after him alone, haven't you? Where are you?"

She pointed the camera and panned the museum. "Field Museum," she said. "He's here someplace, Richard, and he insisted I come alone."

"Damn you, Jess! You have no bloody right to endanger yourself in such a way, not now, now that you've made me love you."

"He's close, Richard, and he thinks we have some sort of connection due to—"

"Foolish, Jess! He's a mad hatter, and you are following

his lead! Harry Laughlin and I are on our way now. Stay put. Stay close to that crowd there."

"I'll be careful, of course."

"Don't hang up, you! Keep this line open, and keep the camera filming. I swear this will not be our last conversation. After what this monster did to Amanda Petersaul, Cates, all the others . . . how could you be so foolish as to go off after him alone, Jess?"

"Richard, had I come with an entourage . . . even being on the phone with you now compromises my deal with Gahran."

"You cannot make a deal with the Devil and come out unscathed, Jess. You of all people know that!"

She thought of her many scars over the years inflicted by others such as Matisak, both physical and psychological.

The radio earphone crackled with a voice now, Giles Gahran. "We don't have a lot of time left, Jessica—darling of my father's wet dreams. I want you with me now. You'll be the prize Father could not have, but I will possess. Make the old man proud, wherever he is."

"Giles, where are you? I'm here. Just direct me . . . guide me."

"You almost sound willing."

"Maybe I am. Maybe I should have gone out of this world with your father, Giles. I haven't exactly had the best life since then. Filled with depression, fear, anxiety, night sweats, nightmares, visited by your father's spirit." She hoped the lies would keep him off balance.

"Come to the top floor, rear stairs, directly on your right or left, either way . . . but no elevators. And come alone. Remember, I can see you from here."

She looked up far overhead, but she could not see Giles on the overhead promenade due to the lighting around the Mojave boneyard exhibit. The *Lovely Bones* banner lifted and lowered with the air spilling from nearby ducts, sending a

shiver through the canvas sign. The smooth river of movement and ripple reminded Jessica of how at the lightest
touch of the brush her horse's back rippled with feeling
from hoof to ear. How could a horse have more feeling in its
epidermis than a man had in his entire being, she wondered
as she took the first white marble step toward her and
Giles's fate.

As she made the half-landing, she could see down over
the crowd. The speaker continued to gloat and praise fellow
archaeologists working the dig back in the southwestern
desert. He was working up toward the money pitch, she realized. Looking down from the second landing, she saw the
enormous boneyard from straight over the top now. It
looked like a jagged pile of arrowhead shaped glass. It's centerpiece appeared to be what the speaker referred to now as
the diablo spinata, and with a long pointer, he touched it
and added, "The Devil's Spine, we came to know it as . . .
called it that when it began to take full shape from out of
the eons-old layers of rock and sand around it. And I can tell
you, ladies and gentlemen, out under a Navajo moon at
night with that thing staring up at you for what seemed a
half a mile at the time, I can tell you, it began to smell of
sulfur, it had so convinced us of it's namesake . . . that we
knew we were indeed tugging on Satan's own tailbone."

The laughter rose up to Jessica as she made the third
landing. The boneyard looked smaller from here, all save
the diablo spinata section.

"Aren't you curious how I came by the radio, Jess?" asked
Giles in her ear.

"Yes, I am."

"And how I knew you would be on this frequency?"

"Wise of you, Giles."

"Tell me, Jess. What did you think of the showing?"

"The showing?"

"Don't fuck with me."

"Oh, yeah . . . the showing in the back bargain basement

area of the Cafe Avanti, yeah, not a large crowd but quite an enthusiastic one. Especially for the locked door exhibit, your last victim. Richard said your work was a bit off the usual trodden path. But you know how low-key those British are. Myself, I thought it curiously derivative of Keith Orion."

"*Derivative . . . Orion! Bullshit!* You're such a lying bitch. How many lies did you tell to my father to lure him away from Mother?"

"Oh . . . is that what this is all about?" she replied, knowing all that she said was going over the line to Richard and Laughlin on the open line. "You think *Matthew* left your mommy to fuck me?" Her voice had taken on a teasing tone.

"He wanted eternity with you," Giles replied. "Maybe if you weren't around . . . who knows? Maybe he could have loved Mother. As it is, she became a *diabla* to his *diablo*. Maybe the two of them reign in hell now."

"Sure . . . and if we all lived in a dream world, Giles, life wouldn't suck for so many of us, would it? You don't get any fucking sympathy from me, Giles."

"Why don't you call me Matt Junior. By the way, what did you think of the sculptures, really? I want an honest answer."

"They were curiously lacking any of the haunting quality or humanity I had anticipated and you were obviously going for." She lied, describing her true reaction in the opposite.

"Lying slut cunt . . . that's what you are. You're just denying your true feelings, ashamed that the sculptures moved you, touched something in you. I know you *liked* the artwork."

"I wish I could say that was so, Giles, but—"

"Liar! You found my art, the spines included, fascinating, didn't you, Jessica? You're an M.E., hell, you've got to love it. The panache of it alone, the daring, the abandon."

"Are you trying to convince me or yourself, Giles?"

"Just get the fuck up here and tell me to my face. I want to see your eyes when you lie, just how cold they can be."

Jessica did wonder who had given up the headphone and mouthpiece set to Giles. She prayed no one else had lost a life due to Giles Gahran's kill spree.

"Curious thing you did out at Navy Pier, Giles. Tell me, were you going to jump?"

"I just had an accident with the box is all."

"Not the way I heard it. You stood up in the gondola, began rocking it. Like you were going to take a swan dive. You like heights, Giles?"

She made the last and final landing. Wearing jeans, she'd placed her camera phone face out and anchored in her hip pocket. She knew that Laughlin and Richard could see what she now saw. Across from her on this lonely final floor of the museum, Giles Gahran held hostage a young black girl barely out of her teens wearing the uniform of a security guard.

He held a small caliber weapon to the terrified girl's brain. Jessica could see bruises on her forehead where he had burrowed the muzzle into her to make his point, and the girl had gone limp, fainted, so that Giles had to drag her about with him like some enormous other self.

"She's not dead," he said immediately to clear this up. "Just went out like a light. I may've choked off her air a bit too long. But she's very much alive."

"That's good, Giles. I know you want to do the right thing here."

"Yeah . . . I do. Now take out your weapon and kick it back down those steps you came up."

"For the girl, OK. You let her go, I kick away my weapon and become your hostage."

"That might do except for one thing. You toss the weapon first. Then I let go of her."

Jessica took in a long deep breath of air as she cautiously took her coat off and discarded it, displaying her shoulder holster. This she then unstrapped and tossed down the stairwell to the half landing below. It made a resounding echo, causing some in the crowd below to look up at the unfolding drama overhead as if it were part of the planned activities of the evening. Stroud's voice wafted up and echoed off the marble columns here. "The Mojaves had a strange ritual and an even stranger deity . . ."

"Satisfied?" Jessica asked Giles. "Now let the girl go."

Giles smiled and eased the unconscious girl to the marble floor. Jessica took a tentative step toward the girl as if she might help her, but Giles jammed the gun in her face.

"Forget about her. She's nobody. It's you and me now, and it's time. Our time, Jess. Something I do to make Father proud."

"Time for what, Giles?" Jessica reached hands out to him. "You going to shoot me? If so do it now, because I'll be damned and dead before I go to any other location with you. I'm no fool to wind up facedown under your bone saw for a slow death."

"Bet you have exquisite spinal fluid running through you, Jessica Coran. Juicy and thick. Thick yellow is . . . healthy. And marrow. I could really enjoy sucking on your—"

"It's not going to happen, Giles. It's here and now. One shot and every policeman and FBI in the building descends on you."

"You came alone. I saw you."

She lifted the phone and spoke into it to Richard. "Richard, where is your location?"

"Main lobby downstairs."

"Lies," countered Giles.

"Richard, show me your location on the camera."

She held up the camera phone to Giles's eyes, and he saw the show of force, uniformed and plainclothes cops spreading out across the museum and covering every exit.

Jessica took this moment of surprise to drop and yank his

ankles from beneath him. Giles came down hard, striking his head on the marble floor, his gun skittering away, rattling crablike as it raked across the marble floor.

"I got him!" shouted Jessica who'd snatched out her second weapon. "The same gun that ended your father's life, Giles. One fucking wrong move from you, and I put you out of your miserable fucking excuse for a life. Now get up!"

Jessica heard the elevator rev up, knowing Richard and others would spill out any moment to relieve her, Richard to scold her further. She heard others racing up the stairs to the collective shock of the crowd below. She took a moment to gather in her breath when the girl on the floor moaned, and Jessica took her eyes off Gahran for a millisecond.

Giles had been pulling himself up with the help of the balustrade, and suddenly he stood balanced atop it, threatening to jump.

The others spilled from the elevator and Jessica shouted for all to stop. She pleaded with Giles to come into her custody. "I'll see you aren't harmed, Giles, and that you aren't treated—"

"Like some sort of freak?" He laughed and sent a colorful bubblegum card billowing her way. As the card fluttered birdlike toward her, Giles shouted, "I'll see you in hell, Doctor!" And he dove swanlike out over the railing. She rushed to the edge, irrationally shouting *no* even at this juncture, just in time to see him pirouette onto his back and land face up, his entire back splayed open in a series of stabbings from the diablo spinata. The *splat* and the spatter of blood on white shirts, eyeglasses and evening gowns combined with the horror of Gahran's sudden arrival amid the elite of Field Museum donors sent up a collective terror-layered gasp.

Even from her distance, Jessica could make out Giles's open eyes staring back up at her, and she heard a whisper in her ear, not Giles's voice, but that of Mad Matthew Matisak's, quietly, eerily saying, *Join me here, Jess, on the spine of Sa-*

tan. She could even hear his maniacal laugh, a sound she had thought long before banished from the last corridor of her mind, vanquished years before by her heart.

Apparently not so.

"Diablo spinata," she repeated the archaeology professor's term for the dinosaur bone that had claimed Giles Gahran, just to hear the sound of it again, she imagined, and just to weigh the sheer irony of it all as she stooped and lifted the bubblegum card he'd contemptuously thrown in her face. It proved a card depicting none other than Mad Matthew Matisak—crime statistics, the man's ranking according to body count listed alongside his brief biography with a notation of his unofficial official website all on one side, while his grim, ruddy and handsome features as a young man before the ravages of his disease graced the front. A sick society had made of Matisak a cult hero.

Laughlin now stared matter-of-factly down at the dead man and said, "Damn, looks like a picket fence went through the creep. Good riddance to rubbish, heh? One for the M.E.'s to yammer about over drinks at the convention, heh, Dr. Coran?"

"That could've been you down there, Jess. It's obviously what he had in mind, send you over to join with his father in a pathetic attempt of one monster trying to please another," Richard said.

"A son trying to please a father, a son who could never please his mother," Jessica replied.

"Why don't you write it up in another of your case file books, Dr. Coran," Laughlin sardonically suggested. "Given the bizarre nature of the case and all, it oughta make a bestseller."

"I'll likely have all the time in the world to write. Gods of the FBI are going to come down hard on us, Richard, when we return to D.C."

"Perhaps . . . perhaps not," Richard replied, holding her close to him.

"Do you know something I don't?"

"Before I discovered you missing at the cafe, I got a call from Eriq Santiva."

"And?"

"He and Hemmings had it out right in the middle of Fischer's office, heated battle as they say, and Eriq came out on top defending our actions, reminding them of your previous successes in New York, Philadelphia, Miami, twice in New Orleans, D.C., Houston, Hawaii and London."

"Did Eriq go so far as to say he condoned our actions in Portland?"

"Better yet."

"What?"

"He brought in Xavier Darwin Reynolds who so impressed Fischer that Hemmings was blown out of the water. Darwin pointed out that the FBI came out as the hero all across America thanks to us yanking an innocent man off death row at the thirteenth hour. And the kid's persuasive, as you know."

"But did Eriq go so far as to tell Fischer that we had his blessings?"

"He went further. He claims the glory. It was his idea."

"My God, Eriq did that?"

"To save our asses, yes. Said he will take the brunt of any disciplinary actions Fischer might want to take, including his dismissal."

"Geez, we can't let Eriq take this on himself this way. Did you tell him I was thinking of taking that position with Virginia state? Did you?" She grabbed her phone up and pressed speed dial for Santiva in Quantico.

Richard stopped her, pressing the phone's off button. "Calm down. There's something else."

"What?"

"Eriq won a 155 million dollar infusion of funds to be used for the Behavioral Science Unit and the FBI M.E. programs to be administered at *your* discretion, Jess. You're on the board that decides just how this money will be used."

She stared at Richard, disbelieving. "I-I don't know what to say."

"Jessica Coran? Without words? Mute? The world's turned upside down."

"I'll take that as a compliment, I think."

"Does this mean you'll stay with the FBI, Jess?"

"No . . . no amount of money is worth going through this again. Look down there at that lost soul, Richard."

Sharpe looked again at the battered, torn body of the dead young man still in his early twenties. "The kid lived such an unrelentingly brutal emotional nightmare, constantly under assault by his own mother."

Then he saw movement.

At least he thought he saw movement.

It appeared imperceptible, but yes, Giles Gahran Matisak began to slowly squirm.

"God blind me for a fool, Jess, he's alive!"

"What?" She stared down to the body splayed swastika-like and bleeding all over Dr. Stroud's bones, which were apparently the only thing in the exhibit not simulated but the actual diablo spinata transported here from the Mojave.

Now Jessica, too, saw the pinned Devil's child squirm in pain. "Someone ought to put the wretched thing out of its misery," she muttered, her gun pointed.

Richard put a hand over hers, taking the gun from her, saying, "No, Jess. It would only add to your nightmares. Leave it in God's hands."

"He's suffered enough."

"It is rather like watching a rabid animal, isn't it?" asked Laughlin.

"You're right, Richard. I won't do it. I won't do it." She holstered her weapon.

Laughlin said, "If we can save him, you could study him, as you did with Matisak before him."

"What good came of it? Studying this kind of evil does

not make it go away, and neither does burying it. It just keeps coming back, and I'm walking away on two good legs from it now for the final curtain."

Richard draped his arm about her and placed her head on his chest. "Whatever you decide, I'm behind you one hundred percent, Jess."

"With you at my side, Richard, I want to enjoy life more."

"As do I, of course."

"I want us both to escape this madness that surrounds us. We've paid our dues many times over, you in London, me here."

"Time for a little peace and paradise, you mean?"

"We'll never find it on the path we're on, not as FBI agents without a semblance of normalcy in our lives."

"All right then, it's settled! But we must make a pact. Neither of us shall ever be lured back in once we've stepped out of it.

"Done!" She hugged him to her. "Thank God I have you."

"Perhaps I'll find time now to write that book I've carried about in my head all these years."

"By all means, Richard, do it," she said.

"I love you, Jess. I've loved you all my life."

"But you haven't known me all your life."

"Doesn't matter. I've loved you——"

"——all my life!" They said it in unison.

Richard kissed her passionately while the milling confusion of humanity's floating opera here in the museum continued to file past Giles Gahran Matisak's now-still body. Giles lay still now, beyond caring about the amateur photos being shot or where they might wind up. For a moment, Jessica watched men in tuxedos and women in sequined evening gowns all rubbernecking for a better view of the monster who suddenly let out a final death rattle and was gone.

"Horace Keene and his team can take care of this untidy mess," Sharpe firmly said, guiding her along the promenade farther and farther from the horror below. Jessica, nestled in the crook of Richard Sharpe's embrace, allowed him his way toward the far stairwell and exit. She consciously fought the urge to pull from him and go back to take control of the crime scene. But no, she would not do that, not this time. Fuck them one and all, the FBI, Portland authorities, all her critics who felt she had, over the years, developed a heavy-handedness that put others off, and those who felt she had nothing but a cold sociopathic mind herself to be able to function in this man's world.

She liked the feel of her feet moving her body out of this lifestyle here and now. She could do this, easily, with enthusiasm simply turn and walk away. Mentally, she had also turned a corner deep within, one camouflaged all these years by ultimately meaningless cliches about duty and honor and integrity and loyalty to something she had no reason to turn her entire life over to, and to a profession that only rewarded in order to take away later, a profession that constantly asked, What have you done for me lately?

Inside her head, she felt a great sense of freedom rush in to replace all the mendacity that thrived on the system like parasites, fat cutworms, slugs, leeches and lampreys. The freedom she felt allowed her to walk off without a care and to not once look back, but to think only of her future at the ranch with Richard and their animals. To think herself and her sanity and good health and as small a thing as her smile might actually be more important than the next autopsy, than doing an autopsy on the son of Mad Matthew Matisak. Something any competent autopsiest could do.

"Yeah, Horace Keene can take care of this mess," she said, stopping Richard in his tracks. She hugged him close. "I want to live now, really live."

"Cancun's got great airfares right now, and it's been a while since we've gone diving."

"No . . . maybe later in the year, but now it's home. We do have a wedding to plan."

Acknowledgments

Go to *The Beast Within* by Benjamin Walker (another great out-of-print title) for all the spine-tingling details and arcane information on the backbone of mankind! I would also add a major thank-you to Lara Robbins for her years upon years of editorial assistance in copyediting just about all of the *Instinct* titles, from the inception of the series to its current title. I would also like to thank Dr. Jessica Coran for a lovely, decades-long ride as my most endearing character. For the memories, thank you, Jess. She can never be replaced. However, my new series will begin January 2006 with *City for Ransom*. How do these villains and heroes come full-blown into my head? Find out at my website, www.robertwalker.com.